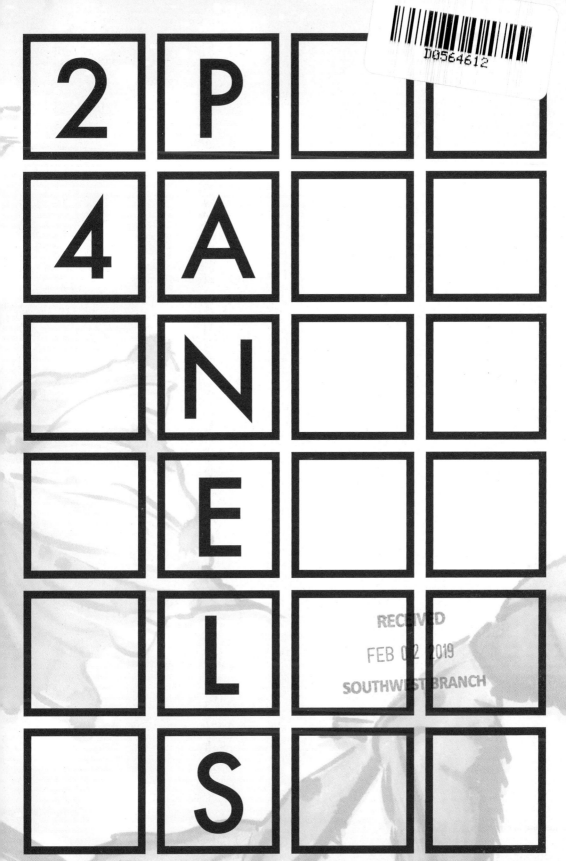

2 4 PANELS

AN ANTHOLOGY COMIC TO AID PTSD NEEDS
OF SURVIVORS OF THE GRENFELL TOWER FIRE

2 PANELS

AN INTRODUCTION 1
Written by Kieron Gillen
Art by Sean Azzopardi
Letters by Hassan Otsmane-Elhaou

BREATHE 6
Written by Gen Ainslow
Art by Drew Wills
Letters by Rob Jones

HEATH MAGIC 9
Written by Leigh Alexander
Art and letters by Tom Humberstone

BURGER JOINT 13
Written by Christof Bogacs
Art and letters by Reda Kahloula

FRUIT PUNCH 16
Written by Trevor Boyd
Art and letters by Bev Johnson

THEY SAY 21
Words and letters by Alex de Campi
Art by Ro Stein and Ted Brandt
Colour by Triona Tree Farrell

THE GLEAMING GREEN . . .27
Written by Paul Cornell
Art and letters by Rachael Smith

KINSHIP 32
Words, art and letters by
Liam Donnelly

UNTITLED 34
Written by Al Ewing
Art by Doug Braithwaite

THE FORT 36
Written by Mike Garley
Art by Alex Moore
Letters by Mike Stock

PEOPLE FIRST 39
Written by Antony Johnston
Art by Robin Hoelzemann
Colour by Pippa Mather

DREAM JOB 42
Words, art and letters by Lizz Lunney

AMYG DALA 44
Written by Sara Kenney
Art by Caspar Wijngaard
Letters by Hassan Otsmane-Elhaou

A LITTLE HOPE 49
Words and art by Dilraj Mann

IF EINSTEIN'S RIGHT 57
Written by Alan Moore
Art by Melinda Gebbie
Letters by Hassan Otsmane-Elhaou

ABREK 61
Written by Emmet O'Cuana
Art by Jeferson Sadzinski
Letters by Cardinal Rae

HUMAN CHILD 66
Written by Laurie Penny
Art by Gavin Mitchell
Letters by Hassan Otsmane-Elhaou

UNTITLED 71
Words, art and letters by Erika Price

PEOPLE LIKE US 74
Written by Joanne Starer
Art by Lynne Yoshii
Letters by Comicraft

THE FAVELAS 77
Written by Daniel Santos
Art by Débora Santos
Letters by Toben Racicot

UNTITLED 82
Art by Paul Swain

A LOGICAL CONCLUSION . 84
Written by Gwen Kortsen
Art by Angela Wraight
Letters by Hassan Otsmane-Elhaou

SILHOUETTE TITANS 89
Written by Ram V
Art by Pablo Clark
Letters by Hassan Otsmane-Elhaou

GRAFTAGE 95
Written by Deshan Tennekoon
Art and letters by Linki Brand

SCRATCHCARDS 99
Written by Dan Watters
Art by Sarah Gordon
Letters by Hassan Otsmane-Elhaou

BIOS 104

IMAGE COMICS, INC. • **Robert Kirkman**: Chief Operating Officer • **Erik Larsen**: Chief Financial Officer • **Todd McFarlane**: President • **Marc Silvestri**: Chief Executive Officer • **Jim Valentino**: Vice President • **Eric Stephenson**: Publisher / Chief Creative Officer • **Corey Hart**: Director of Sales • **Jeff Boison**: Director of Publishing Planning & Book Trade Sales • **Chris Ross**: Director of Digital Sales • **Jeff Stang**: Director of Specialty Sales • **Kat Salazar**: Director of PR & Marketing • **Drew Gill**: Art Director • **Heather Doornink**: Production Director • **Nicole Lapalme**: Controller • **IMAGECOMICS.COM**

24 PANELS. First printing. November 2018. Published by Image Comics, Inc. Office of publication: 2701 NW Vaughn St., Suite 780, Portland, OR 97210. Copyright © 2018 Kieron Gillen, Rhona Martin and Steve Thompson. All rights reserved. "24 PANELS," its logos, and the likenesses of all characters herein are trademarks of Kieron Gillen, Rhona Martin and Steve Thompson, unless otherwise noted. "Image" and the Image Comics logos are registered trademarks of Image Comics, Inc. No part of this publication may be reproduced or transmitted, in any form or by any means (except for short excerpts for journalistic or review purposes), without the express written permission of 24 PANELS, or Image Comics, Inc. All names, characters, events, and locales in this publication are entirely fictional. Any resemblance to actual persons (living or dead), events, or places, without satirical intent, is coincidental. Printed in the USA. For information regarding the CPSIA on this printed material call: 203-595-3636 and provide reference #RICH—820357. For international rights, contact: foreignlicensing@imagecomics.com. ISBN: 978-1-5343-1126-8.

24 Panels
An Introduction

It's Still Happening.

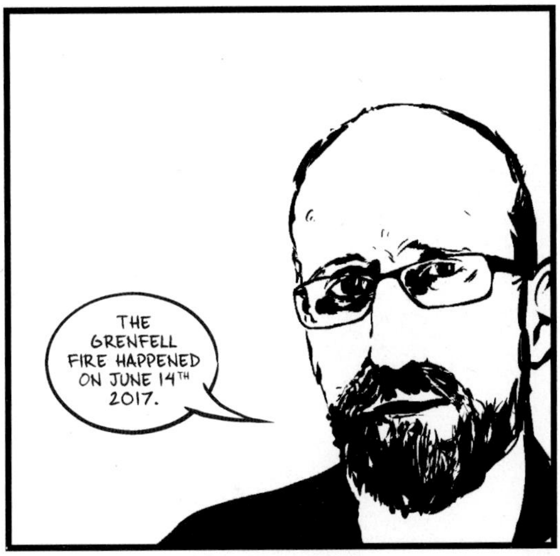
THE GRENFELL FIRE HAPPENED ON JUNE 14TH 2017.

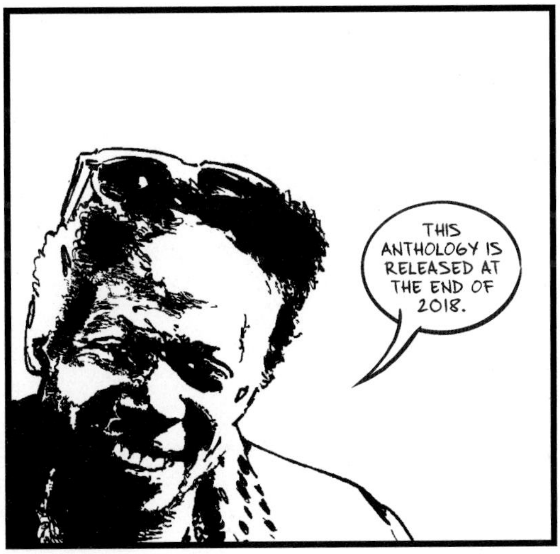
THIS ANTHOLOGY IS RELEASED AT THE END OF 2018.

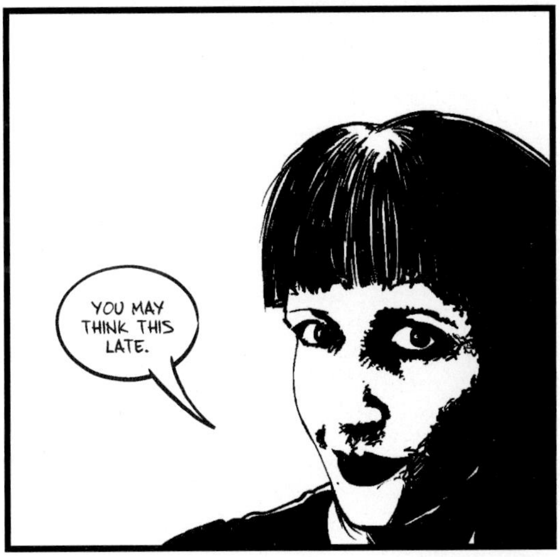
YOU MAY THINK THIS LATE.

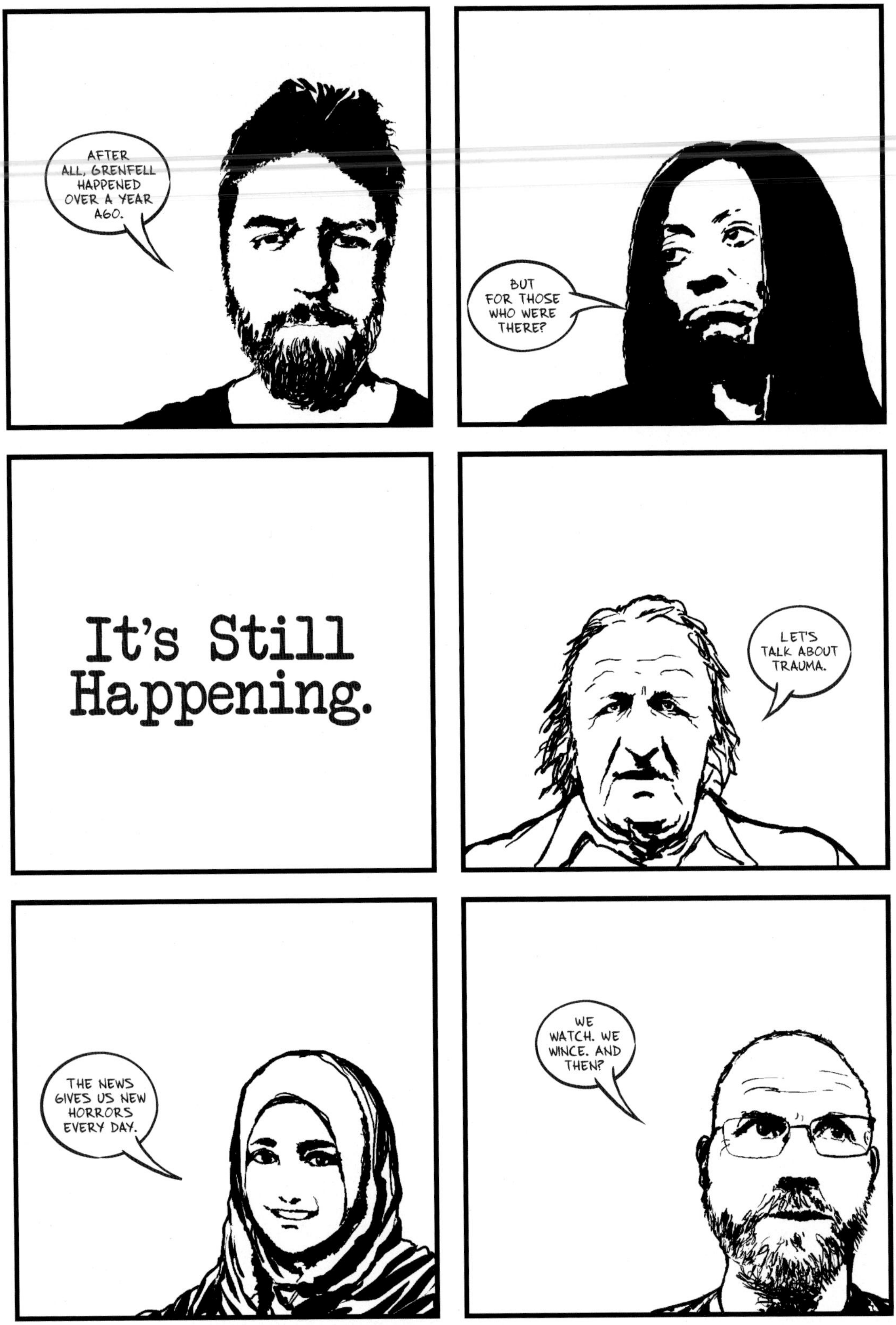
AFTER ALL, GRENFELL HAPPENED OVER A YEAR AGO.
BUT FOR THOSE WHO WERE THERE?
It's Still Happening.
LET'S TALK ABOUT TRAUMA.
THE NEWS GIVES US NEW HORRORS EVERY DAY.
WE WATCH. WE WINCE. AND THEN?

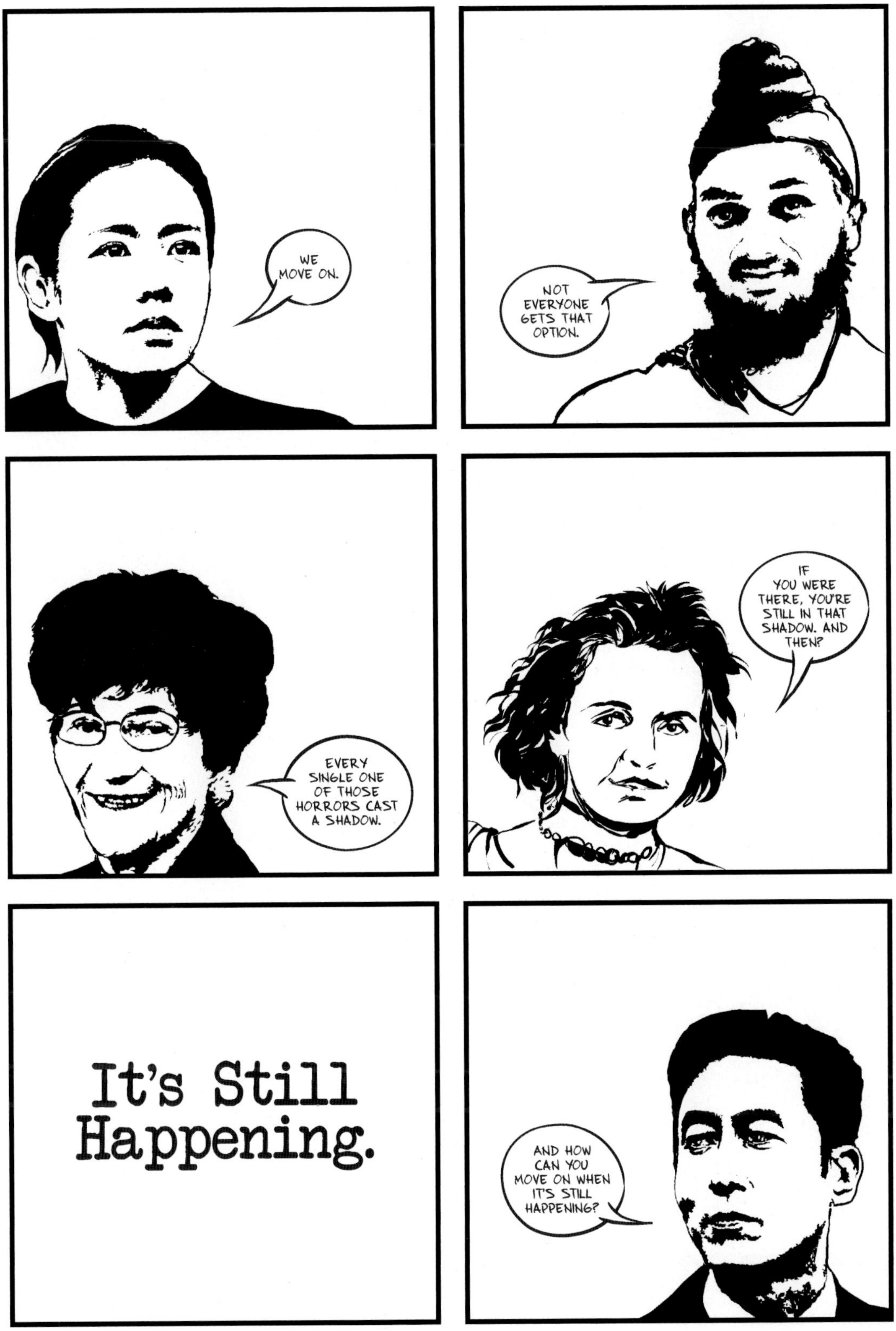
WE MOVE ON.
NOT EVERYONE GETS THAT OPTION.
EVERY SINGLE ONE OF THOSE HORRORS CAST A SHADOW.
IF YOU WERE THERE, YOU'RE STILL IN THAT SHADOW. AND THEN?
It's Still Happening.
AND HOW CAN YOU MOVE ON WHEN IT'S STILL HAPPENING?

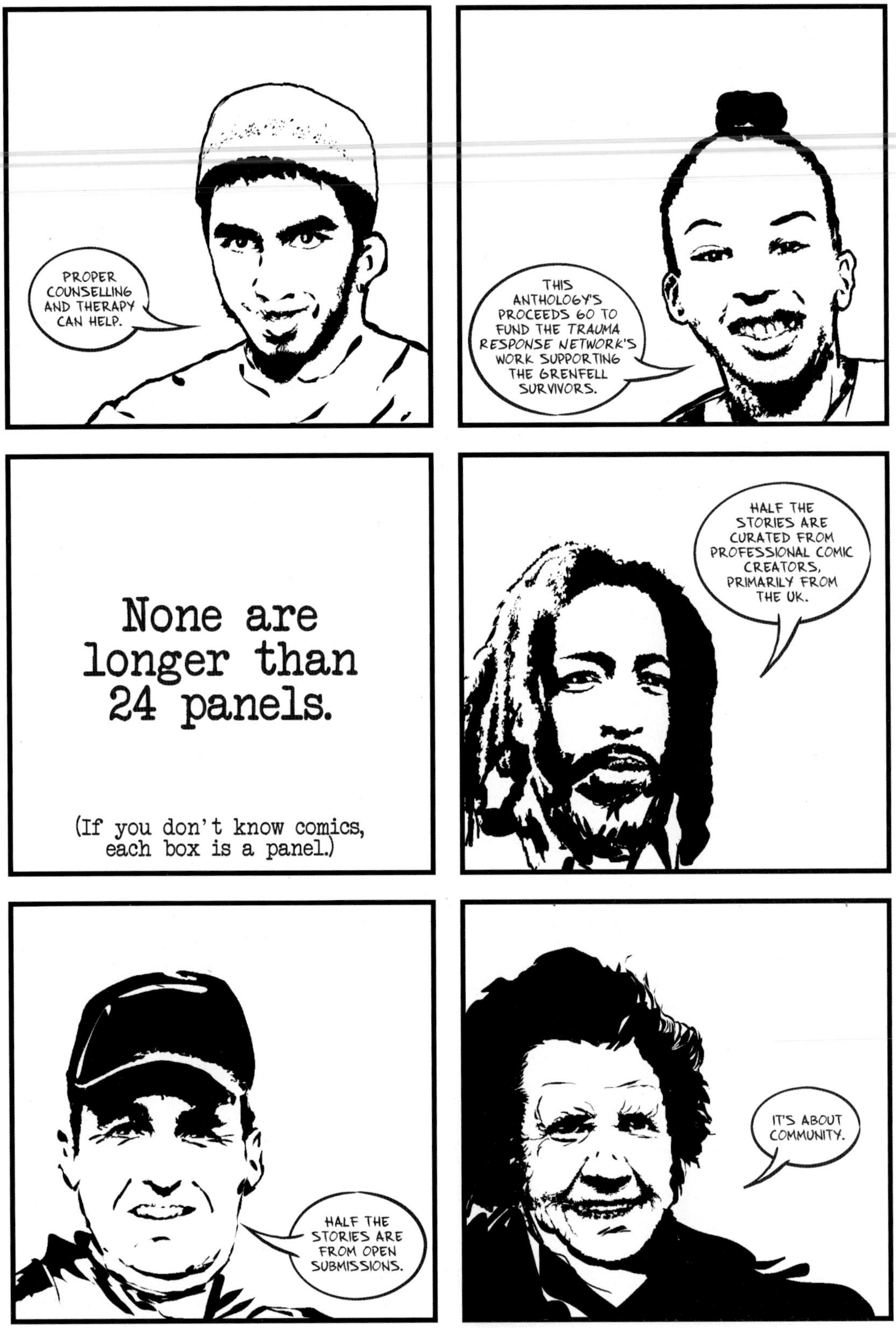
PROPER COUNSELLING AND THERAPY CAN HELP.
THIS ANTHOLOGY'S PROCEEDS GO TO FUND THE TRAUMA RESPONSE NETWORK'S WORK SUPPORTING THE GRENFELL SURVIVORS.
None are longer than 24 panels.
(If you don't know comics, each box is a panel.)
HALF THE STORIES ARE CURATED FROM PROFESSIONAL COMIC CREATORS, PRIMARILY FROM THE UK.
HALF THE STORIES ARE FROM OPEN SUBMISSIONS.
IT'S ABOUT COMMUNITY.

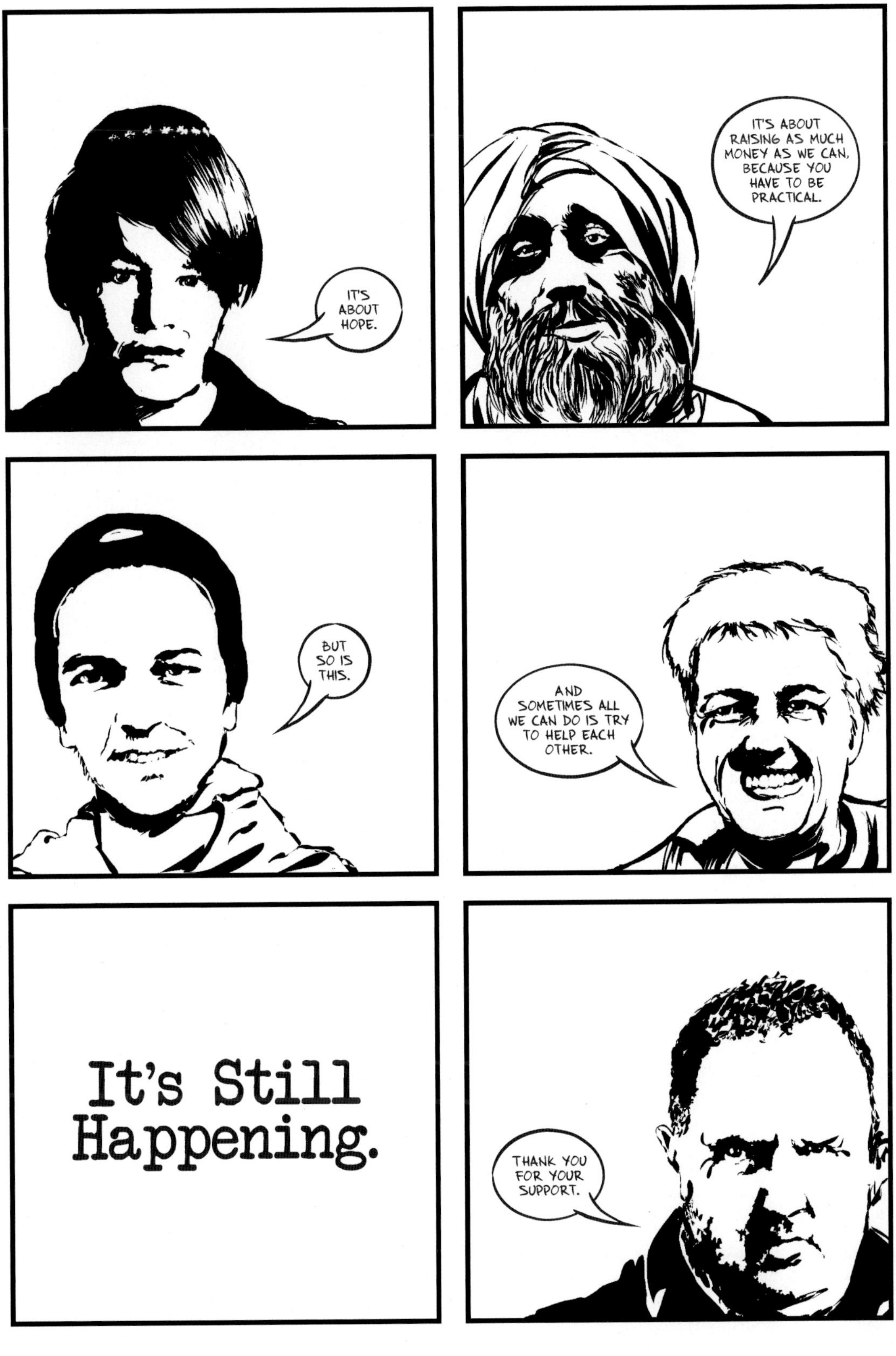
IT'S ABOUT HOPE.
IT'S ABOUT RAISING AS MUCH MONEY AS WE CAN, BECAUSE YOU HAVE TO BE PRACTICAL.
BUT SO IS THIS.
AND SOMETIMES ALL WE CAN DO IS TRY TO HELP EACH OTHER.
It's Still Happening.
THANK YOU FOR YOUR SUPPORT.

*"I **DON'T** THINK I CAN DO THIS."*

*"**THIS** IS GRIEF COUNSELING
FOR AVOIDANT PERSONALITIES:*

*"I'M **FINE**,
EVERYTHING'S **FINE**,
WE'RE **ALL FINE**
HERE..."*

*"AND YOU JUST KEEP CHUGGING
ON BURYING YOUR **DREAMS**...*

*"AND **TERRORS**...*

*"AND **RAGE**...*

*"AND **HOPES**...*

*"AND HOPING THAT NO ONE
WILL NOTICE YOU DROWNING.*

*"BECAUSE YOU HOLD YOUR FEELINGS
BENEATH THE SURFACE, BUT **NEVER**
LET THEM TOUCH THE CORE OF YOU.*

*"HOW DO YOU BREAK
OUT WITHOUT BREAKING
DOWN?*

*"HOW DO YOU COAST ALONG **PROCESSING**
(REPRESSING? DENYING? AVOIDING?) WHEN
YOU DON'T HAVE THE **TIME** OR **SPACE** OR
INCLINATION TO HAVE A MELTDOWN?*

*"HOW DO YOU NOT
COLLAPSE IN OR
EXPLODE OUT?"*

"I CAN'T

"I CAN'T

"I CAN'T--

"--SPEAK, CONFIDE, OPEN UP, VENT, INHALE WITHOUT TIGHTNESS IN MY THROAT.

*"IT'S **FINE**, OKAY?*

*"I'M **ALWAYS** FINE.*

I AM HERE FOR YOU.

I **DON'T NEED** YOU TO BE HERE FOR ME.

"I WON'T CRY.

*"I'LL JUST HOLD THIS TIGHTNESS AGAINST MY CHEST AND **NEVER** LET IT GO.*

*"I WILL TAKE ON **ANY** PAIN THAT YOU ASK OF ME.*

"I WON'T ASK ANYTHING IN RETURN.

"I WON'T NEED HELP."

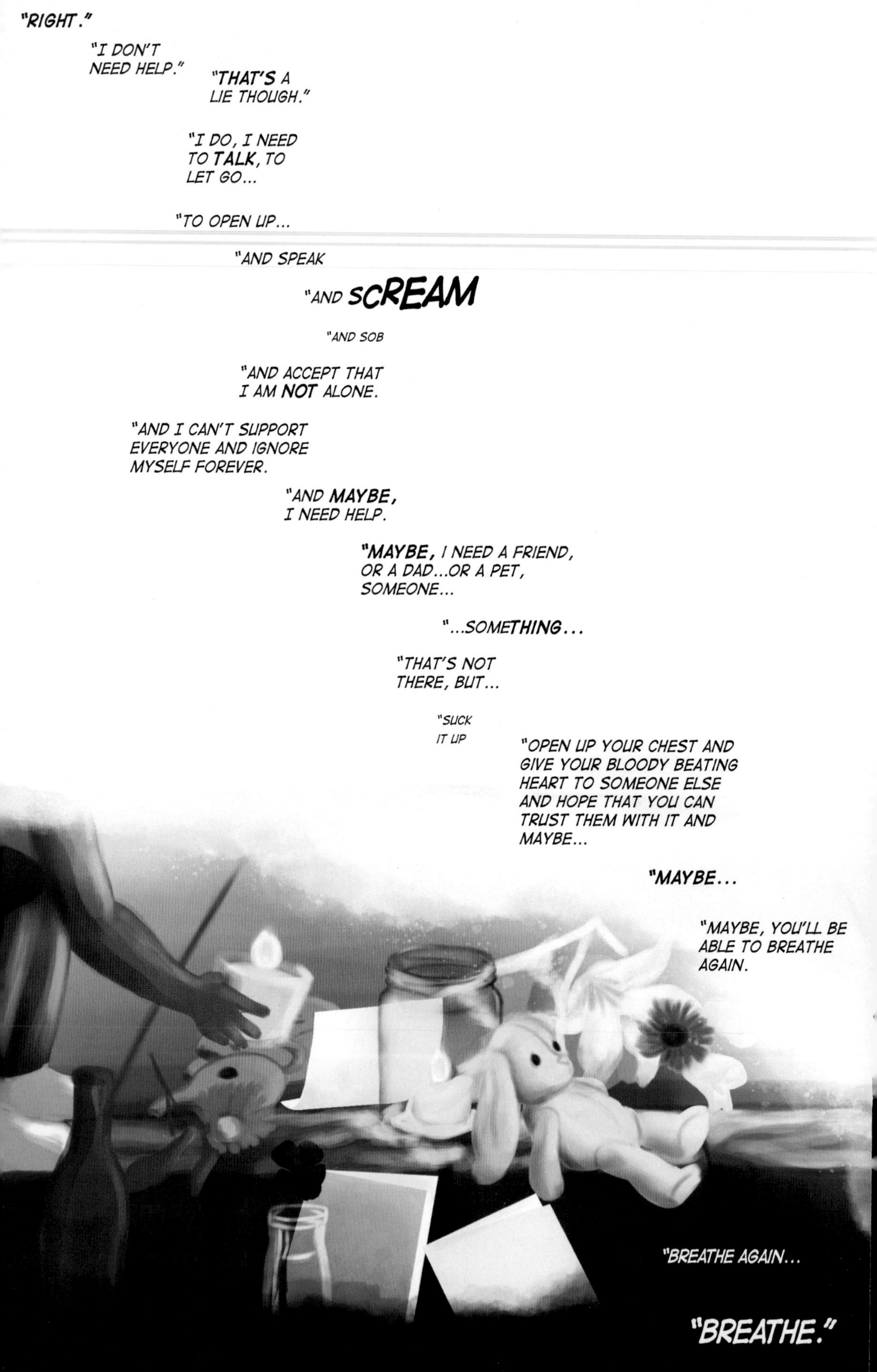
"RIGHT."
"I DON'T NEED HELP."
"THAT'S A LIE THOUGH."
"I DO, I NEED TO TALK, TO LET GO...
"TO OPEN UP...
"AND SPEAK
"AND SCREAM
"AND SOB
"AND ACCEPT THAT I AM NOT ALONE.
"AND I CAN'T SUPPORT EVERYONE AND IGNORE MYSELF FOREVER.
"AND MAYBE, I NEED HELP.
"MAYBE, I NEED A FRIEND, OR A DAD...OR A PET, SOMEONE...
"...SOMETHING...
"THAT'S NOT THERE, BUT...
"SUCK IT UP
"OPEN UP YOUR CHEST AND GIVE YOUR BLOODY BEATING HEART TO SOMEONE ELSE AND HOPE THAT YOU CAN TRUST THEM WITH IT AND MAYBE...
"MAYBE...
"MAYBE, YOU'LL BE ABLE TO BREATHE AGAIN.
"BREATHE AGAIN...
"BREATHE."

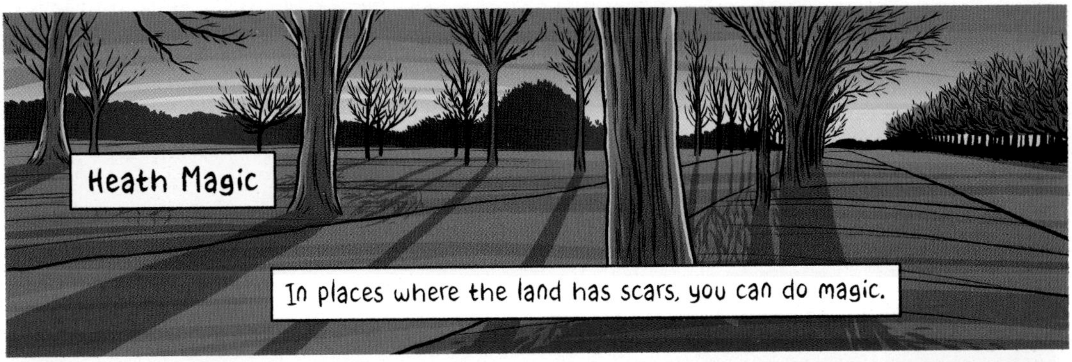
Heath Magic
In places where the land has scars, you can do magic.

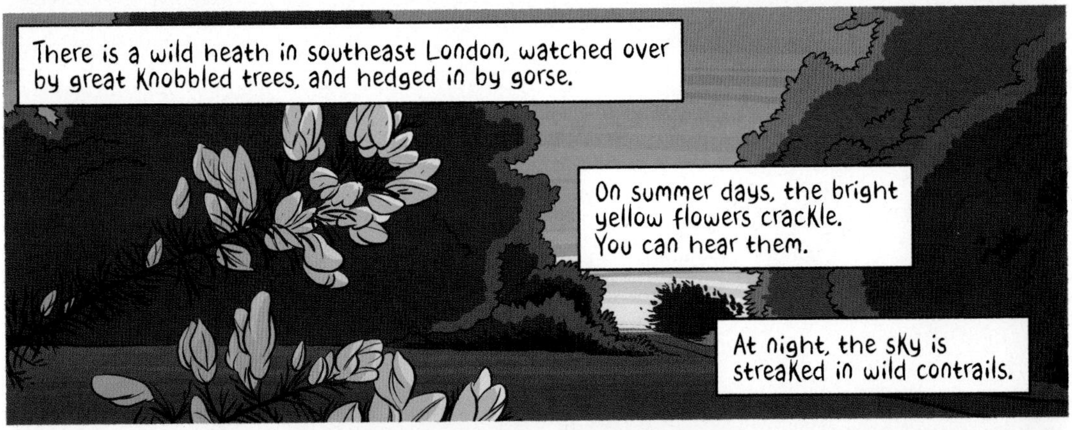
There is a wild heath in southeast London, watched over by great knobbled trees, and hedged in by gorse.
On summer days, the bright yellow flowers crackle. You can hear them.
At night, the sky is streaked in wild contrails.

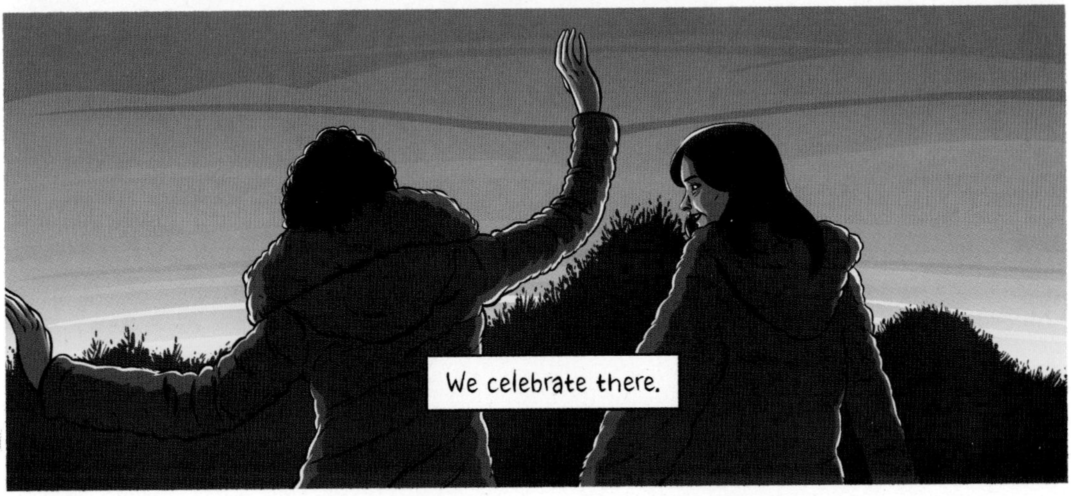
We celebrate there.

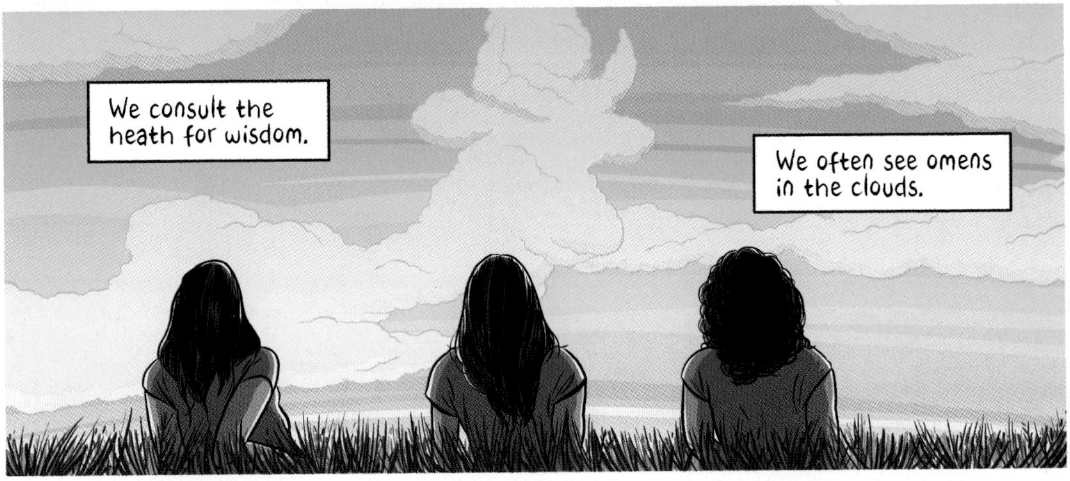
We consult the heath for wisdom.
We often see omens in the clouds.

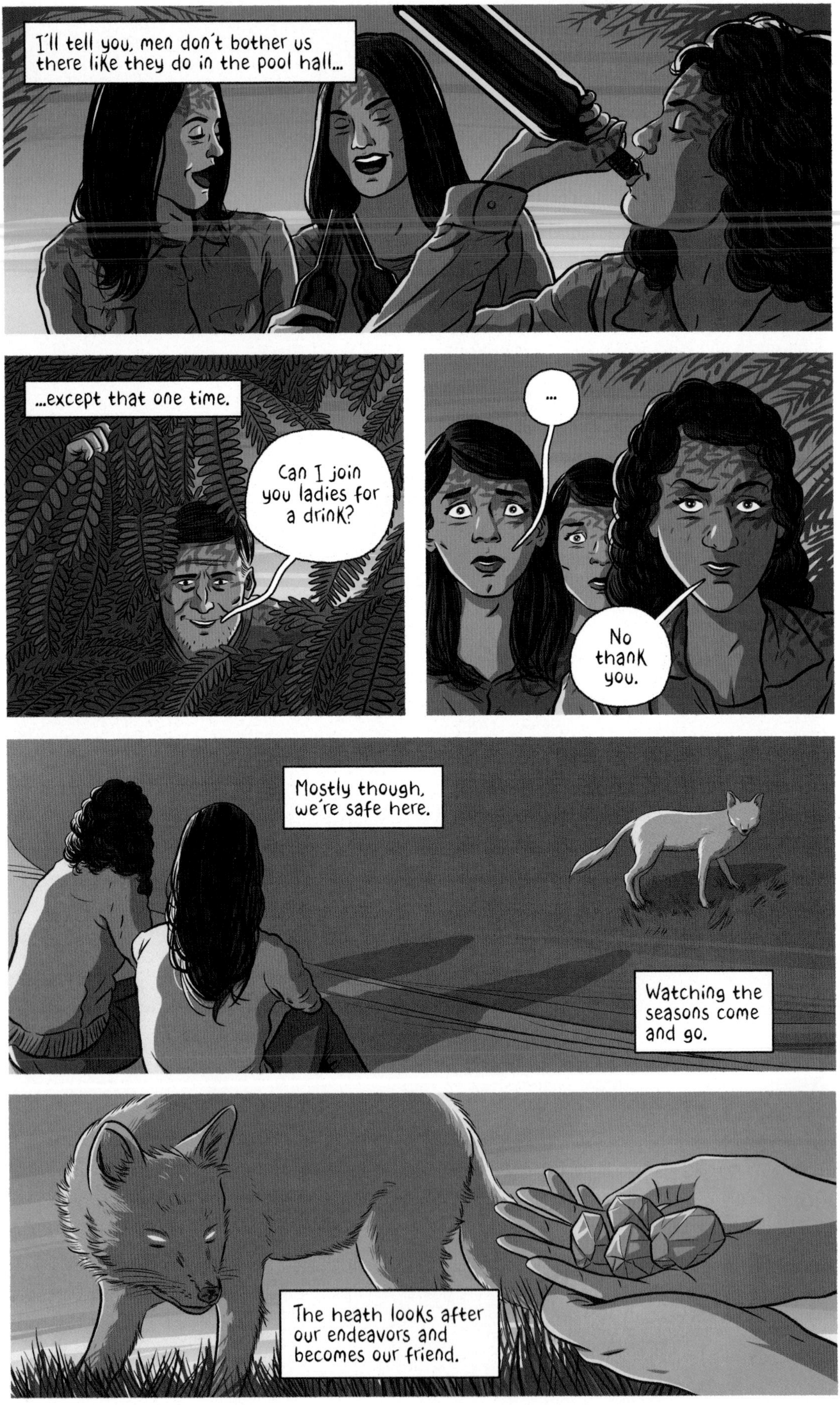
I'll tell you, men don't bother us there like they do in the pool hall...
...except that one time.
Can I join you ladies for a drink?
...
No thank you.
Mostly though, we're safe here.
Watching the seasons come and go.
The heath looks after our endeavors and becomes our friend.

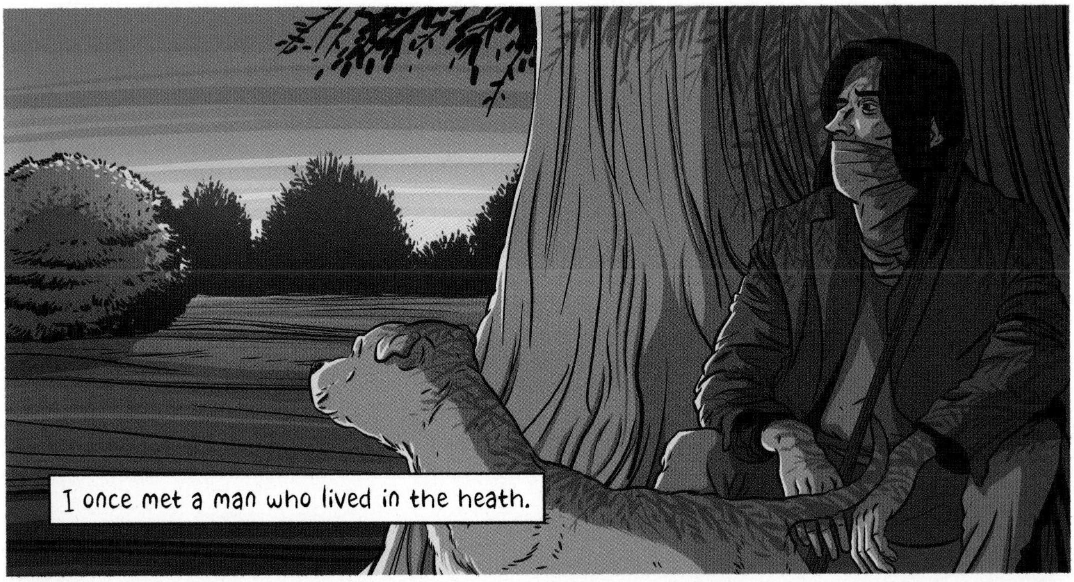
I once met a man who lived in the heath.

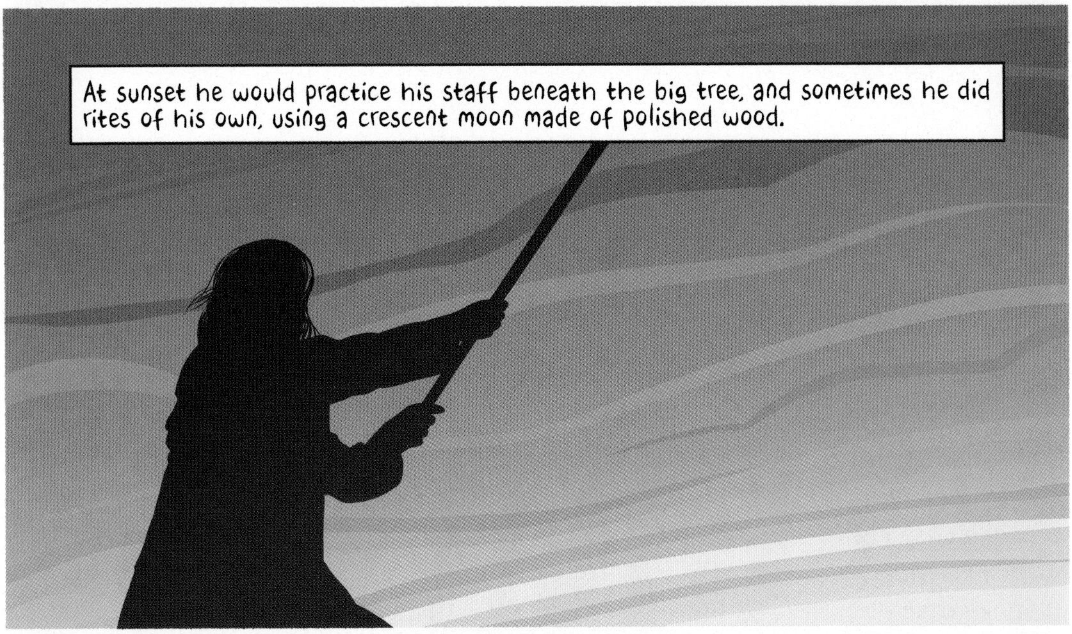
At sunset he would practice his staff beneath the big tree, and sometimes he did rites of his own, using a crescent moon made of polished wood.

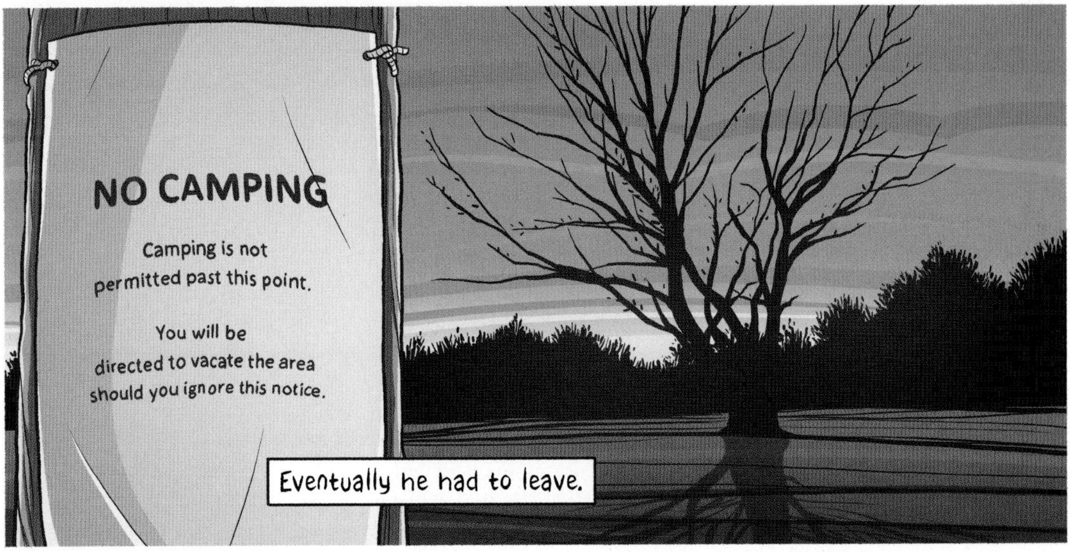
NO CAMPING
Camping is not permitted past this point.
You will be directed to vacate the area should you ignore this notice.
Eventually he had to leave.

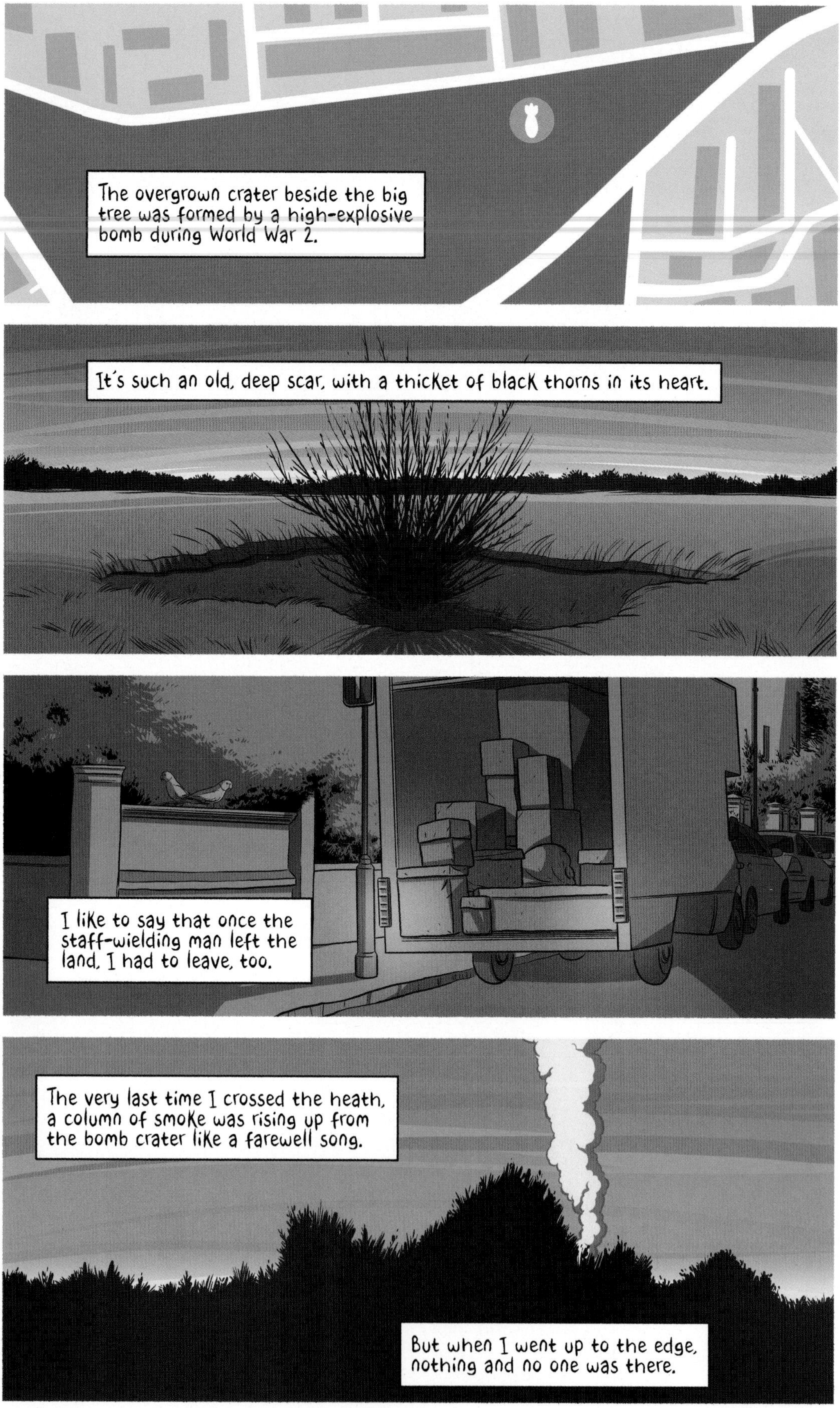
The overgrown crater beside the big tree was formed by a high-explosive bomb during World War 2.
It's such an old, deep scar, with a thicket of black thorns in its heart.
I like to say that once the staff-wielding man left the land, I had to leave, too.
The very last time I crossed the heath, a column of smoke was rising up from the bomb crater like a farewell song.
But when I went up to the edge, nothing and no one was there.

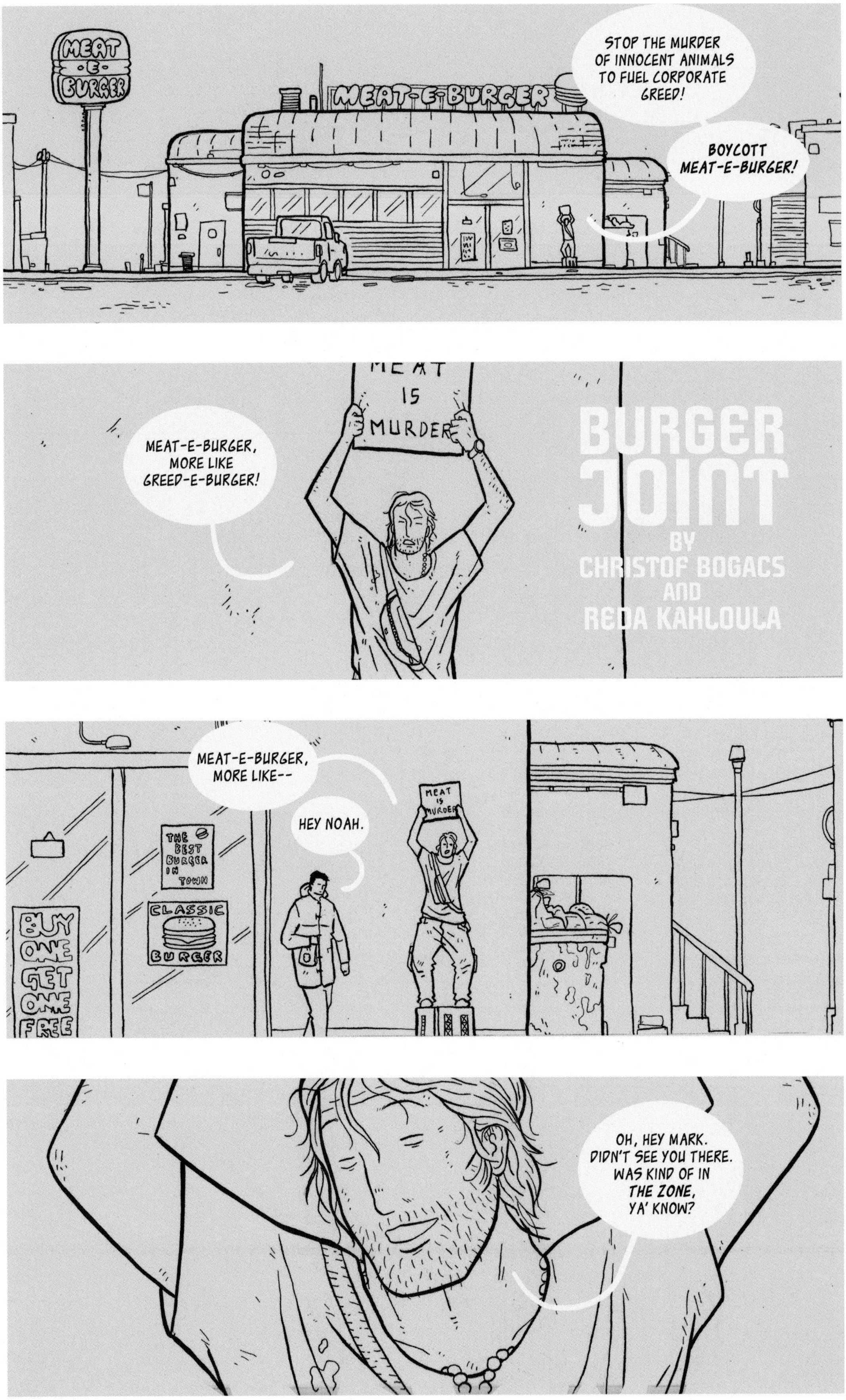
MEAT -E- BURGER
MEAT-E-BURGER
STOP THE MURDER OF INNOCENT ANIMALS TO FUEL CORPORATE GREED!
BOYCOTT MEAT-E-BURGER!
MEAT IS MURDER
MEAT-E-BURGER, MORE LIKE GREED-E-BURGER!
BURGER JOINT
BY CHRISTOF BOGACS AND REDA KAHLOULA
MEAT-E-BURGER, MORE LIKE--
HEY NOAH.
MEAT IS MURDER
THE BEST BURGER IN TOWN
CLASSIC BURGER
BUY ONE GET ONE FREE
OH, HEY MARK. DIDN'T SEE YOU THERE. WAS KIND OF IN THE ZONE, YA' KNOW?

SO, HOW GOES SAVING THE WORLD?

IT'S NOT GLAMOROUS, BUT HEY, AT LEAST IT ISN'T SOAKED IN *TRANS FATS.*

YOU?

JUST MORE OF THE SAME. WORK, SLEEP, EAT. YOU KNOW THE DRILL.

SPEAK FOR YOURSELF. I'M ALWAYS PUMPED TO COME OUT HERE AND FIGHT THE GOOD FIGHT.

GOOD FIGHT!?! DUDE, YOU'RE WAVING A SIGN AND YELLING SLOGANS. YOU'RE NOT EXACTLY GANDHI.

MOCK ALL YOU WANT, BUT, IF I CAN GET JUST ONE PERSON TO EAT SOMEWHERE ELSE, I CAN GO TO SLEEP KNOWING I'VE MADE THE WORLD A *BETTER* PLACE.

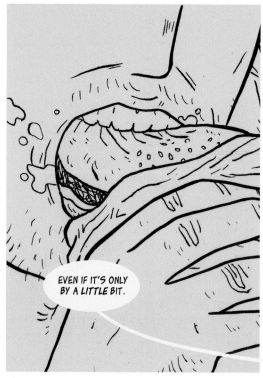

EVEN IF IT'S ONLY BY A *LITTLE* BIT.

THAT DOES SOUND NICE. BUT HONESTLY, I'M JUST GLAD I'VE GOT A JOB THAT PAYS THE BILLS.

SPEAKING OF, I BETTER GET BACK TO IT.

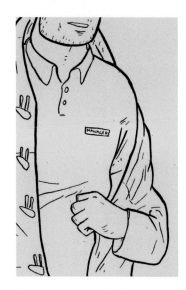

MANAGER

MANAGER

YOU WANT TO FINISH MY BURGER BY THE WAY?

VERY FUNNY.

CAN'T BLAME A MAN FOR TRYING. SAME TIME TOMORROW?

YOU KNOW IT.

MEAT-E-BURGER MORE LIKE GREED-E-BURGER! MEAT-E-BURGER MORE LIKE GREED-E-BURGER!

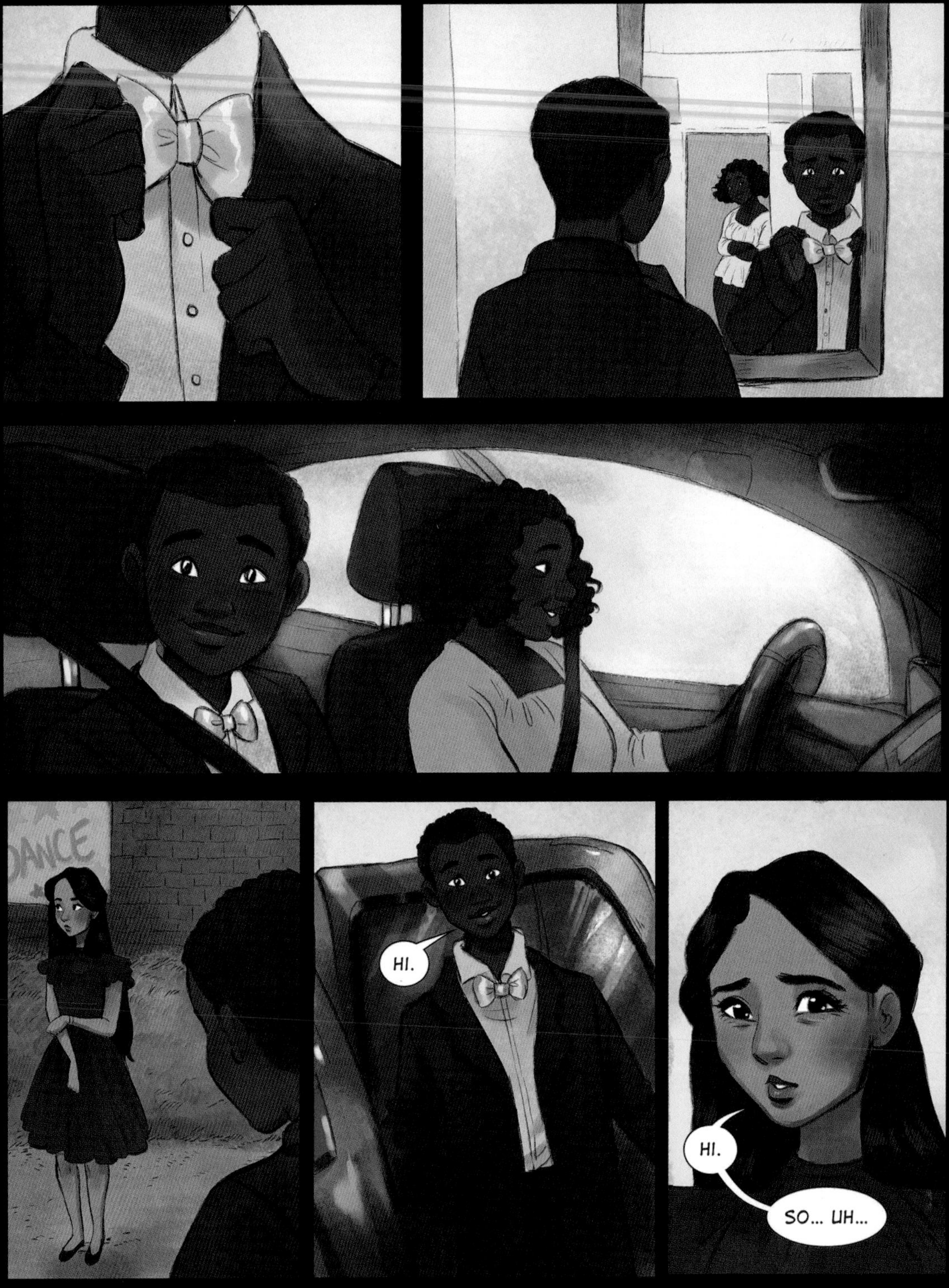
DANCE
HI.
HI.
SO... UH...

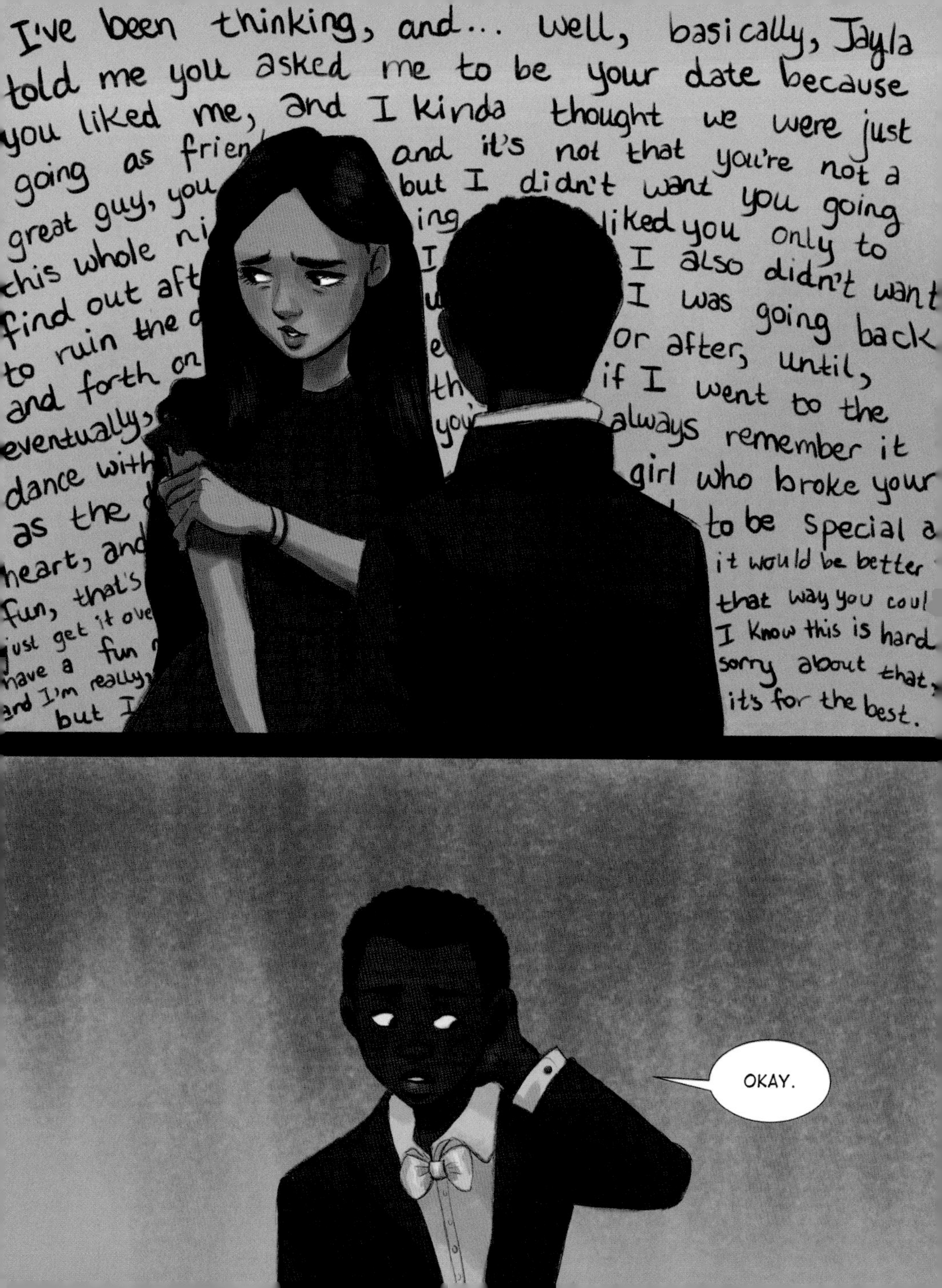
I've been thinking, and... well, basically, Jayla
told me you asked me to be your date because
you liked me, and I kinda thought we were just
going as frien
and it's not that you're not a
great guy, you
but I didn't want you going
this whole ni
ing
liked you only to
find out aft
I
I also didn't want
to ruin the
I was going back
and forth on
or after, until,
eventually,
if I went to the
dance with
always remember it
as the
girl who broke your
heart, and
to be special a
fun, that's
it would be better
just get it ove
that way you coul
have a fun
I know this is hard
and I'm really
sorry about that,
but I
it's for the best.
OKAY.

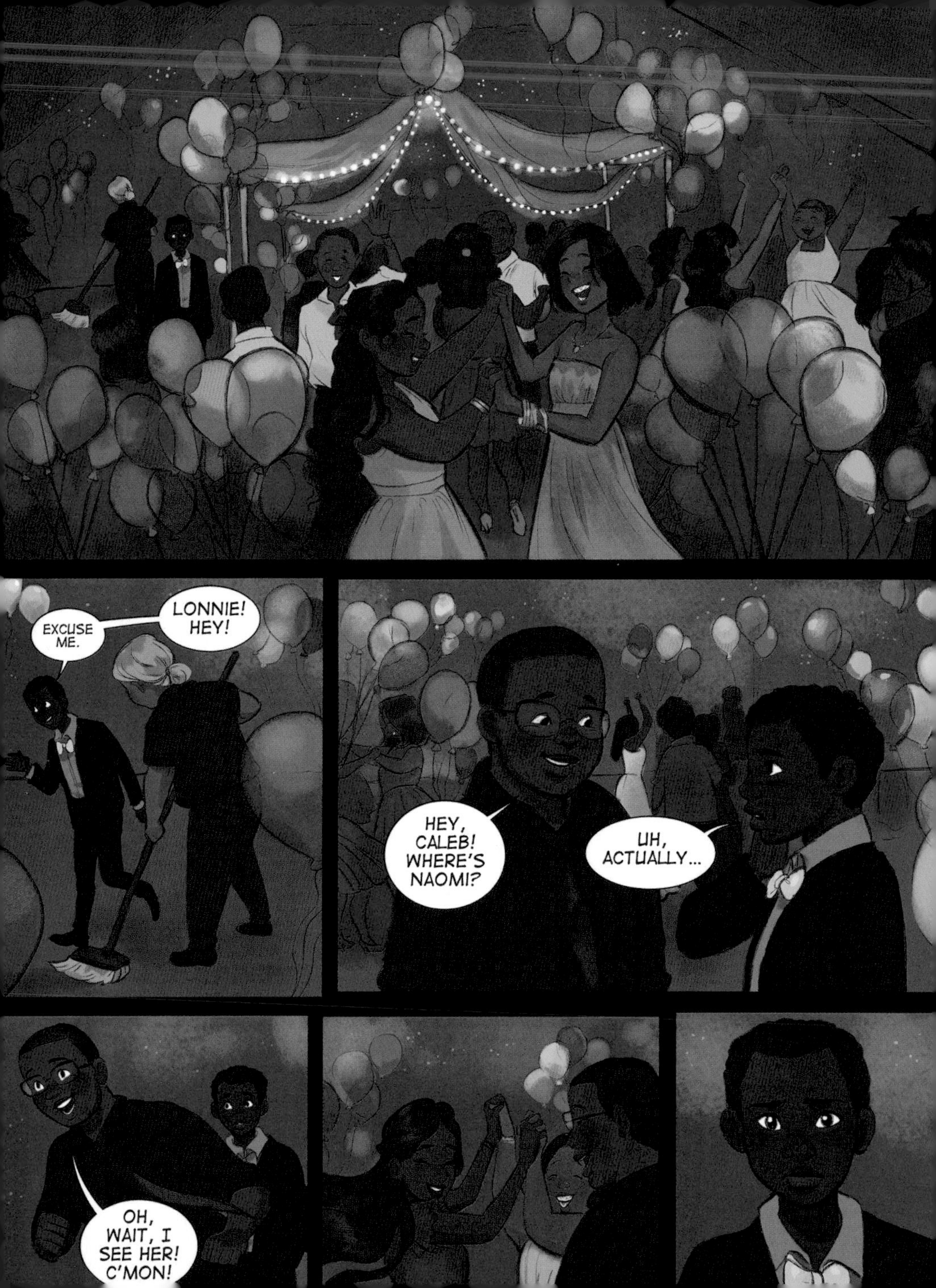
EXCUSE ME.
LONNIE! HEY!
HEY, CALEB! WHERE'S NAOMI?
UH, ACTUALLY...
OH, WAIT, I SEE HER! C'MON!

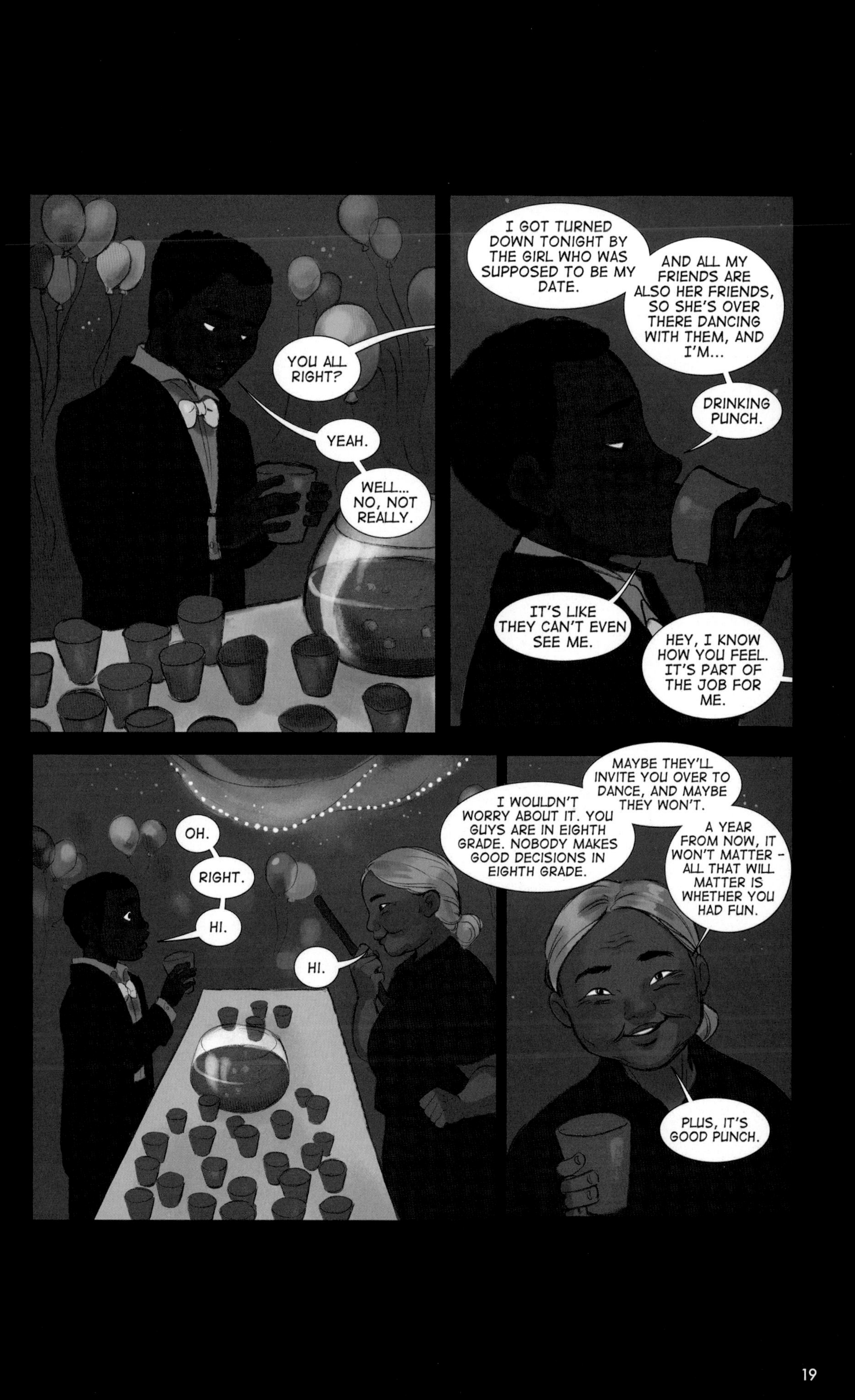
YOU ALL RIGHT?
YEAH.
WELL... NO, NOT REALLY.
I GOT TURNED DOWN TONIGHT BY THE GIRL WHO WAS SUPPOSED TO BE MY DATE.
AND ALL MY FRIENDS ARE ALSO HER FRIENDS, SO SHE'S OVER THERE DANCING WITH THEM, AND I'M...
DRINKING PUNCH.
IT'S LIKE THEY CAN'T EVEN SEE ME.
HEY, I KNOW HOW YOU FEEL. IT'S PART OF THE JOB FOR ME.
OH.
RIGHT.
HI.
HI.
I WOULDN'T WORRY ABOUT IT. YOU GUYS ARE IN EIGHTH GRADE. NOBODY MAKES GOOD DECISIONS IN EIGHTH GRADE.
MAYBE THEY'LL INVITE YOU OVER TO DANCE, AND MAYBE THEY WON'T.
A YEAR FROM NOW, IT WON'T MATTER - ALL THAT WILL MATTER IS WHETHER YOU HAD FUN.
PLUS, IT'S GOOD PUNCH.

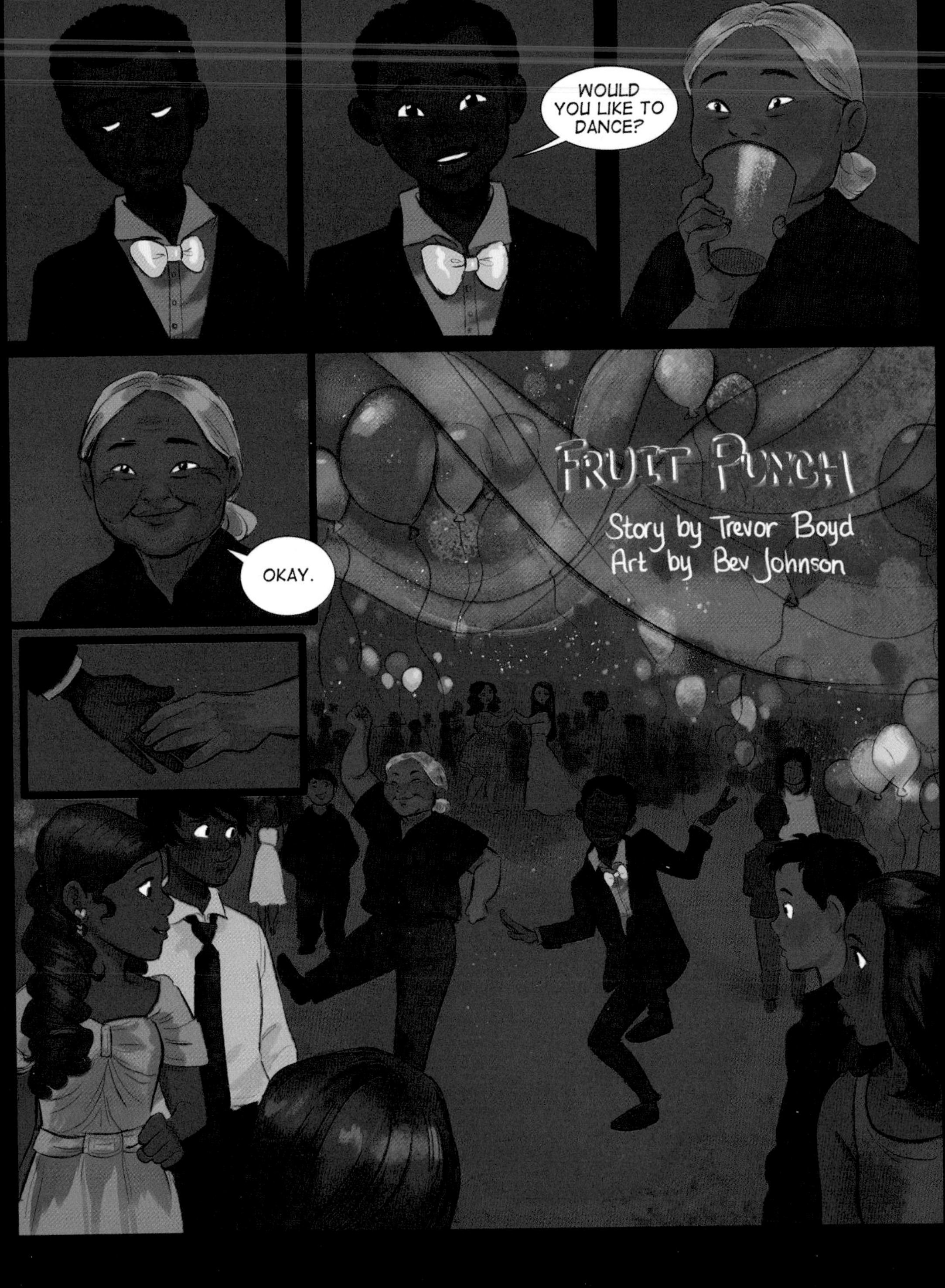

WOULD YOU LIKE TO DANCE?
OKAY.
FRUIT PUNCH
Story by Trevor Boyd
Art by Bev Johnson

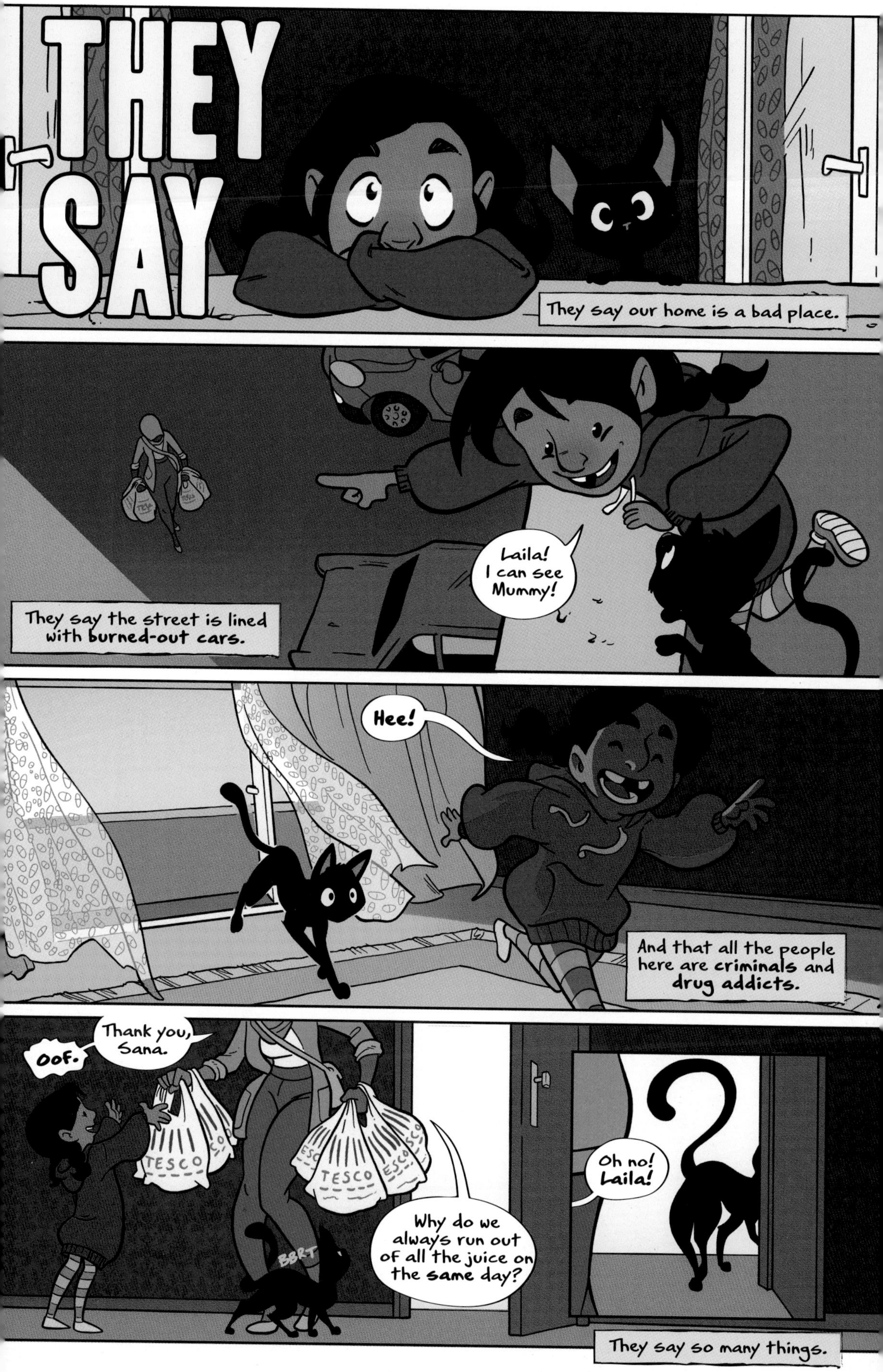
THEY SAY
They say our home is a bad place.
They say the street is lined with burned-out cars.
Laila! I can see Mummy!
Hee!
And that all the people here are criminals and drug addicts.
Oof.
Thank you, Sana.
TESCO
BBRT
Why do we always run out of all the juice on the same day?
Oh no! Laila!
They say so many things.

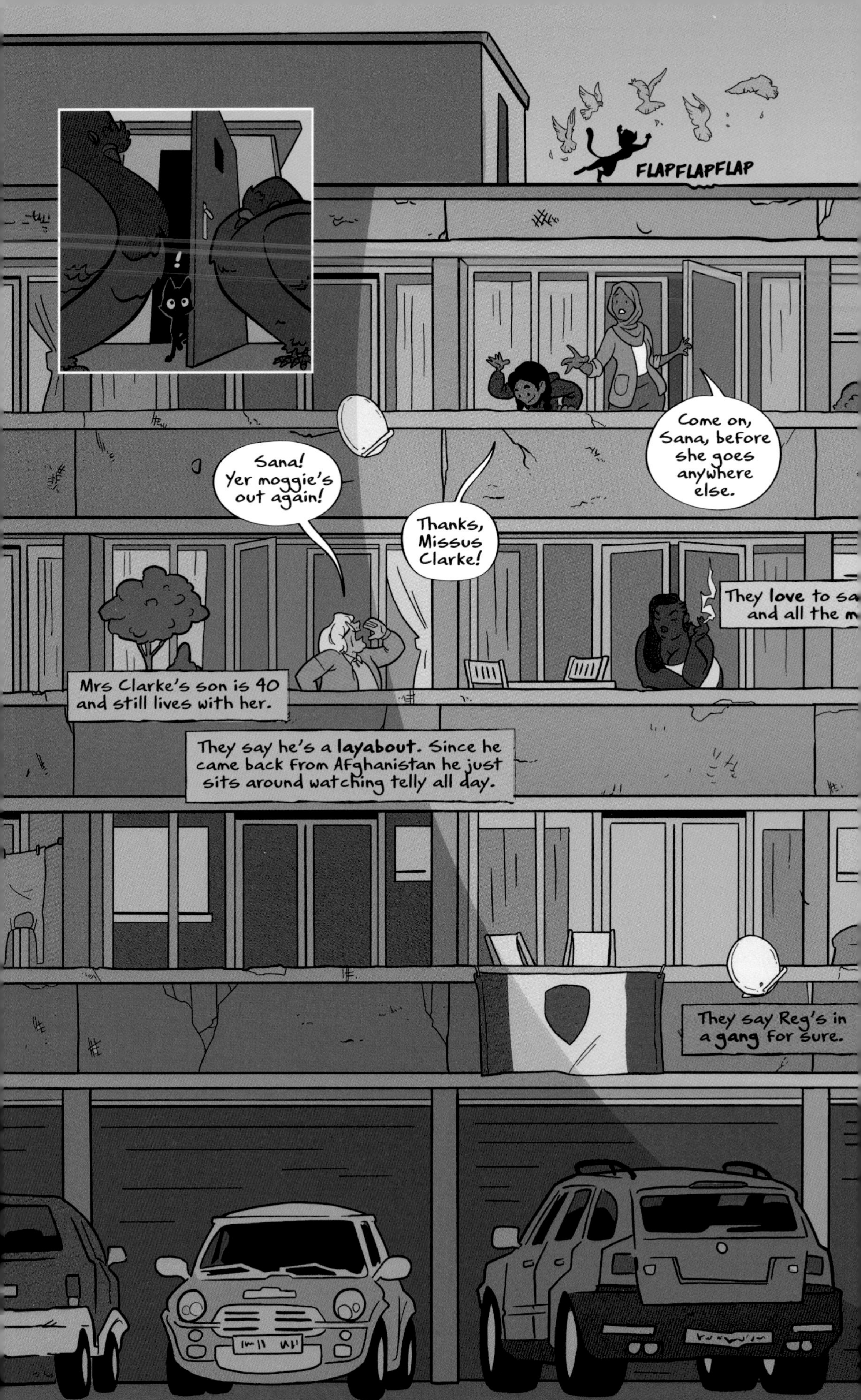
!
FLAPFLAPFLAP
Sana! Yer moggie's out again!
Thanks, Missus Clarke!
Come on, Sana, before she goes anywhere else.
They love to sa
and all the m
Mrs Clarke's son is 40 and still lives with her.
They say he's a **layabout.** Since he came back from Afghanistan he just sits around watching telly all day.
They say Reg's in a gang for sure.

words: ALEX de CAMPI
pencils: RO STEIN
inks: TED BRANDT
colours: TRIONA TREE FARRELL

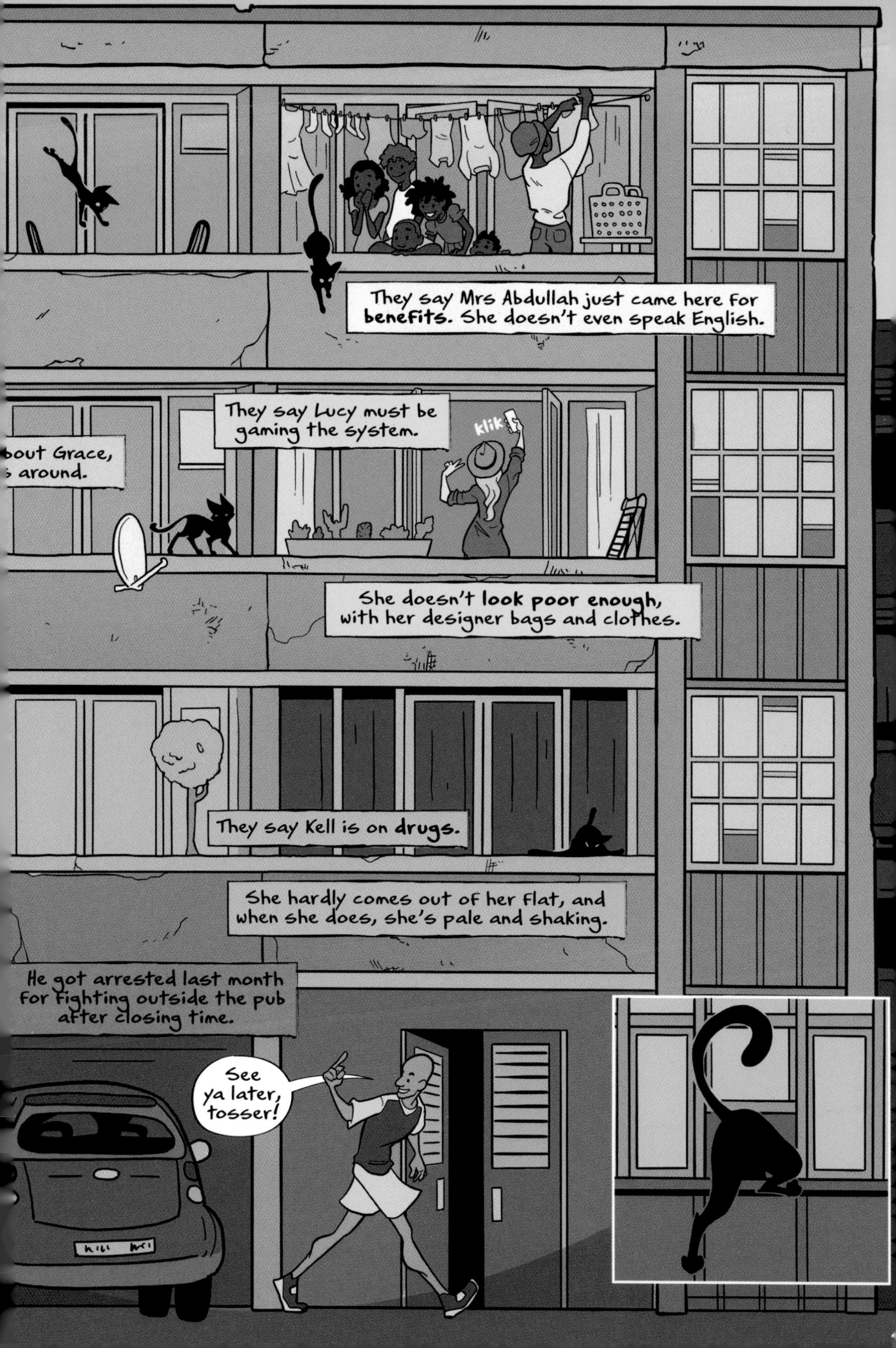

They say Mrs Abdullah just came here for benefits. She doesn't even speak English.
bout Grace, s around.
They say Lucy must be gaming the system.
klik
She doesn't look poor enough, with her designer bags and clothes.
They say Kell is on drugs.
She hardly comes out of her flat, and when she does, she's pale and shaking.
He got arrested last month for fighting outside the pub after closing time.
See ya later, tosser!

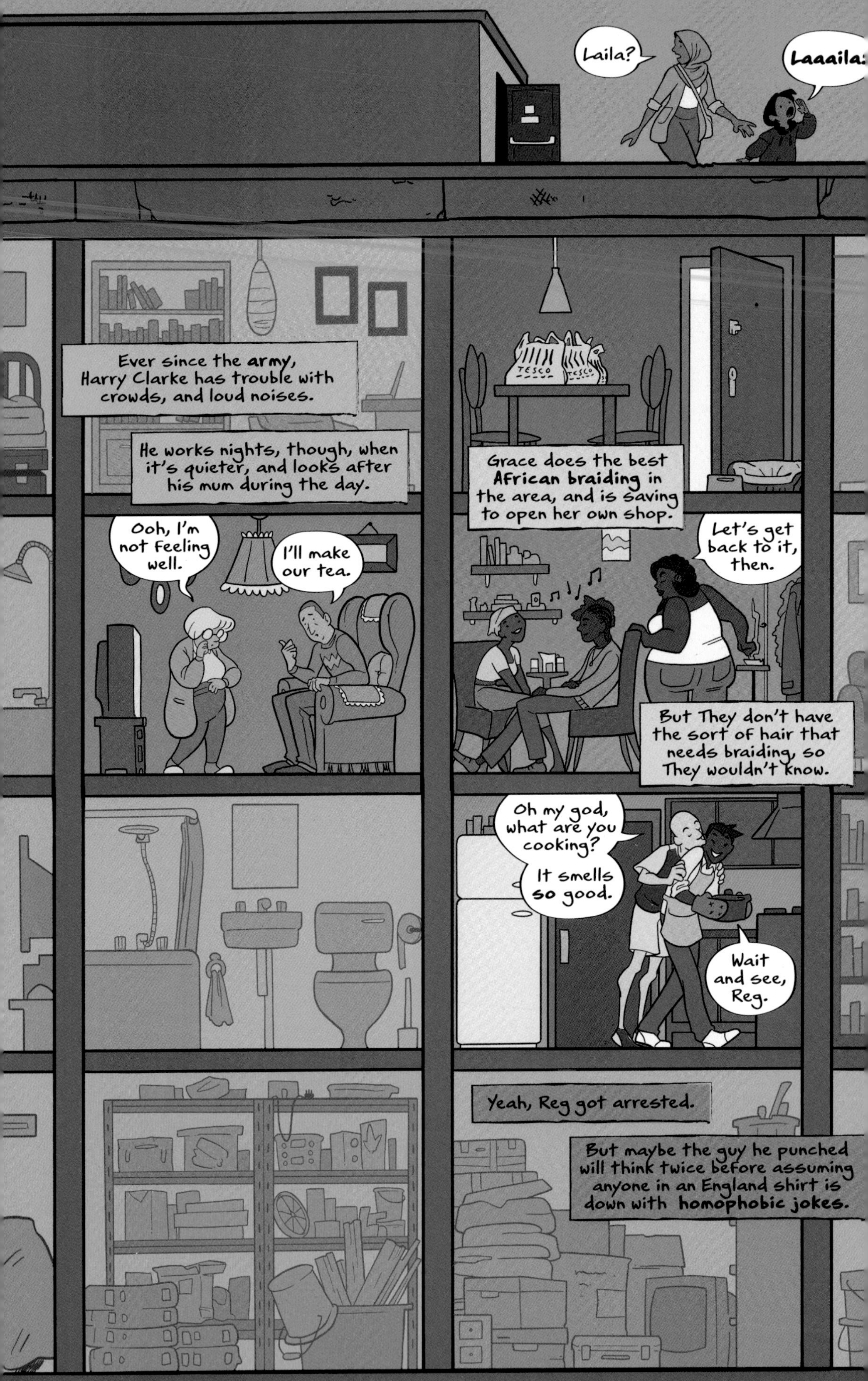

Laila?
Laaaila!
Ever since the army, Harry Clarke has trouble with crowds, and loud noises.
He works nights, though, when it's quieter, and looks after his mum during the day.
Ooh, I'm not feeling well.
I'll make our tea.
Grace does the best African braiding in the area, and is saving to open her own shop.
Let's get back to it, then.
But They don't have the sort of hair that needs braiding, so They wouldn't know.
Oh my god, what are you cooking?
It smells so good.
Wait and see, Reg.
Yeah, Reg got arrested.
But maybe the guy he punched will think twice before assuming anyone in an England shirt is down with homophobic jokes.

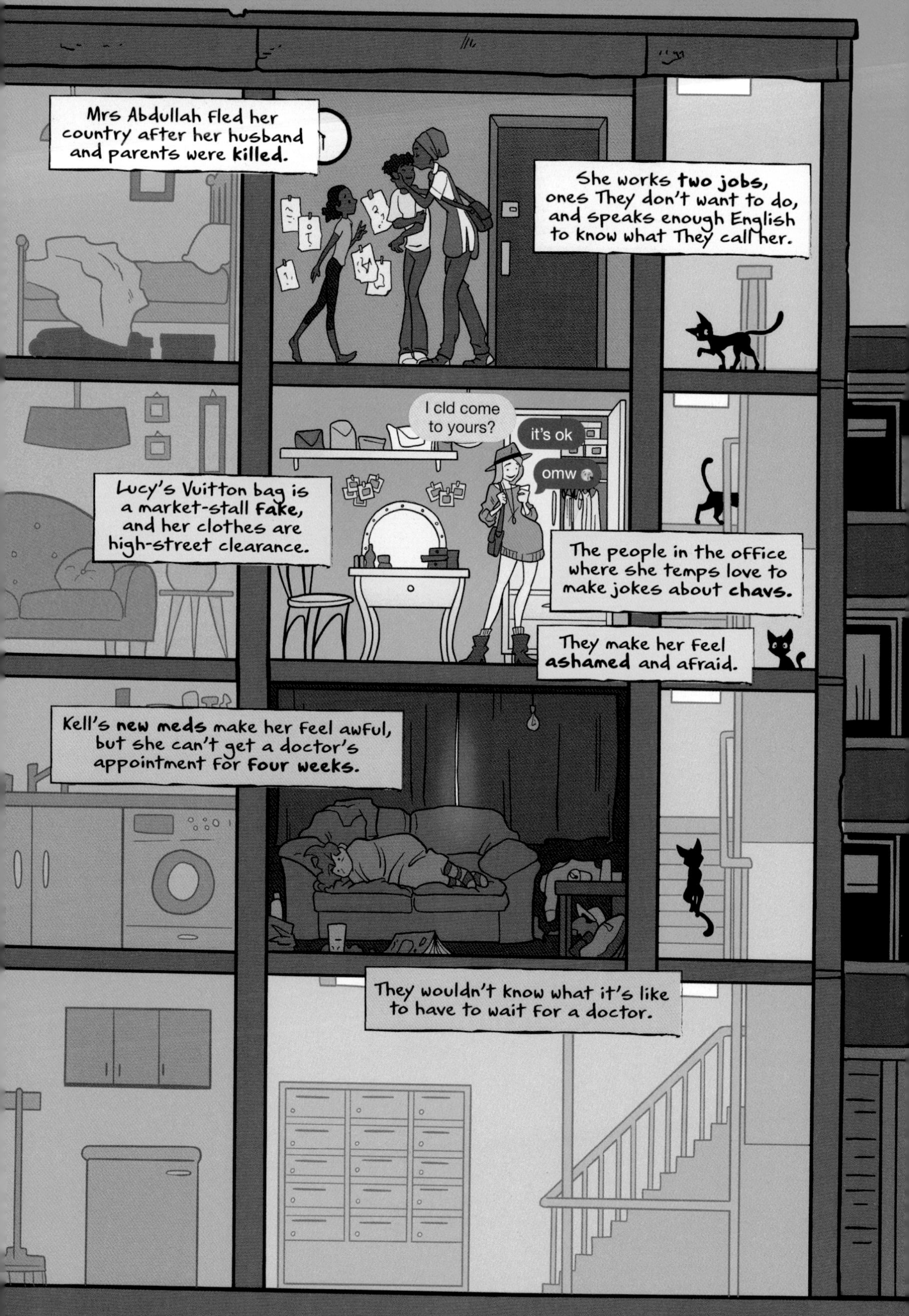

Mrs Abdullah fled her country after her husband and parents were killed.
She works two jobs, ones they don't want to do, and speaks enough English to know what they call her.
I cld come to yours?
it's ok
omw
Lucy's Vuitton bag is a market-stall fake, and her clothes are high-street clearance.
The people in the office where she temps love to make jokes about chavs.
They make her feel ashamed and afraid.
Kell's new meds make her feel awful, but she can't get a doctor's appointment for four weeks.
They wouldn't know what it's like to have to wait for a doctor.

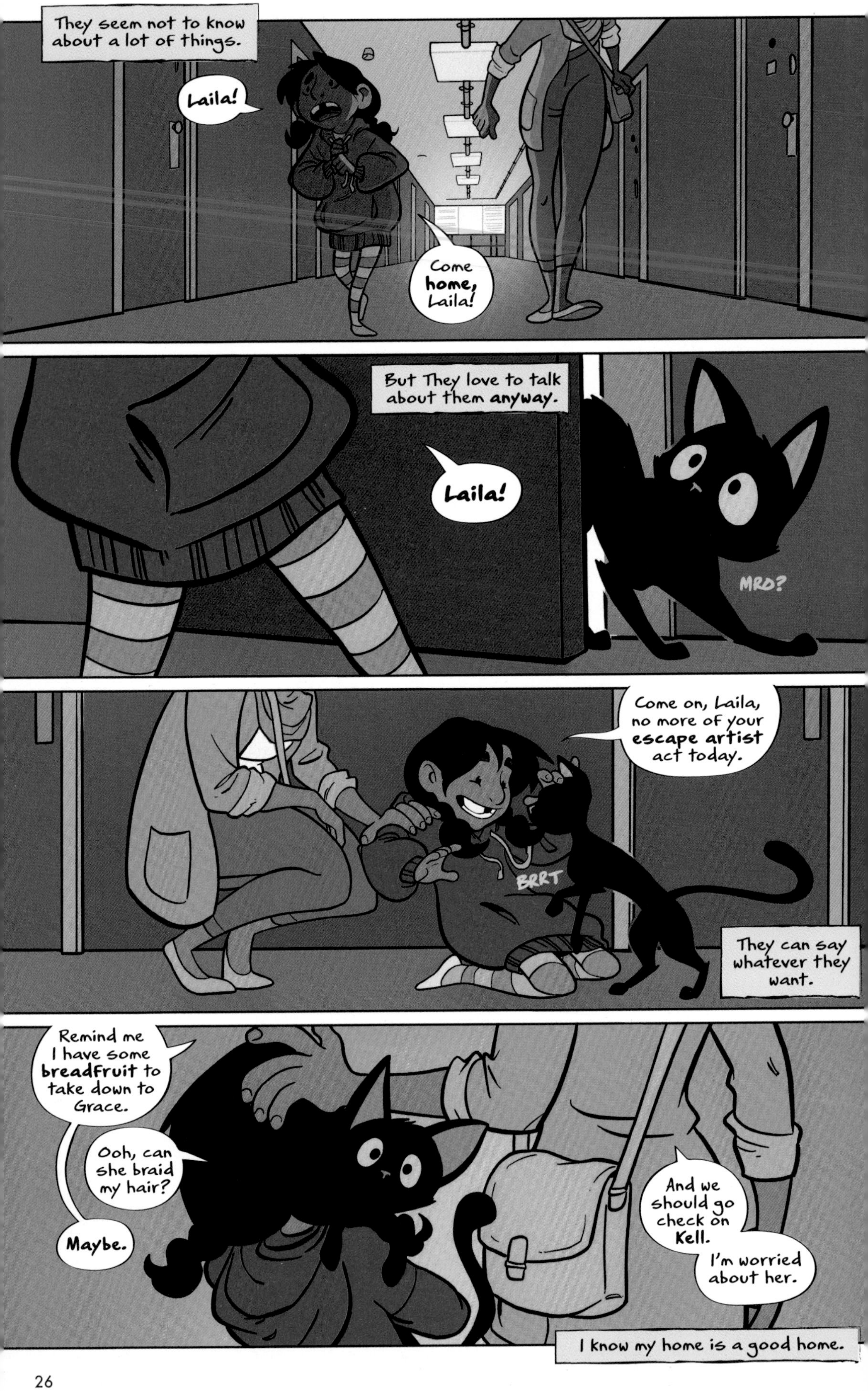
They seem not to know about a lot of things.
Laila!
Come home, Laila!
But They love to talk about them anyway.
Laila!
MRO?
Come on, Laila, no more of your escape artist act today.
BRRT
They can say whatever they want.
Remind me I have some breadfruit to take down to Grace.
Ooh, can she braid my hair?
Maybe.
And we should go check on Kell.
I'm worried about her.
I know my home is a good home.

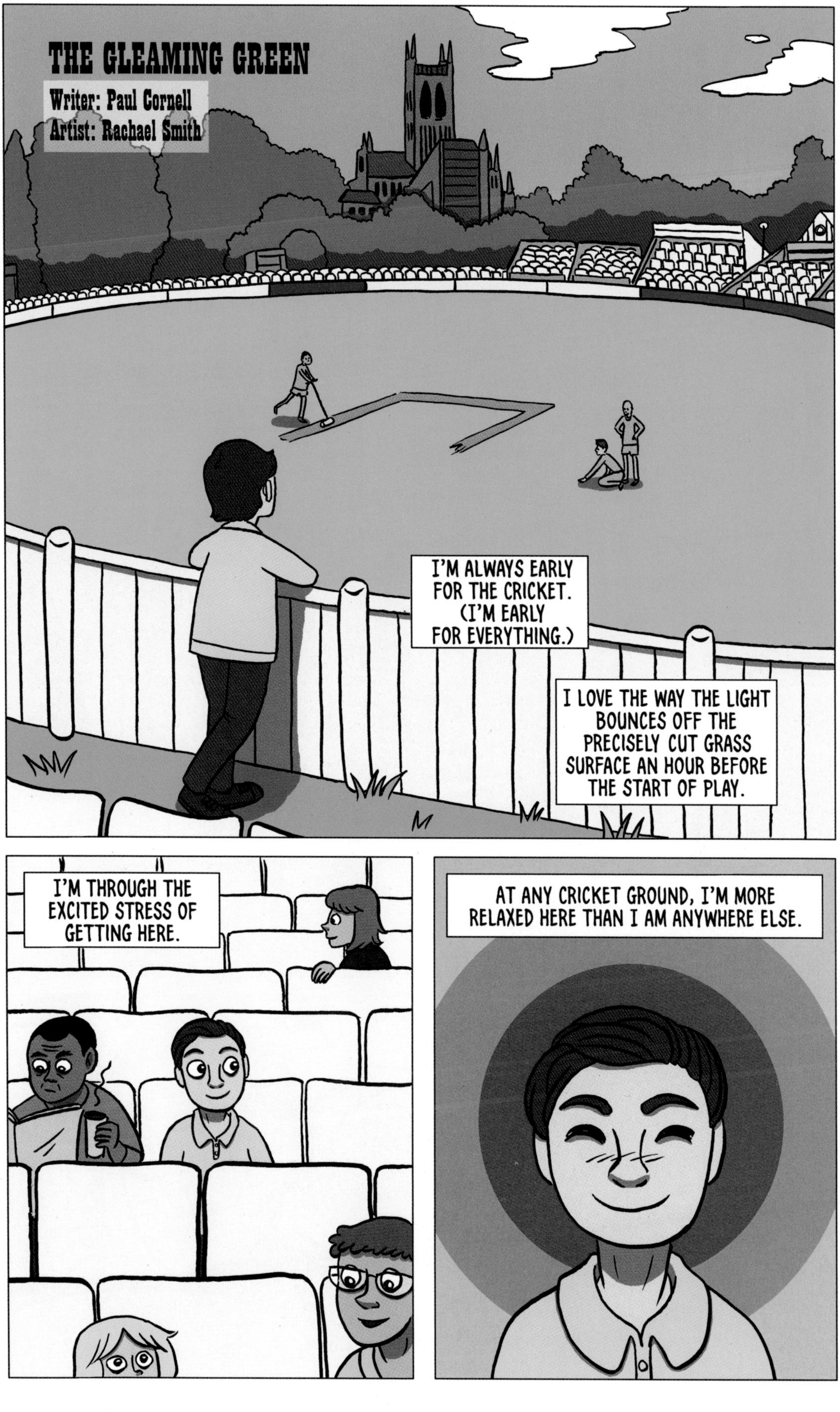
THE GLEAMING GREEN
Writer: Paul Cornell
Artist: Rachael Smith
I'M ALWAYS EARLY FOR THE CRICKET. (I'M EARLY FOR EVERYTHING.)
I LOVE THE WAY THE LIGHT BOUNCES OFF THE PRECISELY CUT GRASS SURFACE AN HOUR BEFORE THE START OF PLAY.
I'M THROUGH THE EXCITED STRESS OF GETTING HERE.
AT ANY CRICKET GROUND, I'M MORE RELAXED HERE THAN I AM ANYWHERE ELSE.

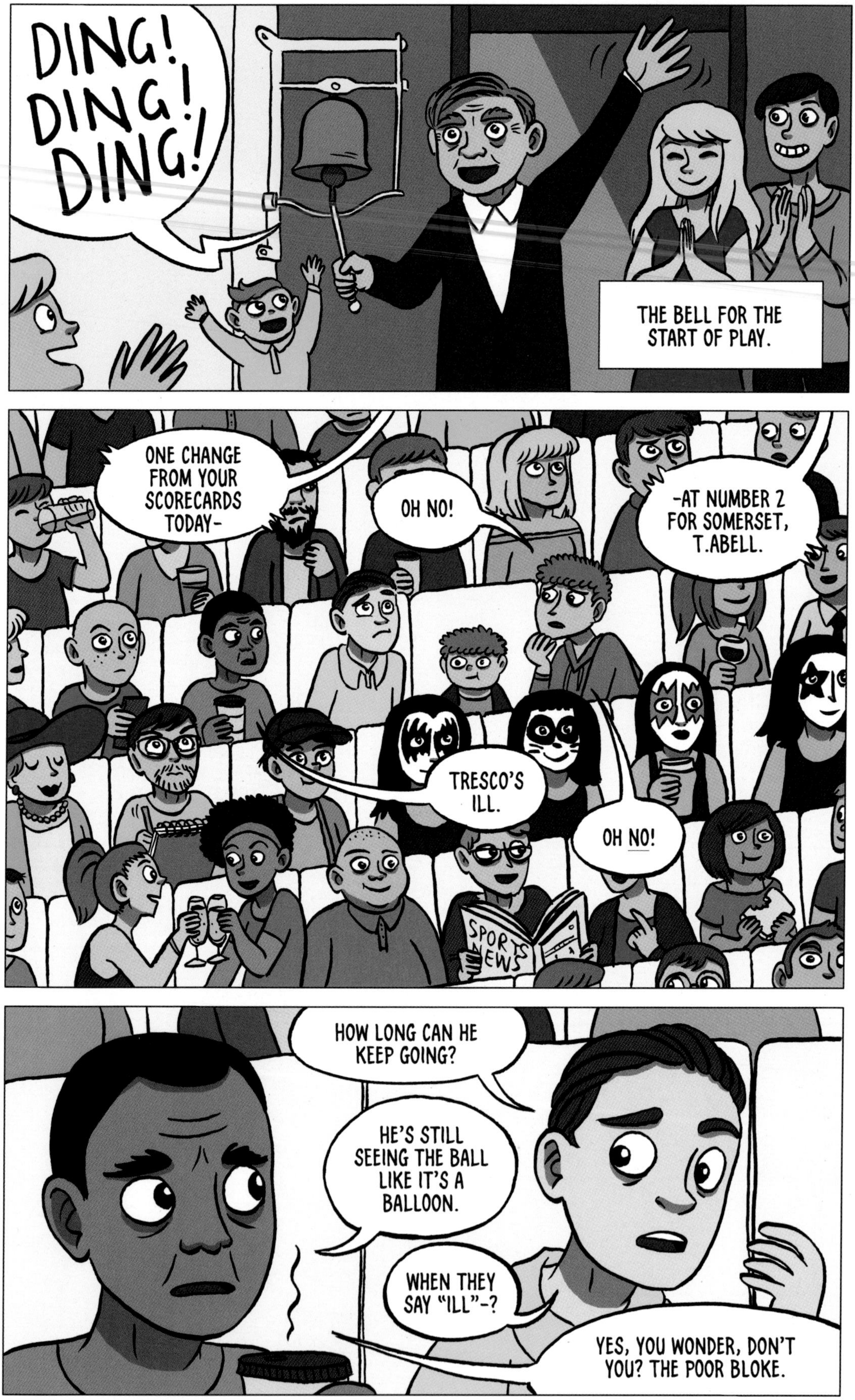
DING! DING! DING!
THE BELL FOR THE START OF PLAY.
ONE CHANGE FROM YOUR SCORECARDS TODAY-
OH NO!
-AT NUMBER 2 FOR SOMERSET, T.ABELL.
TRESCO'S ILL.
OH NO!
SPORTS NEWS
HOW LONG CAN HE KEEP GOING?
HE'S STILL SEEING THE BALL LIKE IT'S A BALLOON.
WHEN THEY SAY "ILL"-?
YES, YOU WONDER, DON'T YOU? THE POOR BLOKE.

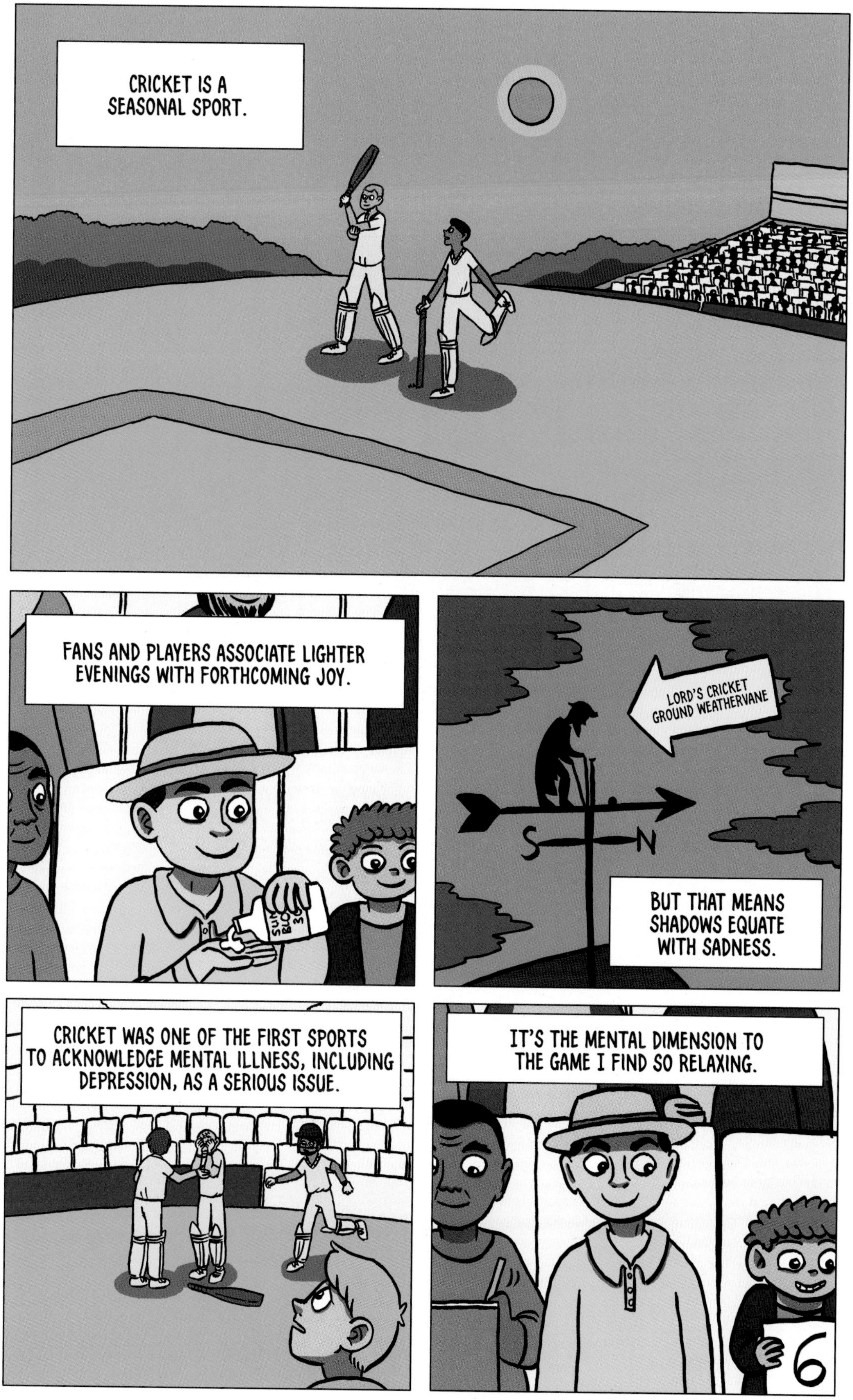
CRICKET IS A SEASONAL SPORT.
FANS AND PLAYERS ASSOCIATE LIGHTER EVENINGS WITH FORTHCOMING JOY.
LORD'S CRICKET GROUND WEATHERVANE
S
N
BUT THAT MEANS SHADOWS EQUATE WITH SADNESS.
CRICKET WAS ONE OF THE FIRST SPORTS TO ACKNOWLEDGE MENTAL ILLNESS, INCLUDING DEPRESSION, AS A SERIOUS ISSUE.
IT'S THE MENTAL DIMENSION TO THE GAME I FIND SO RELAXING.
6

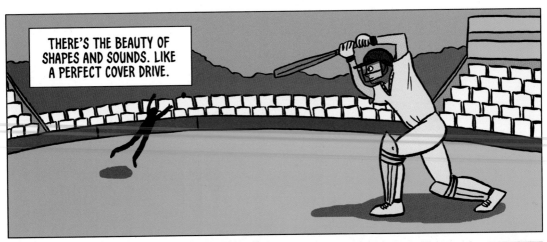

THERE'S THE BEAUTY OF SHAPES AND SOUNDS. LIKE A PERFECT COVER DRIVE.

THEN THERE'S THE SATISFACTION OF CHANGING DATA SETS.

ABELL NEEDS FIVE MORE FOR 2500 CAREER RUNS. AND THERE ARE SOME SURPRISINGLY LOW PARTNERSHIP RECORDS ON THIS GROUND...

AS A CHILD I WAS DIAGNOSED AS AUTISTIC. I DON'T IDENTIFY AS THAT NOW, BUT MY SON, TOM, DEFINITELY IS.

THE PROCESSION OF NUMBERS IN CRICKET PLEASES ME **DEEPLY**. I THINK THAT'S AN EXPRESSION OF THOSE GENES.

I WILL NOW LIST ALL MY THOMAS ENGINES...

STOIC ENGLISH IDENTITY STEREOTYPES, CRICKET INCLUDED, ARE KIND OF AUTISM-FRIENDLY, BUT AUTISM DOESN'T PRECLUDE HIGH EMOTION...

HE'S THE CAPTAIN, BUT HIS AVERAGE IS **SO** LOW. THE **PRESSURE** ON HIM. THAT TIME HE DROPPED **HIMSELF** FROM THE TEAM...

THE HIGH EMOTION OF KNOWING PLAYERS WHO STAY WITH TEAMS FOR DECADES...

AND IT ALL EBBS AND FLOWS ON THE PITCH AS THE SHADOWS CHANGE WITH THE DAY. AND INSPIRED BY IT-

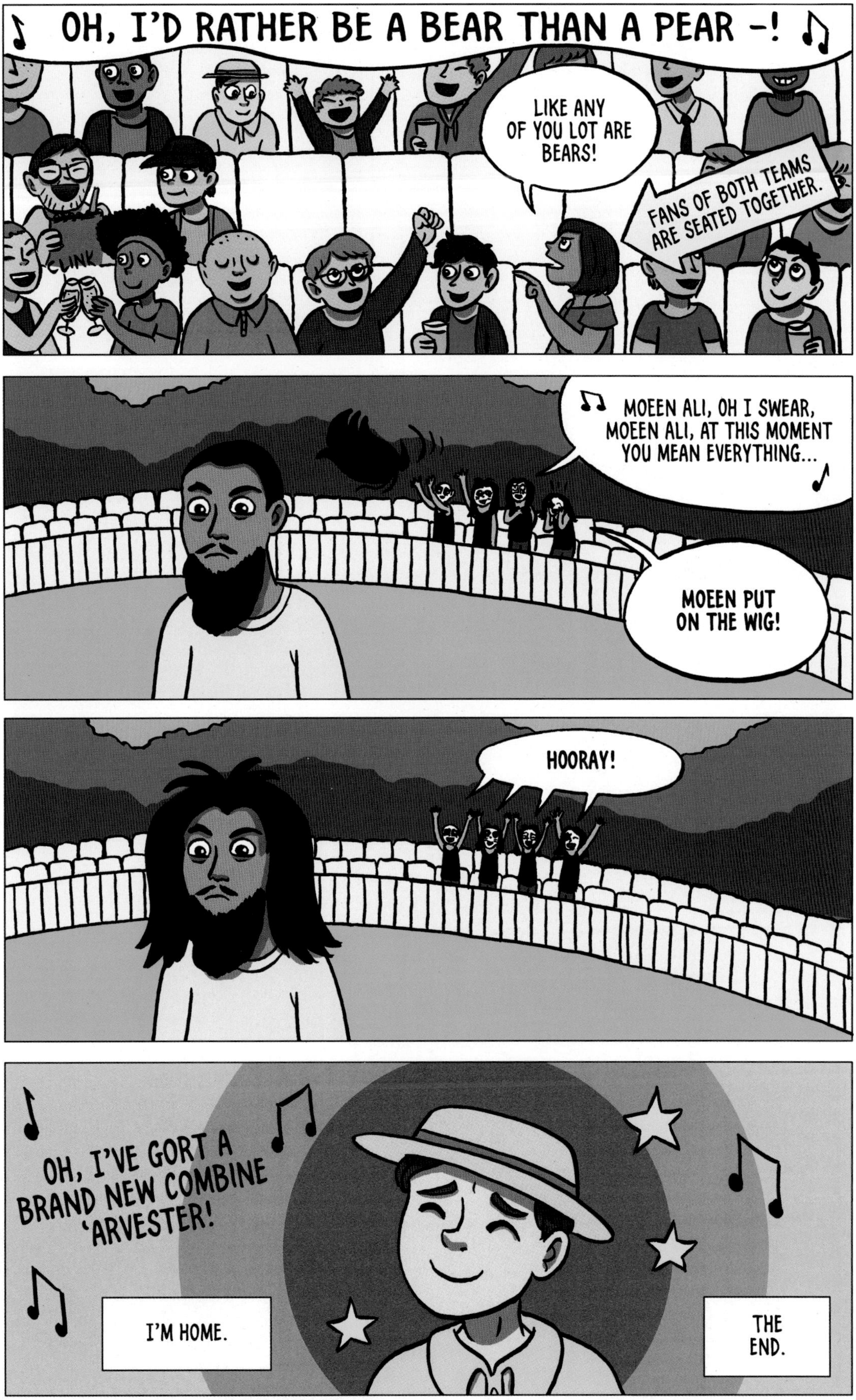

OH, I'D RATHER BE A BEAR THAN A PEAR –!
LIKE ANY OF YOU LOT ARE BEARS!
FANS OF BOTH TEAMS ARE SEATED TOGETHER.
CLINK
MOEEN ALI, OH I SWEAR, MOEEN ALI, AT THIS MOMENT YOU MEAN EVERYTHING...
MOEEN PUT ON THE WIG!
HOORAY!
OH, I'VE GORT A BRAND NEW COMBINE 'ARVESTER!
I'M HOME.
THE END.

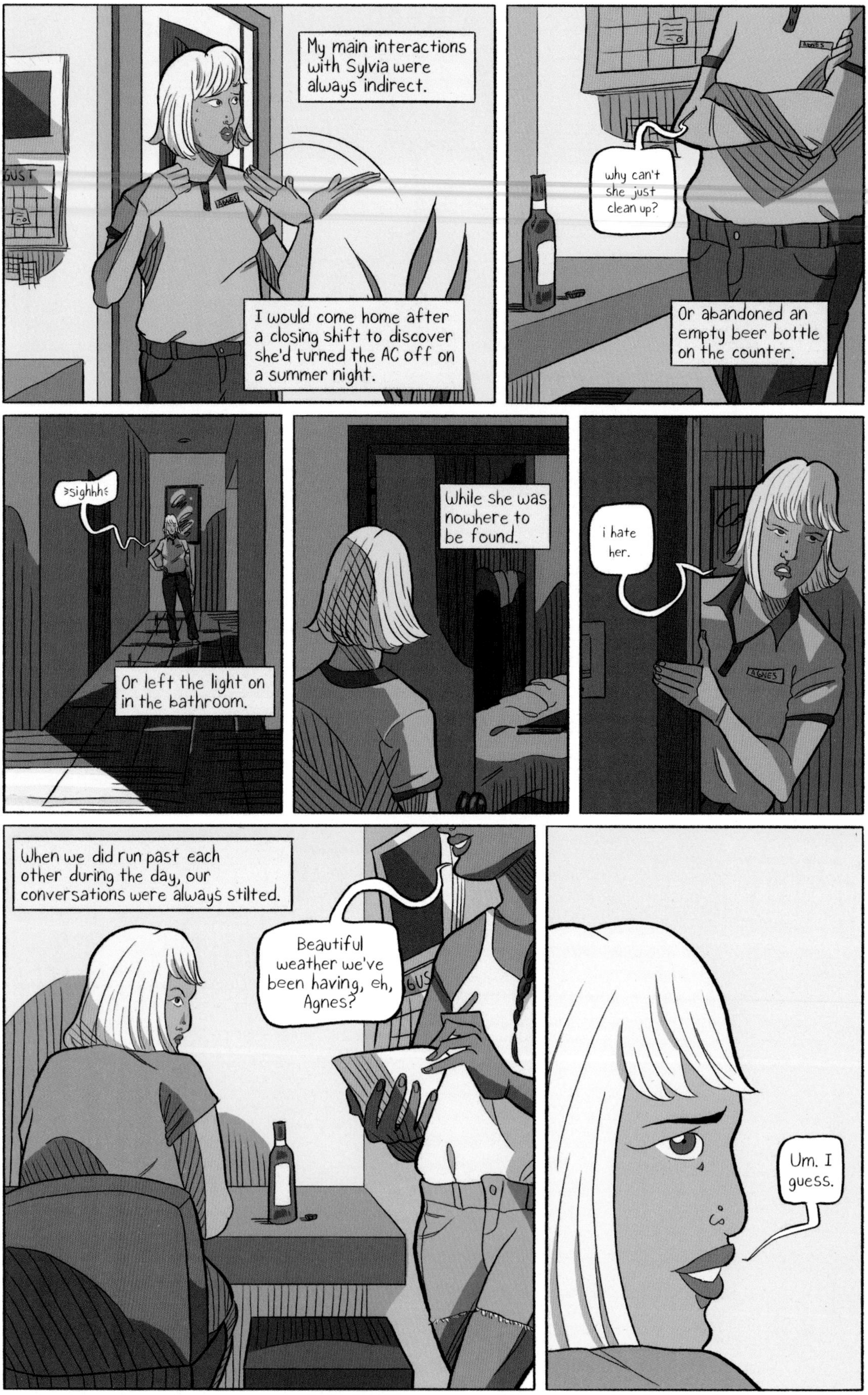
My main interactions with Sylvia were always indirect.
I would come home after a closing shift to discover she'd turned the AC off on a summer night.
why can't she just clean up?
Or abandoned an empty beer bottle on the counter.
≽sighhh≼
Or left the light on in the bathroom.
While she was nowhere to be found.
i hate her.
When we did run past each other during the day, our conversations were always stilted.
Beautiful weather we've been having, eh, Agnes?
Um. I guess.

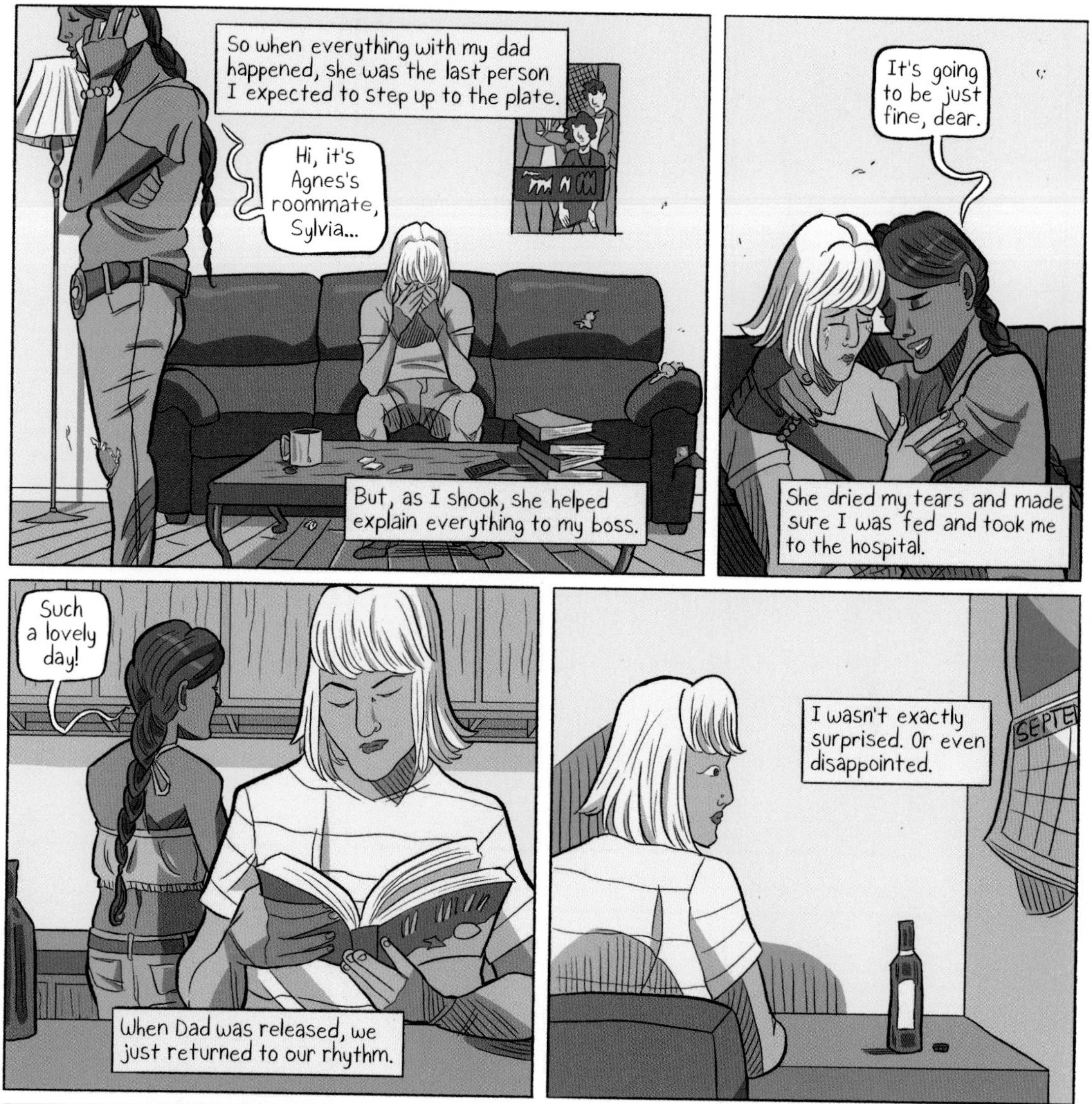
So when everything with my dad happened, she was the last person I expected to step up to the plate.
Hi, it's Agnes's roommate, Sylvia...
But, as I shook, she helped explain everything to my boss.
It's going to be just fine, dear.
She dried my tears and made sure I was fed and took me to the hospital.
Such a lovely day!
When Dad was released, we just returned to our rhythm.
I wasn't exactly surprised. Or even disappointed.
SEPTE

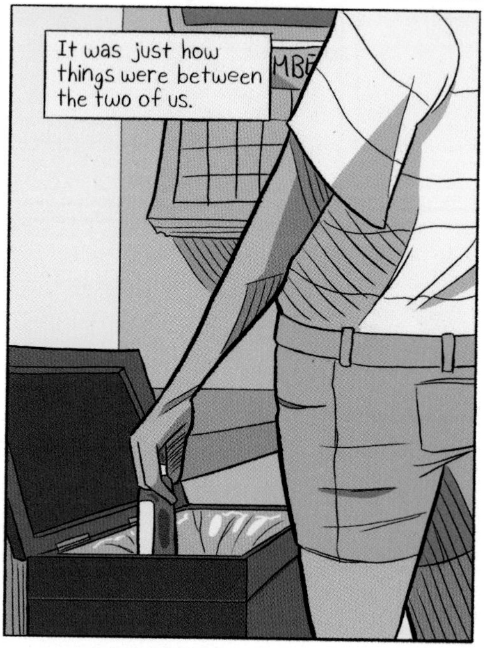
It was just how things were between the two of us.
MBE

clink!

"KINSHIP"

Words + Art by
Liam Donnelly

24 PANELS; DBL PAGE SPREAD

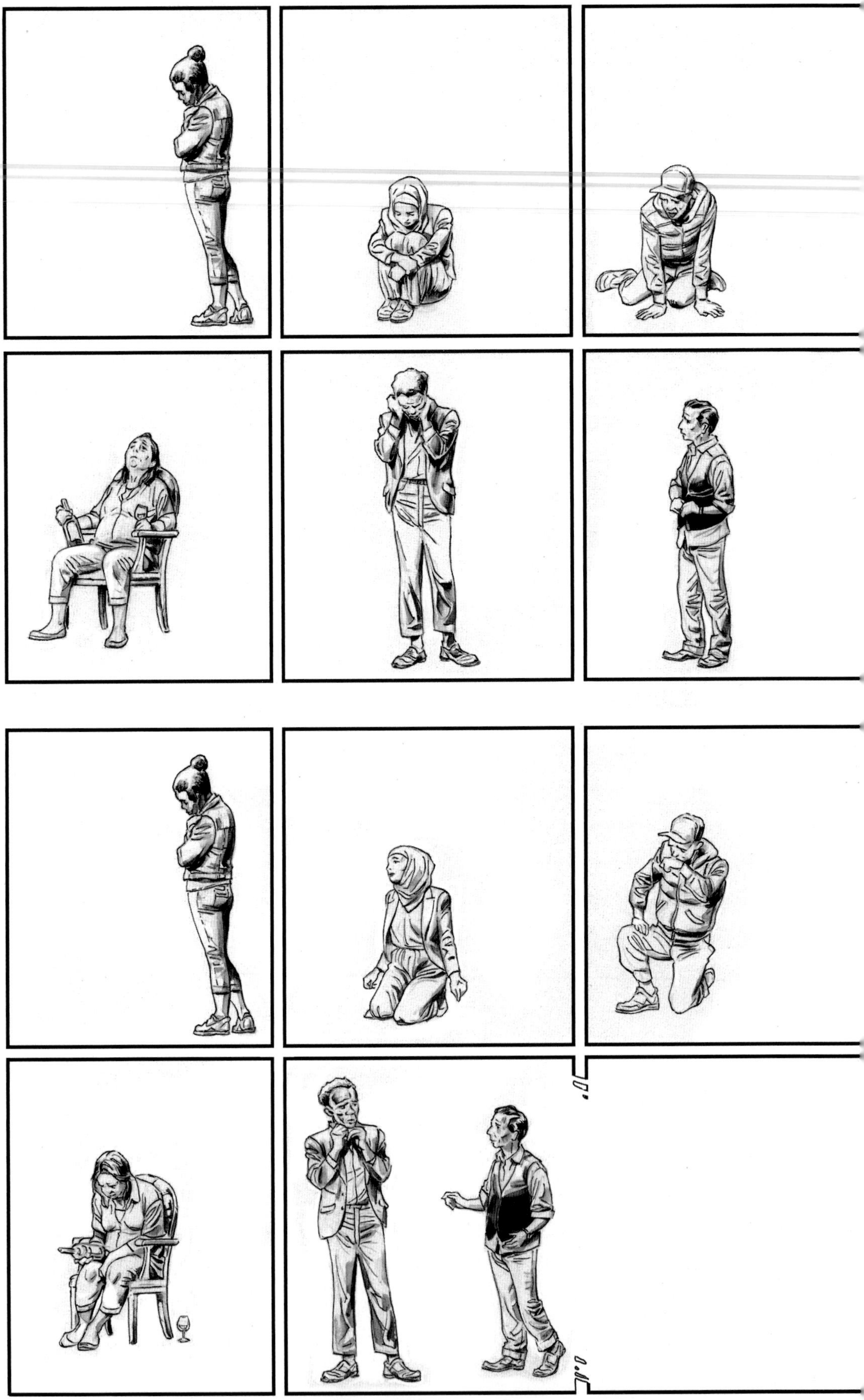

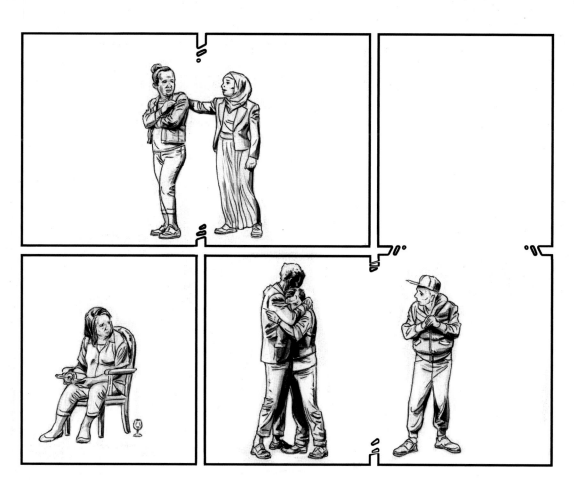

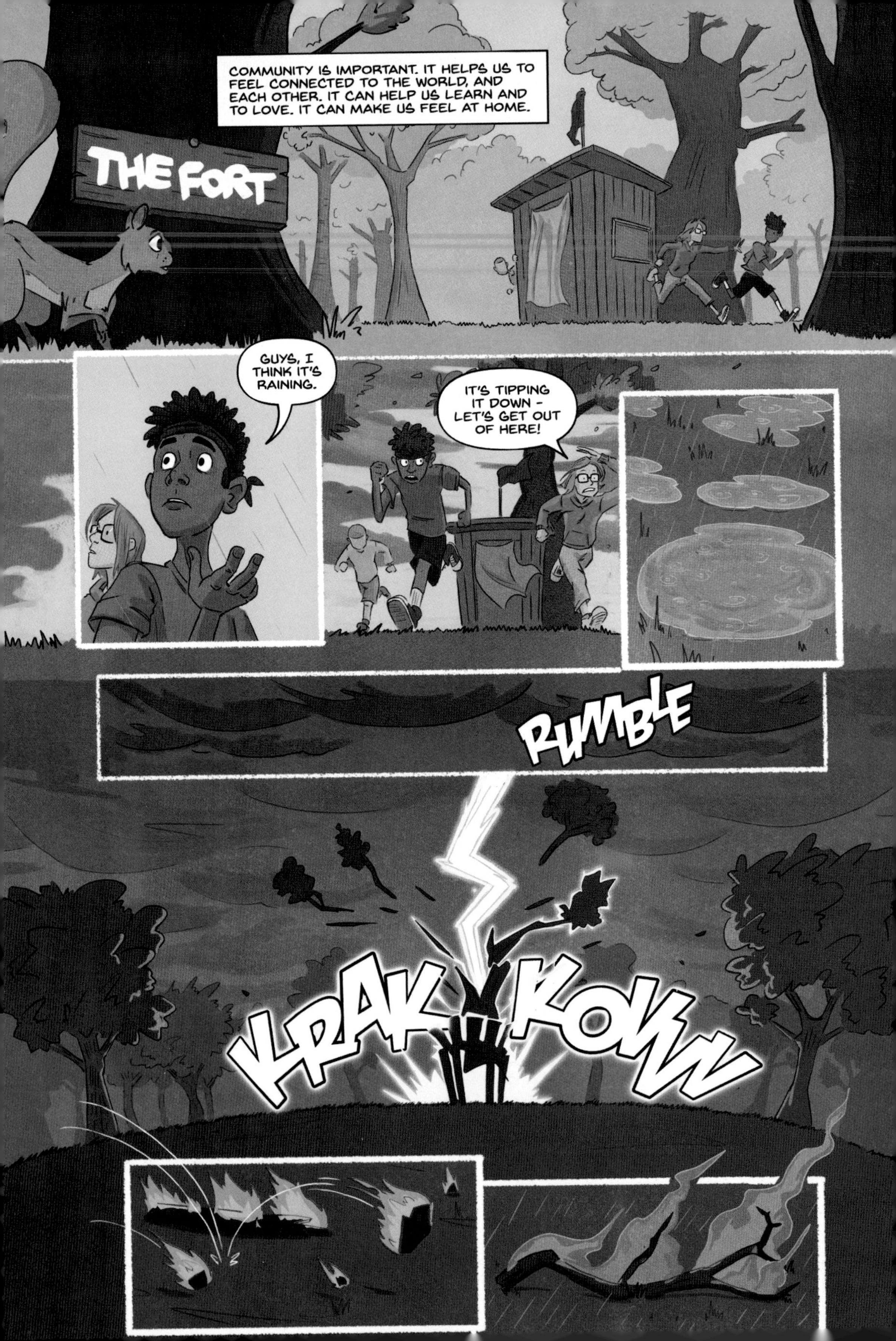
COMMUNITY IS IMPORTANT. IT HELPS US TO FEEL CONNECTED TO THE WORLD, AND EACH OTHER. IT CAN HELP US LEARN AND TO LOVE. IT CAN MAKE US FEEL AT HOME.
THE FORT
GUYS, I THINK IT'S RAINING.
IT'S TIPPING IT DOWN - LET'S GET OUT OF HERE!
RUMBLE
KRAK KOWW

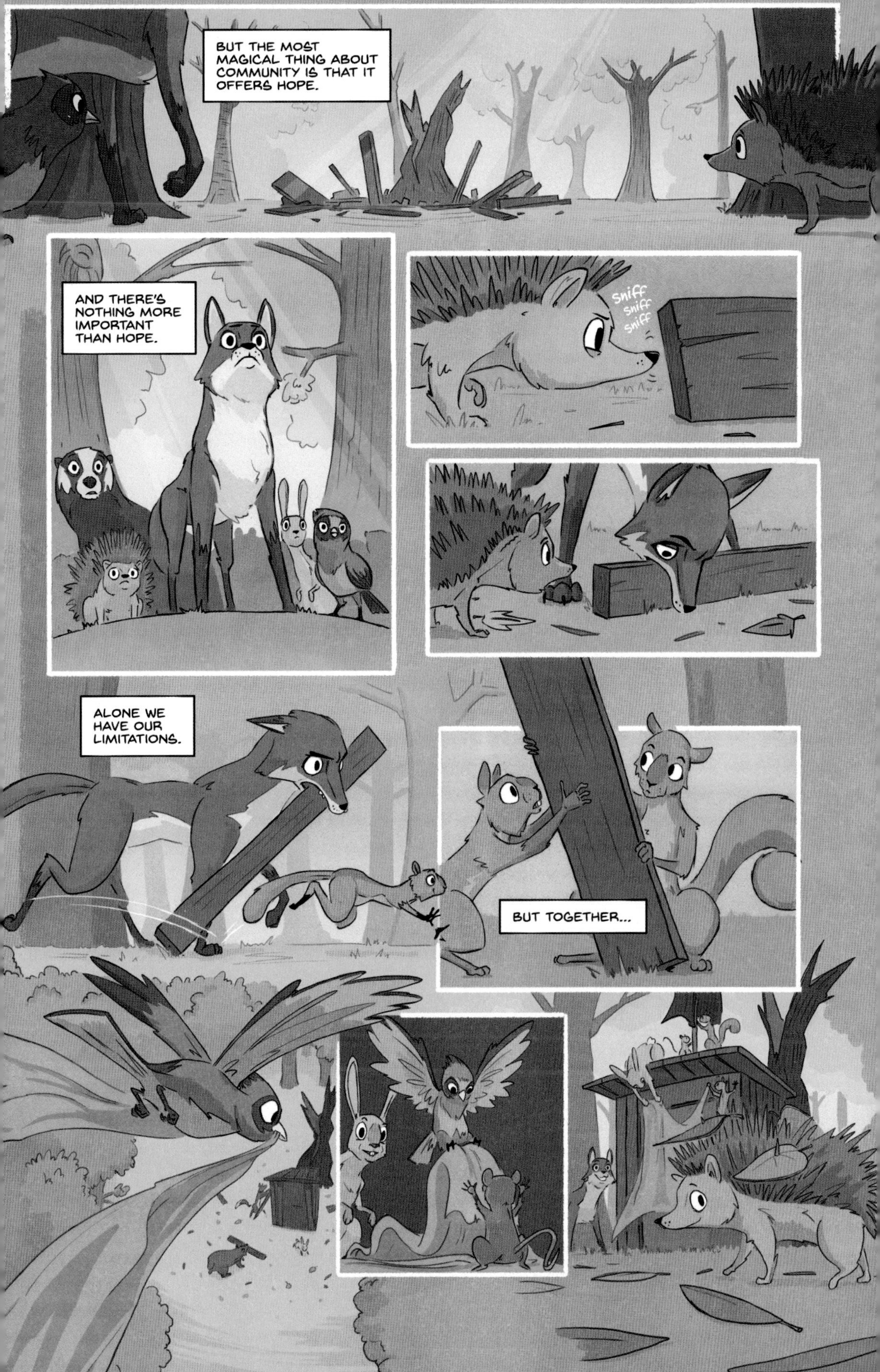

BUT THE MOST MAGICAL THING ABOUT COMMUNITY IS THAT IT OFFERS HOPE.
AND THERE'S NOTHING MORE IMPORTANT THAN HOPE.
Sniff sniff sniff
ALONE WE HAVE OUR LIMITATIONS.
BUT TOGETHER...

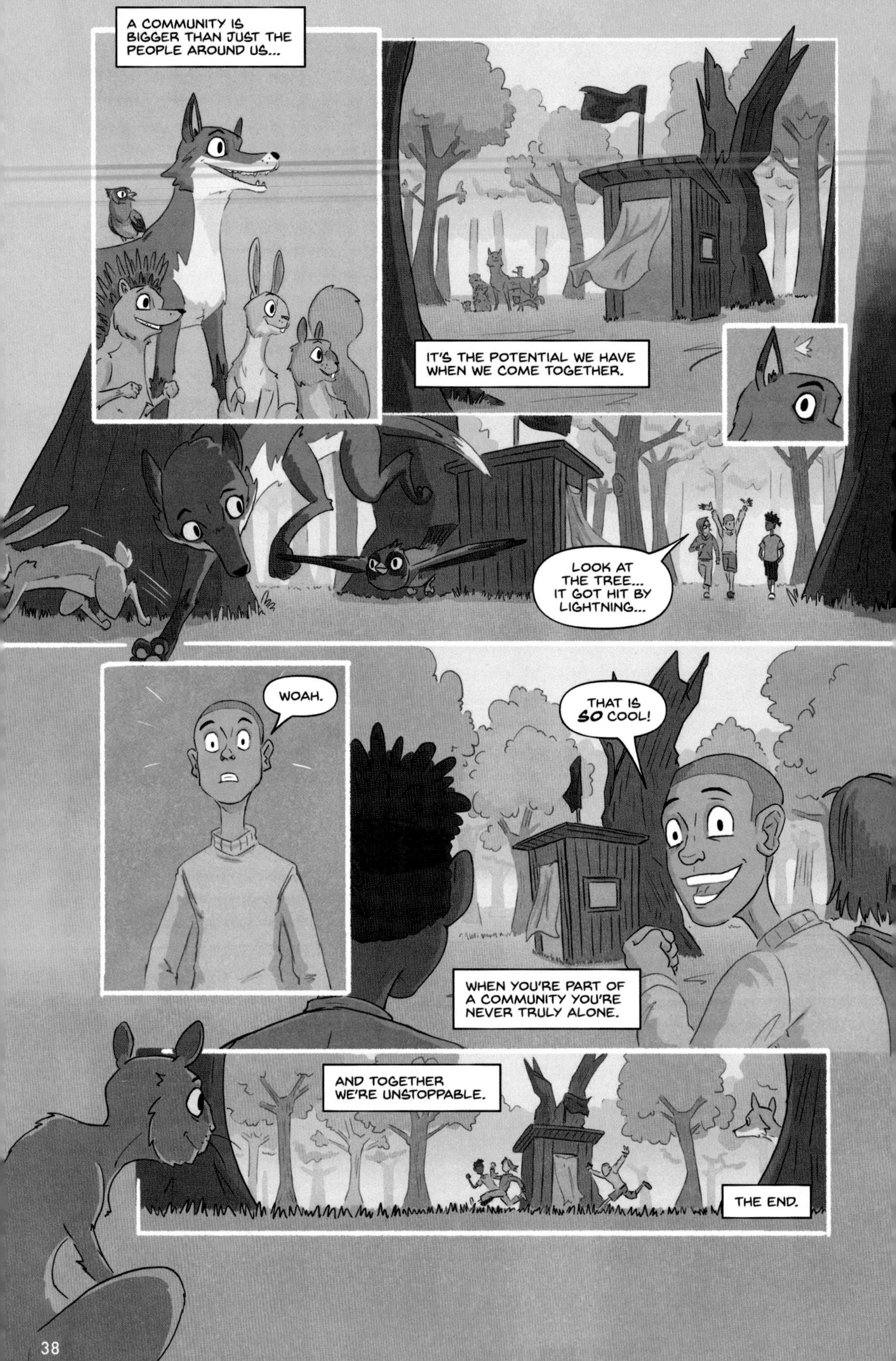
A COMMUNITY IS BIGGER THAN JUST THE PEOPLE AROUND US...
IT'S THE POTENTIAL WE HAVE WHEN WE COME TOGETHER.
LOOK AT THE TREE... IT GOT HIT BY LIGHTNING...
WOAH.
THAT IS *SO* COOL!
WHEN YOU'RE PART OF A COMMUNITY YOU'RE NEVER TRULY ALONE.
AND TOGETHER WE'RE UNSTOPPABLE.
THE END.

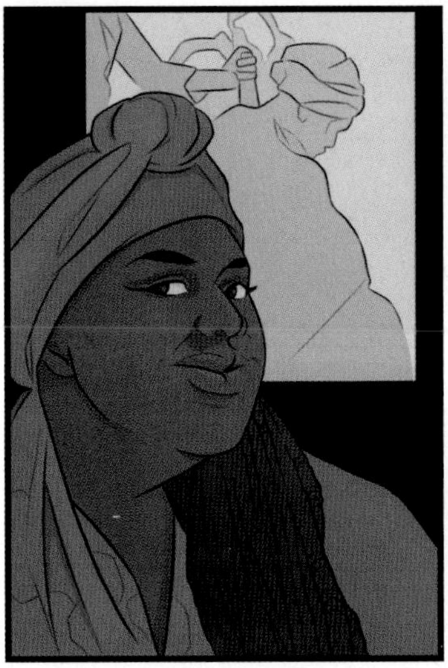

KHADIJA SAYE

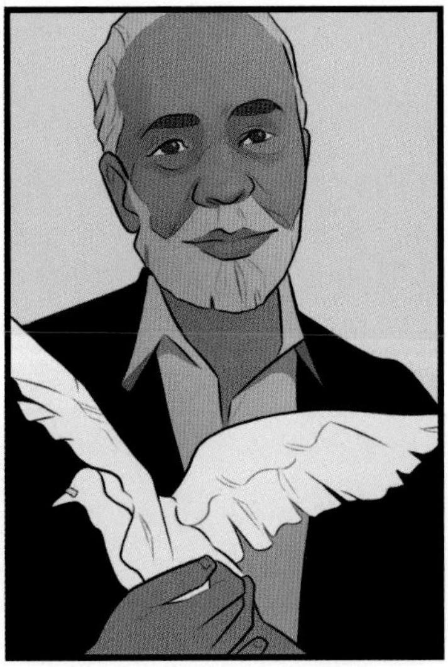

ALI YAWAR JAFARI

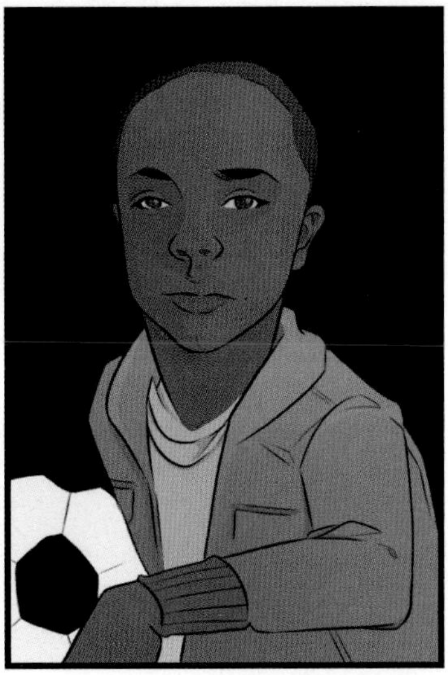

ISAAC PAULOS

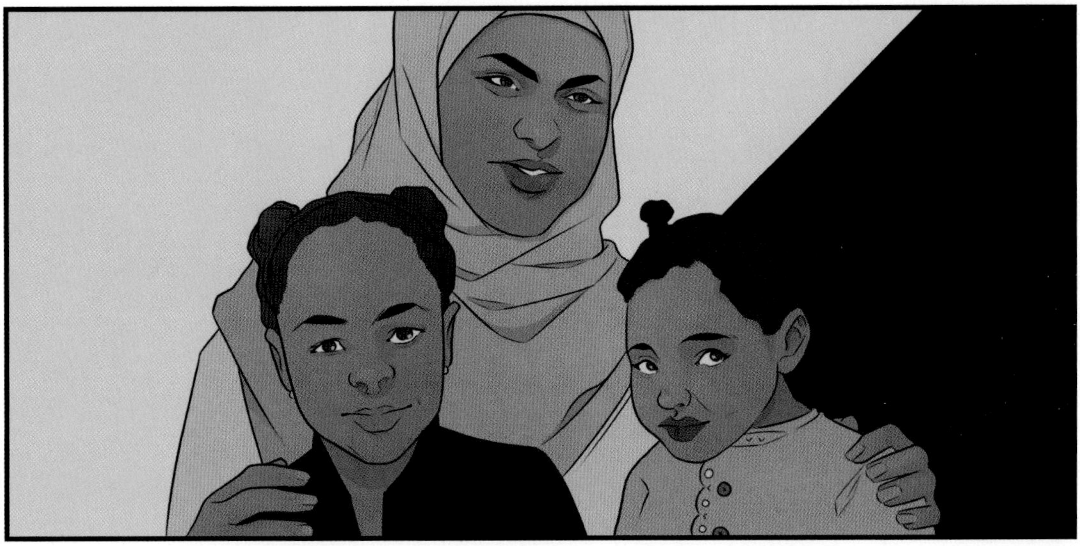

RANIA IBRAHIM AND HANIA AND FETHIA HASSAN

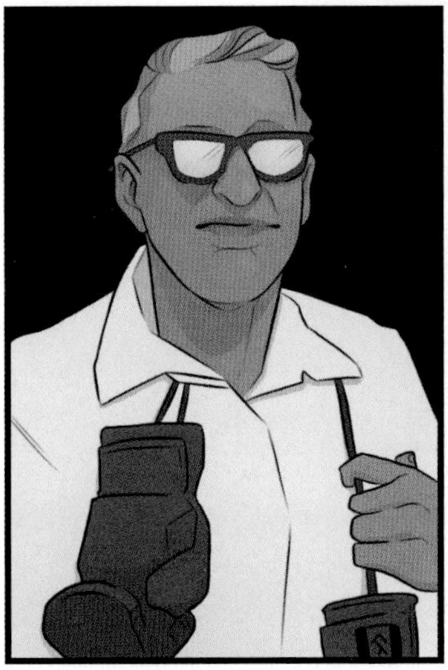

ANTHONY DISSON

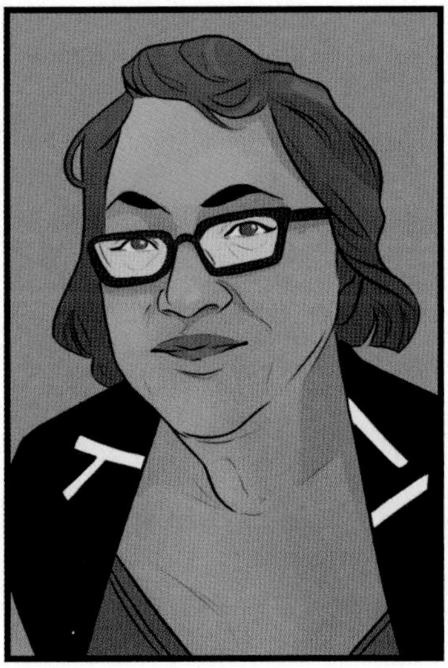

LIGAYA MOORE

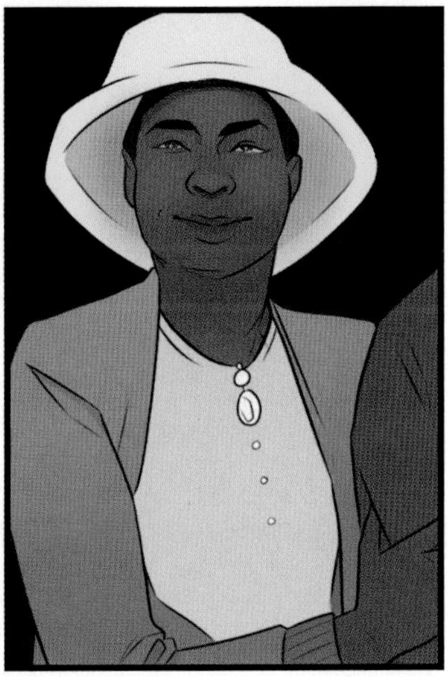

MARJORIE VITAL

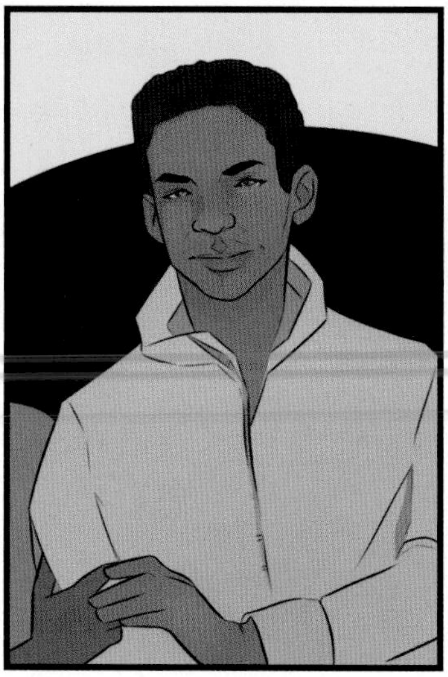

ERNIE VITAL

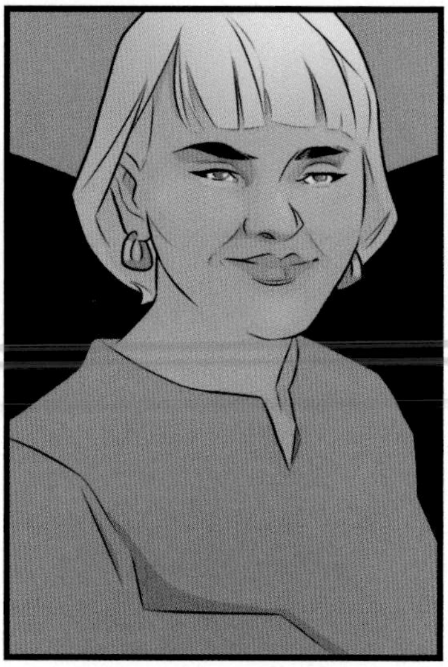

DEBORAH LAMPRELL

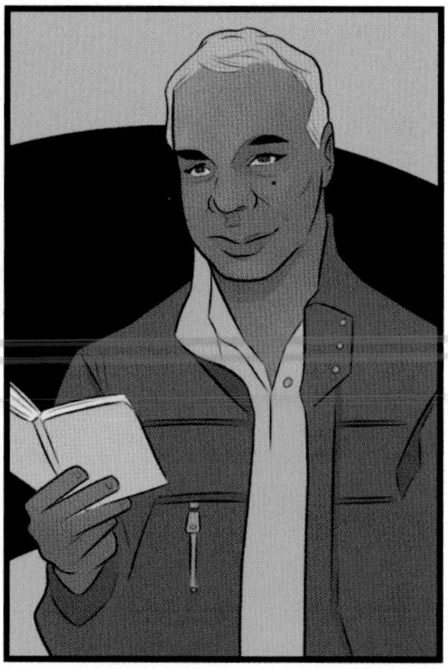

HESHAM RAHMAN

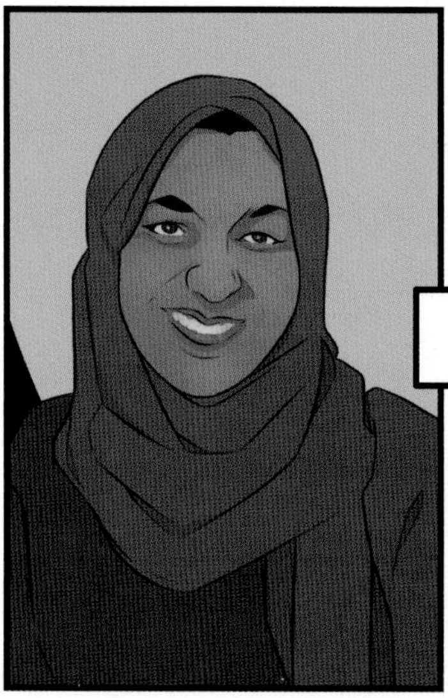

KHADIJA KHALOUFI

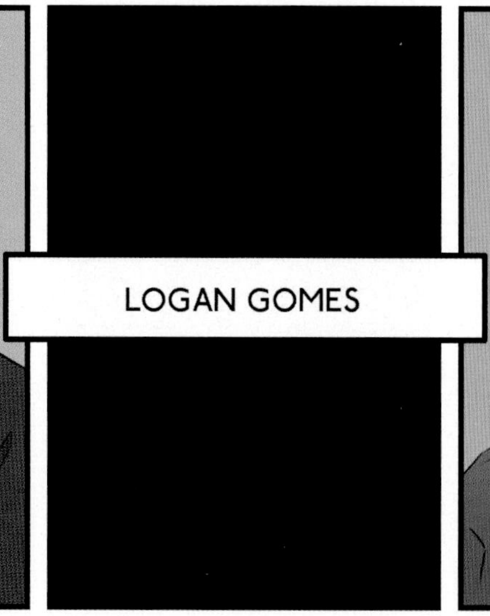
LOGAN GOMES

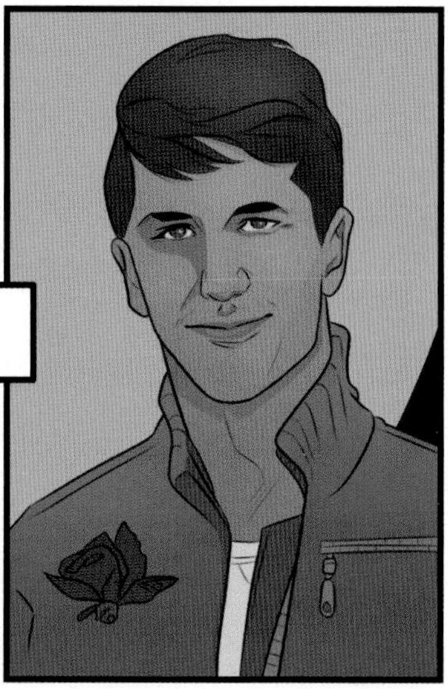

MARCO GOTTARDI

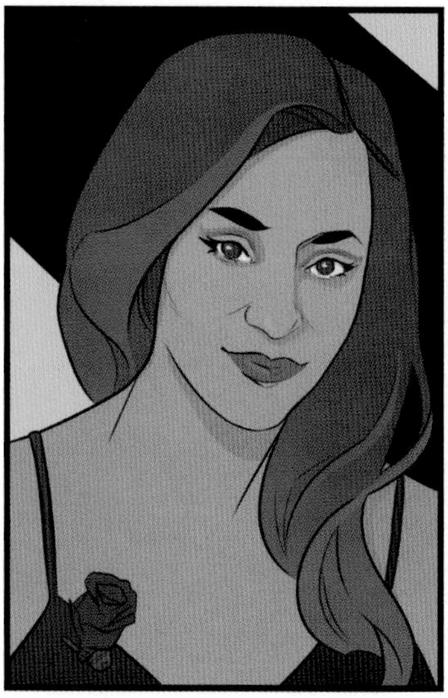

GLORIA TREVISAN

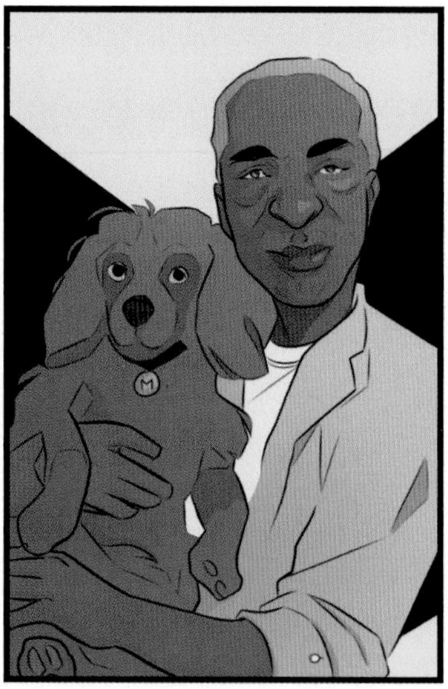

RAYMOND 'MOSES' BERNARD

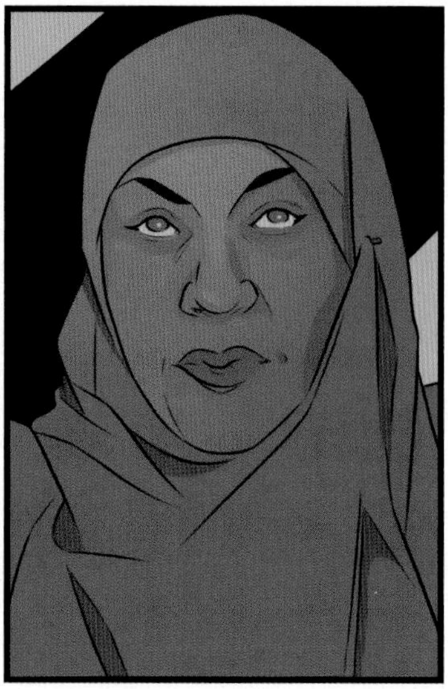

SIRRIA CHOUCAIR

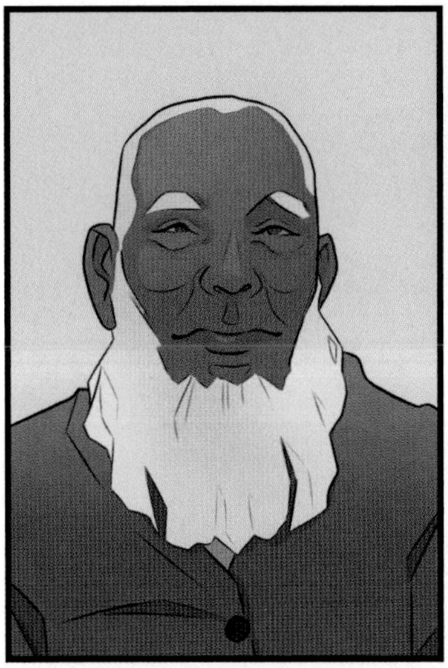

KAMRU MIAH

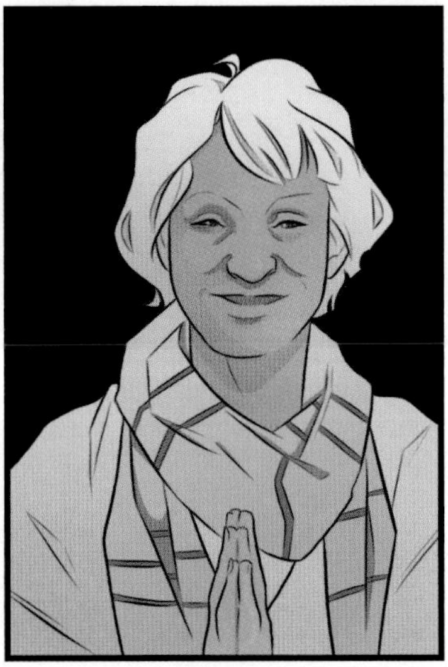

SHEILA

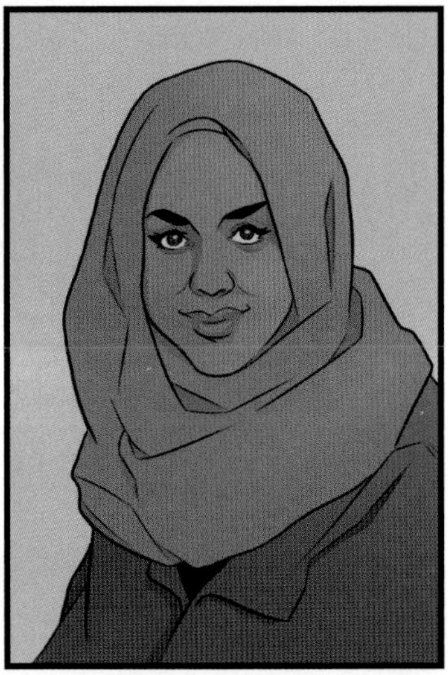

HUSNA BEGUM

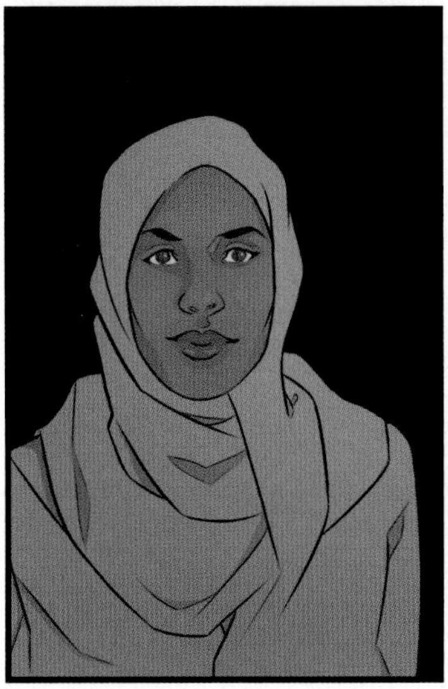

AMNA MAHMUD IDRIS

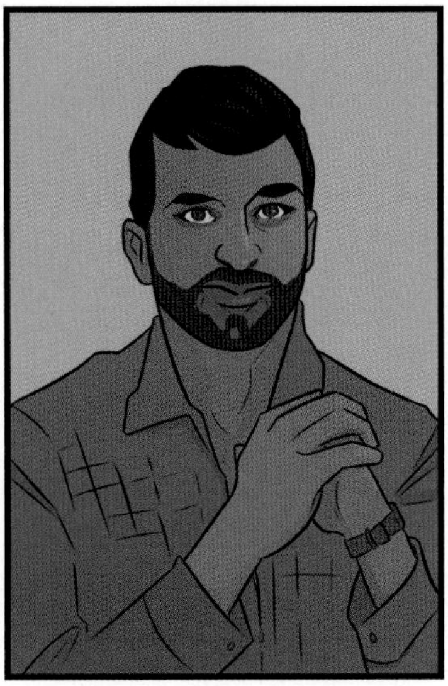

MOHAMMED ALHAJALI

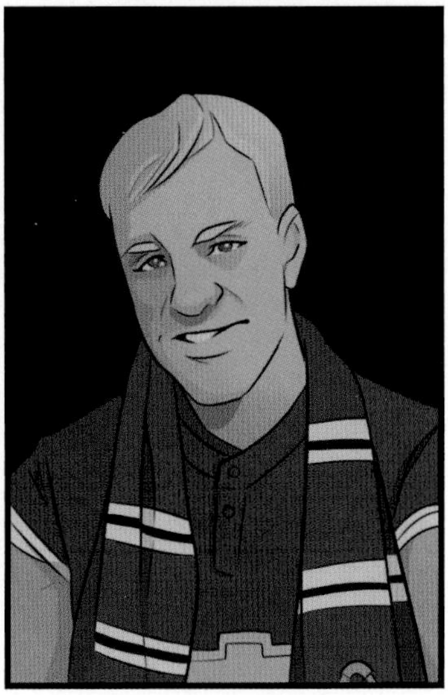

GARY MAUNDERS

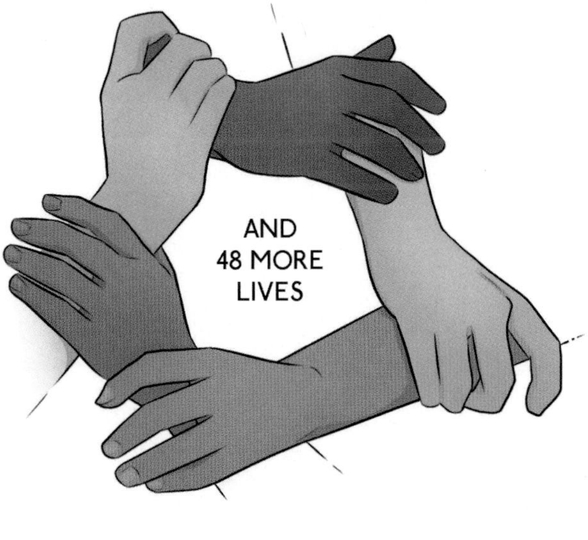
AND
48 MORE
LIVES

...DREAM JOB

A CHOOSE YOUR OWN STORY COMIC!

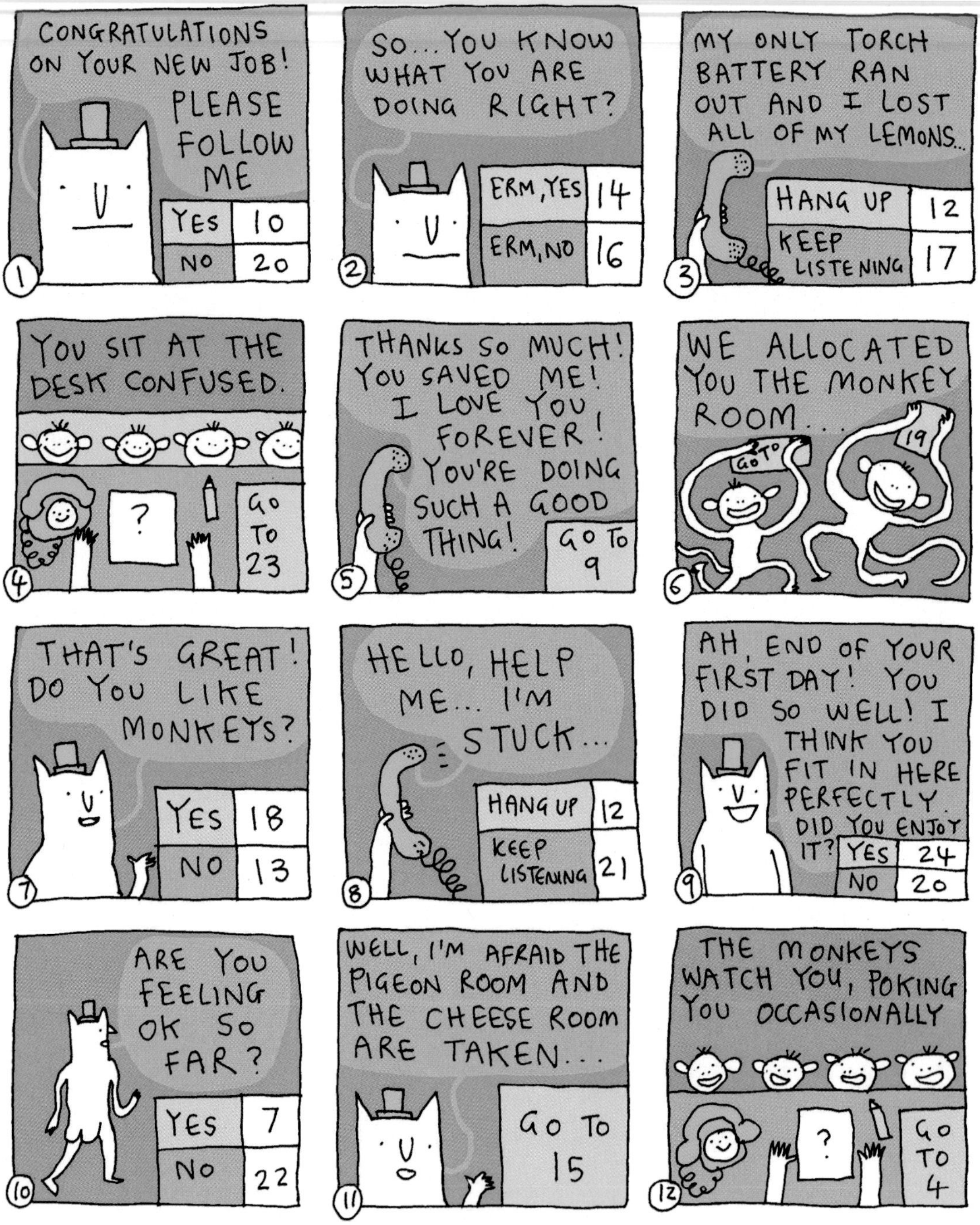

CONGRATULATIONS ON YOUR NEW JOB!
PLEASE FOLLOW ME
YES 10
NO 20
1
SO... YOU KNOW WHAT YOU ARE DOING RIGHT?
ERM, YES 14
ERM, NO 16
2
MY ONLY TORCH BATTERY RAN OUT AND I LOST ALL OF MY LEMONS...
HANG UP 12
KEEP LISTENING 17
3
YOU SIT AT THE DESK CONFUSED.
?
GO TO 23
4
THANKS SO MUCH! YOU SAVED ME! I LOVE YOU FOREVER! YOU'RE DOING SUCH A GOOD THING!
GO TO 9
5
WE ALLOCATED YOU THE MONKEY ROOM...
GO TO
19
6
THAT'S GREAT! DO YOU LIKE MONKEYS?
YES 18
NO 13
7
HELLO, HELP ME... I'M STUCK...
HANG UP 12
KEEP LISTENING 21
8
AH, END OF YOUR FIRST DAY! YOU DID SO WELL! I THINK YOU FIT IN HERE PERFECTLY. DID YOU ENJOY IT?
YES 24
NO 20
9
ARE YOU FEELING OK SO FAR?
YES 7
NO 22
10
WELL, I'M AFRAID THE PIGEON ROOM AND THE CHEESE ROOM ARE TAKEN...
GO TO 15
11
THE MONKEYS WATCH YOU, POKING YOU OCCASIONALLY
?
GO TO 4
12

DID YOU GUESS WHAT YOUR JOB IS?

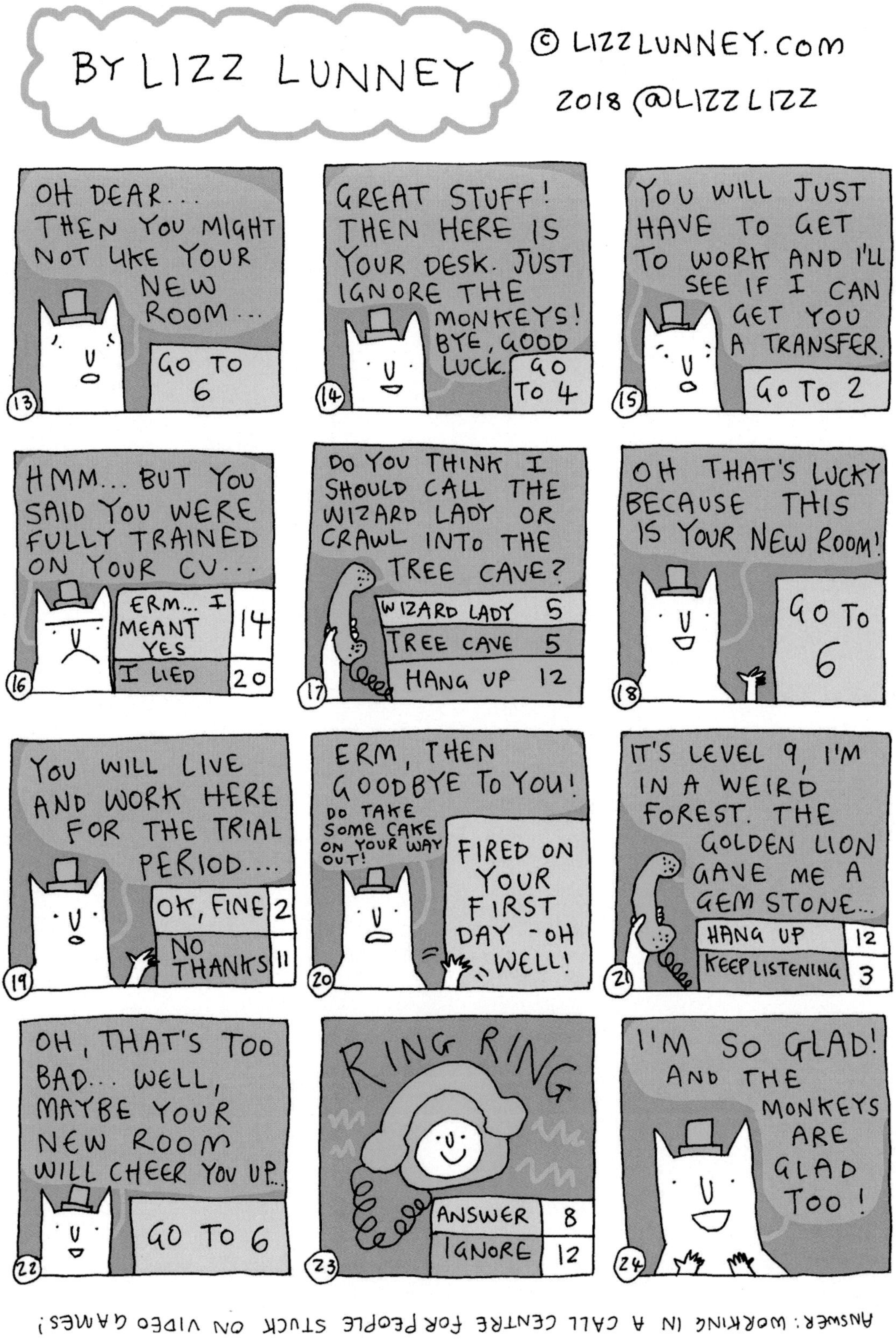

BY LIZZ LUNNEY
© LIZZLUNNEY.COM
2018 @LIZZLIZZ
13 OH DEAR... THEN YOU MIGHT NOT LIKE YOUR NEW ROOM...
GO TO 6
14 GREAT STUFF! THEN HERE IS YOUR DESK. JUST IGNORE THE MONKEYS! BYE, GOOD LUCK.
GO TO 4
15 YOU WILL JUST HAVE TO GET TO WORK AND I'LL SEE IF I CAN GET YOU A TRANSFER.
GO TO 2
16 HMM... BUT YOU SAID YOU WERE FULLY TRAINED ON YOUR CV...
ERM... I MEANT YES 14
I LIED 20
17 DO YOU THINK I SHOULD CALL THE WIZARD LADY OR CRAWL INTO THE TREE CAVE?
WIZARD LADY 5
TREE CAVE 5
HANG UP 12
18 OH THAT'S LUCKY BECAUSE THIS IS YOUR NEW ROOM!
GO TO 6
19 YOU WILL LIVE AND WORK HERE FOR THE TRIAL PERIOD....
OK, FINE 2
NO THANKS 11
20 ERM, THEN GOODBYE TO YOU!
DO TAKE SOME CAKE ON YOUR WAY OUT!
FIRED ON YOUR FIRST DAY - OH WELL!
21 IT'S LEVEL 9, I'M IN A WEIRD FOREST. THE GOLDEN LION GAVE ME A GEM STONE...
HANG UP 12
KEEP LISTENING 3
22 OH, THAT'S TOO BAD... WELL, MAYBE YOUR NEW ROOM WILL CHEER YOU UP...
GO TO 6
23 RING RING
ANSWER 8
IGNORE 12
24 I'M SO GLAD! AND THE MONKEYS ARE GLAD TOO!
ANSWER: WORKING IN A CALL CENTRE FOR PEOPLE STUCK ON VIDEO GAMES!

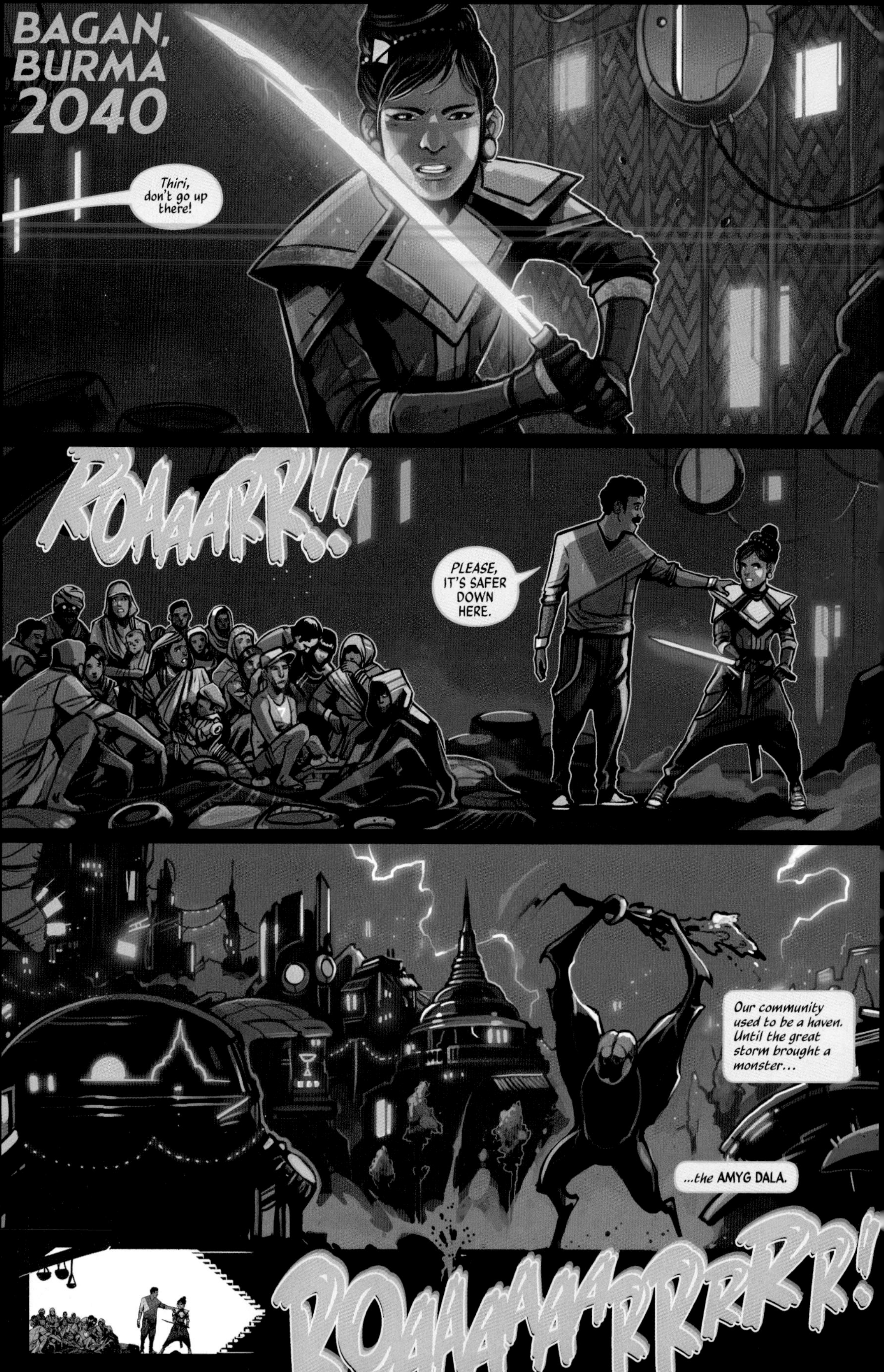
BAGAN, BURMA 2040
Thiri, don't go up there!
ROAAARR!!
PLEASE, IT'S SAFER DOWN HERE.
Our community used to be a haven. Until the great storm brought a monster...
...the AMYG DALA.
ROAAAAARRRRR!

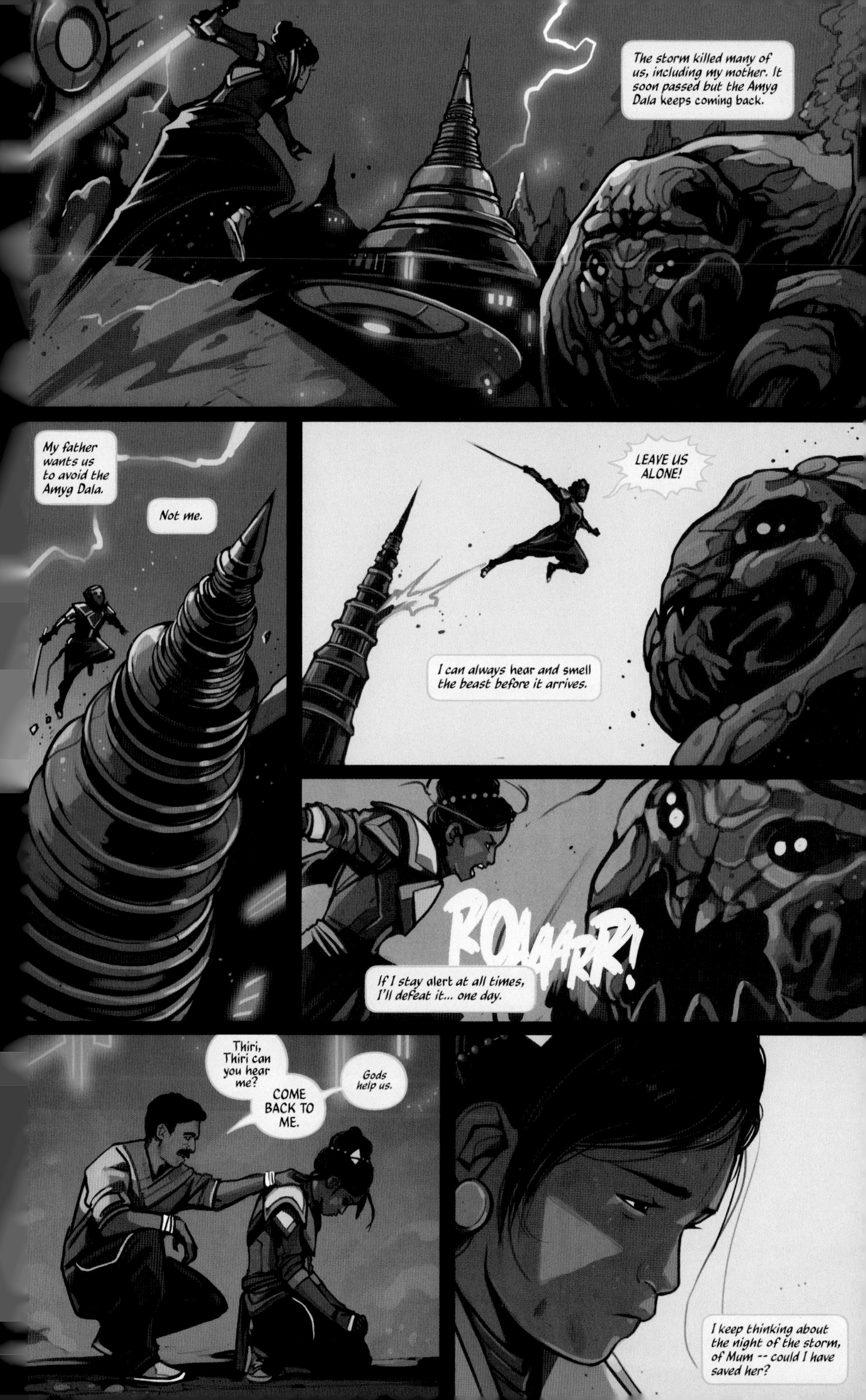
The storm killed many of us, including my mother. It soon passed but the Amyg Dala keeps coming back.
My father wants us to avoid the Amyg Dala.
Not me.
LEAVE US ALONE!
I can always hear and smell the beast before it arrives.
ROAAARR!
If I stay alert at all times, I'll defeat it... one day.
Thiri, Thiri can you hear me?
COME BACK TO ME.
Gods help us.
I keep thinking about the night of the storm, of Mum -- could I have saved her?

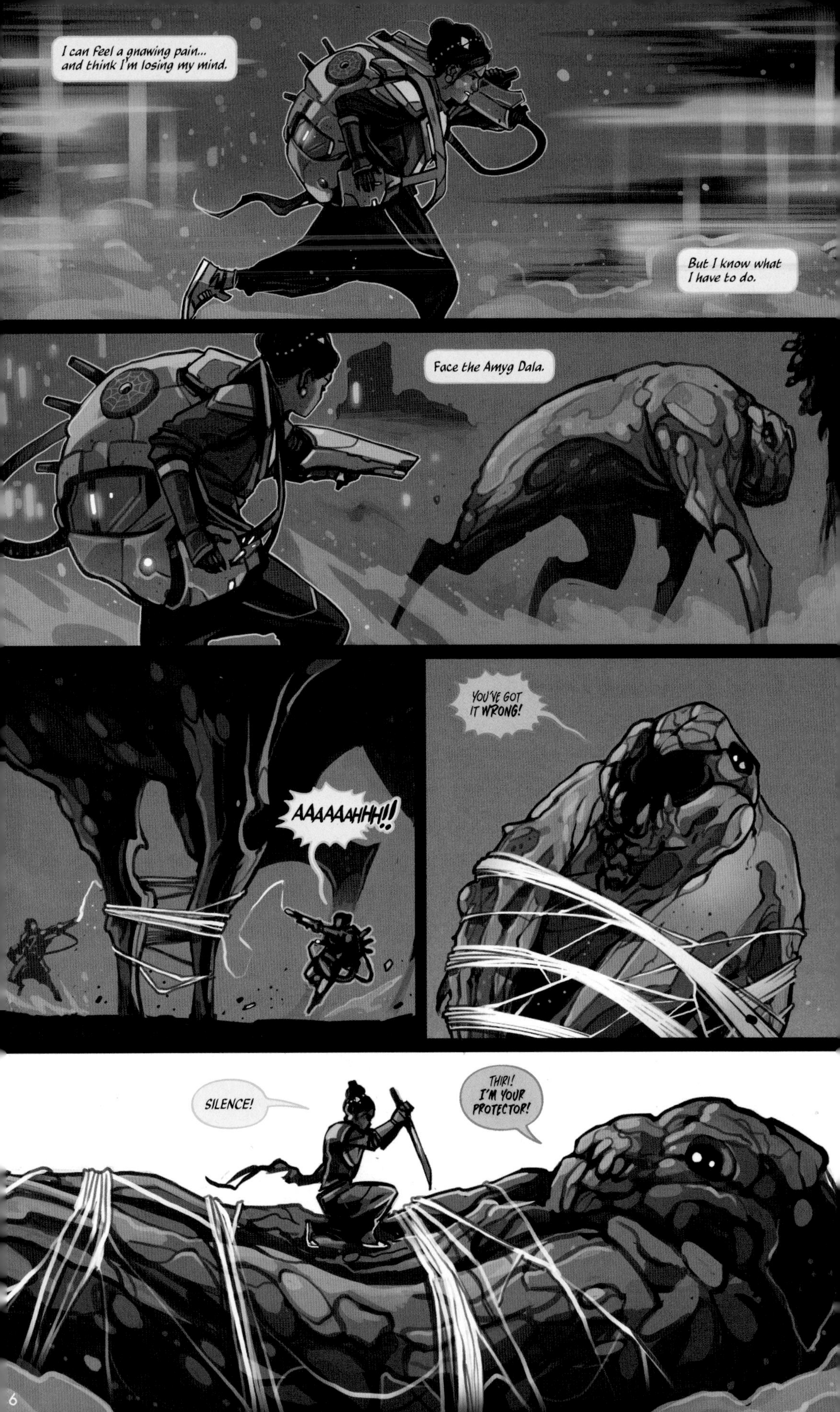

I can feel a gnawing pain...
and think I'm losing my mind.
But I know what
I have to do.
Face the Amyg Dala.
AAAAAAHHH!!
YOU'VE GOT IT WRONG!
SILENCE!
THIRI! I'M YOUR PROTECTOR!

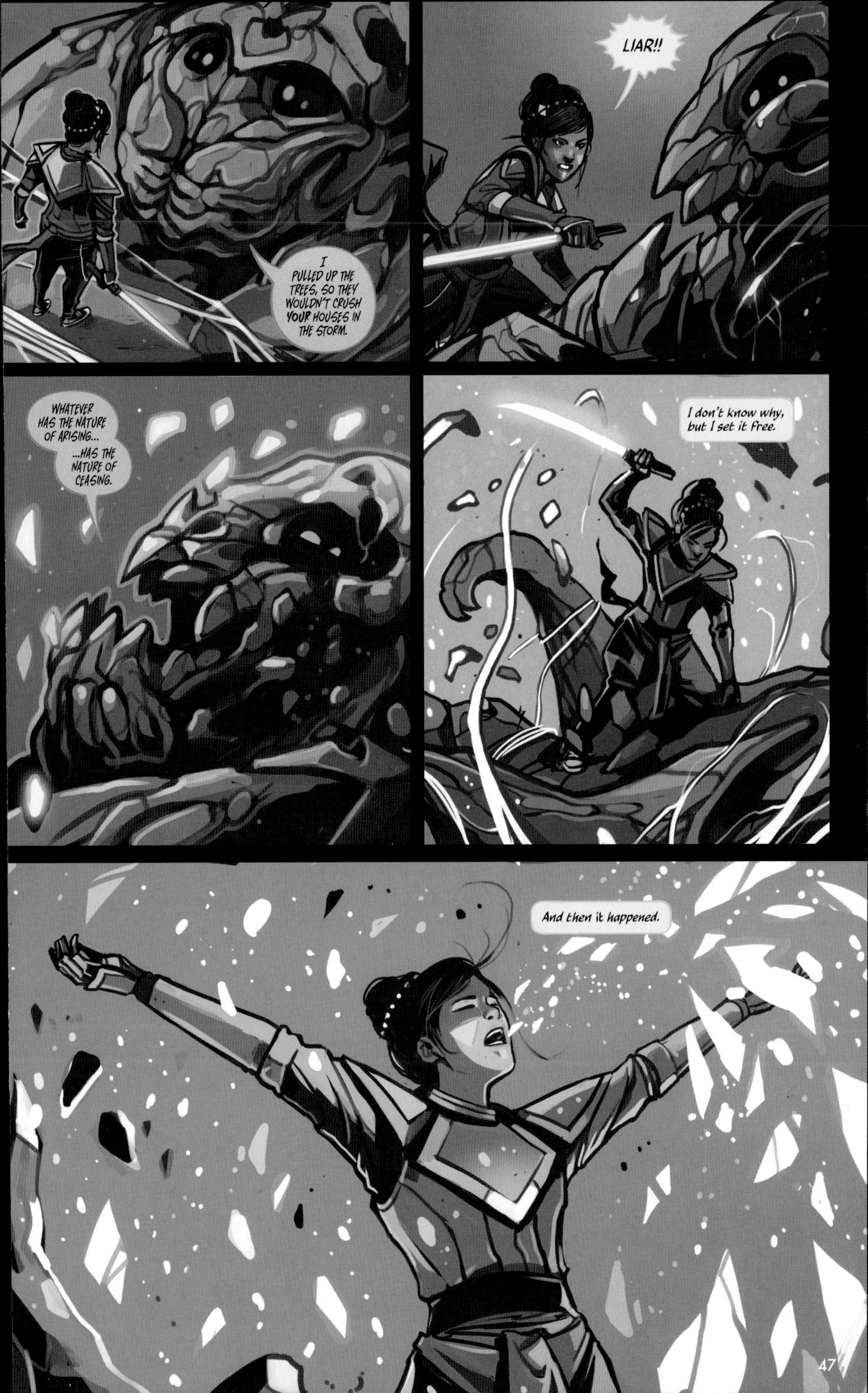
I PULLED UP THE TREES, SO THEY WOULDN'T CRUSH YOUR HOUSES IN THE STORM.
LIAR!!
WHATEVER HAS THE NATURE OF ARISING...
...HAS THE NATURE OF CEASING.
I don't know why, but I set it free.
And then it happened.

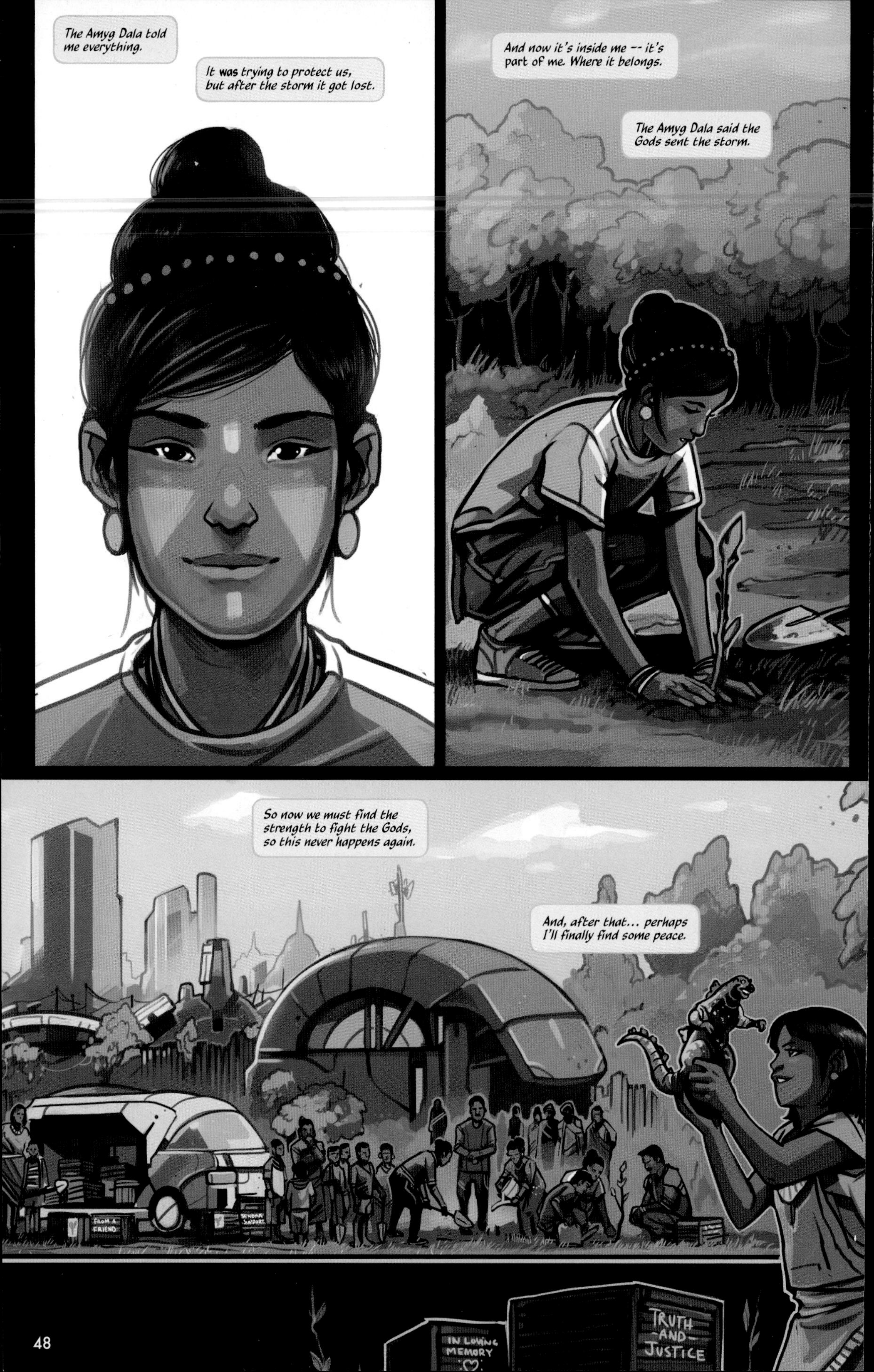
The Amyg Dala told me everything.
It was trying to protect us, but after the storm it got lost.
And now it's inside me -- it's part of me. Where it belongs.
The Amyg Dala said the Gods sent the storm.
So now we must find the strength to fight the Gods, so this never happens again.
And, after that... perhaps I'll finally find some peace.
FROM A FRIEND
SENDING SUPPORT
IN LOVING MEMORY
TRUTH AND JUSTICE

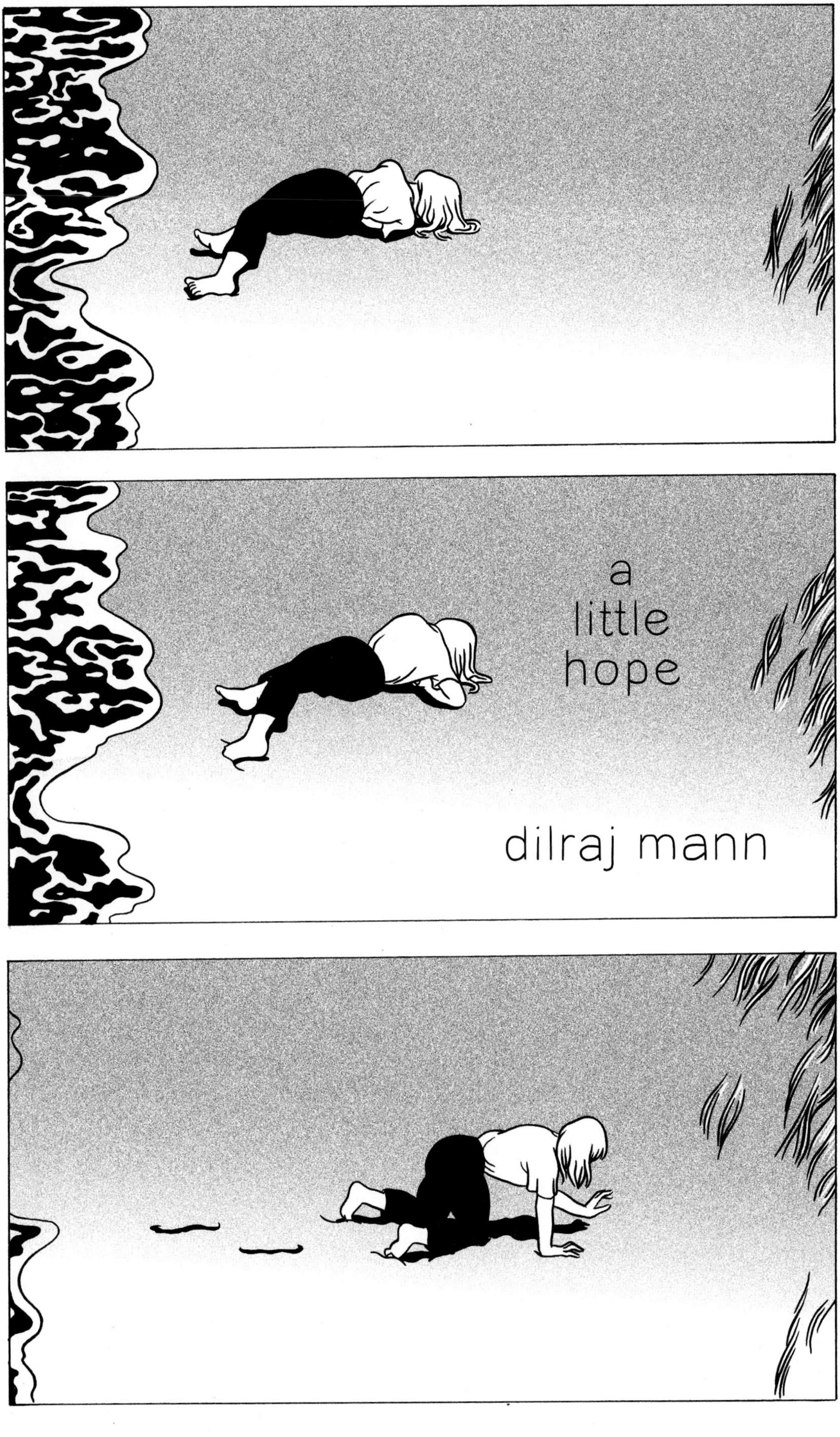
a
little
hope
dilraj mann

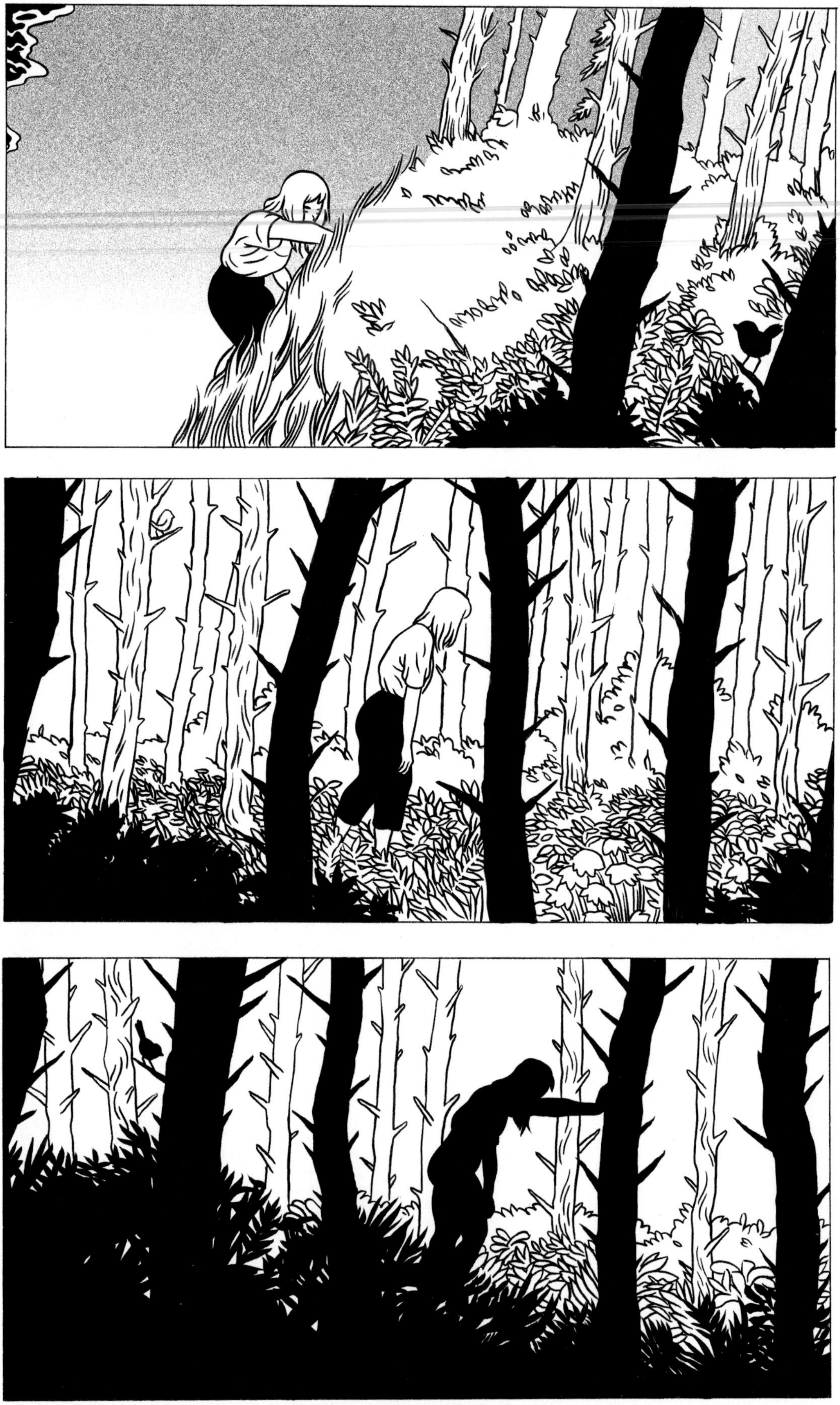

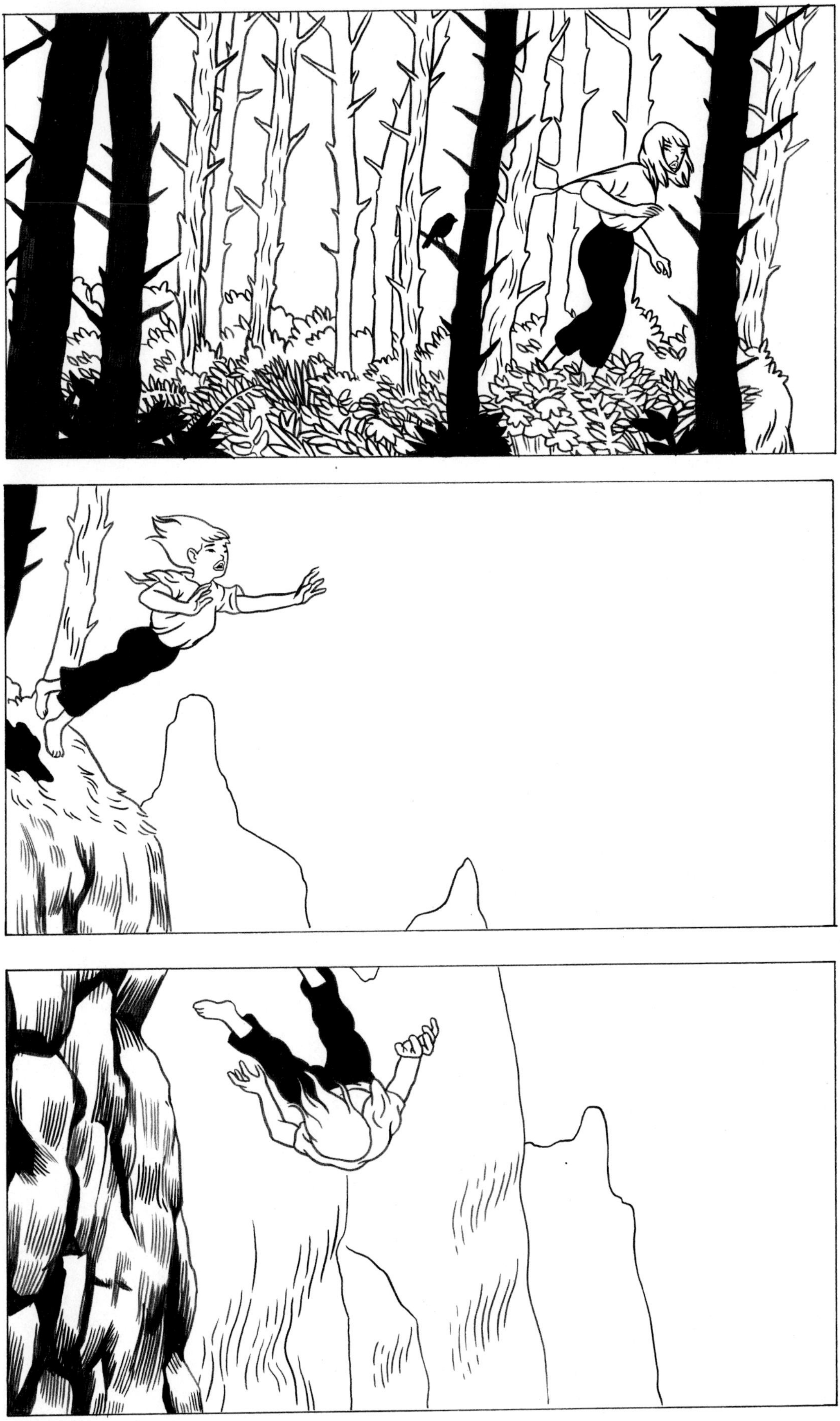

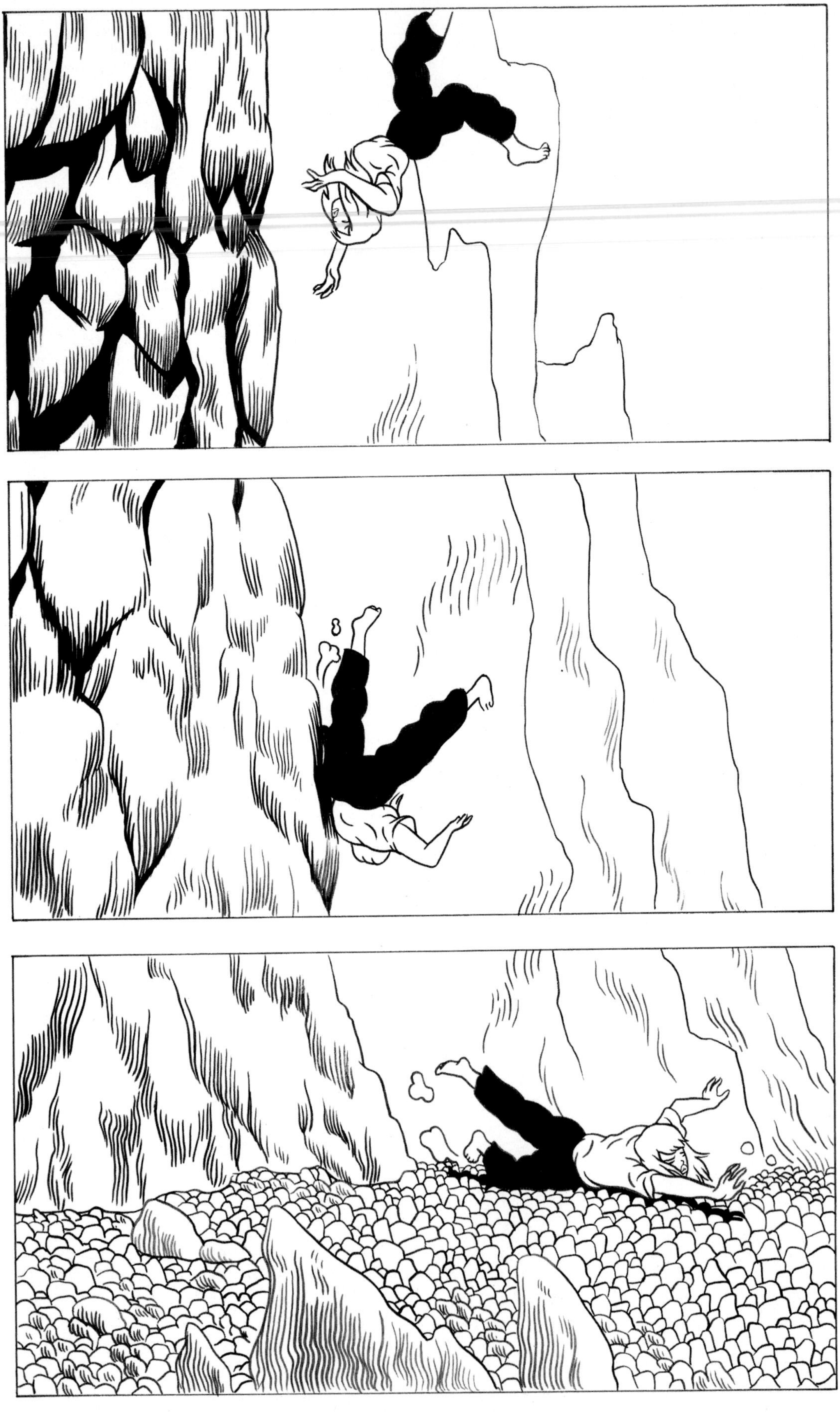

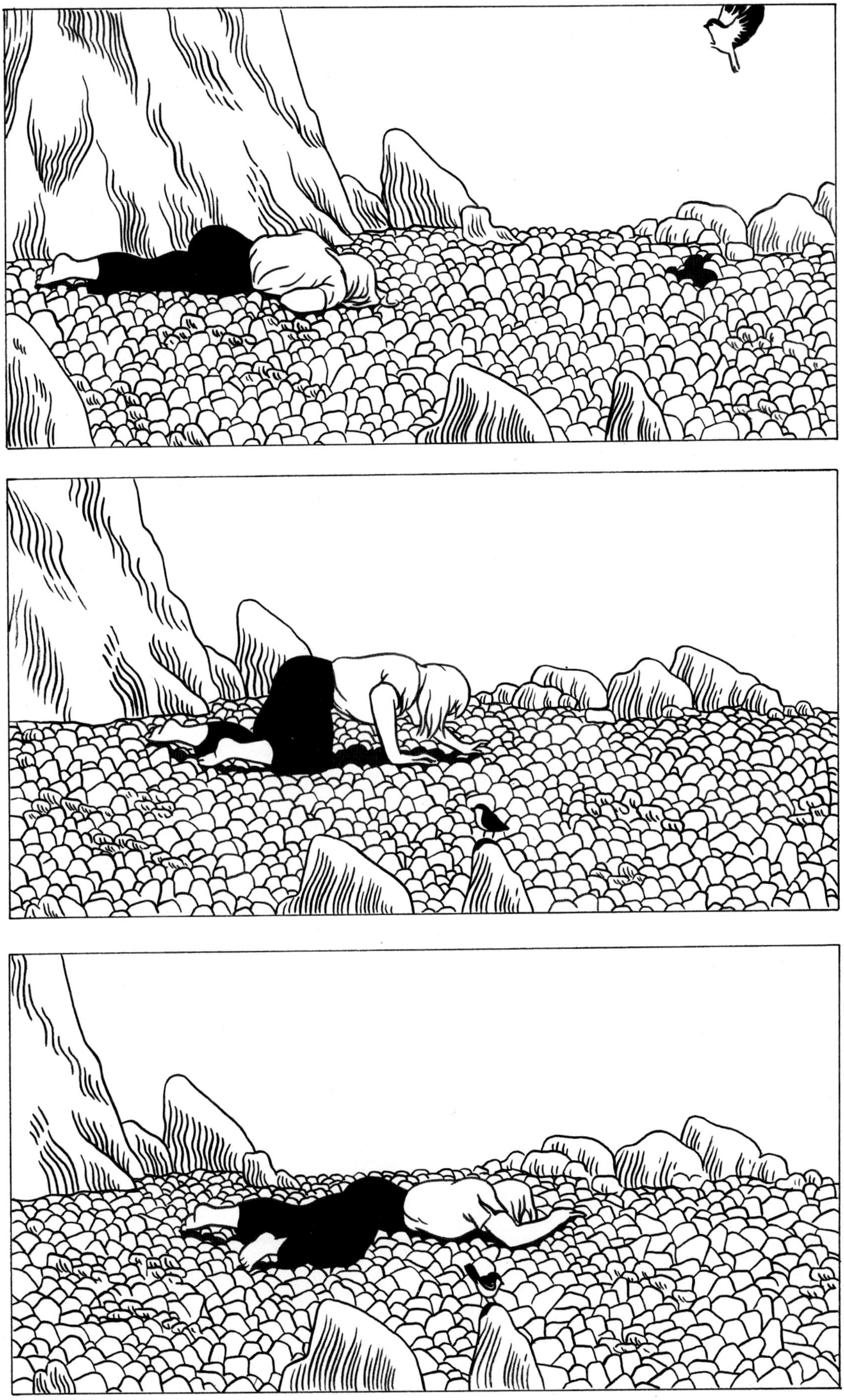

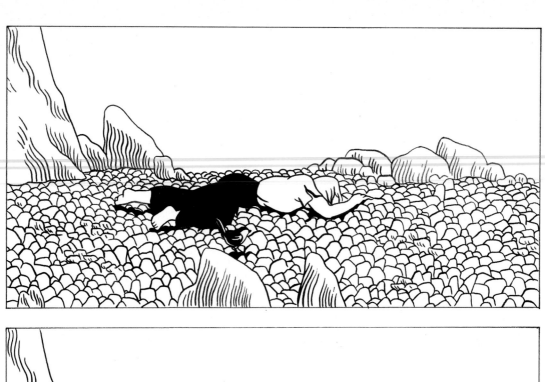

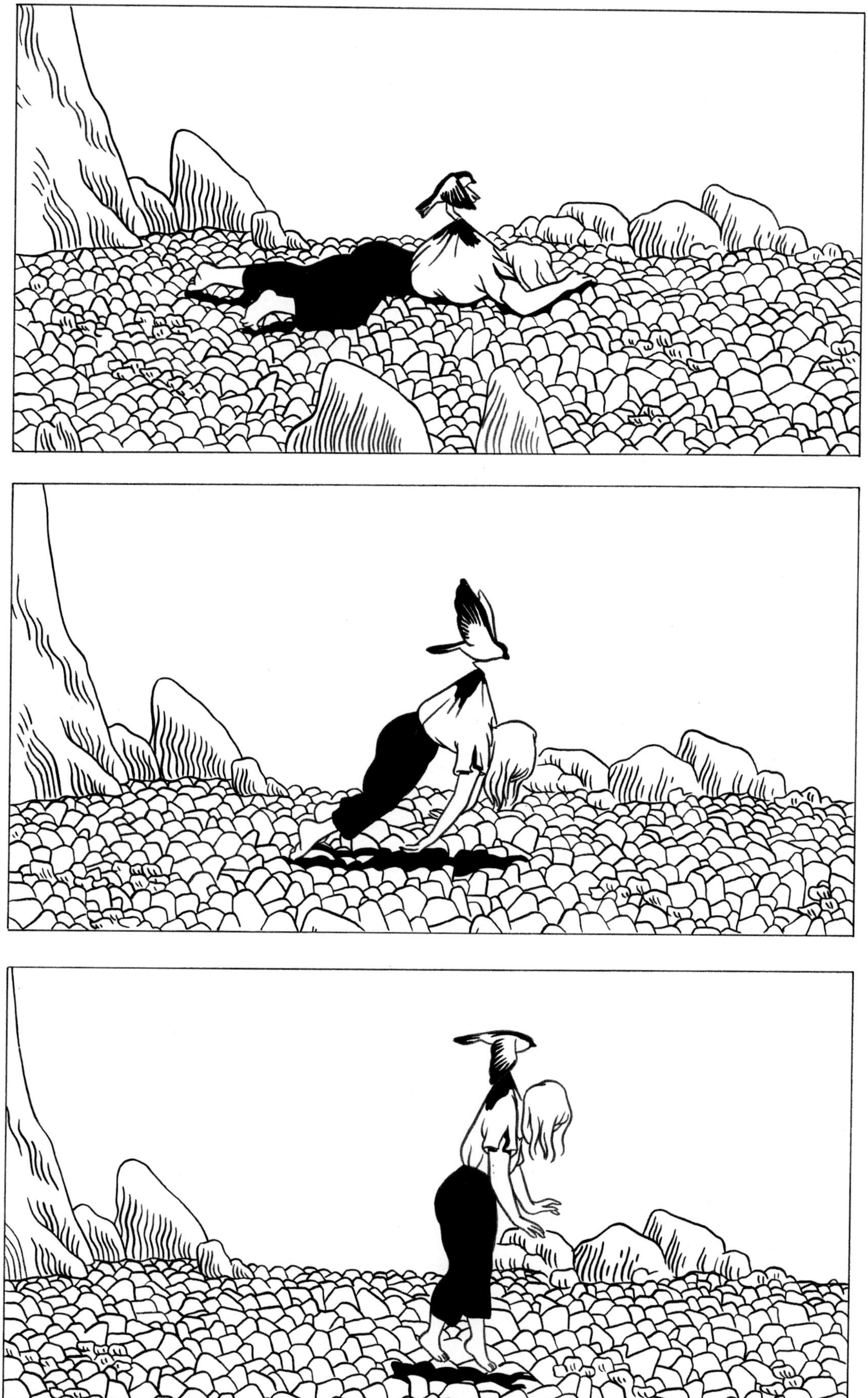

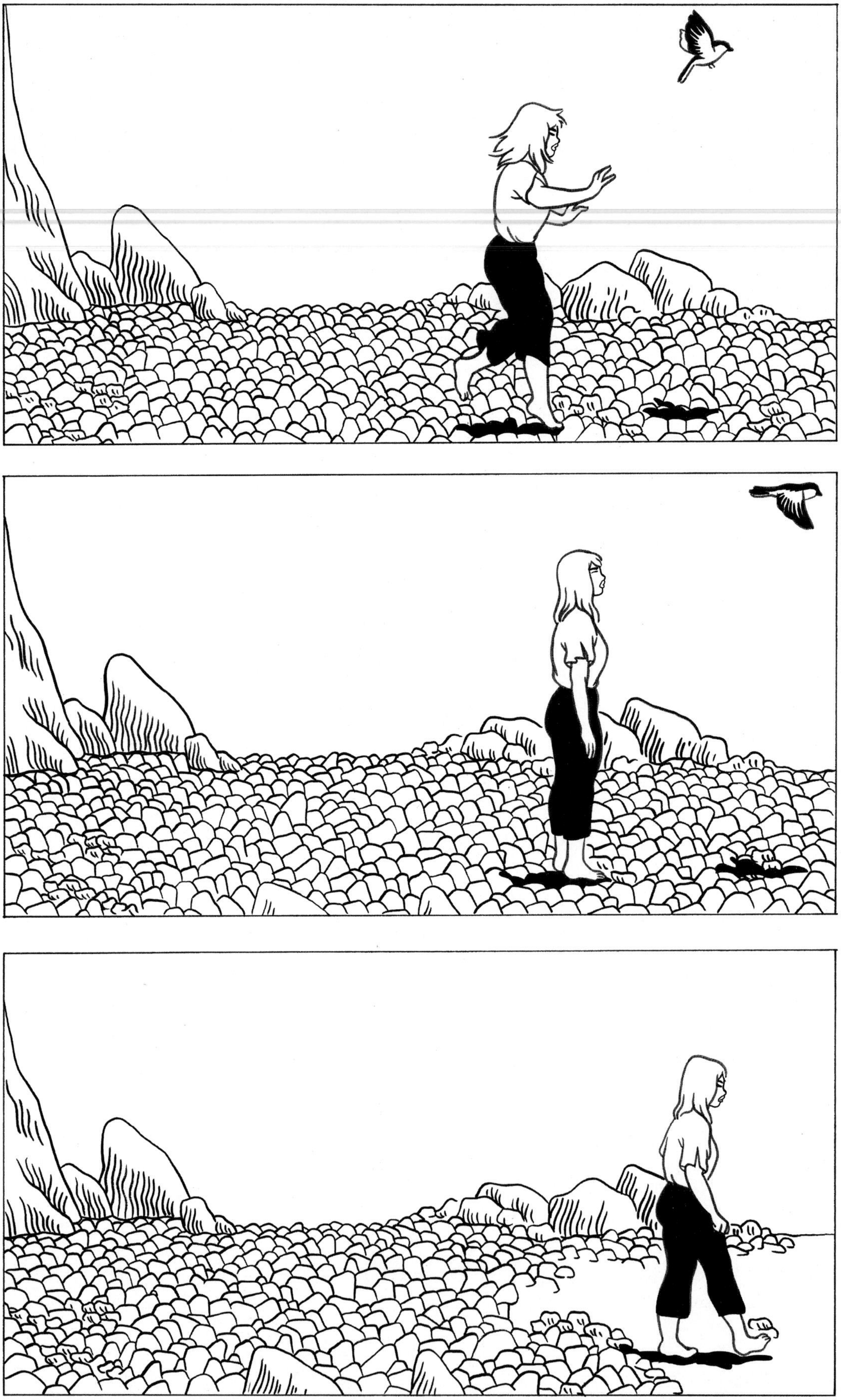

after fredrik raddum

"If Einstein's right.."

by Alan Moore & Melinda Gebbie
Letters by Hassan Otsmane-Elhaou

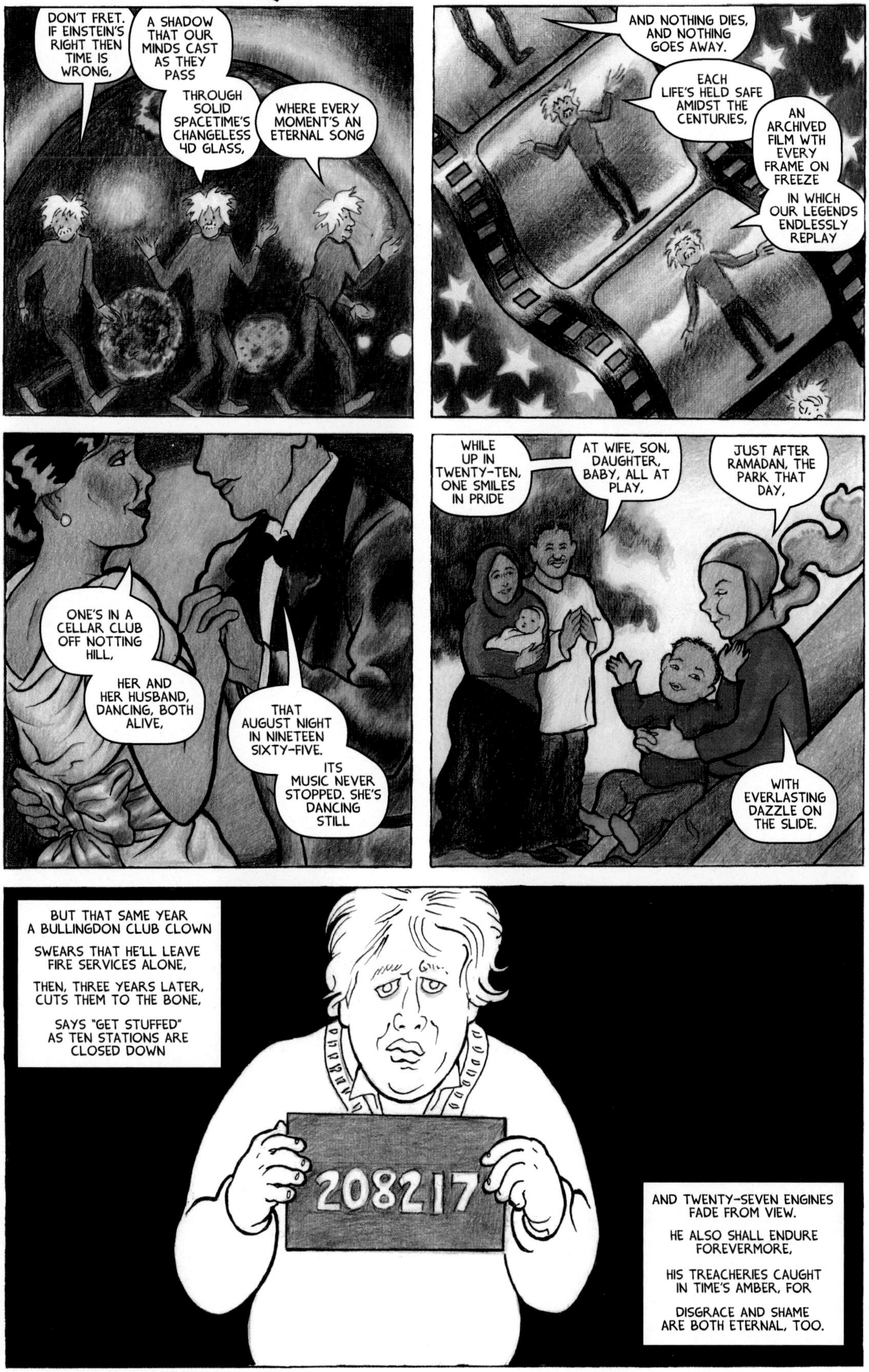
DON'T FRET. IF EINSTEIN'S RIGHT THEN TIME IS WRONG,
A SHADOW THAT OUR MINDS CAST AS THEY PASS
THROUGH SOLID SPACETIME'S CHANGELESS 4D GLASS,
WHERE EVERY MOMENT'S AN ETERNAL SONG
AND NOTHING DIES, AND NOTHING GOES AWAY.
EACH LIFE'S HELD SAFE AMIDST THE CENTURIES,
AN ARCHIVED FILM WTH EVERY FRAME ON FREEZE
IN WHICH OUR LEGENDS ENDLESSLY REPLAY
ONE'S IN A CELLAR CLUB OFF NOTTING HILL,
HER AND HER HUSBAND, DANCING, BOTH ALIVE,
THAT AUGUST NIGHT IN NINETEEN SIXTY-FIVE.
ITS MUSIC NEVER STOPPED. SHE'S DANCING STILL
WHILE UP IN TWENTY-TEN, ONE SMILES IN PRIDE
AT WIFE, SON, DAUGHTER, BABY, ALL AT PLAY,
JUST AFTER RAMADAN, THE PARK THAT DAY,
WITH EVERLASTING DAZZLE ON THE SLIDE.
BUT THAT SAME YEAR A BULLINGDON CLUB CLOWN
SWEARS THAT HE'LL LEAVE FIRE SERVICES ALONE,
THEN, THREE YEARS LATER, CUTS THEM TO THE BONE,
SAYS "GET STUFFED" AS TEN STATIONS ARE CLOSED DOWN
2082I7
AND TWENTY-SEVEN ENGINES FADE FROM VIEW.
HE ALSO SHALL ENDURE FOREVERMORE,
HIS TREACHERIES CAUGHT IN TIME'S AMBER, FOR
DISGRACE AND SHAME ARE BOTH ETERNAL, TOO.

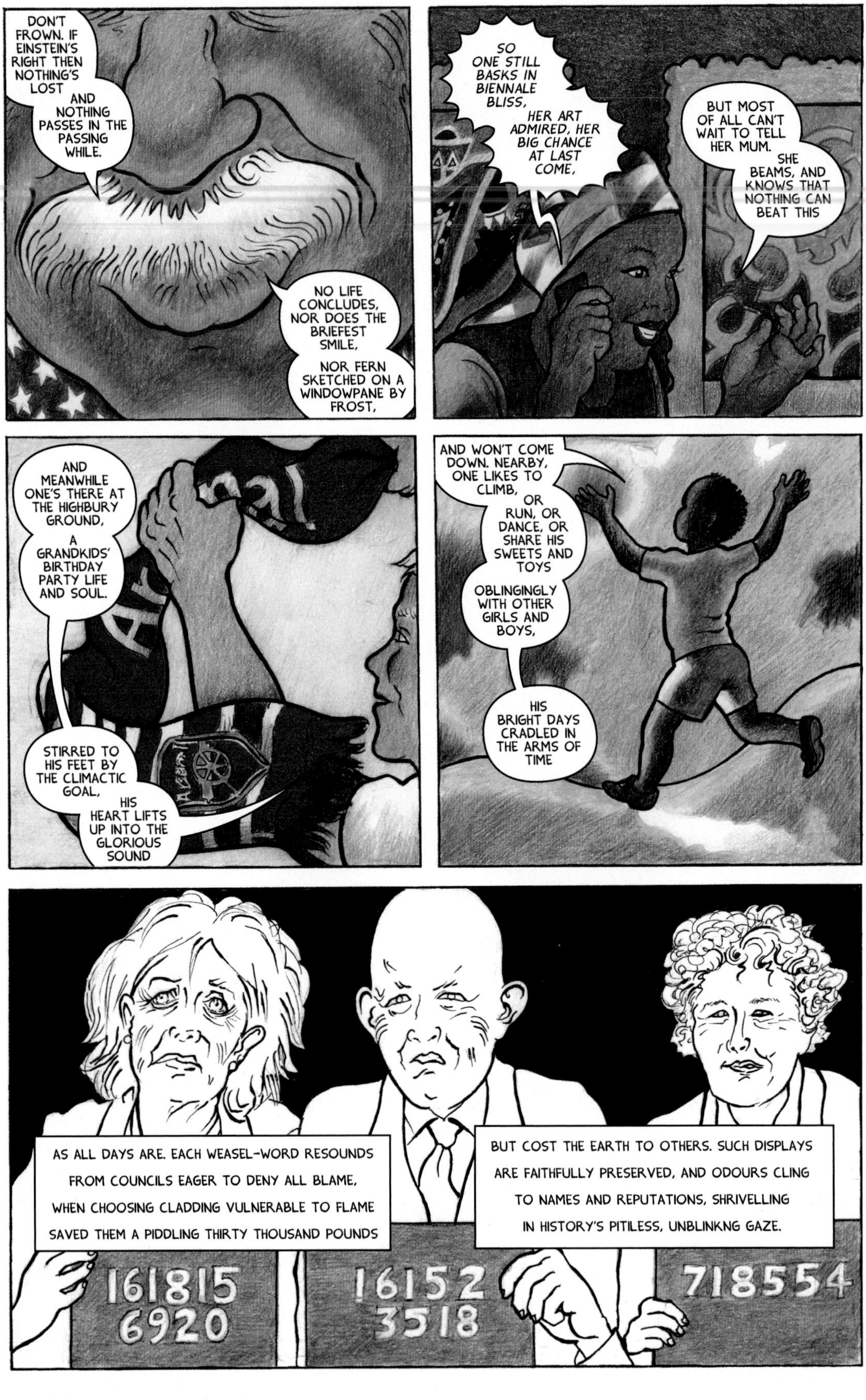
DON'T FROWN. IF EINSTEIN'S RIGHT THEN NOTHING'S LOST
AND NOTHING PASSES IN THE PASSING WHILE.
NO LIFE CONCLUDES, NOR DOES THE BRIEFEST SMILE,
NOR FERN SKETCHED ON A WINDOWPANE BY FROST,
SO ONE STILL BASKS IN BIENNALE BLISS,
HER ART ADMIRED, HER BIG CHANCE AT LAST COME,
BUT MOST OF ALL CAN'T WAIT TO TELL HER MUM.
SHE BEAMS, AND KNOWS THAT NOTHING CAN BEAT THIS
AND MEANWHILE ONE'S THERE AT THE HIGHBURY GROUND,
A GRANDKIDS' BIRTHDAY PARTY LIFE AND SOUL.
STIRRED TO HIS FEET BY THE CLIMACTIC GOAL,
HIS HEART LIFTS UP INTO THE GLORIOUS SOUND
AND WON'T COME DOWN. NEARBY, ONE LIKES TO CLIMB,
OR RUN, OR DANCE, OR SHARE HIS SWEETS AND TOYS
OBLINGINGLY WITH OTHER GIRLS AND BOYS,
HIS BRIGHT DAYS CRADLED IN THE ARMS OF TIME
AS ALL DAYS ARE. EACH WEASEL-WORD RESOUNDS FROM COUNCILS EAGER TO DENY ALL BLAME, WHEN CHOOSING CLADDING VULNERABLE TO FLAME SAVED THEM A PIDDLING THIRTY THOUSAND POUNDS
BUT COST THE EARTH TO OTHERS. SUCH DISPLAYS ARE FAITHFULLY PRESERVED, AND ODOURS CLING TO NAMES AND REPUTATIONS, SHRIVELLING IN HISTORY'S PITILESS, UNBLINKNG GAZE.
161815 6920
16152 3518
718554

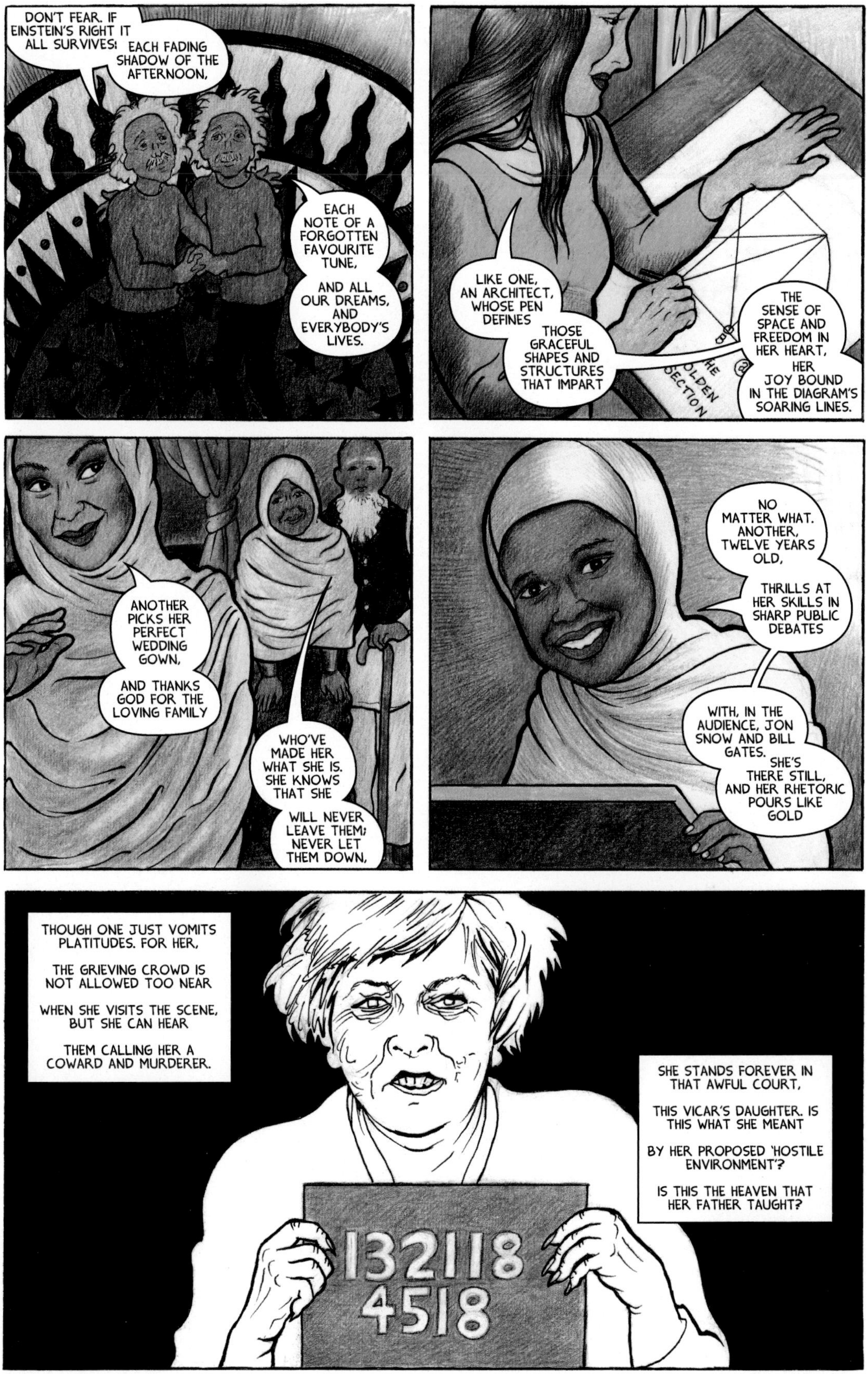
DON'T FEAR. IF EINSTEIN'S RIGHT IT ALL SURVIVES!
EACH FADING SHADOW OF THE AFTERNOON,
EACH NOTE OF A FORGOTTEN FAVOURITE TUNE,
AND ALL OUR DREAMS, AND EVERYBODY'S LIVES.
LIKE ONE, AN ARCHITECT, WHOSE PEN DEFINES
THOSE GRACEFUL SHAPES AND STRUCTURES THAT IMPART
THE SENSE OF SPACE AND FREEDOM IN HER HEART,
HER JOY BOUND IN THE DIAGRAM'S SOARING LINES.
ANOTHER PICKS HER PERFECT WEDDING GOWN,
AND THANKS GOD FOR THE LOVING FAMILY
WHO'VE MADE HER WHAT SHE IS. SHE KNOWS THAT SHE
WILL NEVER LEAVE THEM; NEVER LET THEM DOWN,
NO MATTER WHAT. ANOTHER, TWELVE YEARS OLD,
THRILLS AT HER SKILLS IN SHARP PUBLIC DEBATES
WITH, IN THE AUDIENCE, JON SNOW AND BILL GATES.
SHE'S THERE STILL, AND HER RHETORIC POURS LIKE GOLD
THOUGH ONE JUST VOMITS PLATITUDES. FOR HER,
THE GRIEVING CROWD IS NOT ALLOWED TOO NEAR
WHEN SHE VISITS THE SCENE, BUT SHE CAN HEAR
THEM CALLING HER A COWARD AND MURDERER.
SHE STANDS FOREVER IN THAT AWFUL COURT,
THIS VICAR'S DAUGHTER. IS THIS WHAT SHE MEANT
BY HER PROPOSED 'HOSTILE ENVIRONMENT'?
IS THIS THE HEAVEN THAT HER FATHER TAUGHT?
132118
4518

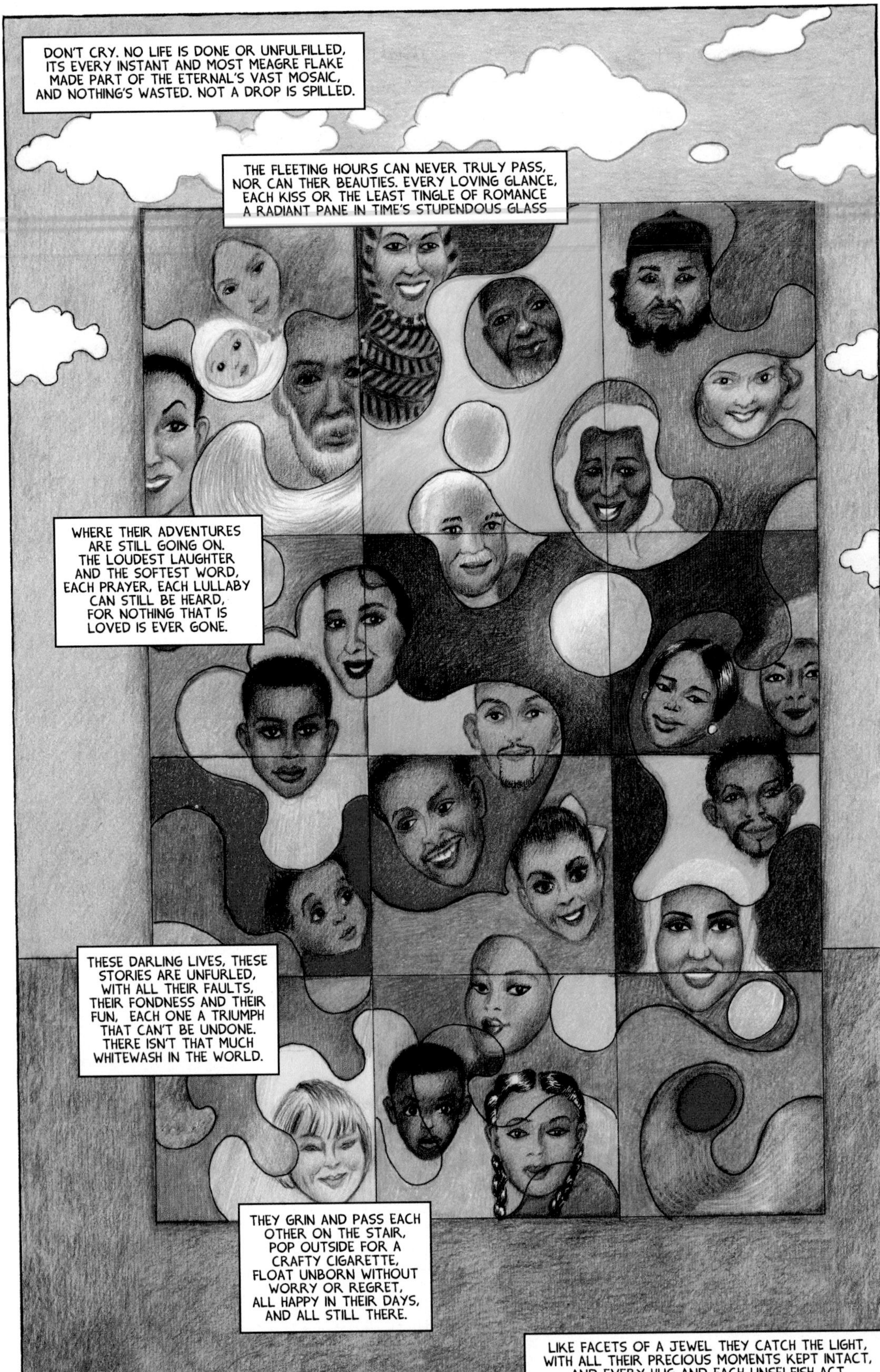
DON'T CRY. NO LIFE IS DONE OR UNFULFILLED, ITS EVERY INSTANT AND MOST MEAGRE FLAKE MADE PART OF THE ETERNAL'S VAST MOSAIC, AND NOTHING'S WASTED. NOT A DROP IS SPILLED.
THE FLEETING HOURS CAN NEVER TRULY PASS, NOR CAN THER BEAUTIES. EVERY LOVING GLANCE, EACH KISS OR THE LEAST TINGLE OF ROMANCE A RADIANT PANE IN TIME'S STUPENDOUS GLASS
WHERE THEIR ADVENTURES ARE STILL GOING ON. THE LOUDEST LAUGHTER AND THE SOFTEST WORD, EACH PRAYER, EACH LULLABY CAN STILL BE HEARD, FOR NOTHING THAT IS LOVED IS EVER GONE.
THESE DARLING LIVES, THESE STORIES ARE UNFURLED, WITH ALL THEIR FAULTS, THEIR FONDNESS AND THEIR FUN, EACH ONE A TRIUMPH THAT CAN'T BE UNDONE. THERE ISN'T THAT MUCH WHITEWASH IN THE WORLD.
THEY GRIN AND PASS EACH OTHER ON THE STAIR, POP OUTSIDE FOR A CRAFTY CIGARETTE, FLOAT UNBORN WITHOUT WORRY OR REGRET, ALL HAPPY IN THEIR DAYS, AND ALL STILL THERE.
LIKE FACETS OF A JEWEL THEY CATCH THE LIGHT, WITH ALL THEIR PRECIOUS MOMENTS KEPT INTACT, AND EVERY HUG AND EACH UNSELFISH ACT SHALL LONG OUTLIVE THE STARS, IF EINSTEIN'S RIGHT.

For Leah & Amber.

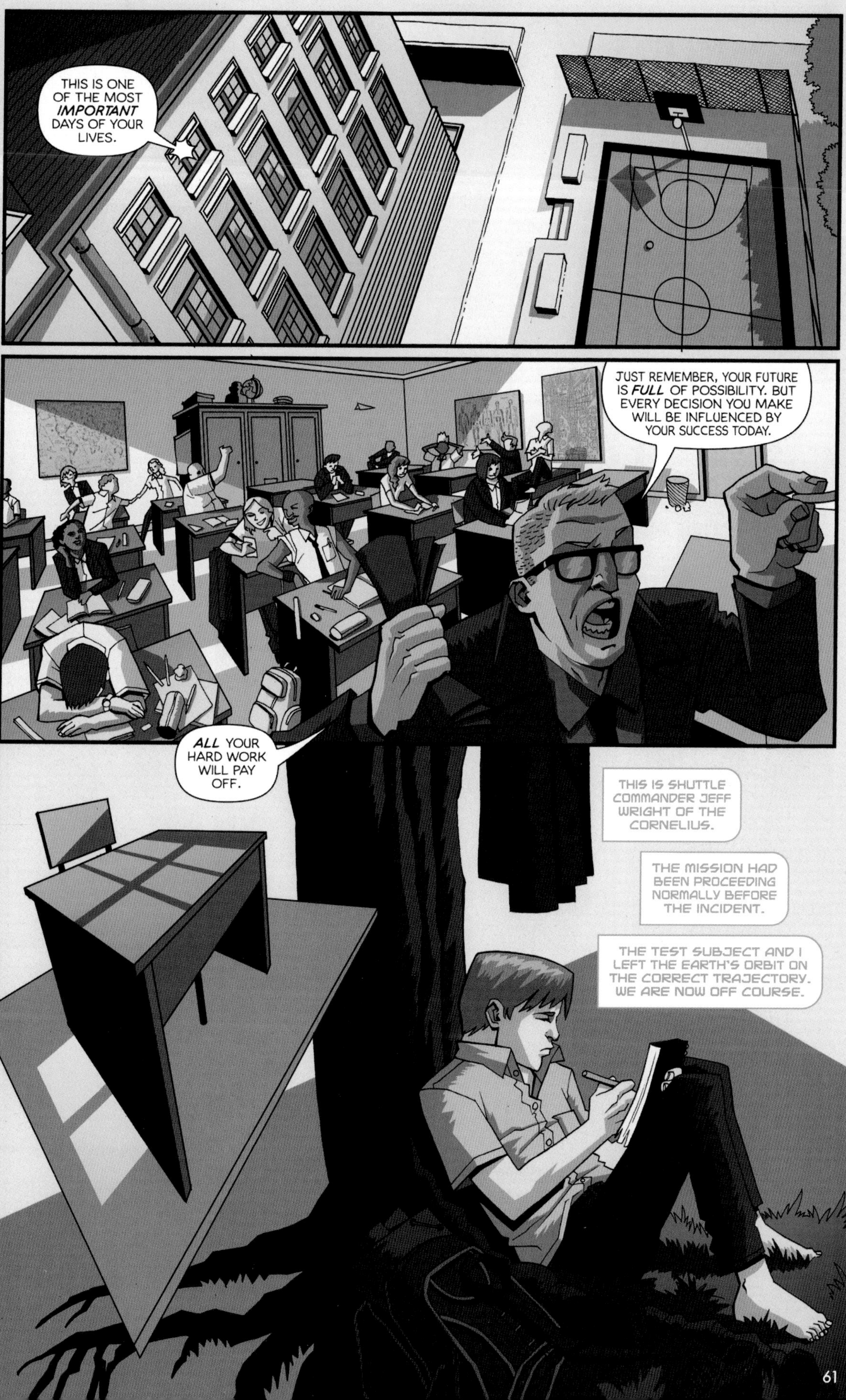
THIS IS ONE OF THE MOST *IMPORTANT* DAYS OF YOUR LIVES.
JUST REMEMBER, YOUR FUTURE IS *FULL* OF POSSIBILITY. BUT EVERY DECISION YOU MAKE WILL BE INFLUENCED BY YOUR SUCCESS TODAY.
ALL YOUR HARD WORK WILL PAY OFF.
THIS IS SHUTTLE COMMANDER JEFF WRIGHT OF THE CORNELIUS.
THE MISSION HAD BEEN PROCEEDING NORMALLY BEFORE THE INCIDENT.
THE TEST SUBJECT AND I LEFT THE EARTH'S ORBIT ON THE CORRECT TRAJECTORY. WE ARE NOW OFF COURSE.

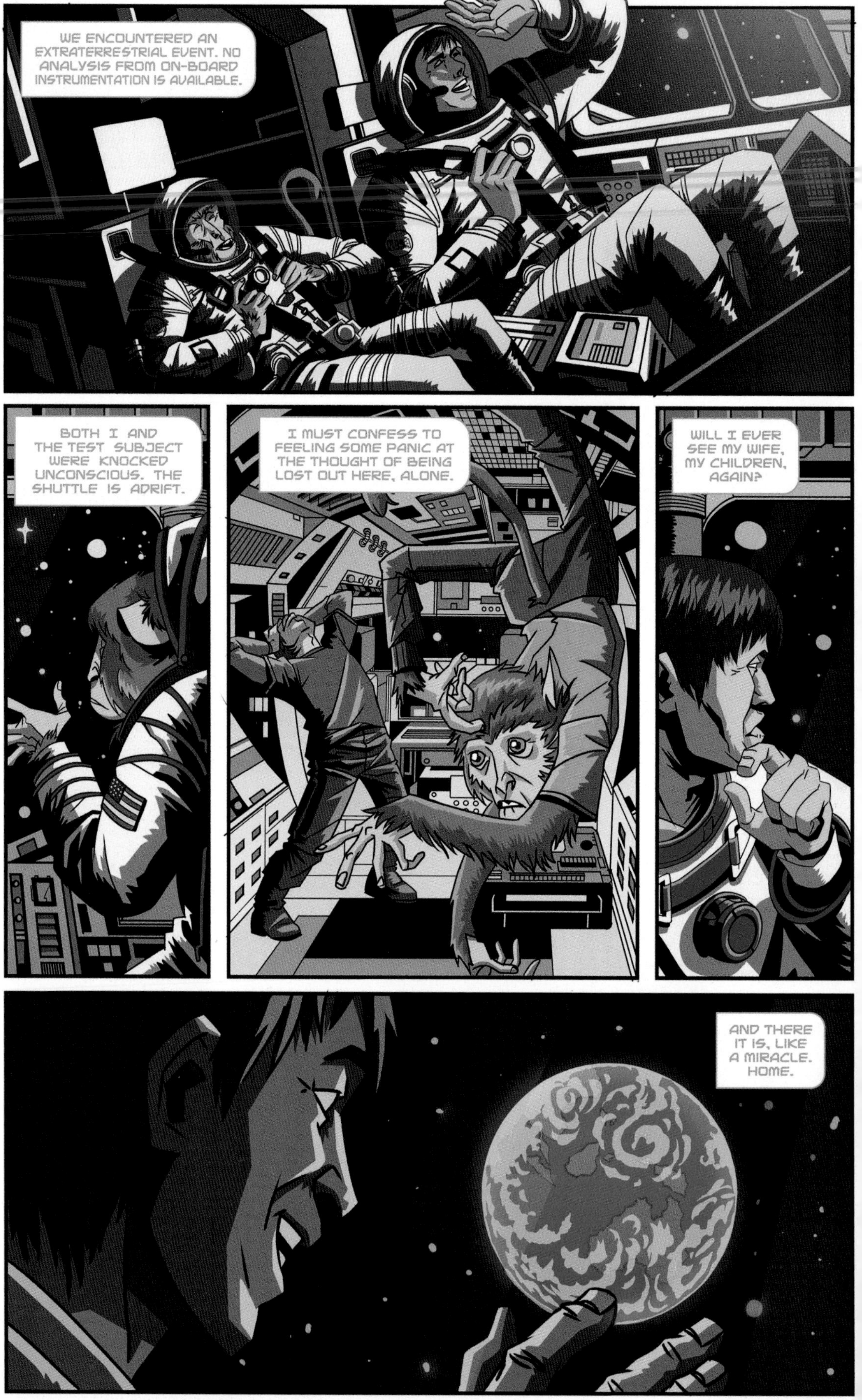
WE ENCOUNTERED AN EXTRATERRESTRIAL EVENT. NO ANALYSIS FROM ON-BOARD INSTRUMENTATION IS AVAILABLE.
BOTH I AND THE TEST SUBJECT WERE KNOCKED UNCONSCIOUS. THE SHUTTLE IS ADRIFT.
I MUST CONFESS TO FEELING SOME PANIC AT THE THOUGHT OF BEING LOST OUT HERE, ALONE.
WILL I EVER SEE MY WIFE, MY CHILDREN, AGAIN?
AND THERE IT IS, LIKE A MIRACLE. HOME.

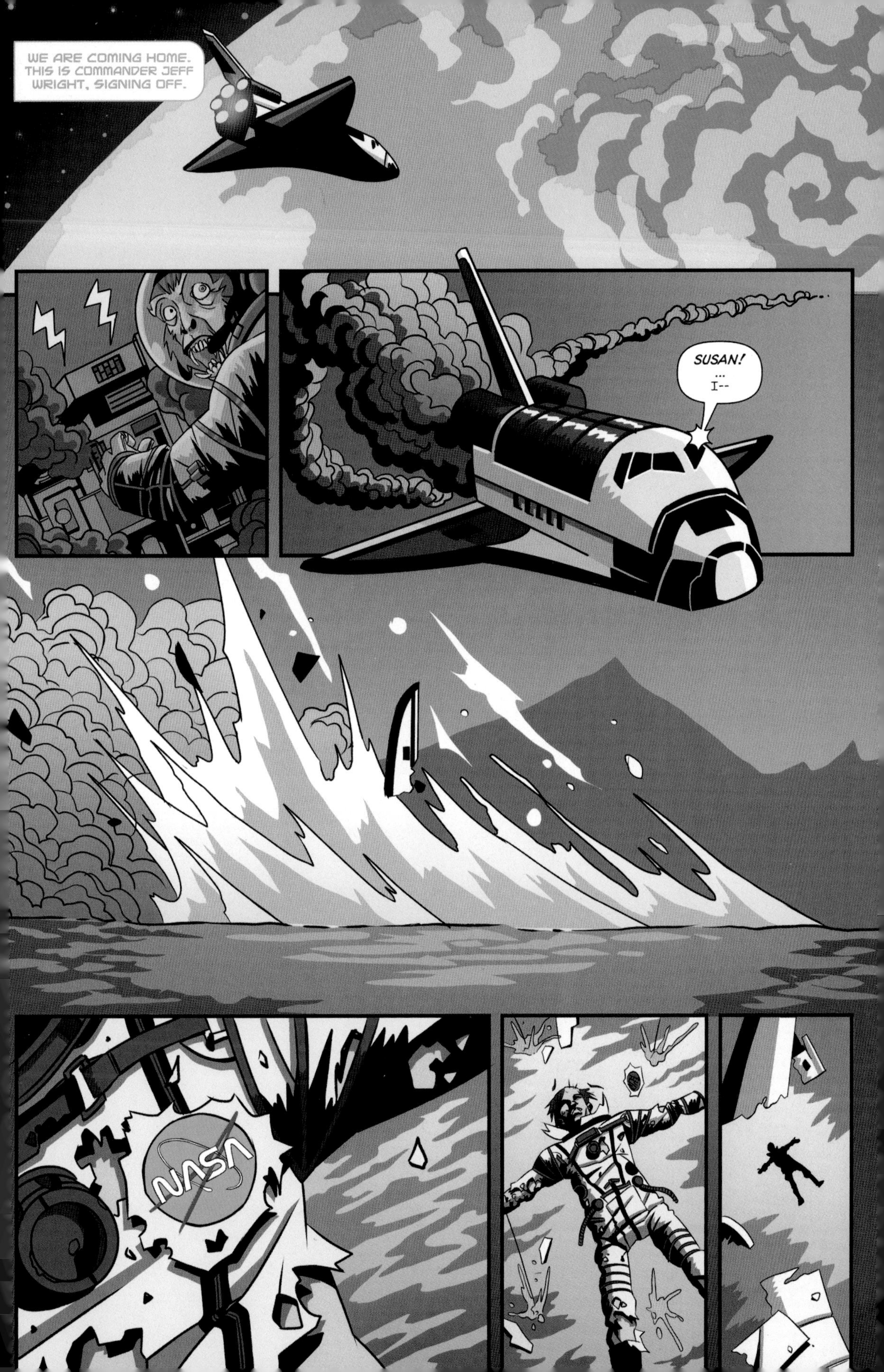
WE ARE COMING HOME. THIS IS COMMANDER JEFF WRIGHT, SIGNING OFF.
SUSAN! ... I--
NASA

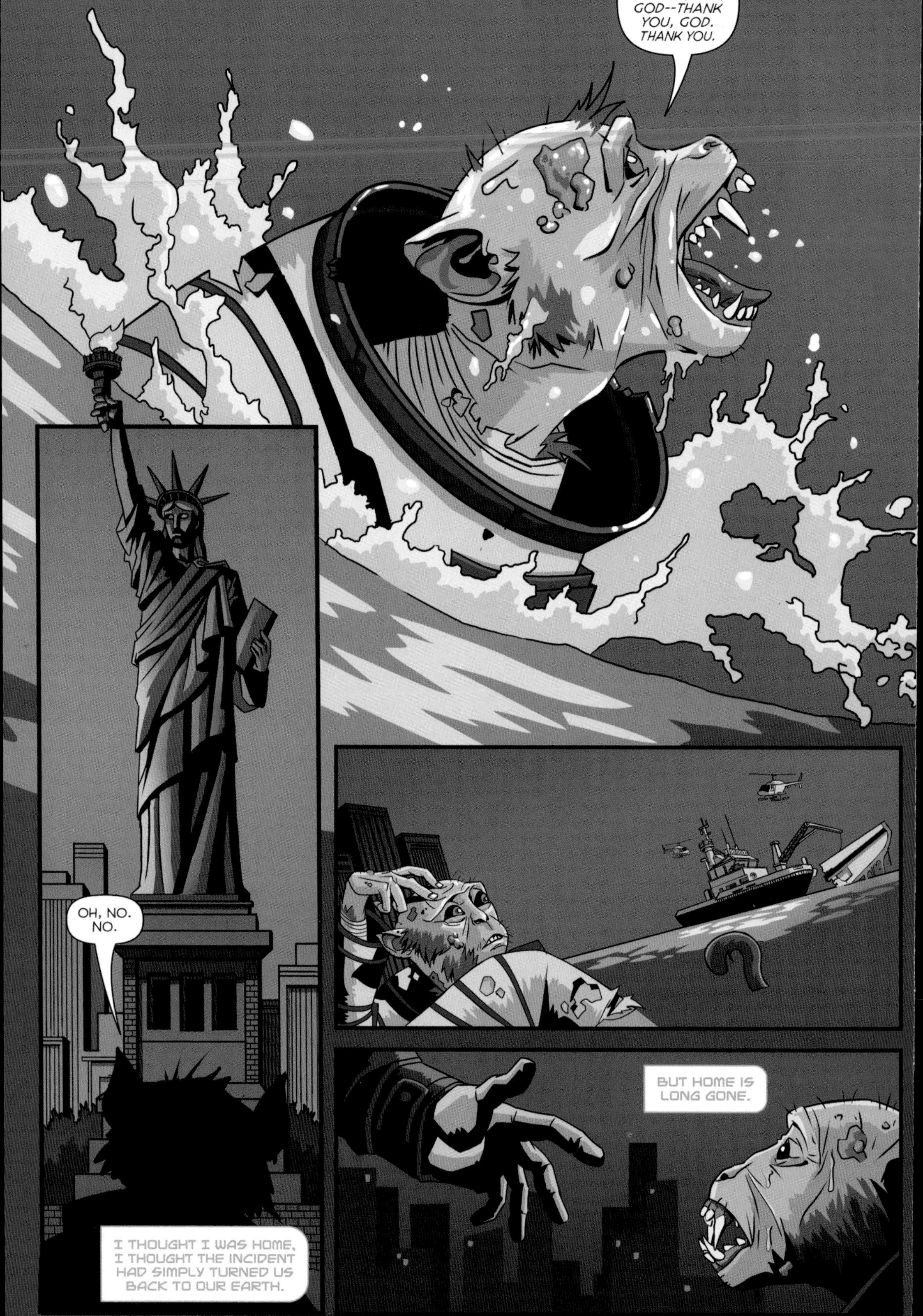

GASP
OH! OH, GOD. OH, GOD, GOD--THANK YOU, GOD. THANK YOU.
OH, NO. NO.
I THOUGHT I WAS HOME, I THOUGHT THE INCIDENT HAD SIMPLY TURNED US BACK TO OUR EARTH.
BUT HOME IS LONG GONE.

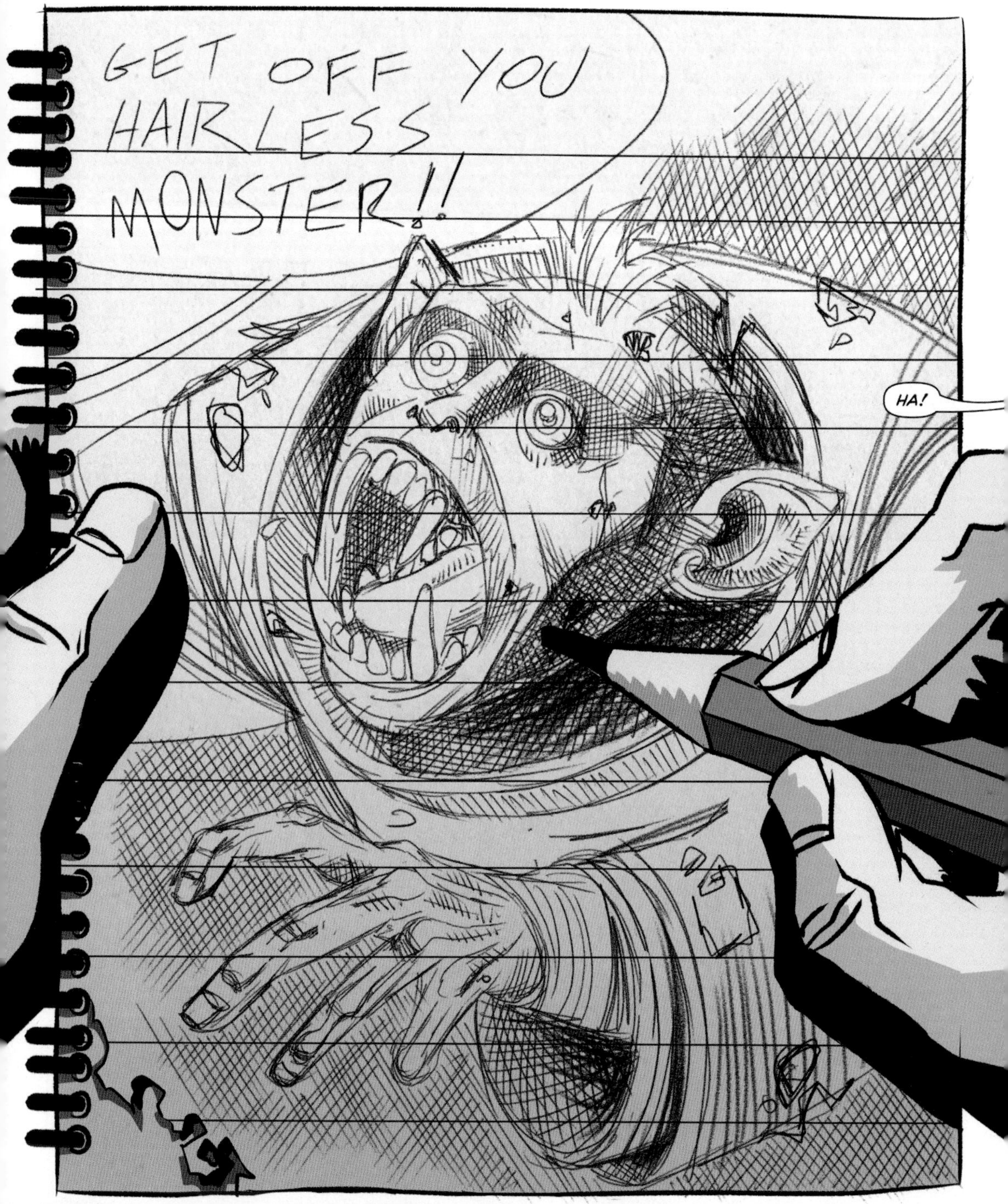
GET OFF YOU HAIRLESS MONSTER!!
HA!

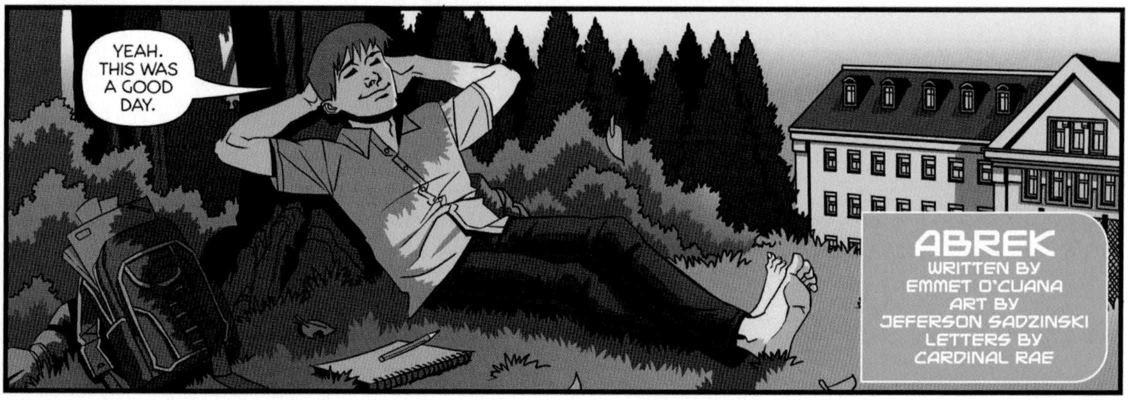
YEAH. THIS WAS A GOOD DAY.
ABREK
WRITTEN BY
EMMET O'CUANA
ART BY
JEFERSON SADZINSKI
LETTERS BY
CARDINAL RAE

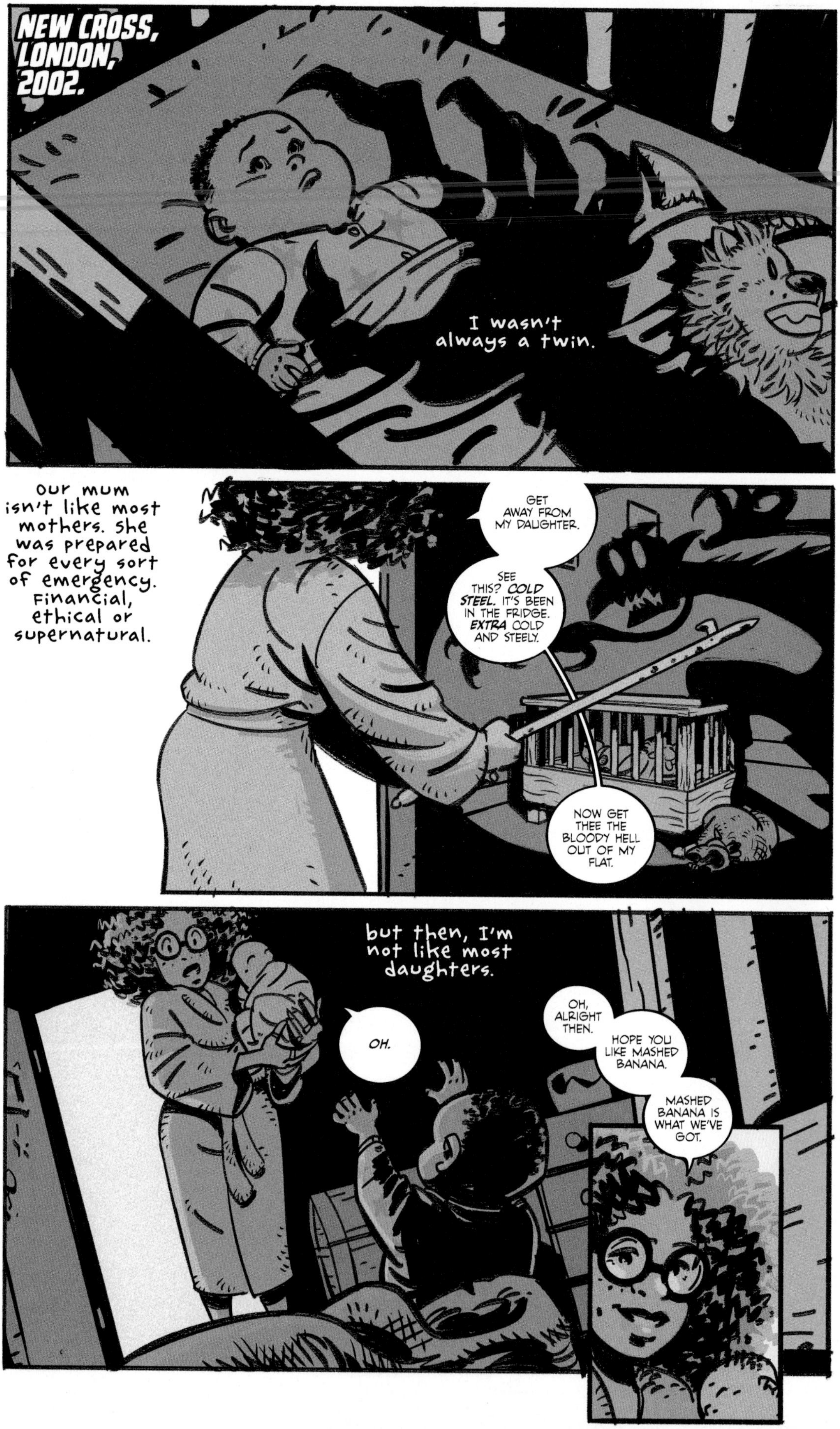
NEW CROSS, LONDON, 2002.
I wasn't always a twin.
Our mum isn't like most mothers. she was prepared for every sort of emergency. Financial, ethical or supernatural.
GET AWAY FROM MY DAUGHTER.
SEE THIS? COLD STEEL. IT'S BEEN IN THE FRIDGE. EXTRA COLD AND STEELY.
NOW GET THEE THE BLOODY HELL OUT OF MY FLAT.
but then, I'm not like most daughters.
OH.
OH, ALRIGHT THEN.
HOPE YOU LIKE MASHED BANANA.
MASHED BANANA IS WHAT WE'VE GOT.

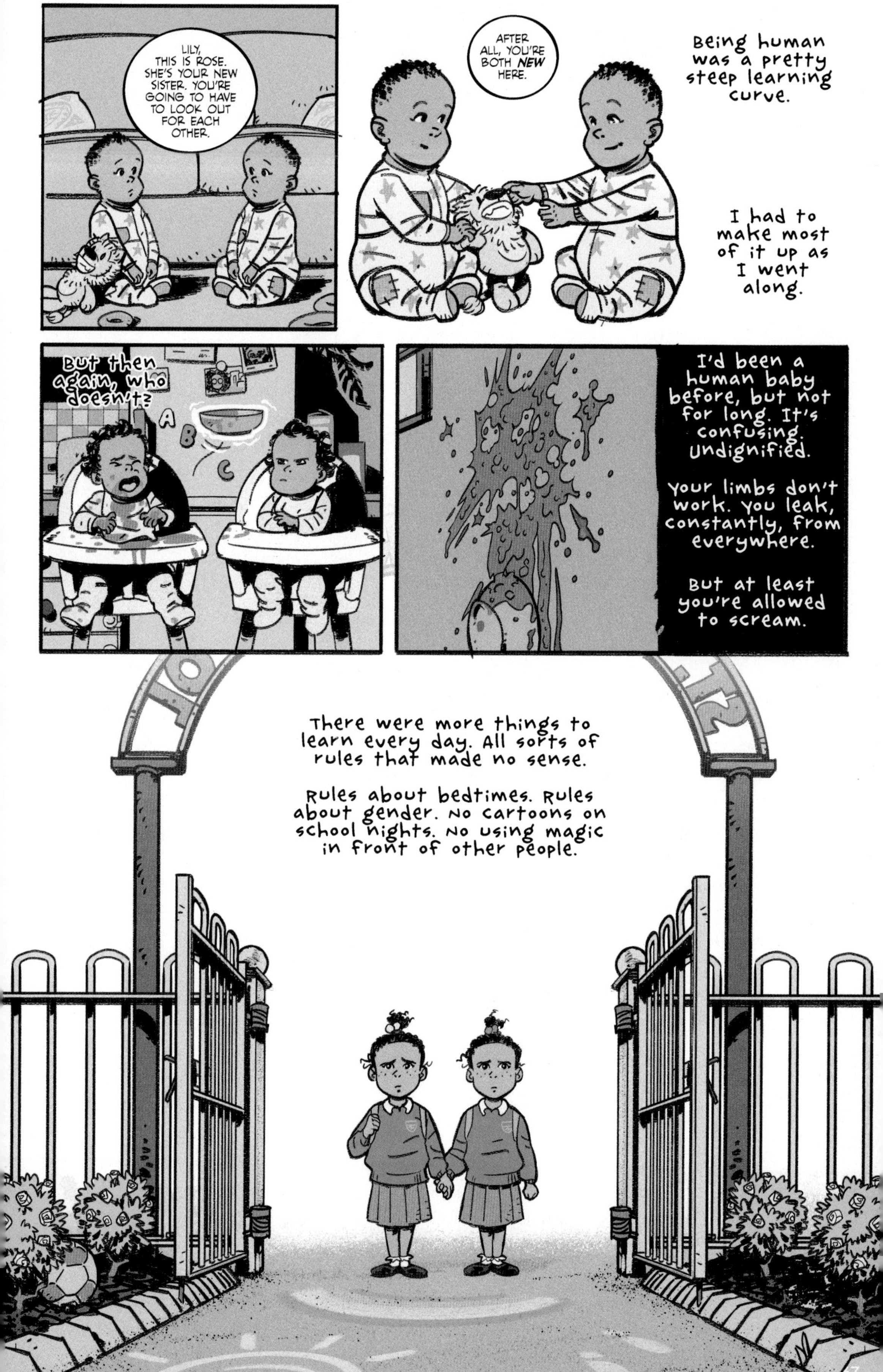

LILY, THIS IS ROSE. SHE'S YOUR NEW SISTER. YOU'RE GOING TO HAVE TO LOOK OUT FOR EACH OTHER.
AFTER ALL, YOU'RE BOTH NEW HERE.
Being human was a pretty steep learning curve.
I had to make most of it up as I went along.
But then again, who doesn't?
A
B
C
I'd been a human baby before, but not for long. It's confusing. Undignified.
Your limbs don't work. You leak, constantly, from everywhere.
But at least you're allowed to scream.
There were more things to learn every day. All sorts of rules that made no sense.
Rules about bedtimes. Rules about gender. No cartoons on school nights. No using magic in front of other people.

mum said that if we stuck to the rules and took care of each other, everything would work out okay in the end.

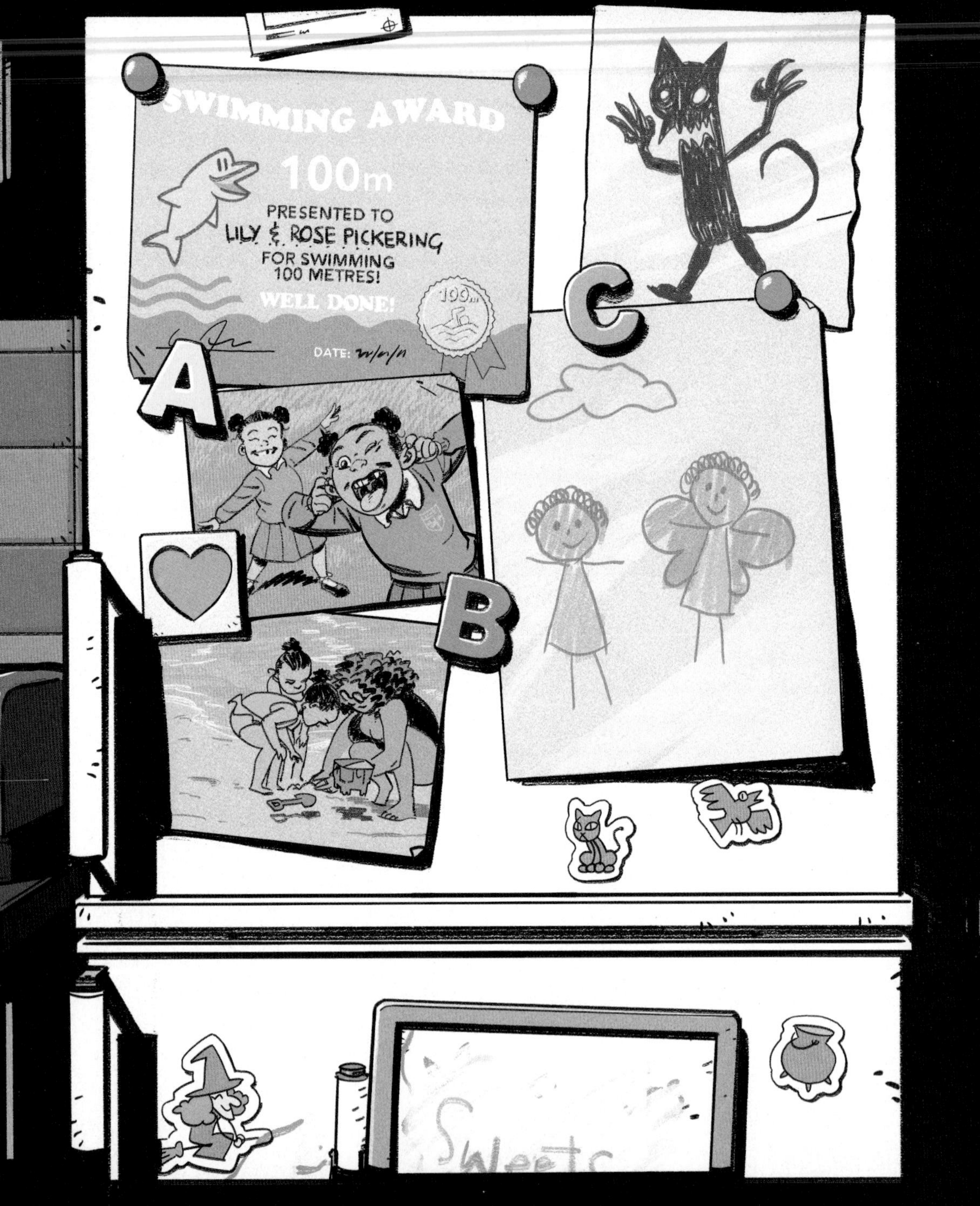
SWIMMING AWARD
100m
PRESENTED TO
LILY & ROSE PICKERING
FOR SWIMMING
100 METRES!
WELL DONE!
DATE:
A
B
C
Sweets

of course, it was never going to be that easy.

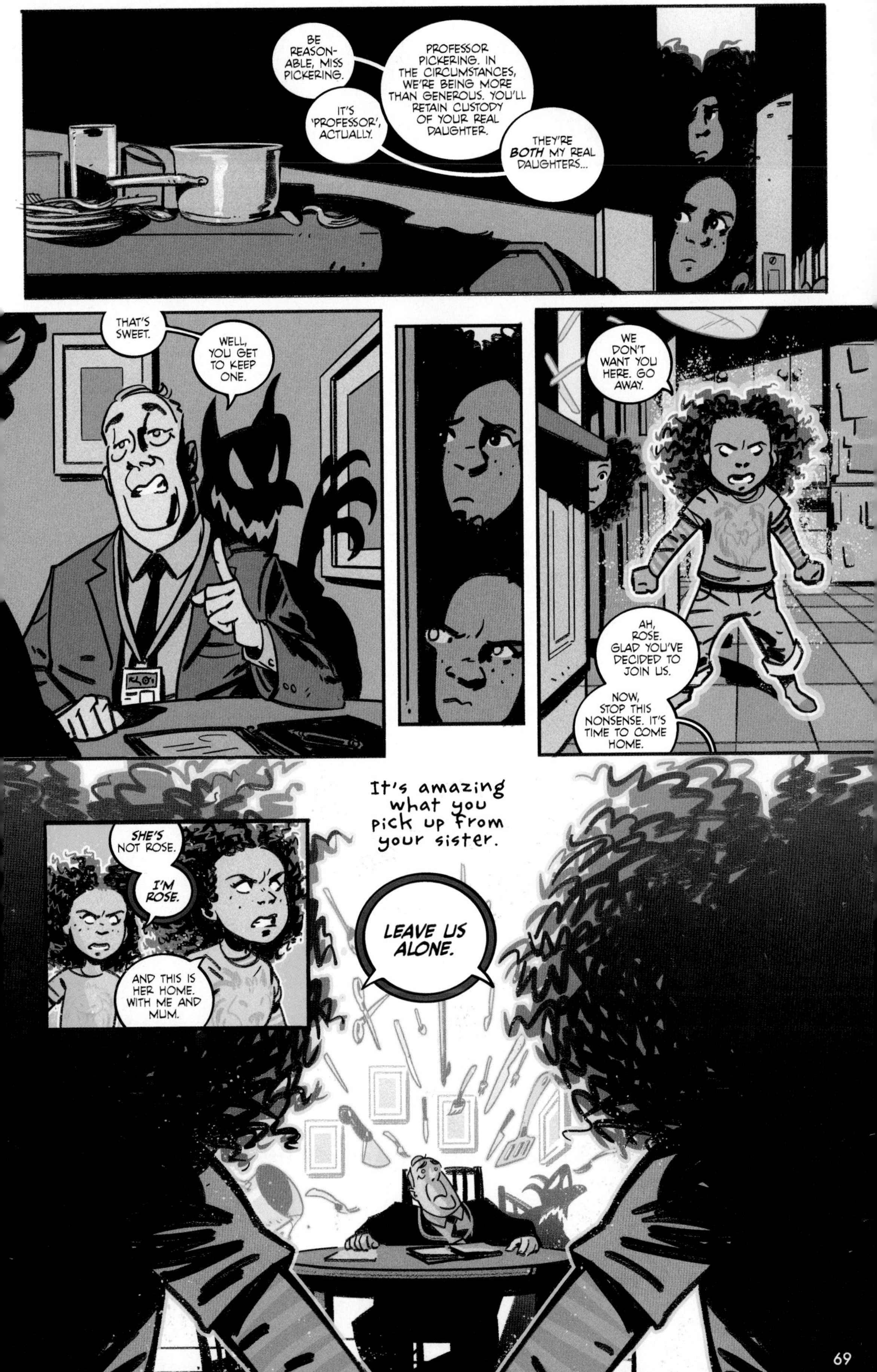

BE REASON-ABLE, MISS PICKERING.
IT'S 'PROFESSOR', ACTUALLY.
PROFESSOR PICKERING. IN THE CIRCUMSTANCES, WE'RE BEING MORE THAN GENEROUS. YOU'LL RETAIN CUSTODY OF YOUR REAL DAUGHTER.
THEY'RE *BOTH* MY REAL DAUGHTERS...
THAT'S SWEET.
WELL, YOU GET TO KEEP ONE.
WE DON'T WANT YOU HERE. GO AWAY.
AH, ROSE. GLAD YOU'VE DECIDED TO JOIN US.
NOW, STOP THIS NONSENSE. IT'S TIME TO COME HOME.
It's amazing what you pick up from your sister.
SHE'S NOT ROSE.
I'M ROSE.
AND THIS IS HER HOME. WITH ME AND MUM.
LEAVE US ALONE.

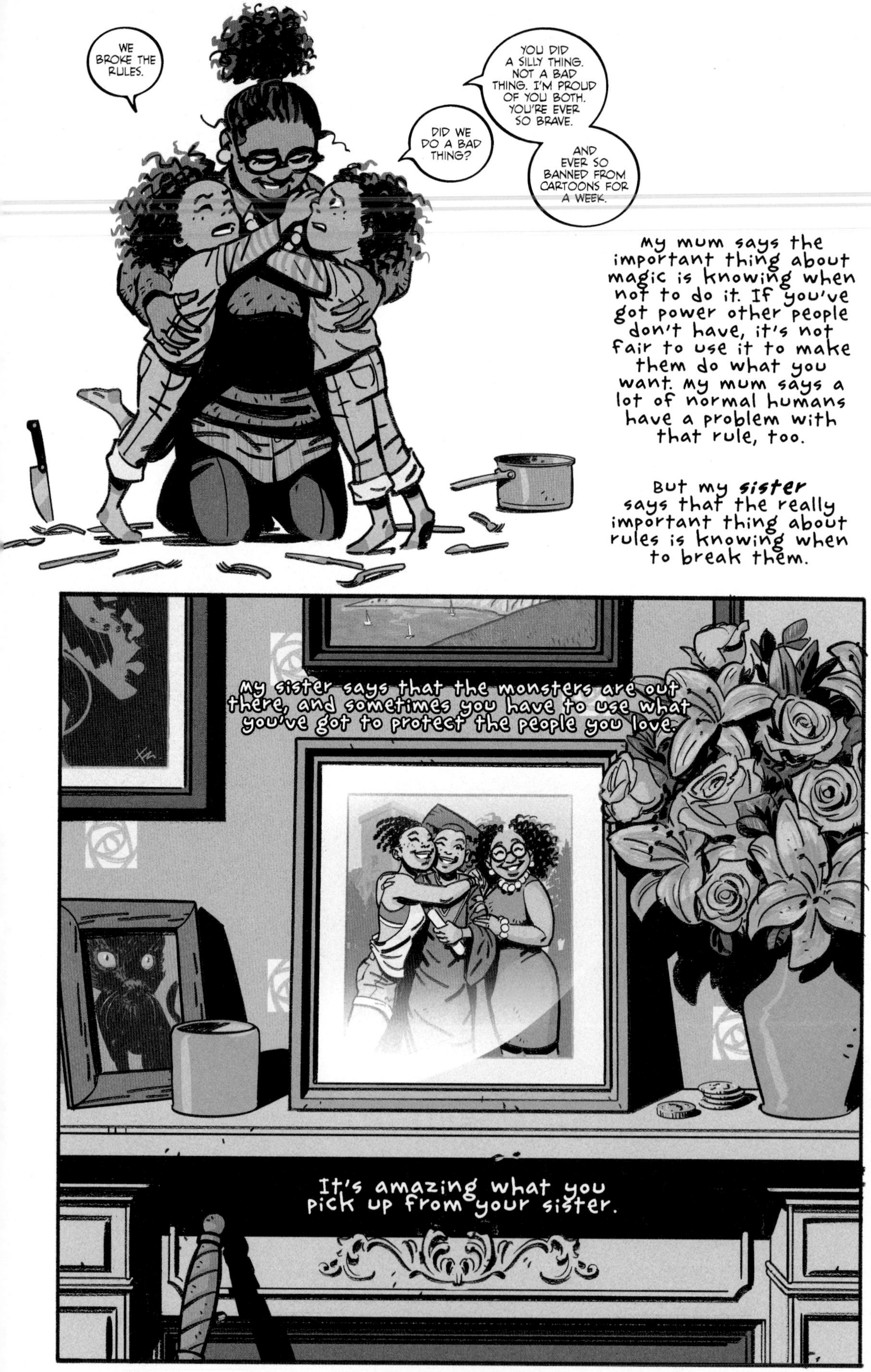
WE BROKE THE RULES.
DID WE DO A BAD THING?
YOU DID A SILLY THING. NOT A BAD THING. I'M PROUD OF YOU BOTH. YOU'RE EVER SO BRAVE.
AND EVER SO BANNED FROM CARTOONS FOR A WEEK.
My mum says the important thing about magic is knowing when not to do it. If you've got power other people don't have, it's not fair to use it to make them do what you want. My mum says a lot of normal humans have a problem with that rule, too.
But my *sister* says that the really important thing about rules is knowing when to break them.
My sister says that the monsters are out there, and sometimes you have to use what you've got to protect the people you love.
It's amazing what you pick up from your sister.

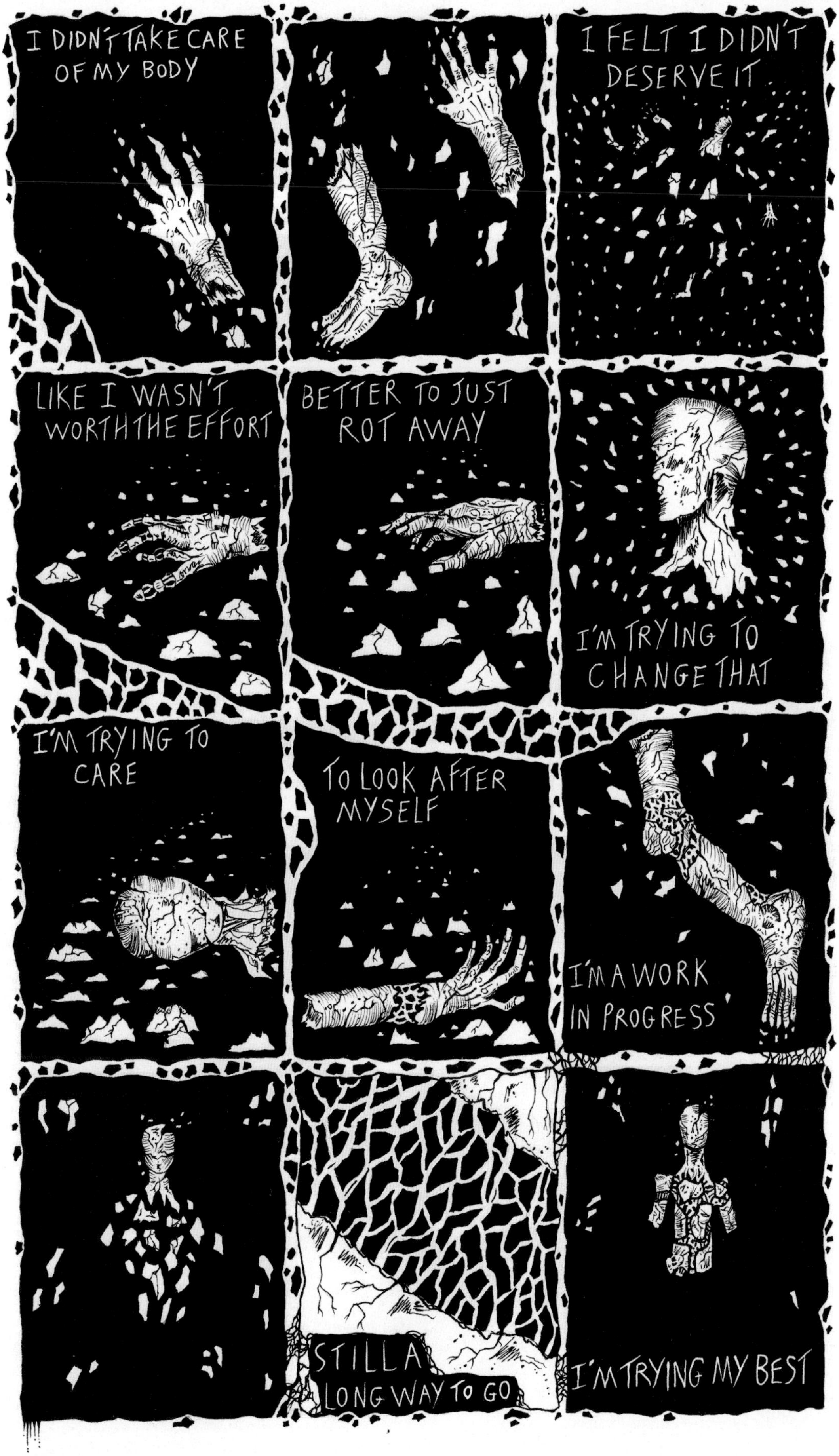
I DIDN'T TAKE CARE OF MY BODY
I FELT I DIDN'T DESERVE IT
LIKE I WASN'T WORTH THE EFFORT
BETTER TO JUST ROT AWAY
I'M TRYING TO CHANGE THAT
I'M TRYING TO CARE
TO LOOK AFTER MYSELF
I'M A WORK IN PROGRESS
STILL A LONG WAY TO GO
I'M TRYING MY BEST

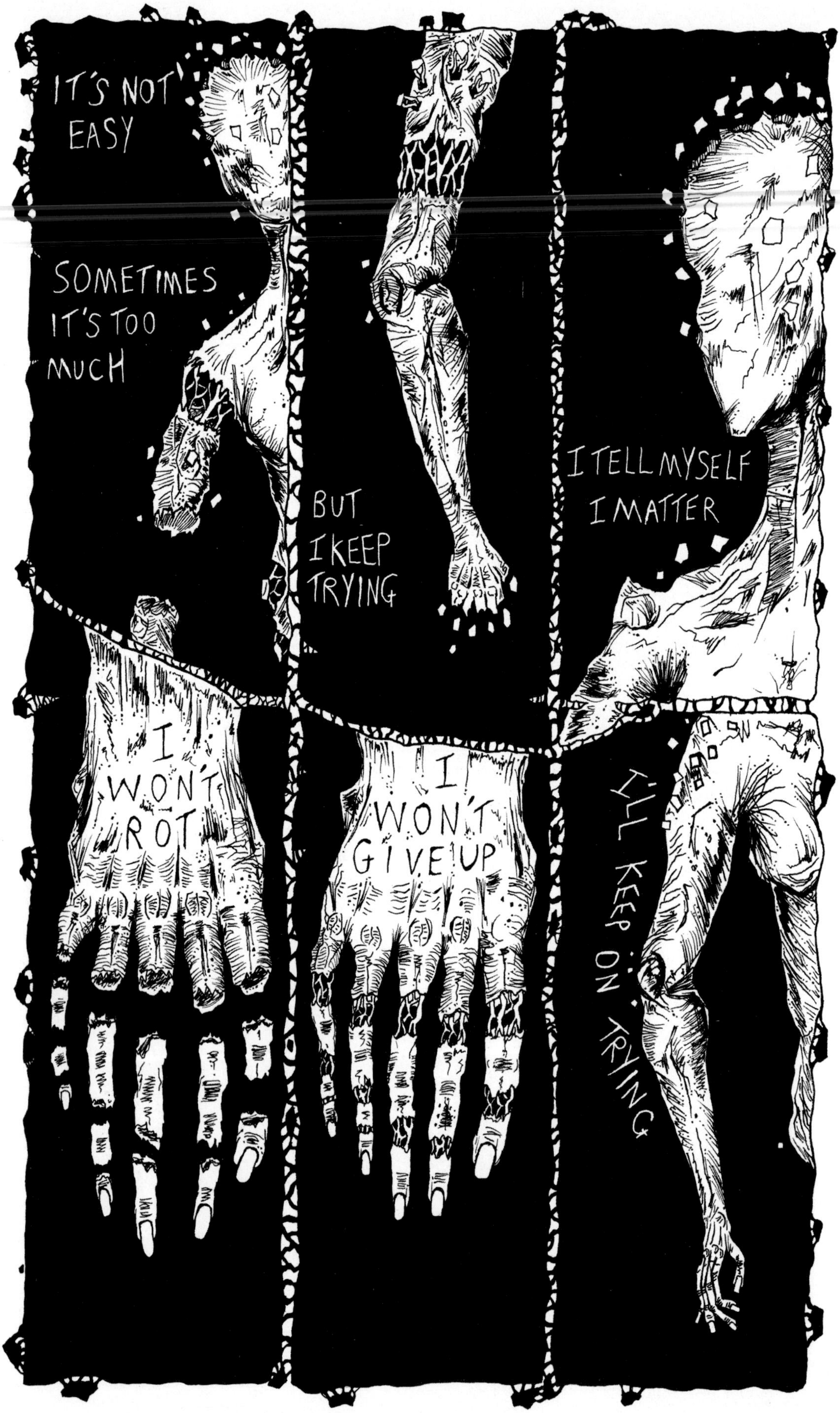

IT'S NOT EASY
SOMETIMES IT'S TOO MUCH
BUT I KEEP TRYING
I TELL MYSELF I MATTER
I WON'T ROT
I WON'T GIVE UP
I'LL KEEP ON TRYING

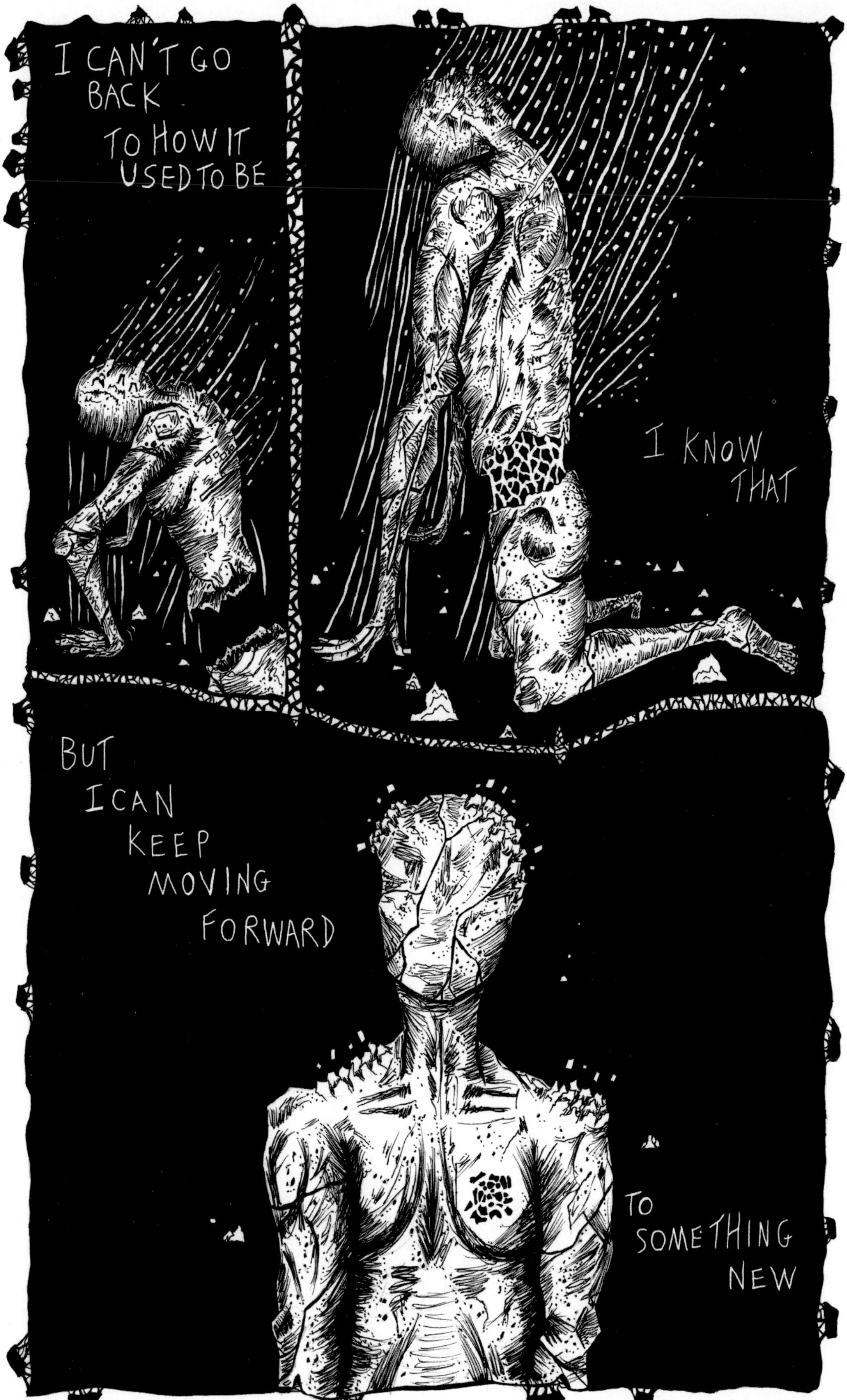
I CAN'T GO BACK TO HOW IT USED TO BE
I KNOW THAT
BUT I CAN KEEP MOVING FORWARD
TO SOMETHING NEW

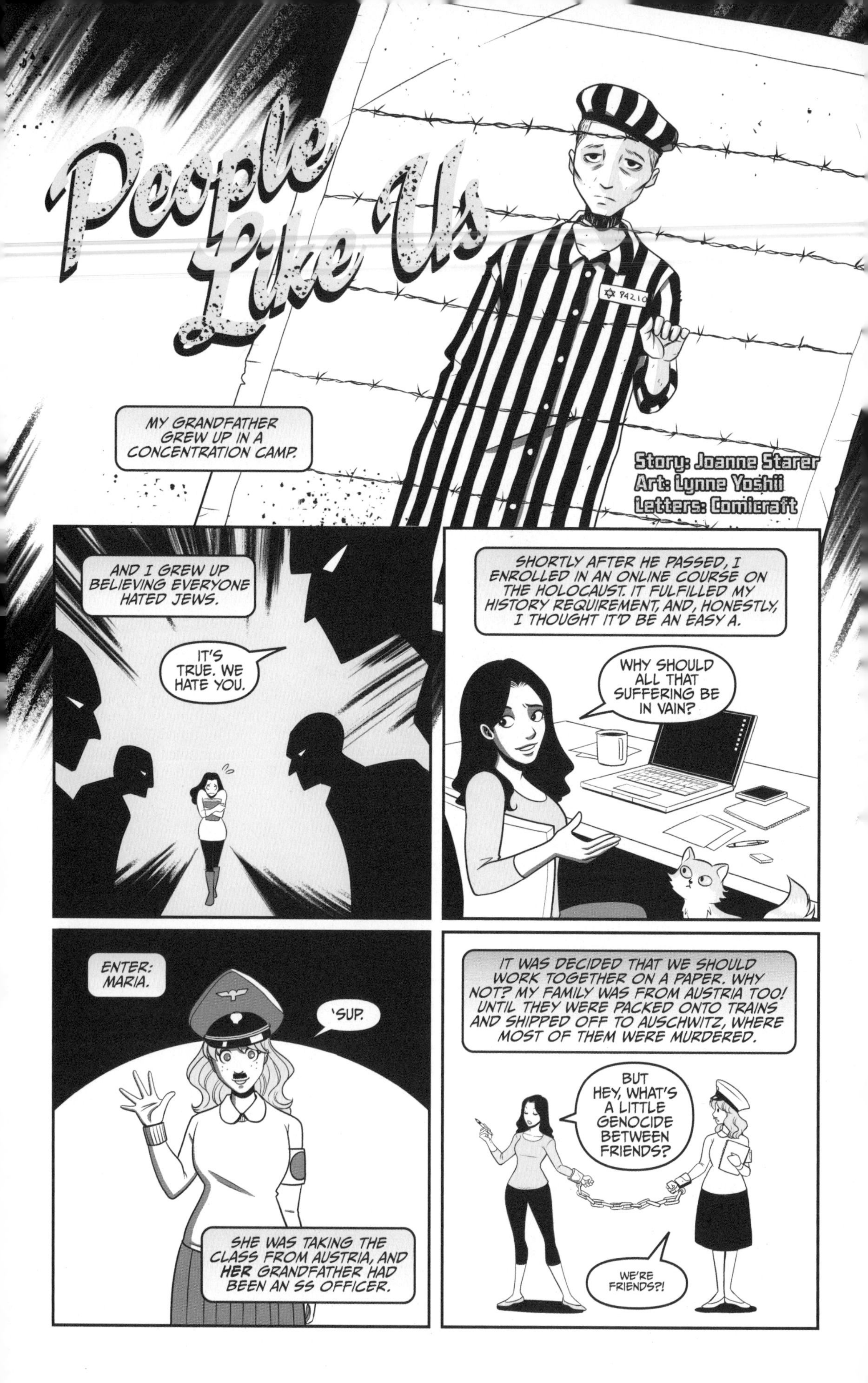
People Like Us
MY GRANDFATHER GREW UP IN A CONCENTRATION CAMP.
Story: Joanne Starer
Art: Lynne Yoshii
Letters: Comicraft
AND I GREW UP BELIEVING EVERYONE HATED JEWS.
IT'S TRUE. WE HATE YOU.
SHORTLY AFTER HE PASSED, I ENROLLED IN AN ONLINE COURSE ON THE HOLOCAUST. IT FULFILLED MY HISTORY REQUIREMENT, AND, HONESTLY, I THOUGHT IT'D BE AN EASY A.
WHY SHOULD ALL THAT SUFFERING BE IN VAIN?
ENTER: MARIA.
'SUP.
SHE WAS TAKING THE CLASS FROM AUSTRIA, AND HER GRANDFATHER HAD BEEN AN SS OFFICER.
IT WAS DECIDED THAT WE SHOULD WORK TOGETHER ON A PAPER. WHY NOT? MY FAMILY WAS FROM AUSTRIA TOO! UNTIL THEY WERE PACKED ONTO TRAINS AND SHIPPED OFF TO AUSCHWITZ, WHERE MOST OF THEM WERE MURDERED.
BUT HEY, WHAT'S A LITTLE GENOCIDE BETWEEN FRIENDS?
WE'RE FRIENDS?!

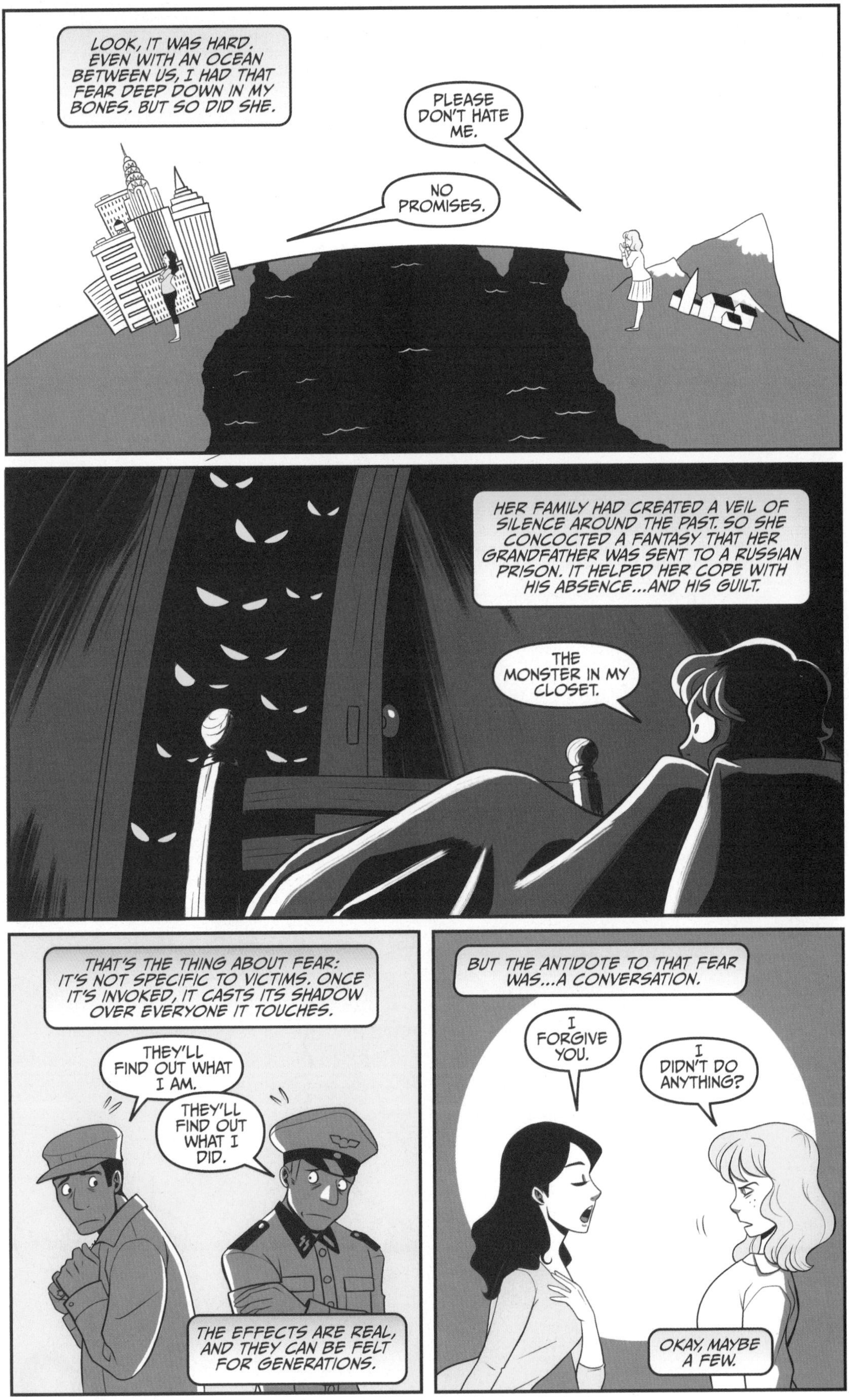
LOOK, IT WAS HARD. EVEN WITH AN OCEAN BETWEEN US, I HAD THAT FEAR DEEP DOWN IN MY BONES. BUT SO DID SHE.
PLEASE DON'T HATE ME.
NO PROMISES.
HER FAMILY HAD CREATED A VEIL OF SILENCE AROUND THE PAST. SO SHE CONCOCTED A FANTASY THAT HER GRANDFATHER WAS SENT TO A RUSSIAN PRISON. IT HELPED HER COPE WITH HIS ABSENCE...AND HIS GUILT.
THE MONSTER IN MY CLOSET.
THAT'S THE THING ABOUT FEAR: IT'S NOT SPECIFIC TO VICTIMS. ONCE IT'S INVOKED, IT CASTS ITS SHADOW OVER EVERYONE IT TOUCHES.
THEY'LL FIND OUT WHAT I AM.
THEY'LL FIND OUT WHAT I DID.
THE EFFECTS ARE REAL, AND THEY CAN BE FELT FOR GENERATIONS.
BUT THE ANTIDOTE TO THAT FEAR WAS...A CONVERSATION.
I FORGIVE YOU.
I DIDN'T DO ANYTHING?
OKAY, MAYBE A FEW.

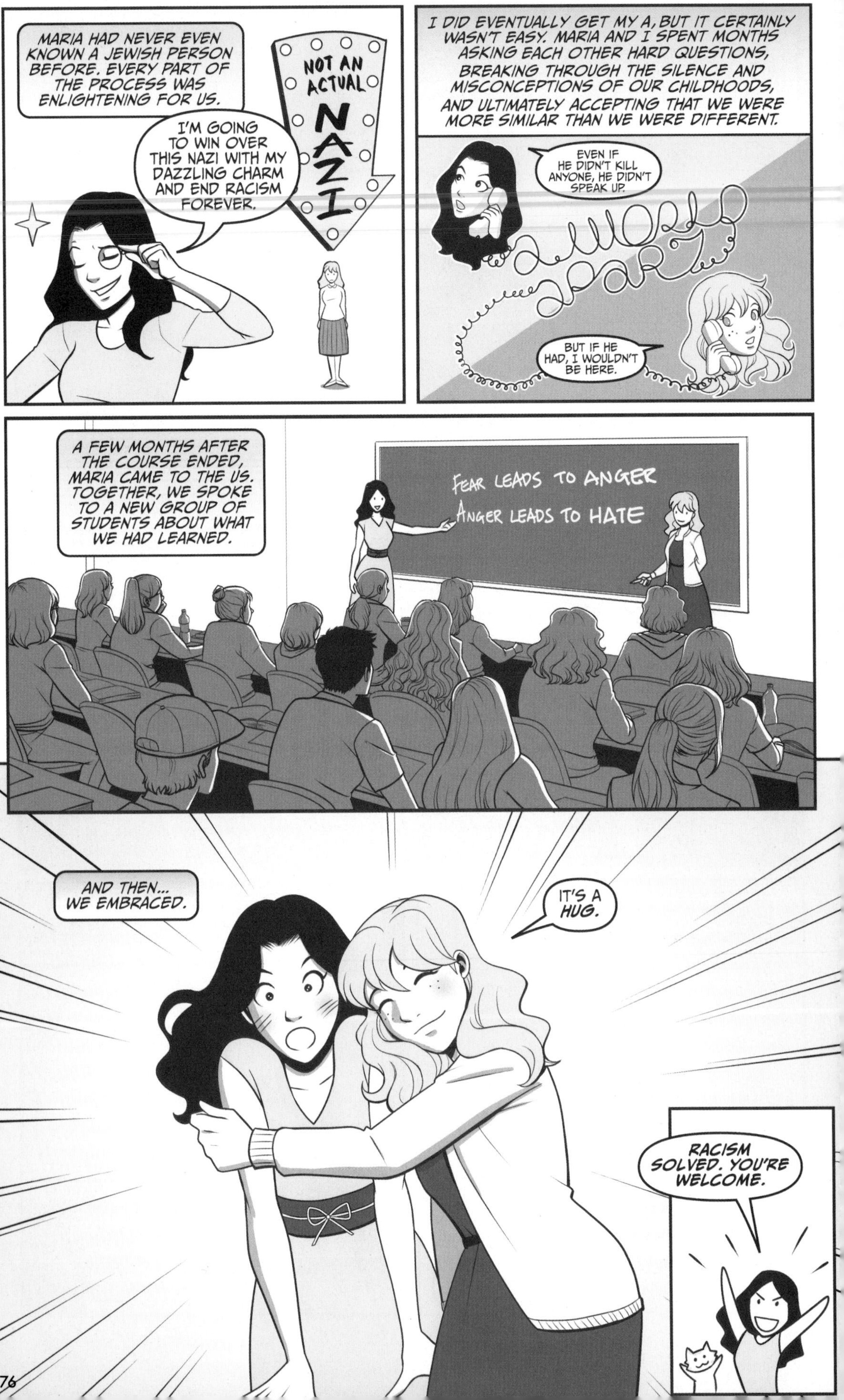
MARIA HAD NEVER EVEN KNOWN A JEWISH PERSON BEFORE. EVERY PART OF THE PROCESS WAS ENLIGHTENING FOR US.
NOT AN ACTUAL NAZI
I'M GOING TO WIN OVER THIS NAZI WITH MY DAZZLING CHARM AND END RACISM FOREVER.
I DID EVENTUALLY GET MY A, BUT IT CERTAINLY WASN'T EASY. MARIA AND I SPENT MONTHS ASKING EACH OTHER HARD QUESTIONS, BREAKING THROUGH THE SILENCE AND MISCONCEPTIONS OF OUR CHILDHOODS, AND ULTIMATELY ACCEPTING THAT WE WERE MORE SIMILAR THAN WE WERE DIFFERENT.
EVEN IF HE DIDN'T KILL ANYONE, HE DIDN'T SPEAK UP.
A WORLD APART
BUT IF HE HAD, I WOULDN'T BE HERE.
A FEW MONTHS AFTER THE COURSE ENDED, MARIA CAME TO THE US. TOGETHER, WE SPOKE TO A NEW GROUP OF STUDENTS ABOUT WHAT WE HAD LEARNED.
FEAR LEADS TO ANGER
ANGER LEADS TO HATE
AND THEN... WE EMBRACED.
IT'S A HUG.
RACISM SOLVED. YOU'RE WELCOME.

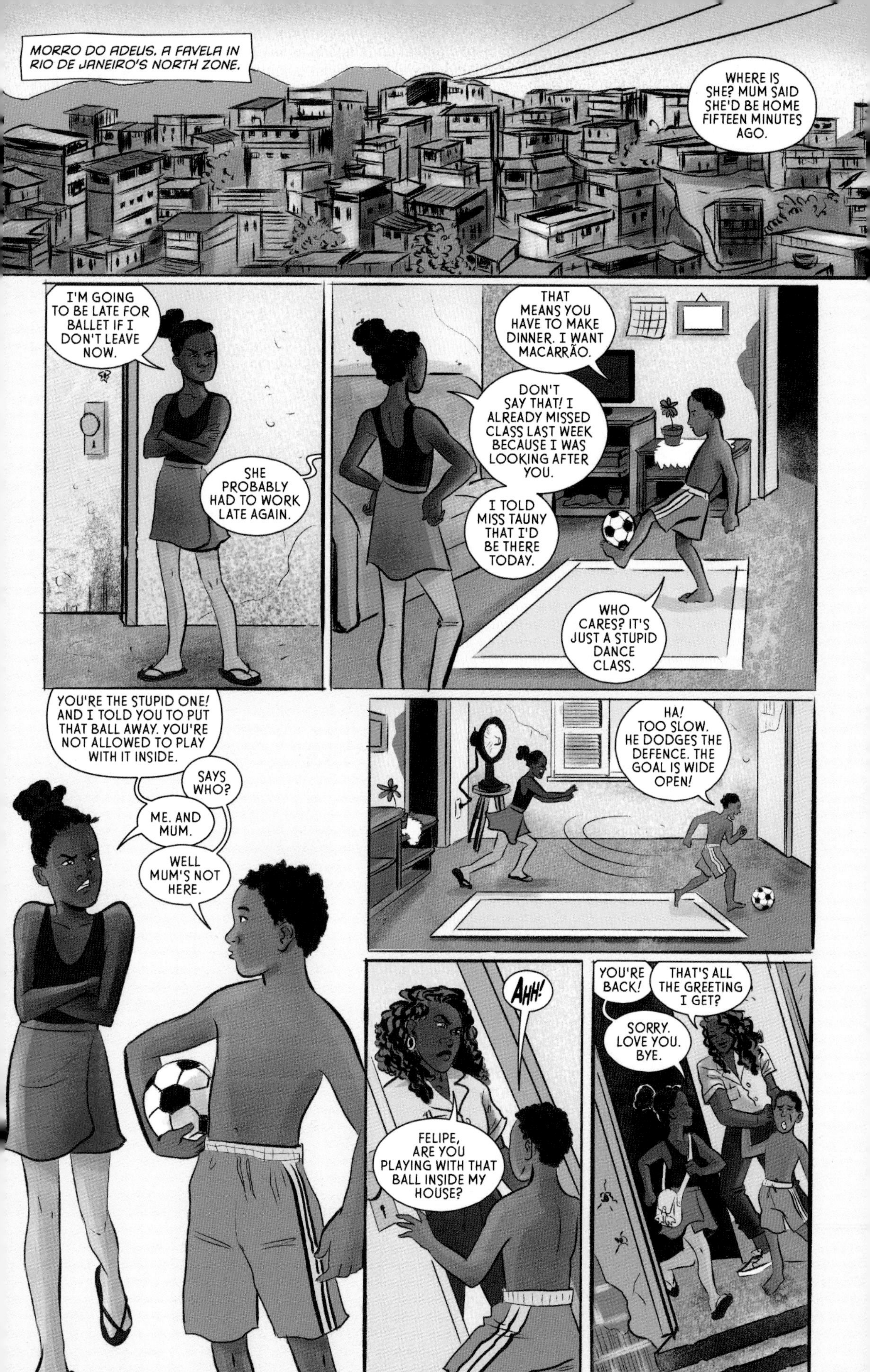
MORRO DO ADEUS, A FAVELA IN RIO DE JANEIRO'S NORTH ZONE.
WHERE IS SHE? MUM SAID SHE'D BE HOME FIFTEEN MINUTES AGO.
I'M GOING TO BE LATE FOR BALLET IF I DON'T LEAVE NOW.
SHE PROBABLY HAD TO WORK LATE AGAIN.
THAT MEANS YOU HAVE TO MAKE DINNER. I WANT MACARRÃO.
DON'T SAY THAT! I ALREADY MISSED CLASS LAST WEEK BECAUSE I WAS LOOKING AFTER YOU.
I TOLD MISS TAUNY THAT I'D BE THERE TODAY.
WHO CARES? IT'S JUST A STUPID DANCE CLASS.
YOU'RE THE STUPID ONE! AND I TOLD YOU TO PUT THAT BALL AWAY. YOU'RE NOT ALLOWED TO PLAY WITH IT INSIDE.
SAYS WHO?
ME. AND MUM.
WELL MUM'S NOT HERE.
HA! TOO SLOW. HE DODGES THE DEFENCE. THE GOAL IS WIDE OPEN!
AHH!
FELIPE, ARE YOU PLAYING WITH THAT BALL INSIDE MY HOUSE?
YOU'RE BACK!
THAT'S ALL THE GREETING I GET?
SORRY. LOVE YOU. BYE.

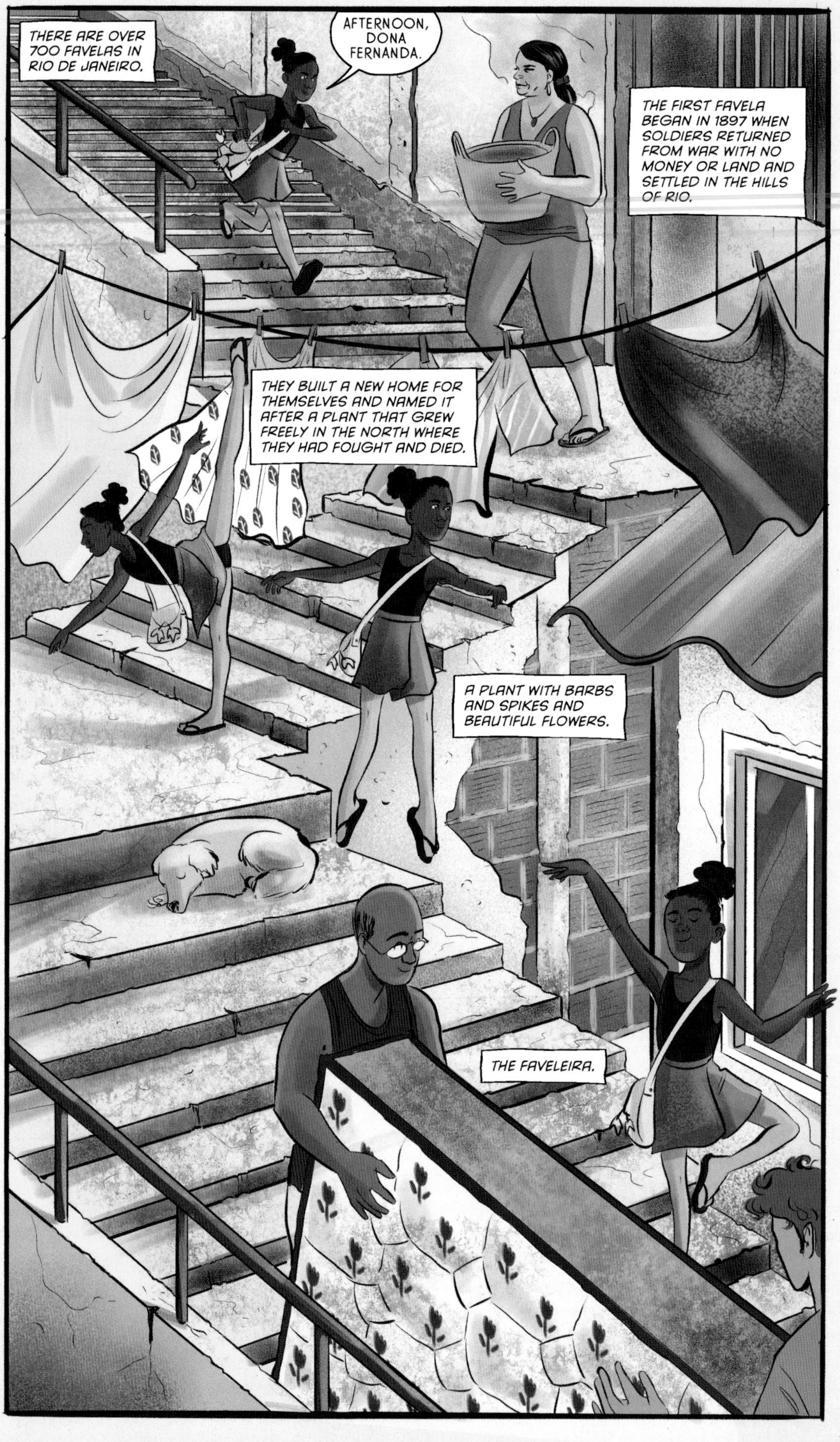
THERE ARE OVER 700 FAVELAS IN RIO DE JANEIRO.
AFTERNOON, DONA FERNANDA.
THE FIRST FAVELA BEGAN IN 1897 WHEN SOLDIERS RETURNED FROM WAR WITH NO MONEY OR LAND AND SETTLED IN THE HILLS OF RIO.
THEY BUILT A NEW HOME FOR THEMSELVES AND NAMED IT AFTER A PLANT THAT GREW FREELY IN THE NORTH WHERE THEY HAD FOUGHT AND DIED.
A PLANT WITH BARBS AND SPIKES AND BEAUTIFUL FLOWERS.
THE FAVELEIRA.

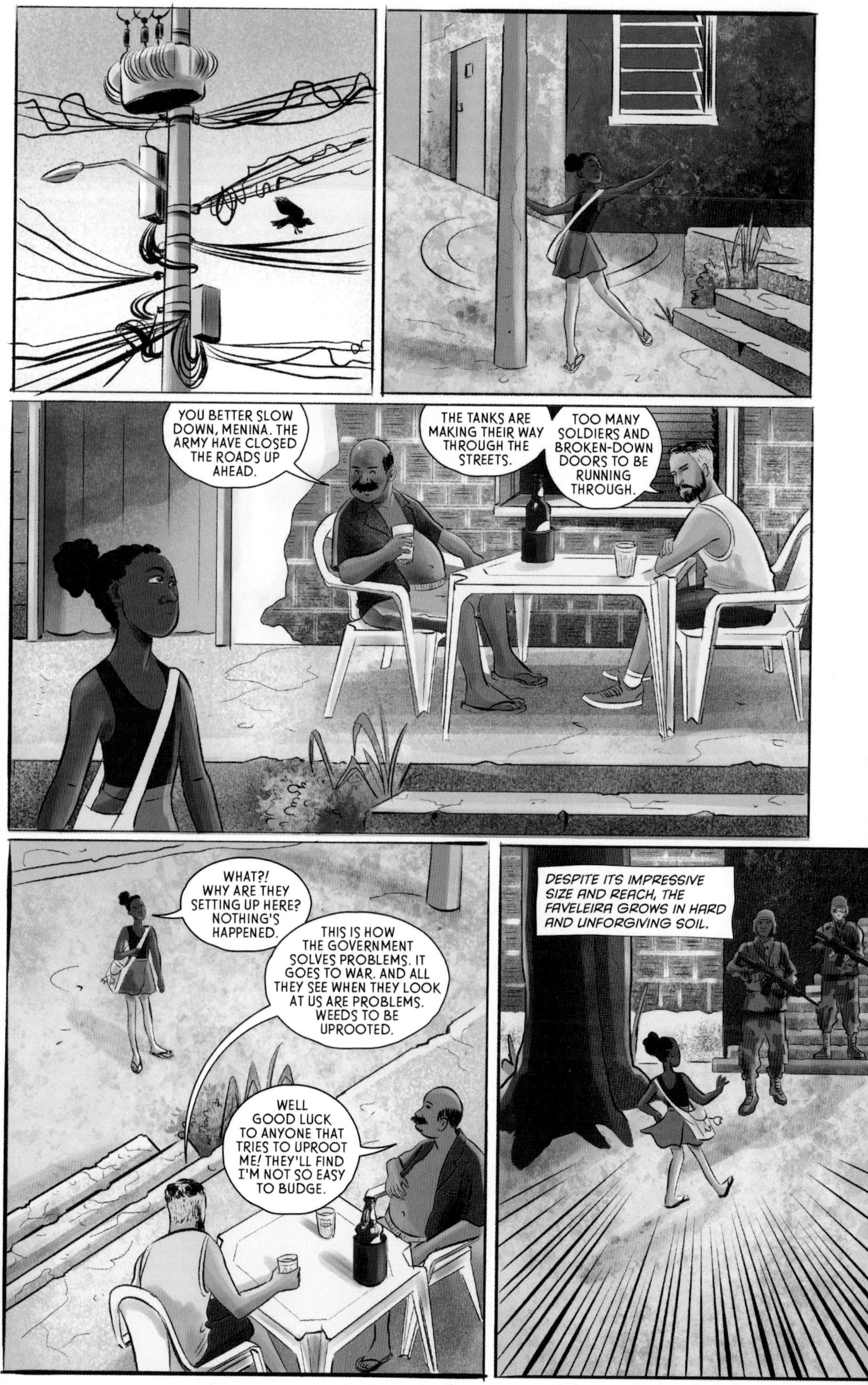
YOU BETTER SLOW DOWN, MENINA. THE ARMY HAVE CLOSED THE ROADS UP AHEAD.
THE TANKS ARE MAKING THEIR WAY THROUGH THE STREETS.
TOO MANY SOLDIERS AND BROKEN-DOWN DOORS TO BE RUNNING THROUGH.
WHAT?! WHY ARE THEY SETTING UP HERE? NOTHING'S HAPPENED.
THIS IS HOW THE GOVERNMENT SOLVES PROBLEMS. IT GOES TO WAR. AND ALL THEY SEE WHEN THEY LOOK AT US ARE PROBLEMS. WEEDS TO BE UPROOTED.
WELL GOOD LUCK TO ANYONE THAT TRIES TO UPROOT ME! THEY'LL FIND I'M NOT SO EASY TO BUDGE.
DESPITE ITS IMPRESSIVE SIZE AND REACH, THE FAVELEIRA GROWS IN HARD AND UNFORGIVING SOIL.

ROAD'S CLOSED. YOU CAN'T COME DOWN THIS WAY.

WHAT DO I CARE WHAT YOU NEED? *GET LOST!*

I JUST NEED TO GET TO CLASS. THIS IS THE ONLY WAY TO--

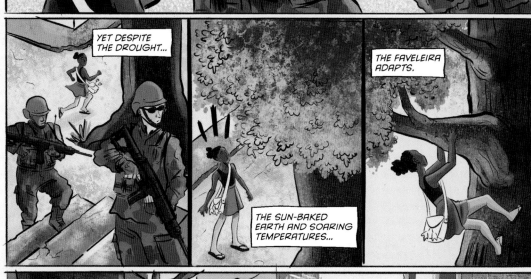

YET DESPITE THE DROUGHT...

THE SUN-BAKED EARTH AND SOARING TEMPERATURES...

THE FAVELEIRA ADAPTS.

IT SPREADS ITS ARMS FAR AND WIDE...

AND THRIVES.

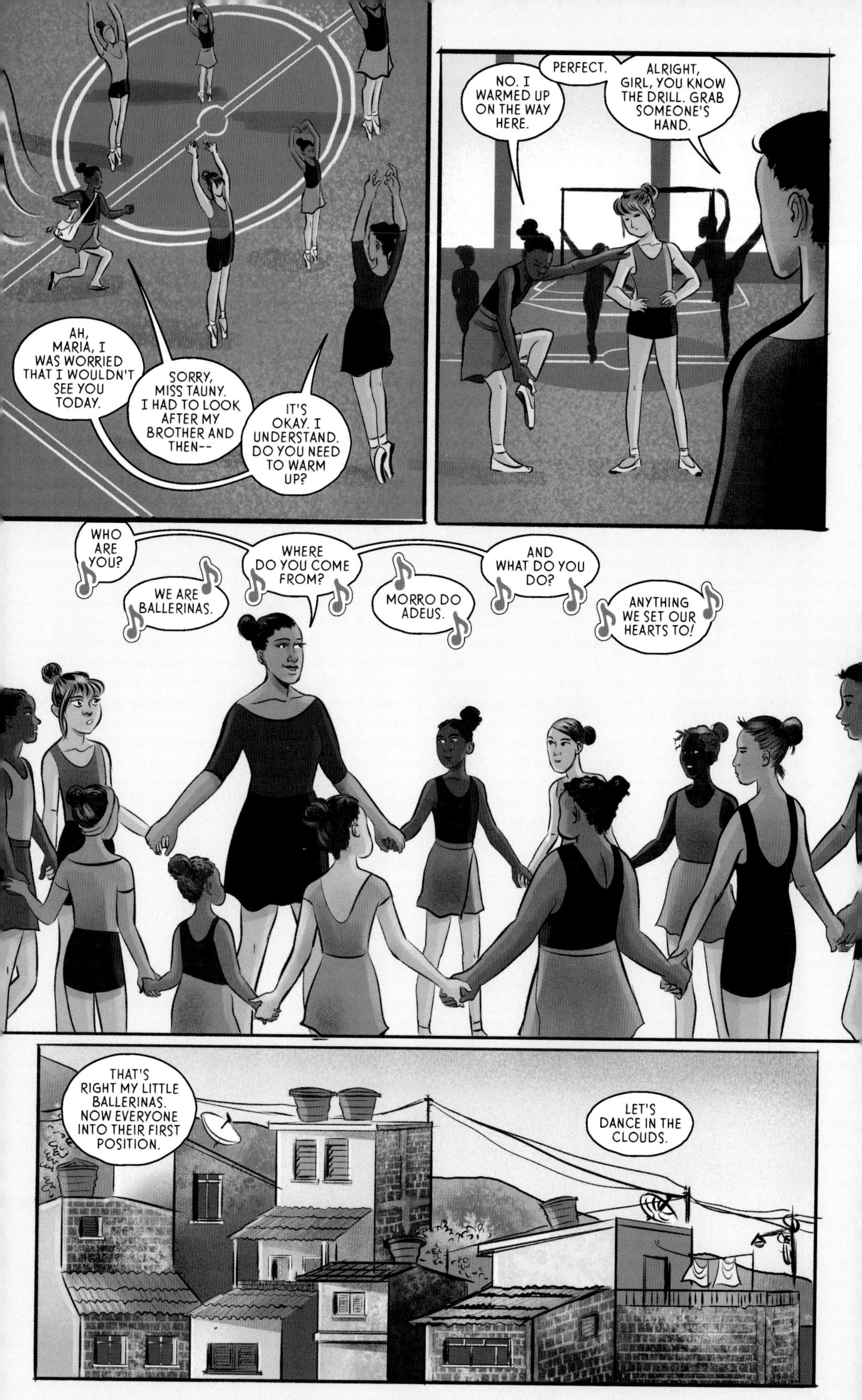
AH, MARIA, I WAS WORRIED THAT I WOULDN'T SEE YOU TODAY.
SORRY, MISS TAUNY. I HAD TO LOOK AFTER MY BROTHER AND THEN--
IT'S OKAY. I UNDERSTAND. DO YOU NEED TO WARM UP?
NO. I WARMED UP ON THE WAY HERE.
PERFECT.
ALRIGHT, GIRL, YOU KNOW THE DRILL. GRAB SOMEONE'S HAND.
WHO ARE YOU?
WE ARE BALLERINAS.
WHERE DO YOU COME FROM?
MORRO DO ADEUS.
AND WHAT DO YOU DO?
ANYTHING WE SET OUR HEARTS TO!
THAT'S RIGHT MY LITTLE BALLERINAS. NOW EVERYONE INTO THEIR FIRST POSITION.
LET'S DANCE IN THE CLOUDS.

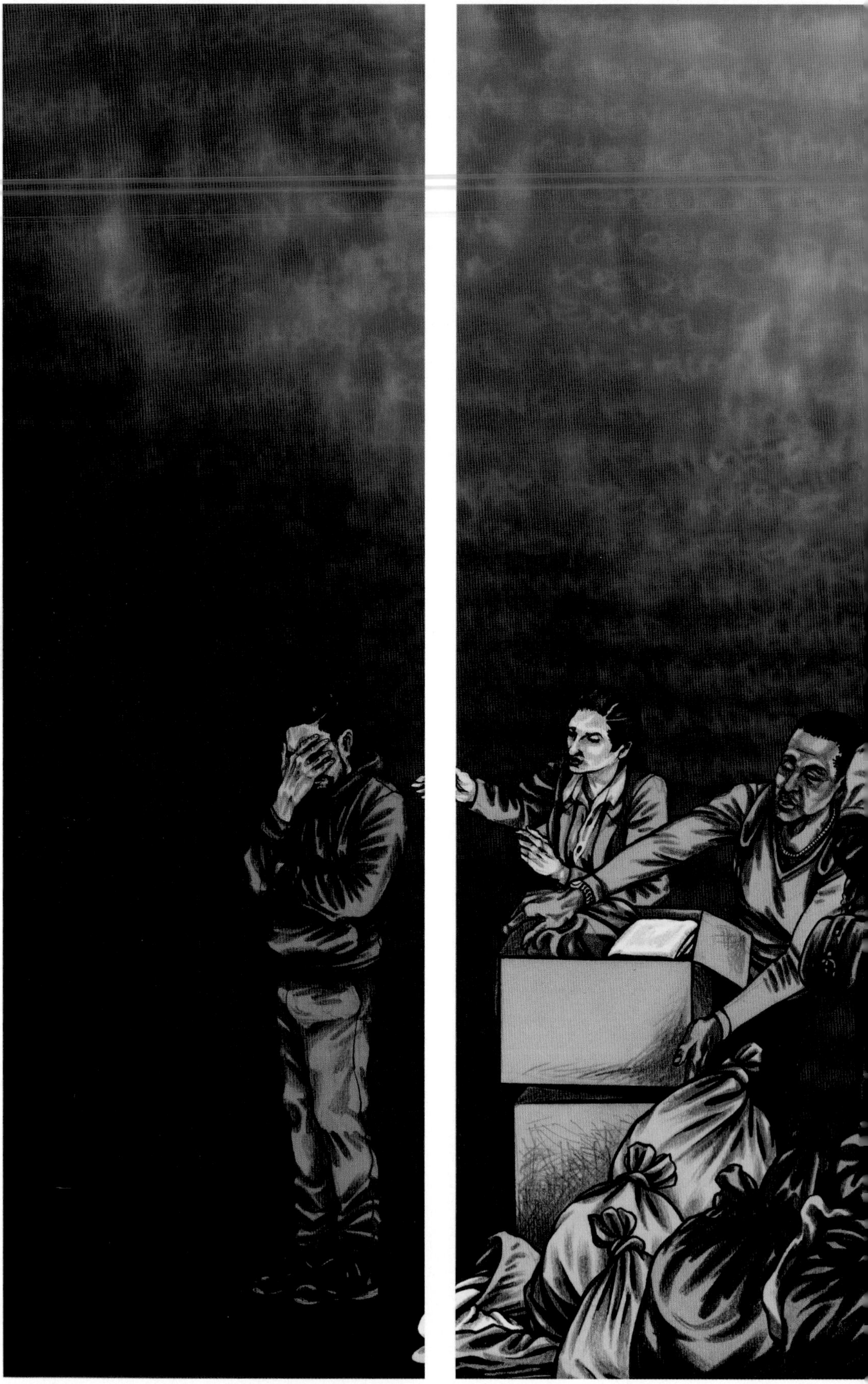

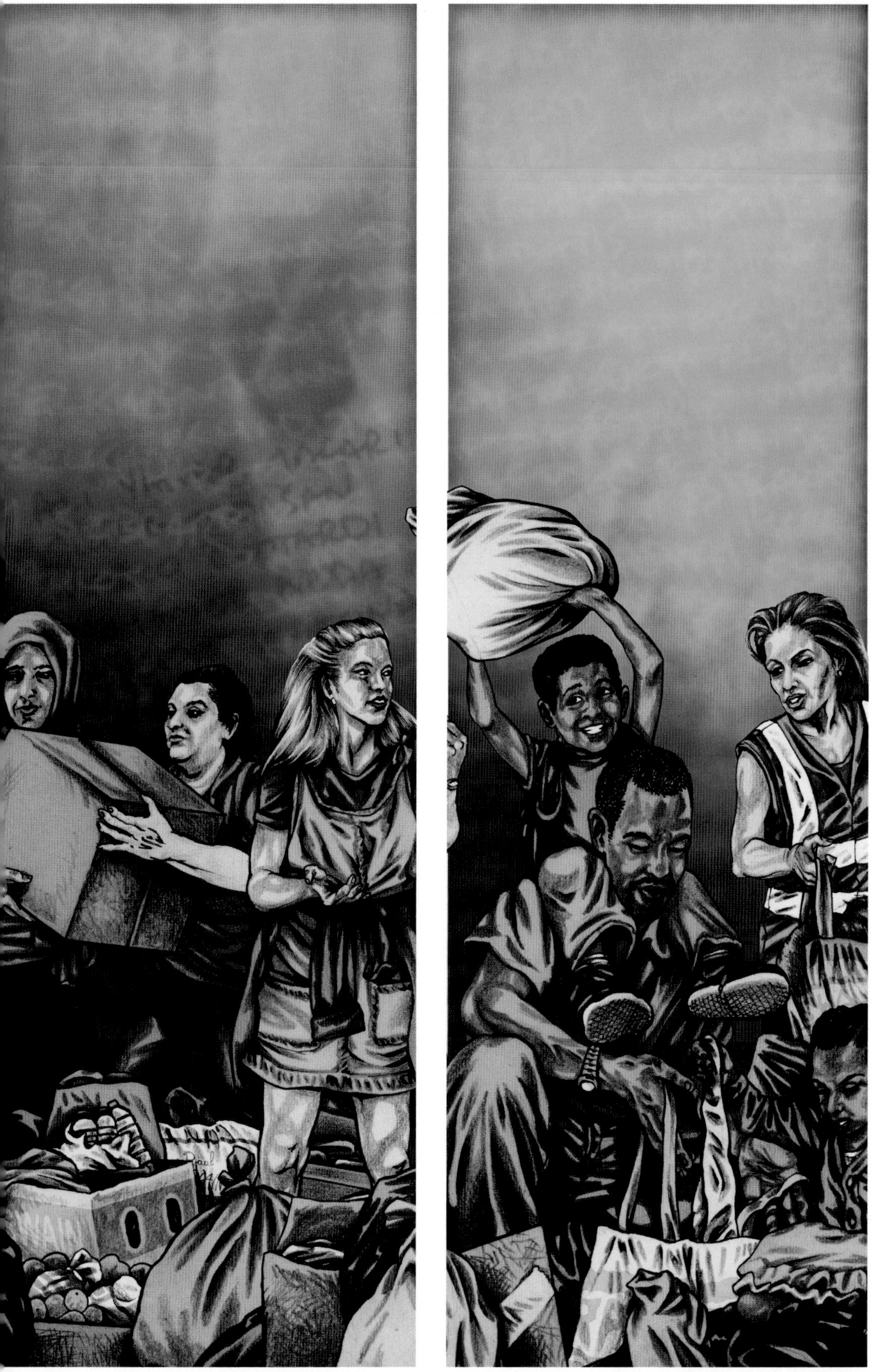

— PAUL SWAIN —

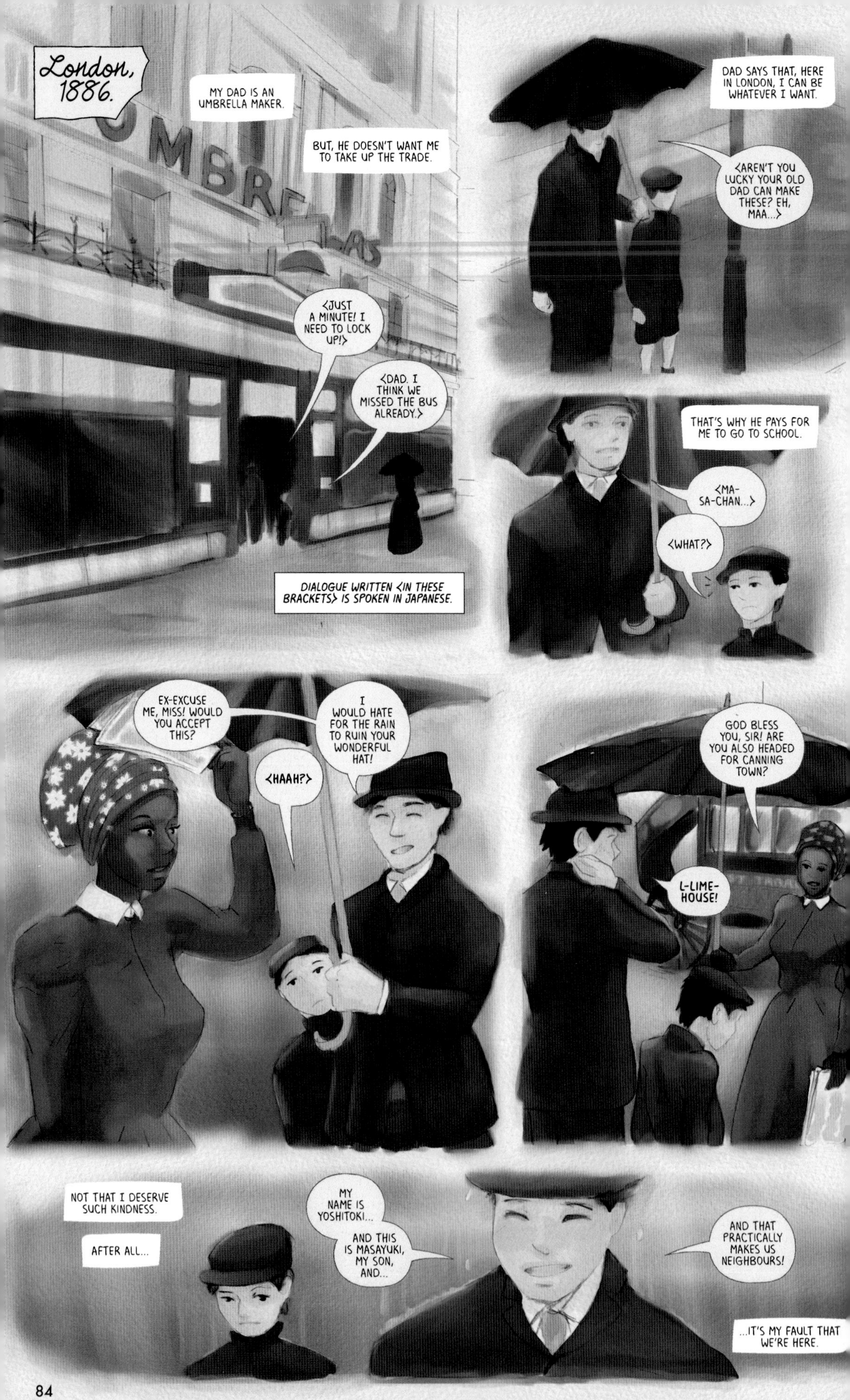
London, 1886.
MY DAD IS AN UMBRELLA MAKER.
BUT, HE DOESN'T WANT ME TO TAKE UP THE TRADE.
OMBRELLAS
<JUST A MINUTE! I NEED TO LOCK UP!>
<DAD. I THINK WE MISSED THE BUS ALREADY.>
DIALOGUE WRITTEN <IN THESE BRACKETS> IS SPOKEN IN JAPANESE.
DAD SAYS THAT, HERE IN LONDON, I CAN BE WHATEVER I WANT.
<AREN'T YOU LUCKY YOUR OLD DAD CAN MAKE THESE? EH, MAA...>
THAT'S WHY HE PAYS FOR ME TO GO TO SCHOOL.
<MA-SA-CHAN...>
<WHAT?>
EX-EXCUSE ME, MISS! WOULD YOU ACCEPT THIS?
I WOULD HATE FOR THE RAIN TO RUIN YOUR WONDERFUL HAT!
<HAAH?>
GOD BLESS YOU, SIR! ARE YOU ALSO HEADED FOR CANNING TOWN?
L-LIME-HOUSE!
NOT THAT I DESERVE SUCH KINDNESS.
AFTER ALL...
MY NAME IS YOSHITOKI...
AND THIS IS MASAYUKI, MY SON, AND...
AND THAT PRACTICALLY MAKES US NEIGHBOURS!
...IT'S MY FAULT THAT WE'RE HERE.

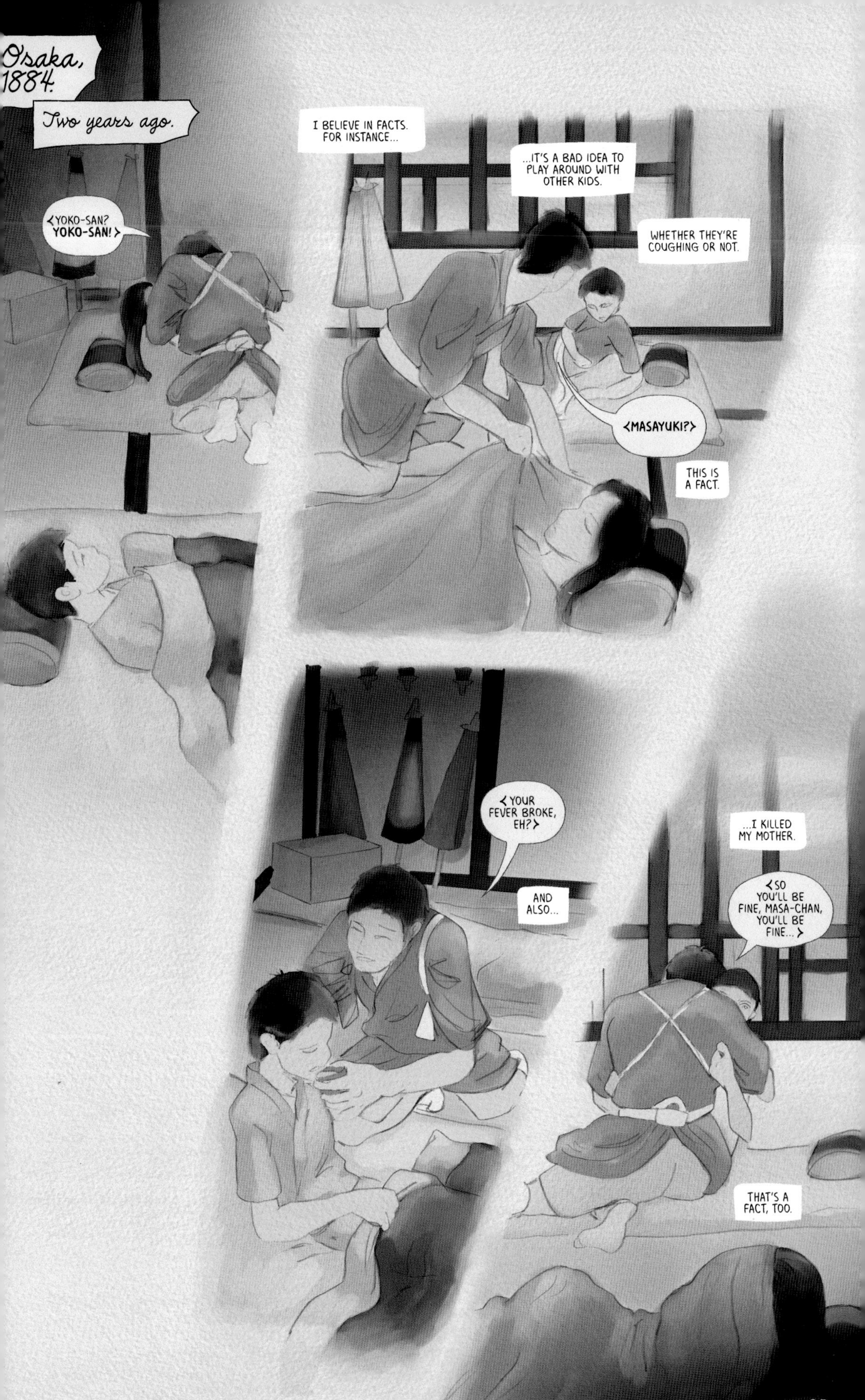
Osaka, 1884.
Two years ago.
<YOKO-SAN? YOKO-SAN!>
I BELIEVE IN FACTS. FOR INSTANCE...
...IT'S A BAD IDEA TO PLAY AROUND WITH OTHER KIDS.
WHETHER THEY'RE COUGHING OR NOT.
<MASAYUKI?>
THIS IS A FACT.
<YOUR FEVER BROKE, EH?>
AND ALSO...
...I KILLED MY MOTHER.
<SO YOU'LL BE FINE, MASA-CHAN, YOU'LL BE FINE...>
THAT'S A FACT, TOO.

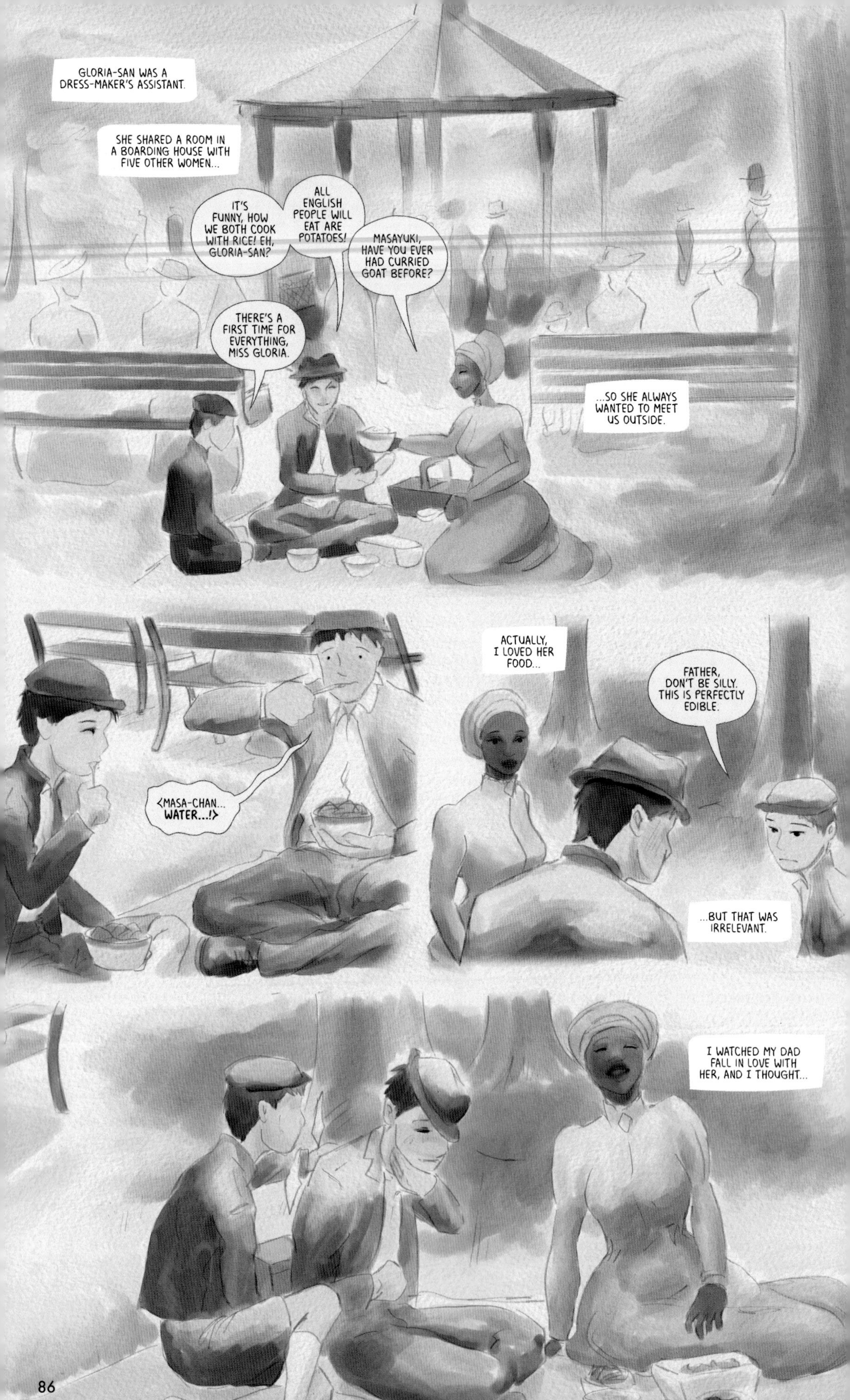
GLORIA-SAN WAS A DRESS-MAKER'S ASSISTANT.
SHE SHARED A ROOM IN A BOARDING HOUSE WITH FIVE OTHER WOMEN...
IT'S FUNNY, HOW WE BOTH COOK WITH RICE! EH, GLORIA-SAN?
ALL ENGLISH PEOPLE WILL EAT ARE POTATOES!
MASAYUKI, HAVE YOU EVER HAD CURRIED GOAT BEFORE?
THERE'S A FIRST TIME FOR EVERYTHING, MISS GLORIA.
...SO SHE ALWAYS WANTED TO MEET US OUTSIDE.
<MASA-CHAN... **WATER...!**>
ACTUALLY, I LOVED HER FOOD...
FATHER, DON'T BE SILLY. THIS IS PERFECTLY EDIBLE.
...BUT THAT WAS IRRELEVANT.
I WATCHED MY DAD FALL IN LOVE WITH HER, AND I THOUGHT...

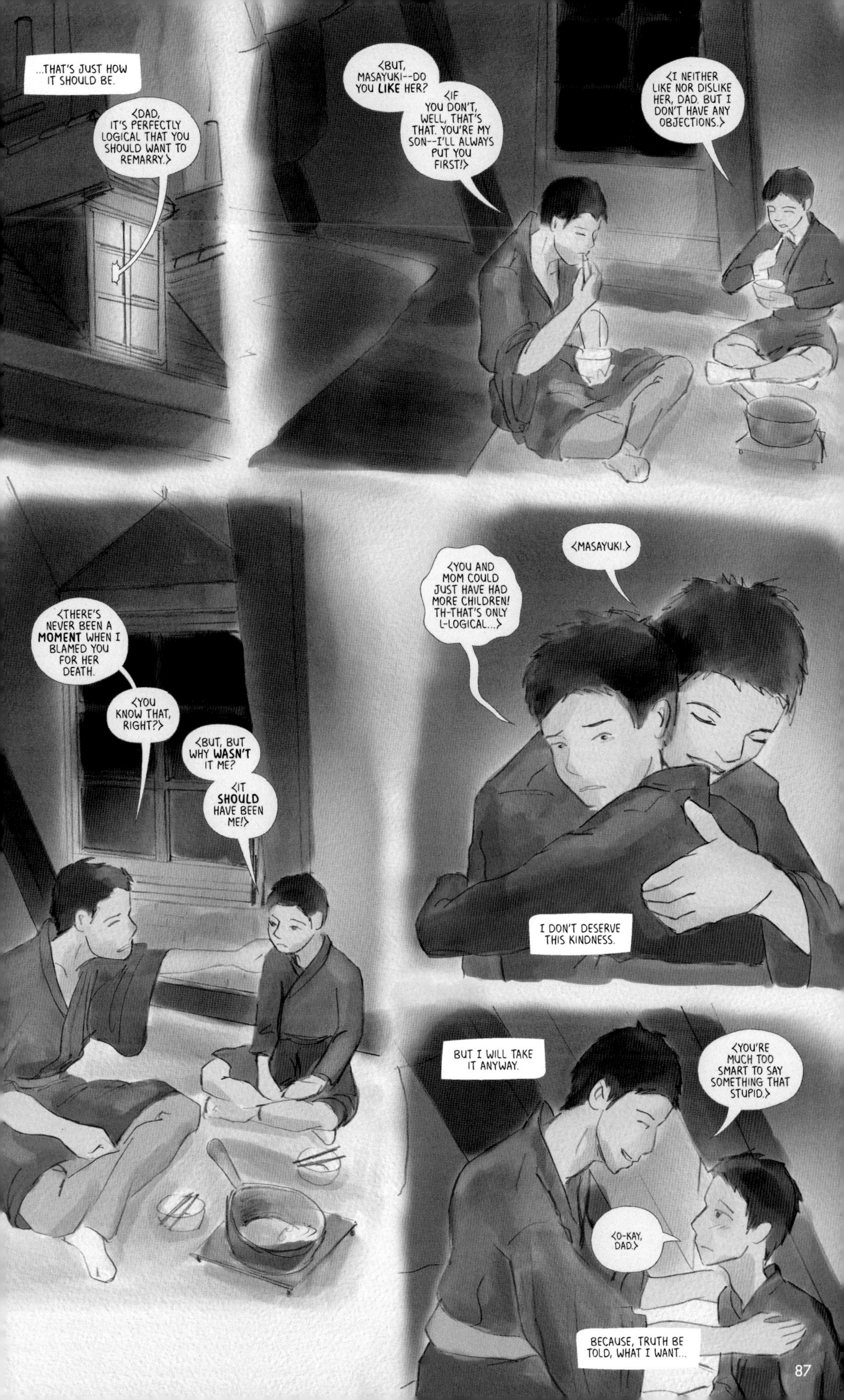
...THAT'S JUST HOW IT SHOULD BE.
<DAD, IT'S PERFECTLY LOGICAL THAT YOU SHOULD WANT TO REMARRY.>
<BUT, MASAYUKI--DO YOU **LIKE** HER?
<IF YOU DON'T, WELL, THAT'S THAT. YOU'RE MY SON--I'LL ALWAYS PUT YOU FIRST!>
<I NEITHER LIKE NOR DISLIKE HER, DAD. BUT I DON'T HAVE ANY OBJECTIONS.>
<THERE'S NEVER BEEN A **MOMENT** WHEN I BLAMED YOU FOR HER DEATH.
<YOU KNOW THAT, RIGHT?>
<BUT, BUT WHY **WASN'T** IT ME?
<IT **SHOULD** HAVE BEEN ME!>
<YOU AND MOM COULD JUST HAVE HAD MORE CHILDREN! TH-THAT'S ONLY L-LOGICAL...>
<MASAYUKI.>
I DON'T DESERVE THIS KINDNESS.
BUT I WILL TAKE IT ANYWAY.
<YOU'RE MUCH TOO SMART TO SAY SOMETHING THAT STUPID.>
<O-KAY, DAD.>
BECAUSE, TRUTH BE TOLD, WHAT I WANT...

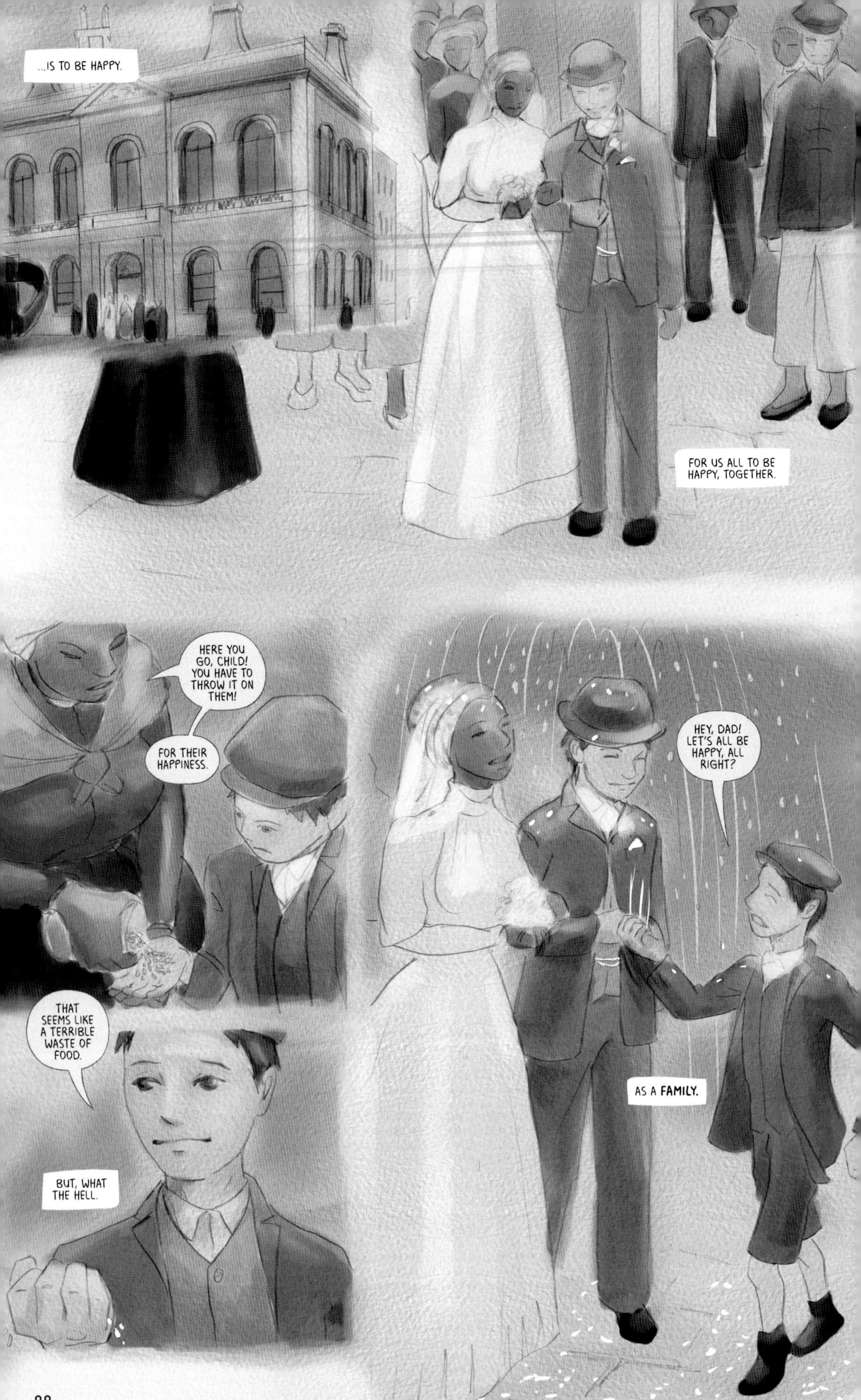

...IS TO BE HAPPY.
FOR US ALL TO BE HAPPY, TOGETHER.
HERE YOU GO, CHILD! YOU HAVE TO THROW IT ON THEM!
FOR THEIR HAPPINESS.
THAT SEEMS LIKE A TERRIBLE WASTE OF FOOD.
BUT, WHAT THE HELL.
HEY, DAD! LET'S ALL BE HAPPY, ALL RIGHT?
AS A **FAMILY**.

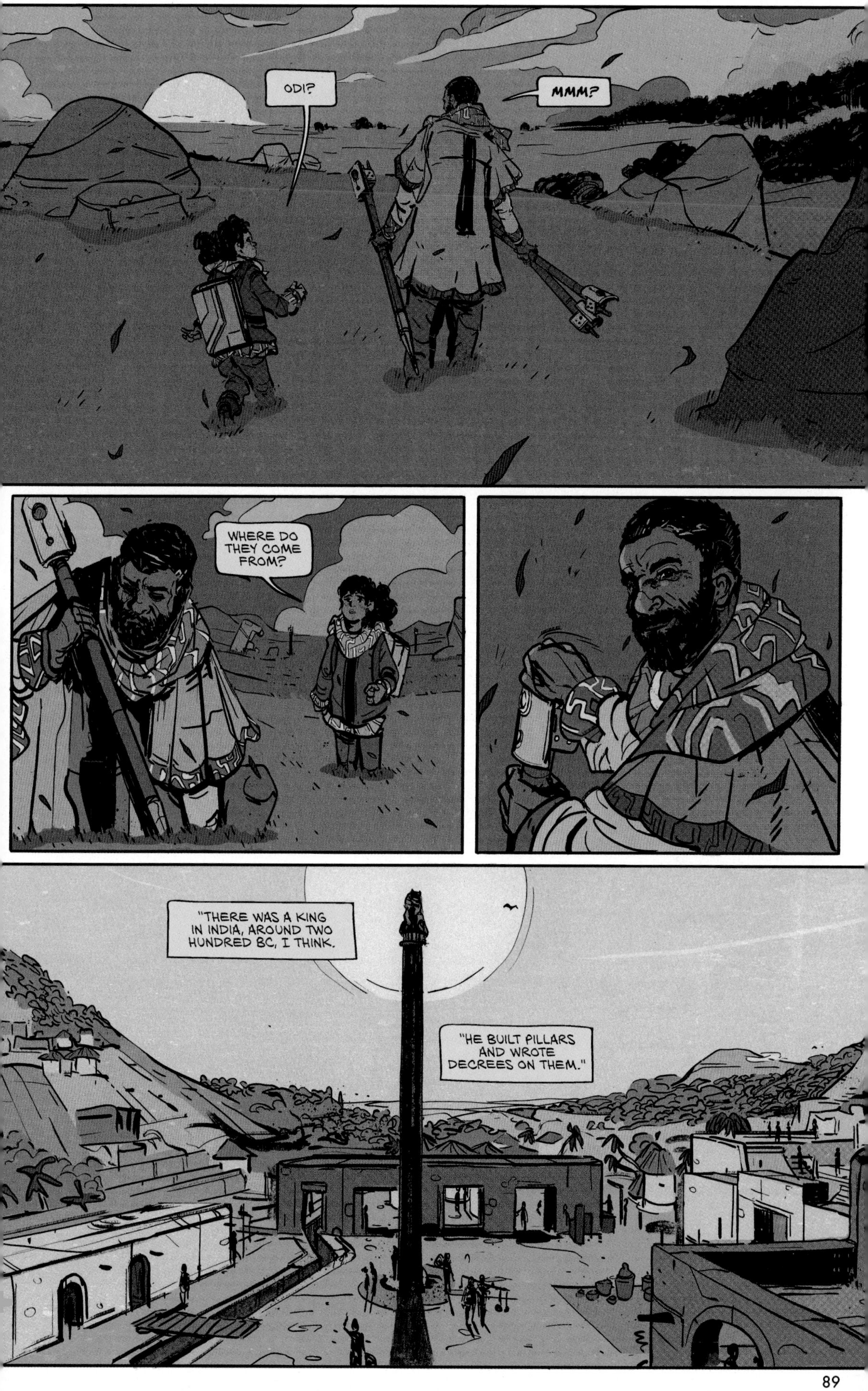
ODI?
MMM?
WHERE DO THEY COME FROM?
"THERE WAS A KING IN INDIA, AROUND TWO HUNDRED BC, I THINK.
"HE BUILT PILLARS AND WROTE DECREES ON THEM."

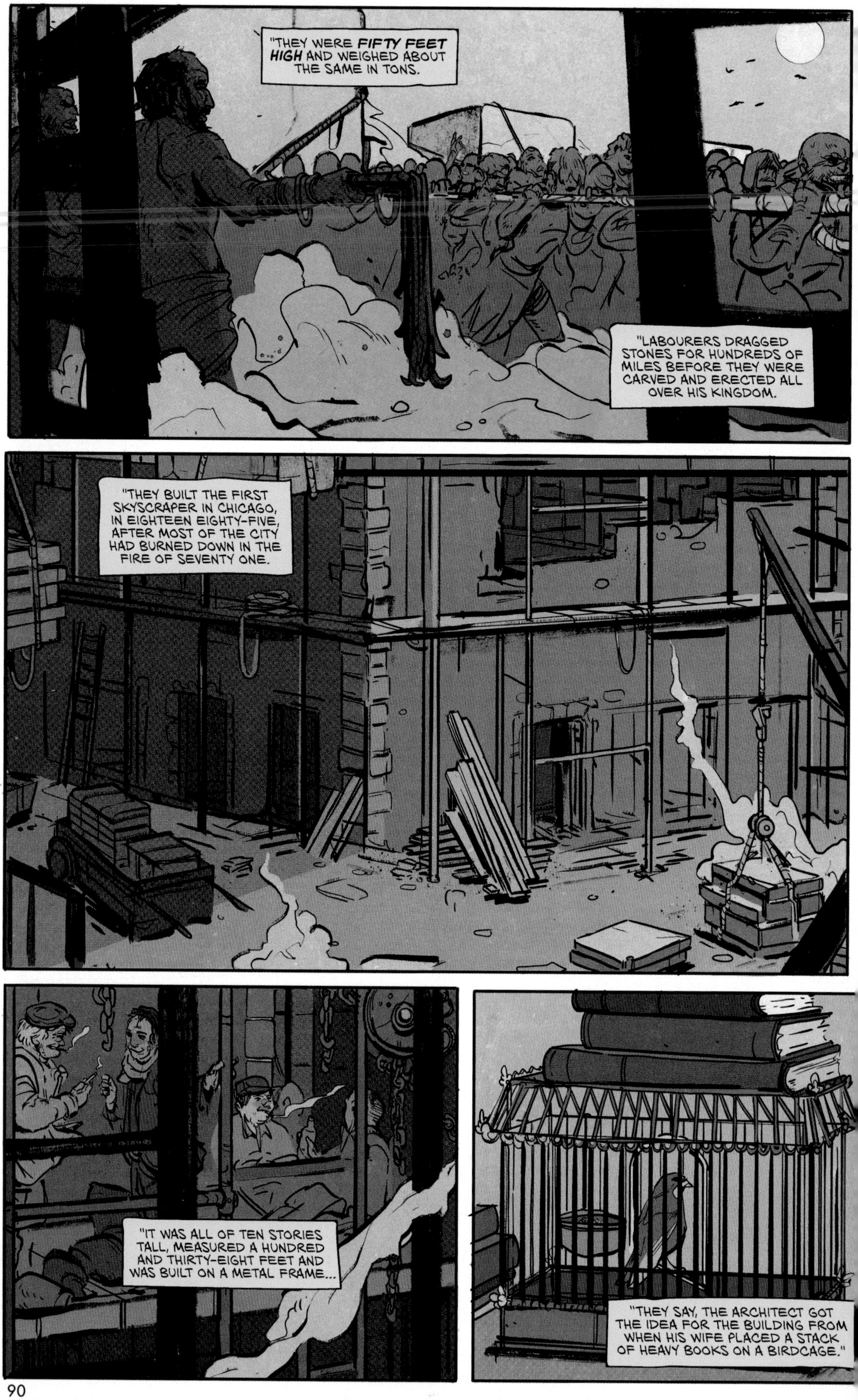
"THEY WERE **FIFTY FEET HIGH** AND WEIGHED ABOUT THE SAME IN TONS.
"LABOURERS DRAGGED STONES FOR HUNDREDS OF MILES BEFORE THEY WERE CARVED AND ERECTED ALL OVER HIS KINGDOM.
"THEY BUILT THE FIRST SKYSCRAPER IN CHICAGO, IN EIGHTEEN EIGHTY-FIVE, AFTER MOST OF THE CITY HAD BURNED DOWN IN THE FIRE OF SEVENTY ONE.
"IT WAS ALL OF TEN STORIES TALL, MEASURED A HUNDRED AND THIRTY-EIGHT FEET AND WAS BUILT ON A METAL FRAME...
"THEY SAY, THE ARCHITECT GOT THE IDEA FOR THE BUILDING FROM WHEN HIS WIFE PLACED A STACK OF HEAVY BOOKS ON A BIRDCAGE."

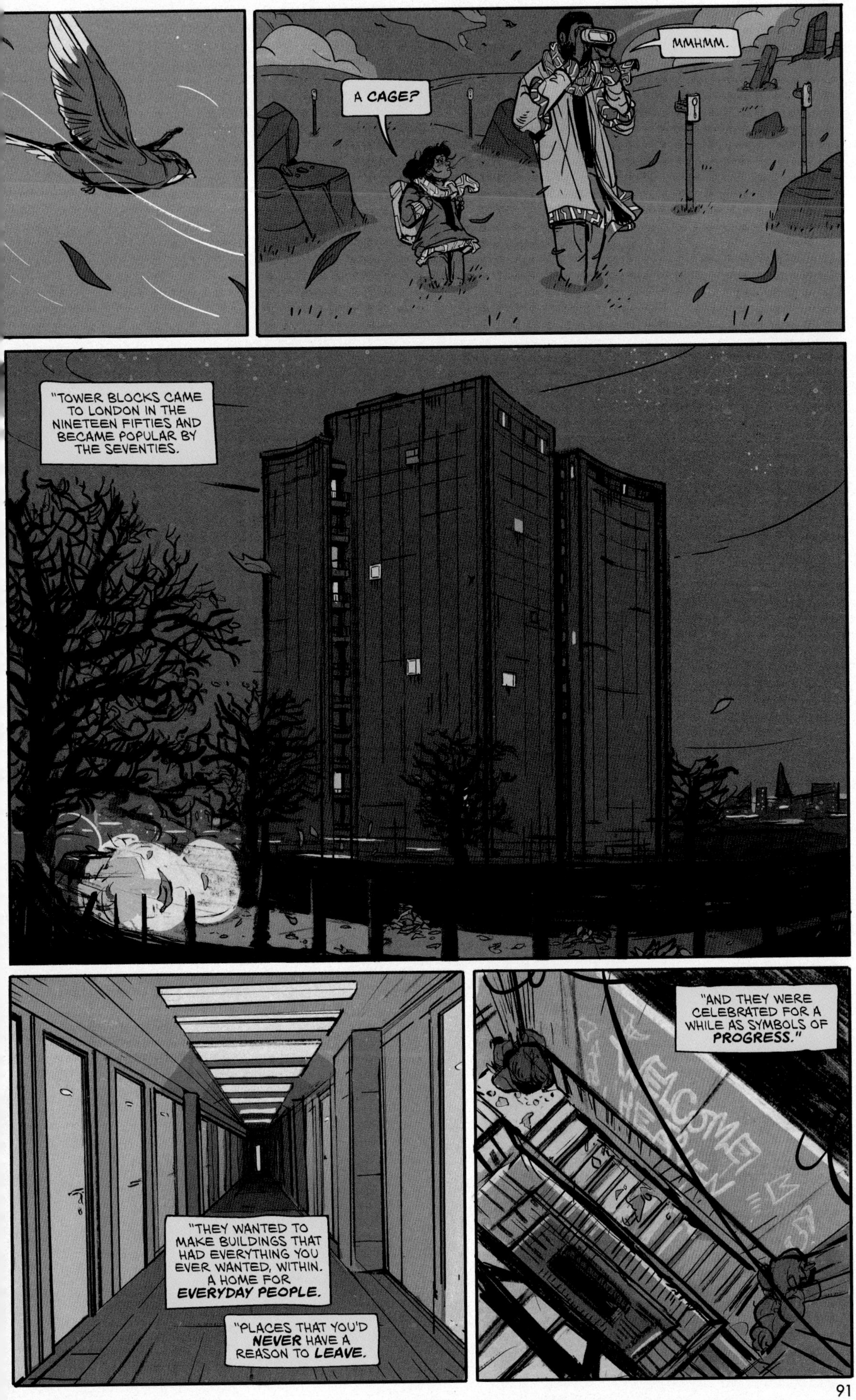
A CAGE?
MMHMM.
"TOWER BLOCKS CAME TO LONDON IN THE NINETEEN FIFTIES AND BECAME POPULAR BY THE SEVENTIES.
"THEY WANTED TO MAKE BUILDINGS THAT HAD EVERYTHING YOU EVER WANTED, WITHIN. A HOME FOR **EVERYDAY PEOPLE.**
"PLACES THAT YOU'D **NEVER** HAVE A REASON TO **LEAVE.**
"AND THEY WERE CELEBRATED FOR A WHILE AS SYMBOLS OF **PROGRESS."**

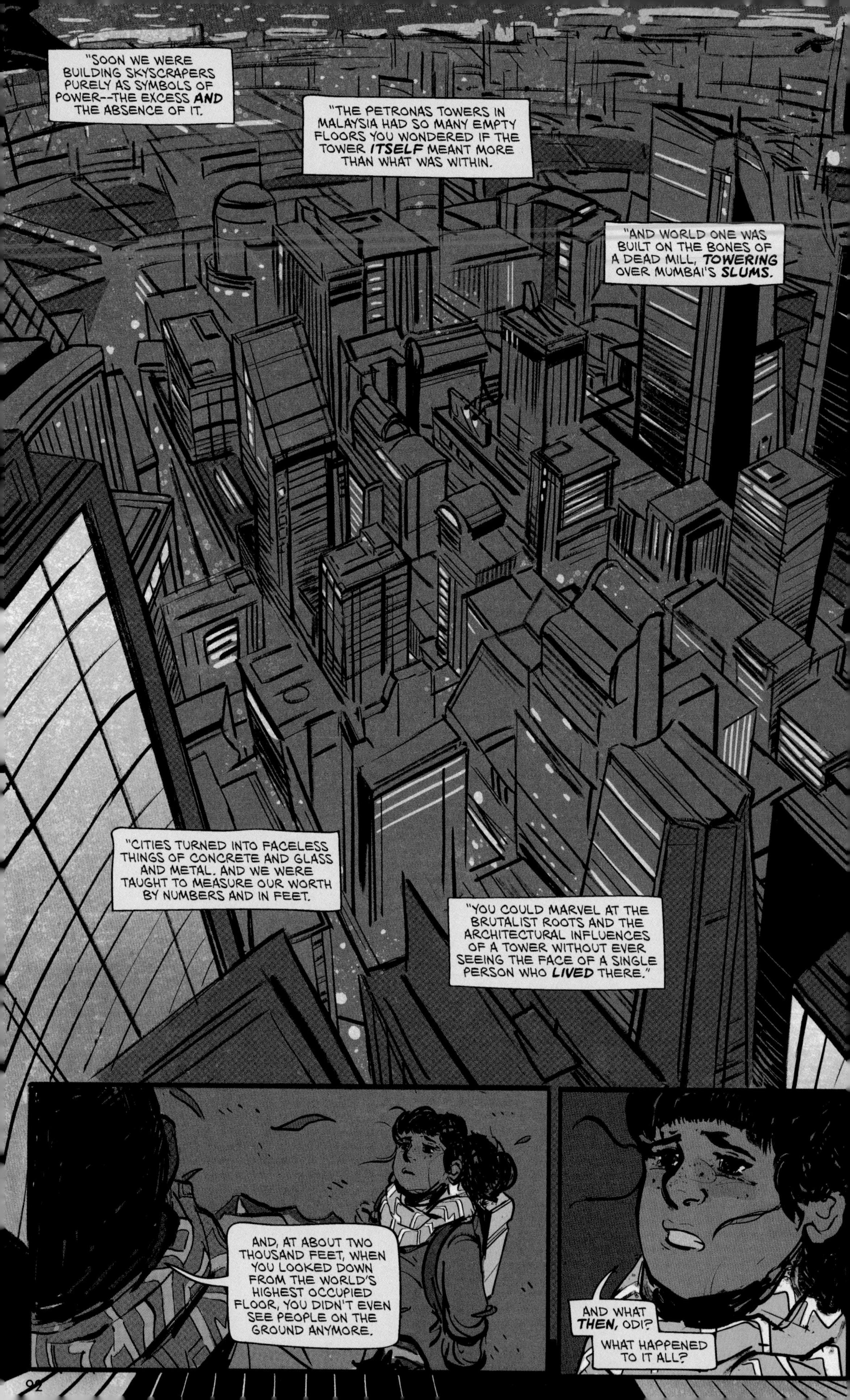
"SOON WE WERE BUILDING SKYSCRAPERS PURELY AS SYMBOLS OF POWER--THE EXCESS AND THE ABSENCE OF IT.
"THE PETRONAS TOWERS IN MALAYSIA HAD SO MANY EMPTY FLOORS YOU WONDERED IF THE TOWER ITSELF MEANT MORE THAN WHAT WAS WITHIN.
"AND WORLD ONE WAS BUILT ON THE BONES OF A DEAD MILL, TOWERING OVER MUMBAI'S SLUMS.
"CITIES TURNED INTO FACELESS THINGS OF CONCRETE AND GLASS AND METAL. AND WE WERE TAUGHT TO MEASURE OUR WORTH BY NUMBERS AND IN FEET.
"YOU COULD MARVEL AT THE BRUTALIST ROOTS AND THE ARCHITECTURAL INFLUENCES OF A TOWER WITHOUT EVER SEEING THE FACE OF A SINGLE PERSON WHO LIVED THERE."
AND, AT ABOUT TWO THOUSAND FEET, WHEN YOU LOOKED DOWN FROM THE WORLD'S HIGHEST OCCUPIED FLOOR, YOU DIDN'T EVEN SEE PEOPLE ON THE GROUND ANYMORE.
AND WHAT THEN, ODI?
WHAT HAPPENED TO IT ALL?

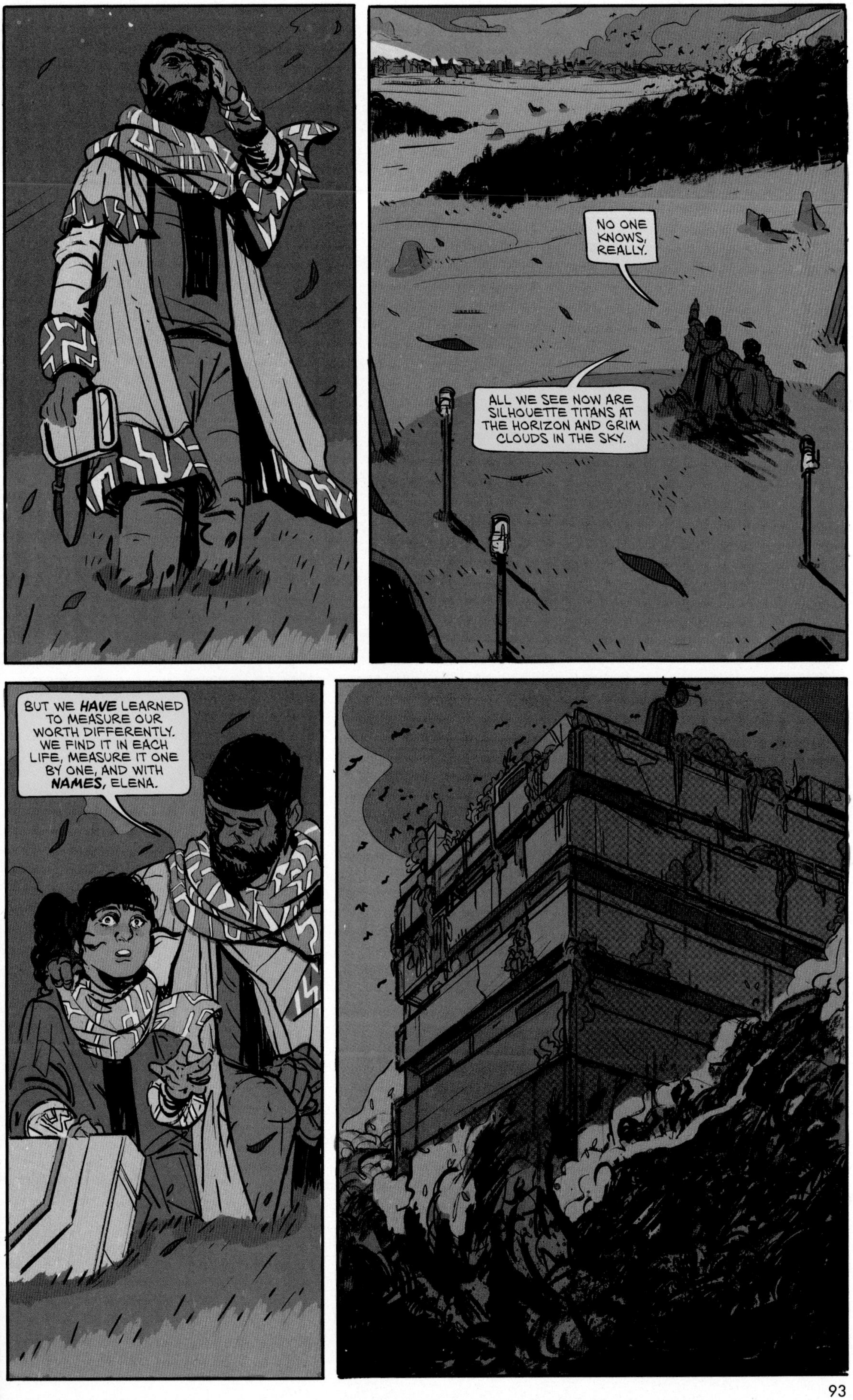
NO ONE KNOWS, REALLY.
ALL WE SEE NOW ARE SILHOUETTE TITANS AT THE HORIZON AND GRIM CLOUDS IN THE SKY.
BUT WE **HAVE** LEARNED TO MEASURE OUR WORTH DIFFERENTLY. WE FIND IT IN EACH LIFE, MEASURE IT ONE BY ONE, AND WITH **NAMES**, ELENA.

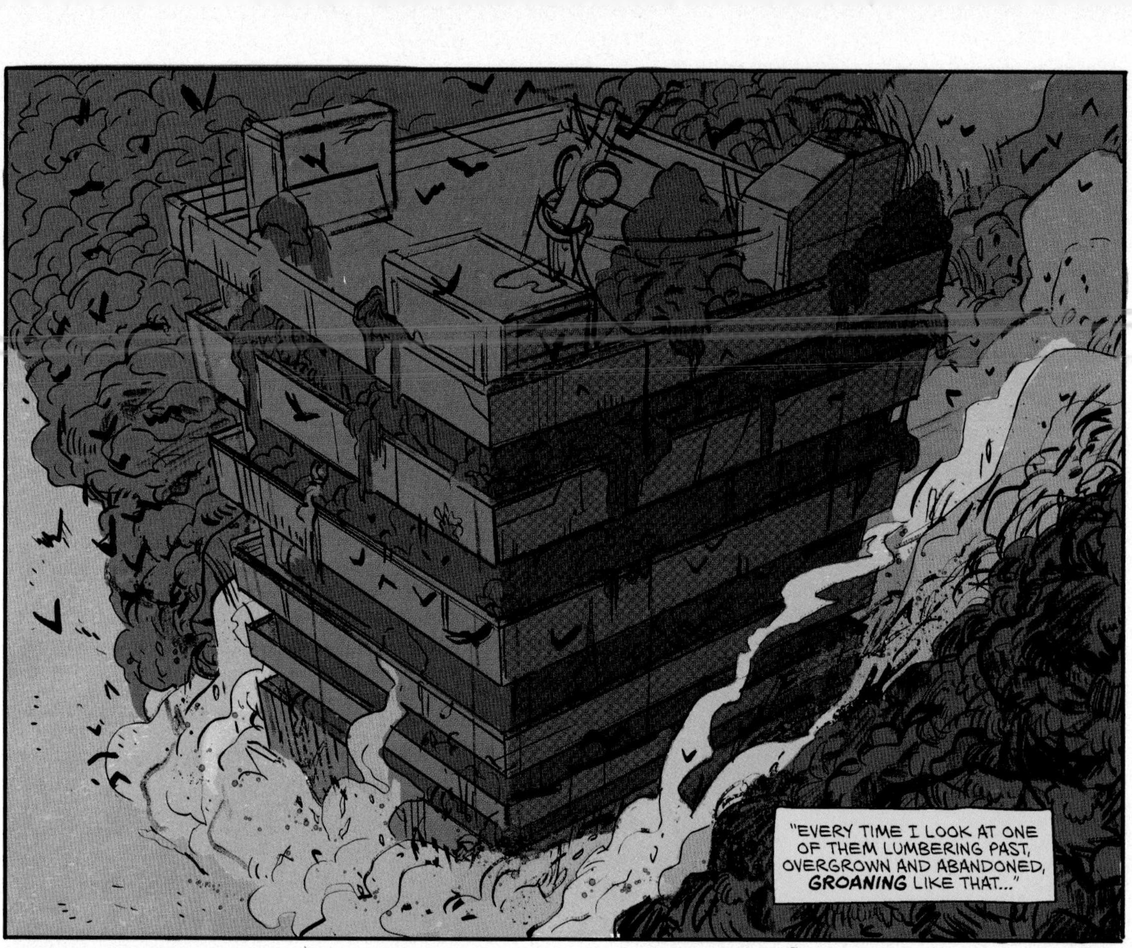
"EVERY TIME I LOOK AT ONE OF THEM LUMBERING PAST, OVERGROWN AND ABANDONED, GROANING LIKE THAT..."

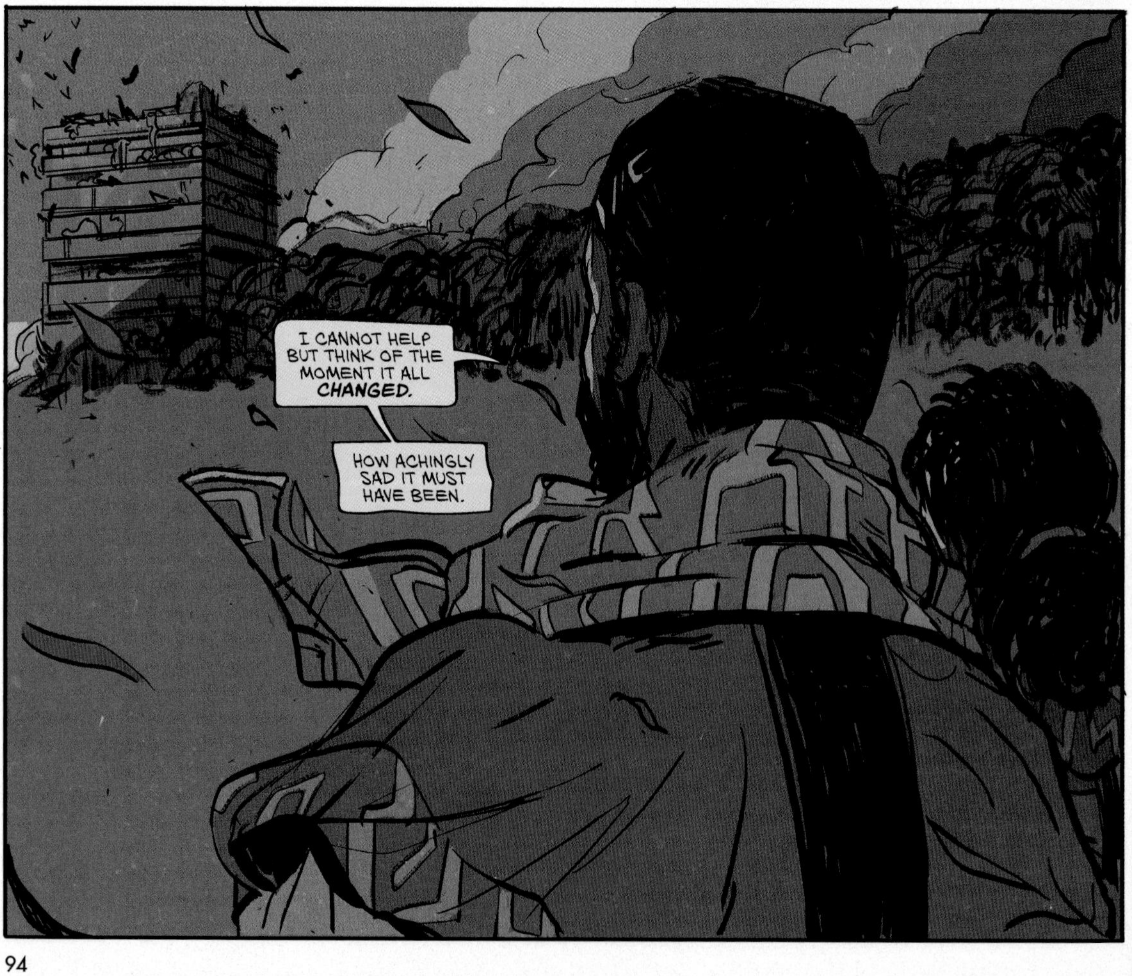
I CANNOT HELP BUT THINK OF THE MOMENT IT ALL CHANGED.
HOW ACHINGLY SAD IT MUST HAVE BEEN.

GRAFTAGE

Words by Deshan Tennekoon, Illustrations by Linki Brand

VIABLE ROOTSTOCK'S RARE AND SEEDS BEING HARD TO COME BY, WE MOSTLY GROW BY GRAFTING.

YOU TRY AND IMPROVE THE SOIL WHILE YOU WAIT.

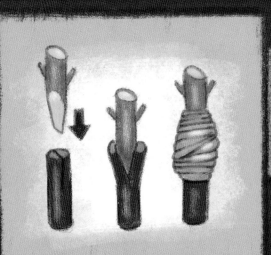

Hope may be grown effectively by the technique of grafting — a popular method, though it calls for readily available sources of hope.

OFF—CHANCE SOMEONE GIVES YOU A DECENT BIT OF STOCK, YOU LOVE IT FEROCIOUSLY, DO YOUR BEST TO MAKE SURE THE GRAFT TAKES.

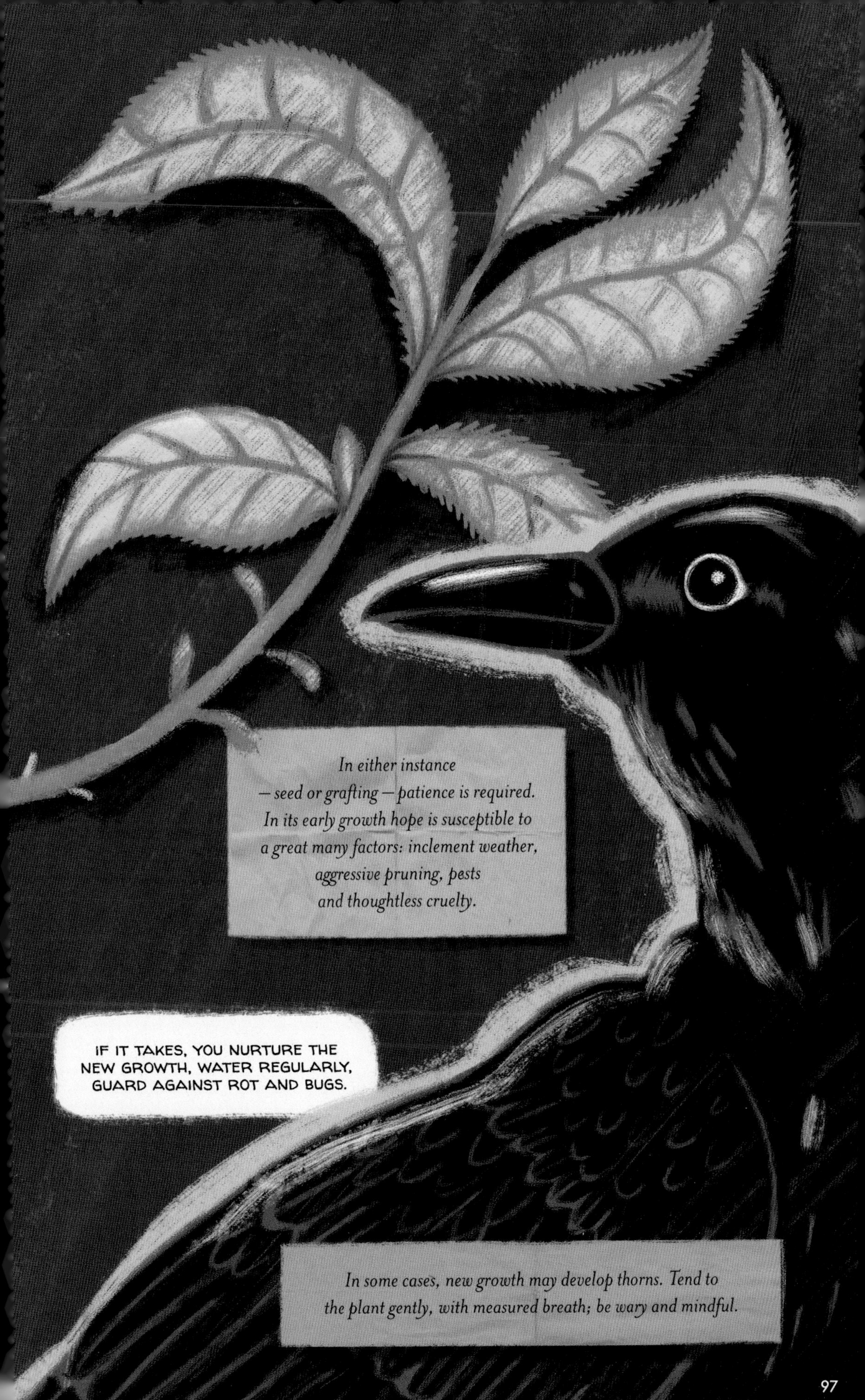
In either instance — seed or grafting — patience is required. In its early growth hope is susceptible to a great many factors: inclement weather, aggressive pruning, pests and thoughtless cruelty.
IF IT TAKES, YOU NURTURE THE NEW GROWTH, WATER REGULARLY, GUARD AGAINST ROT AND BUGS.
In some cases, new growth may develop thorns. Tend to the plant gently, with measured breath; be wary and mindful.

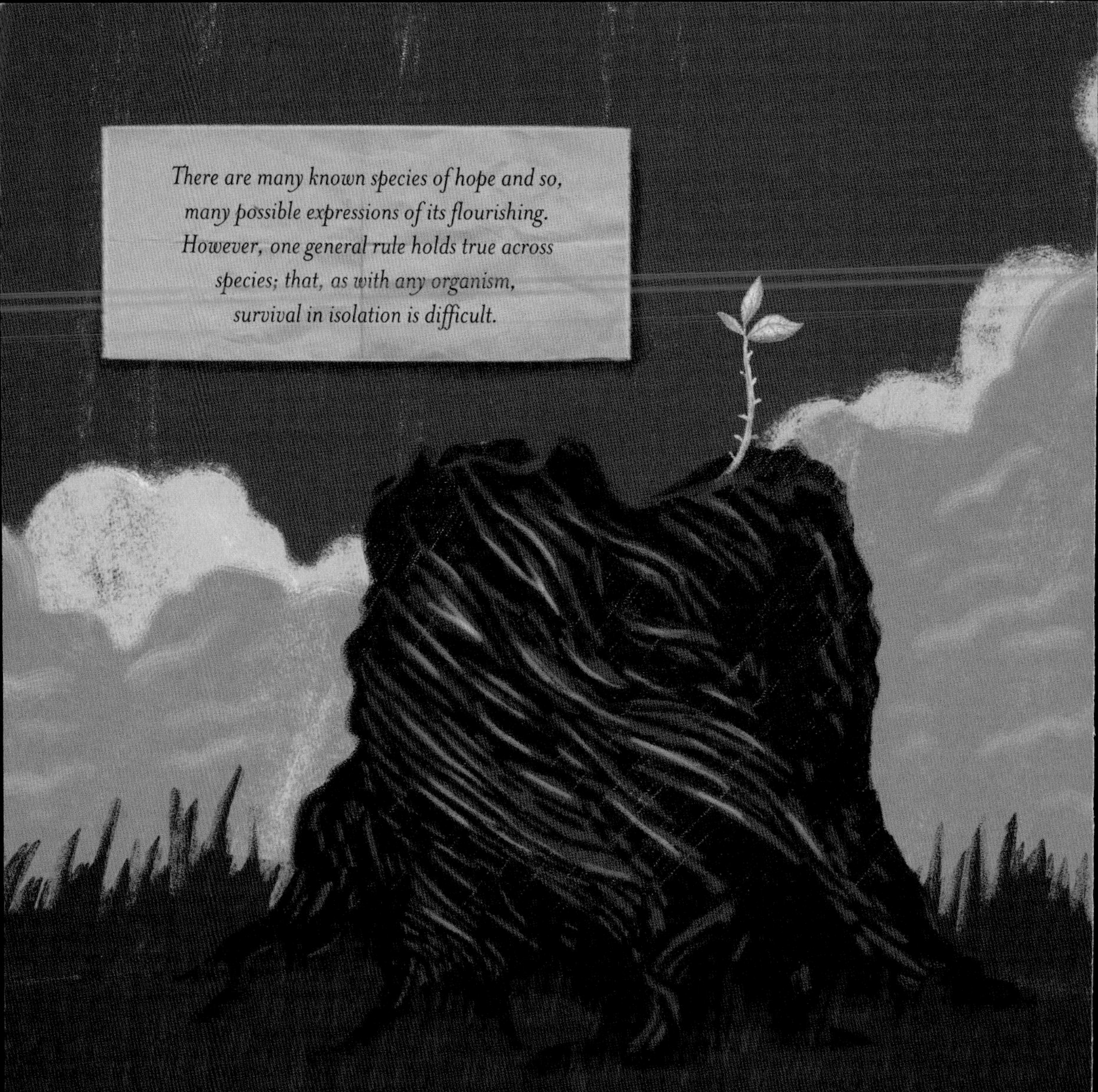
There are many known species of hope and so, many possible expressions of its flourishing. However, one general rule holds true across species; that, as with any organism, survival in isolation is difficult.

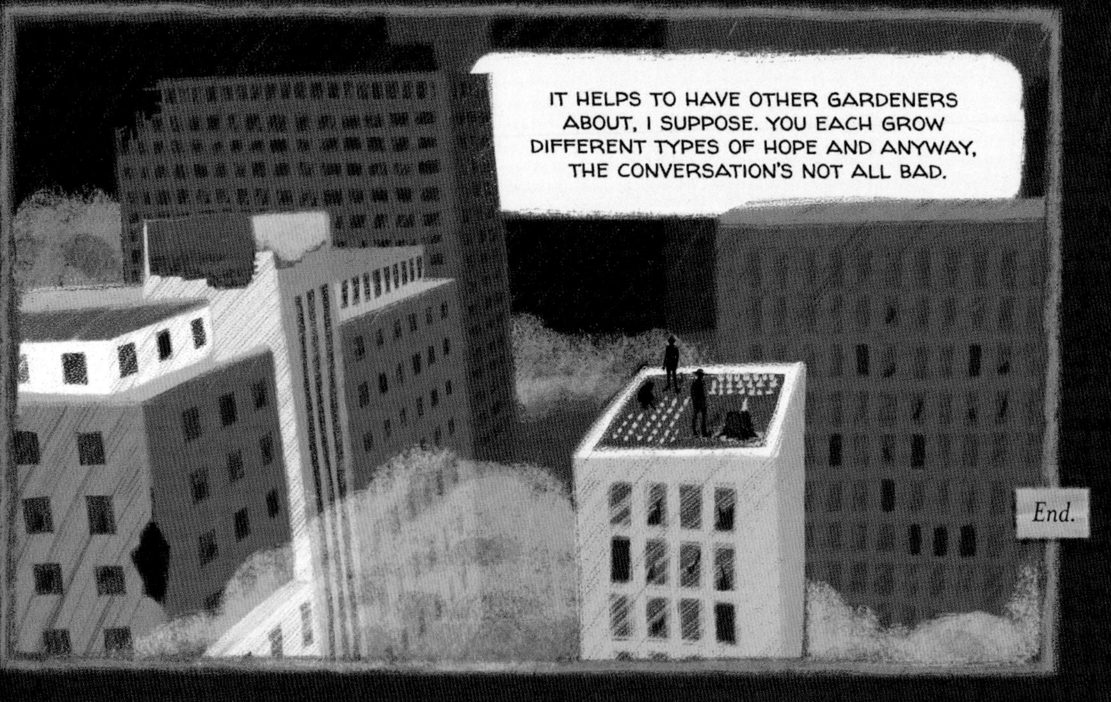
IT HELPS TO HAVE OTHER GARDENERS ABOUT, I SUPPOSE. YOU EACH GROW DIFFERENT TYPES OF HOPE AND ANYWAY, THE CONVERSATION'S NOT ALL BAD.
End.

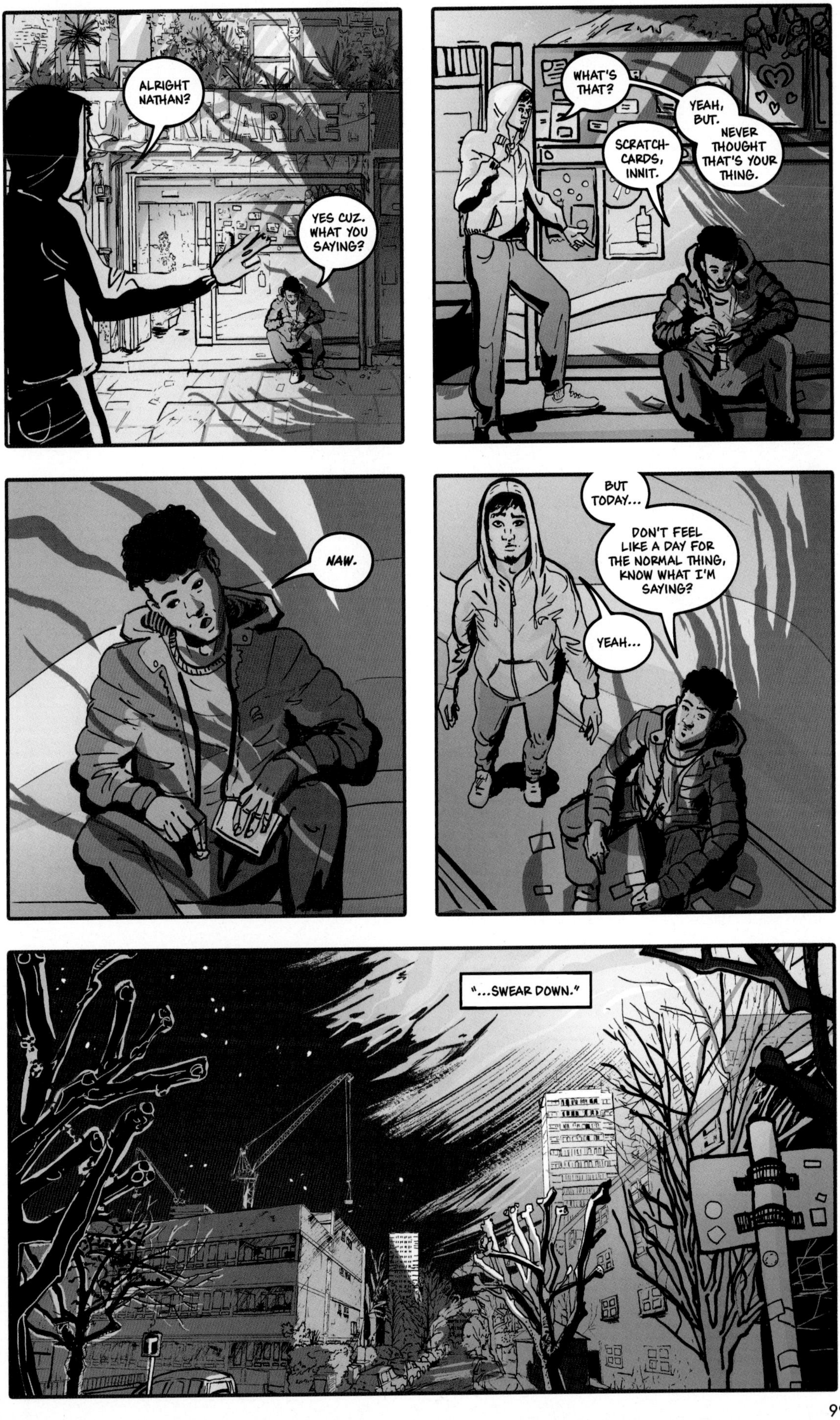
ALRIGHT NATHAN?
YES CUZ. WHAT YOU SAYING?
WHAT'S THAT?
SCRATCH-CARDS, INNIT.
YEAH, BUT.
NEVER THOUGHT THAT'S YOUR THING.
NAW.
BUT TODAY...
DON'T FEEL LIKE A DAY FOR THE NORMAL THING, KNOW WHAT I'M SAYING?
YEAH...
"...SWEAR DOWN."

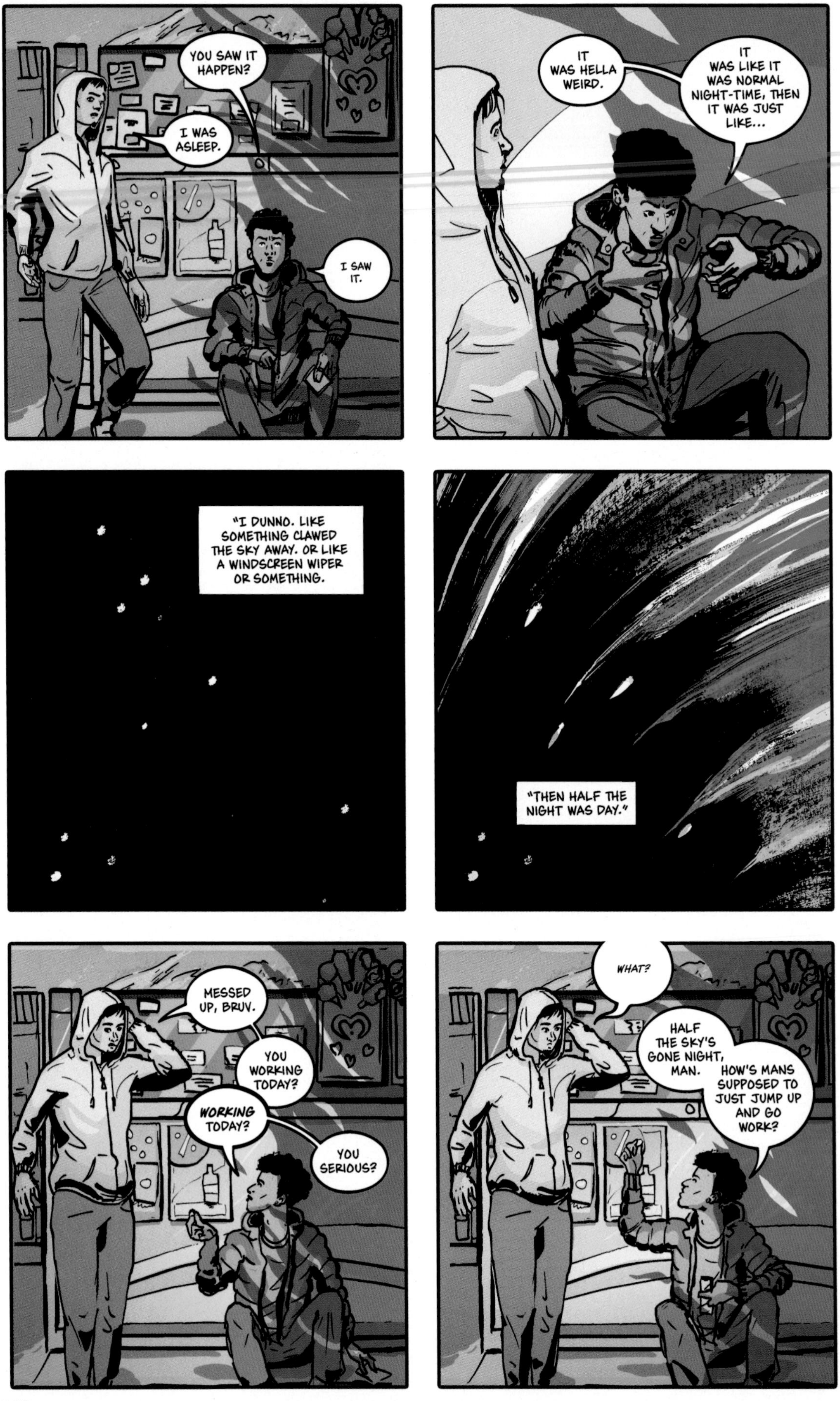
YOU SAW IT HAPPEN?
I WAS ASLEEP.
I SAW IT.
IT WAS HELLA WEIRD.
IT WAS LIKE IT WAS NORMAL NIGHT-TIME, THEN IT WAS JUST LIKE...
"I DUNNO. LIKE SOMETHING CLAWED THE SKY AWAY. OR LIKE A WINDSCREEN WIPER OR SOMETHING.
"THEN HALF THE NIGHT WAS DAY."
MESSED UP, BRUV.
YOU WORKING TODAY?
WORKING TODAY?
YOU SERIOUS?
WHAT?
HALF THE SKY'S GONE NIGHT, MAN.
HOW'S MANS SUPPOSED TO JUST JUMP UP AND GO WORK?

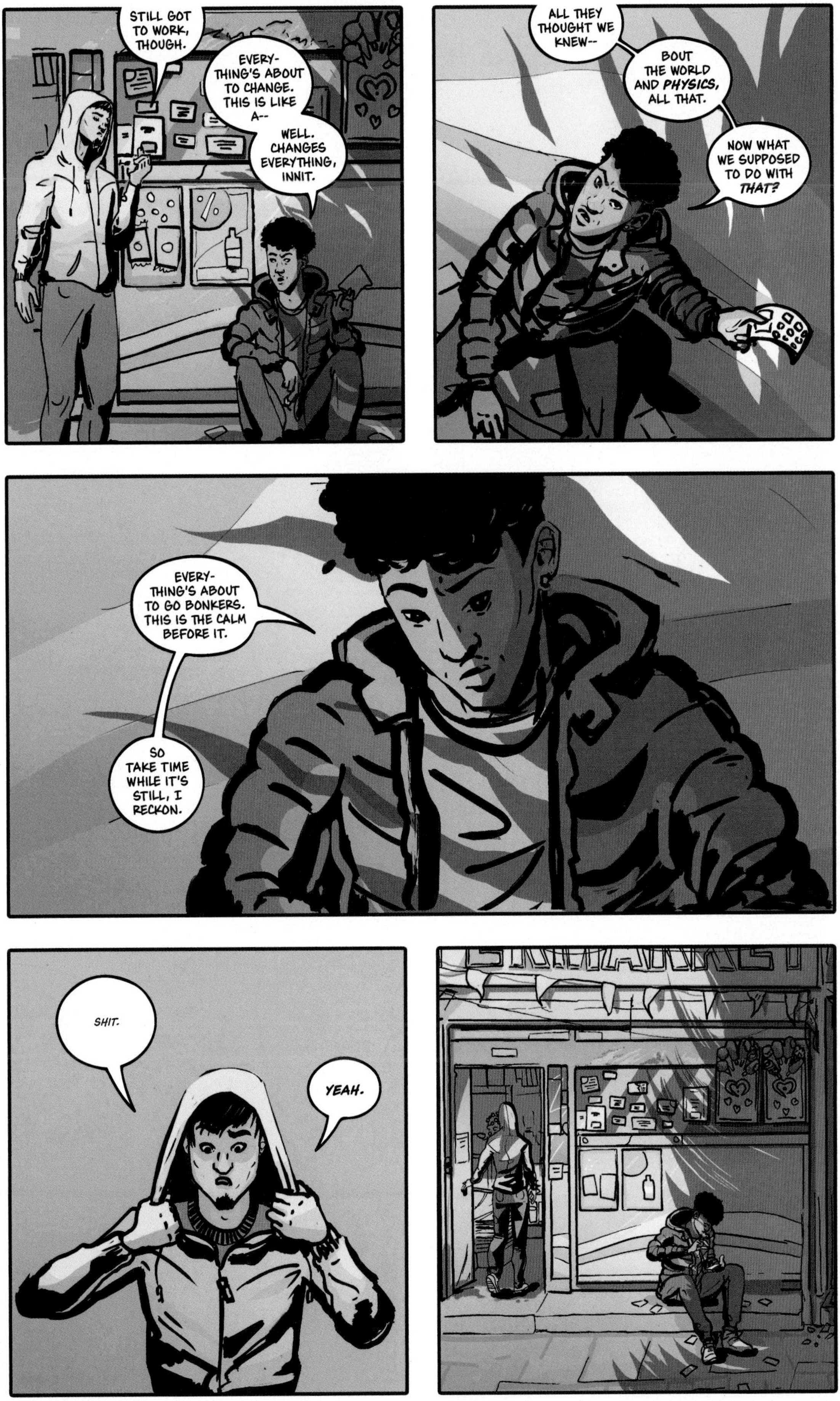
STILL GOT TO WORK, THOUGH.
EVERY-THING'S ABOUT TO CHANGE. THIS IS LIKE A--
WELL. CHANGES EVERYTHING, INNIT.
ALL THEY THOUGHT WE KNEW--
BOUT THE WORLD AND PHYSICS, ALL THAT.
NOW WHAT WE SUPPOSED TO DO WITH THAT?
EVERY-THING'S ABOUT TO GO BONKERS. THIS IS THE CALM BEFORE IT.
SO TAKE TIME WHILE IT'S STILL, I RECKON.
SHIT.
YEAH.

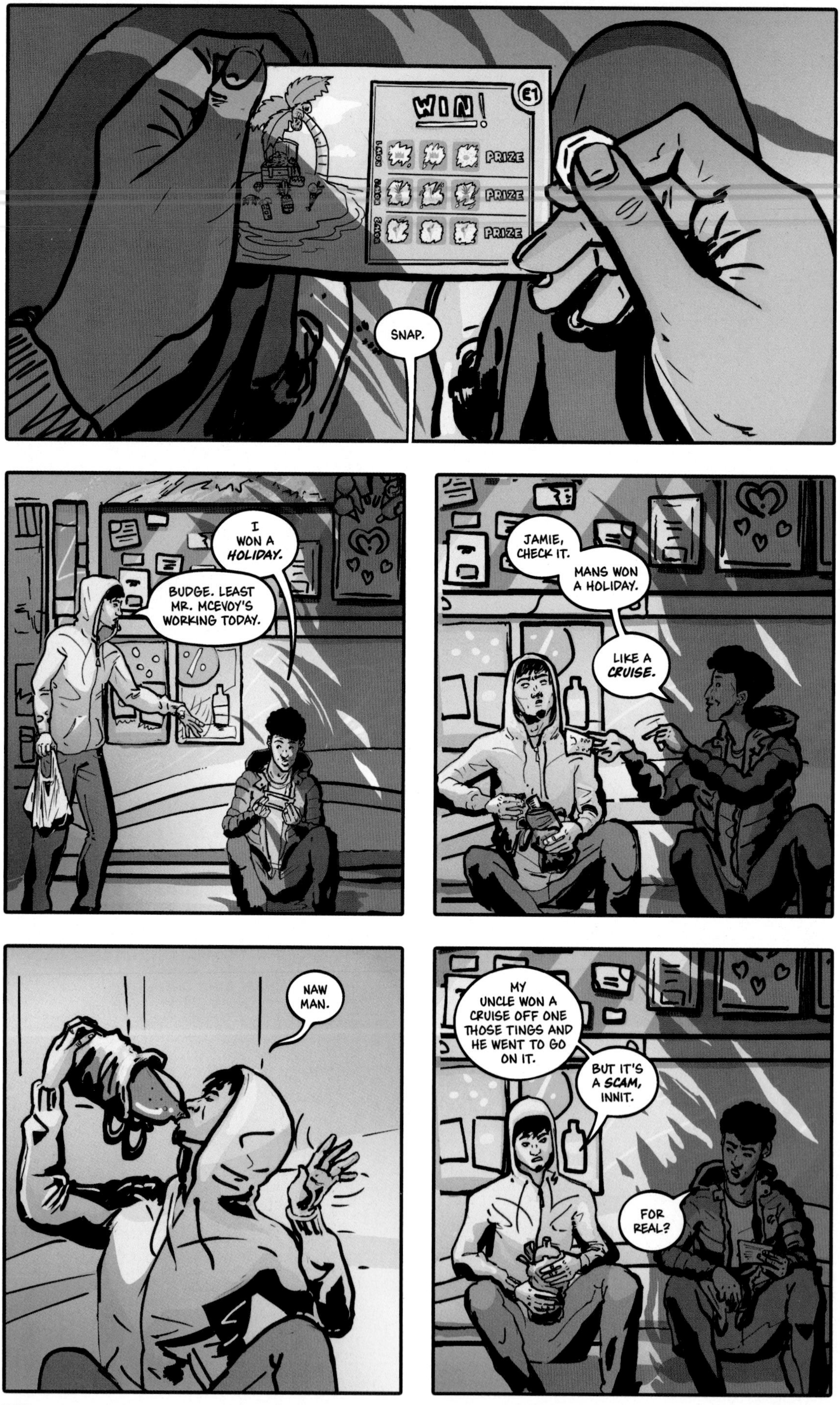
WIN!
PRIZE
PRIZE
PRIZE
SNAP.
I WON A *HOLIDAY.*
BUDGE. LEAST MR. MCEVOY'S WORKING TODAY.
JAMIE, CHECK IT.
MANS WON A HOLIDAY.
LIKE A *CRUISE.*
NAW MAN.
MY UNCLE WON A CRUISE OFF ONE THOSE TINGS AND HE WENT TO GO ON IT.
BUT IT'S A *SCAM,* INNIT.
FOR REAL?

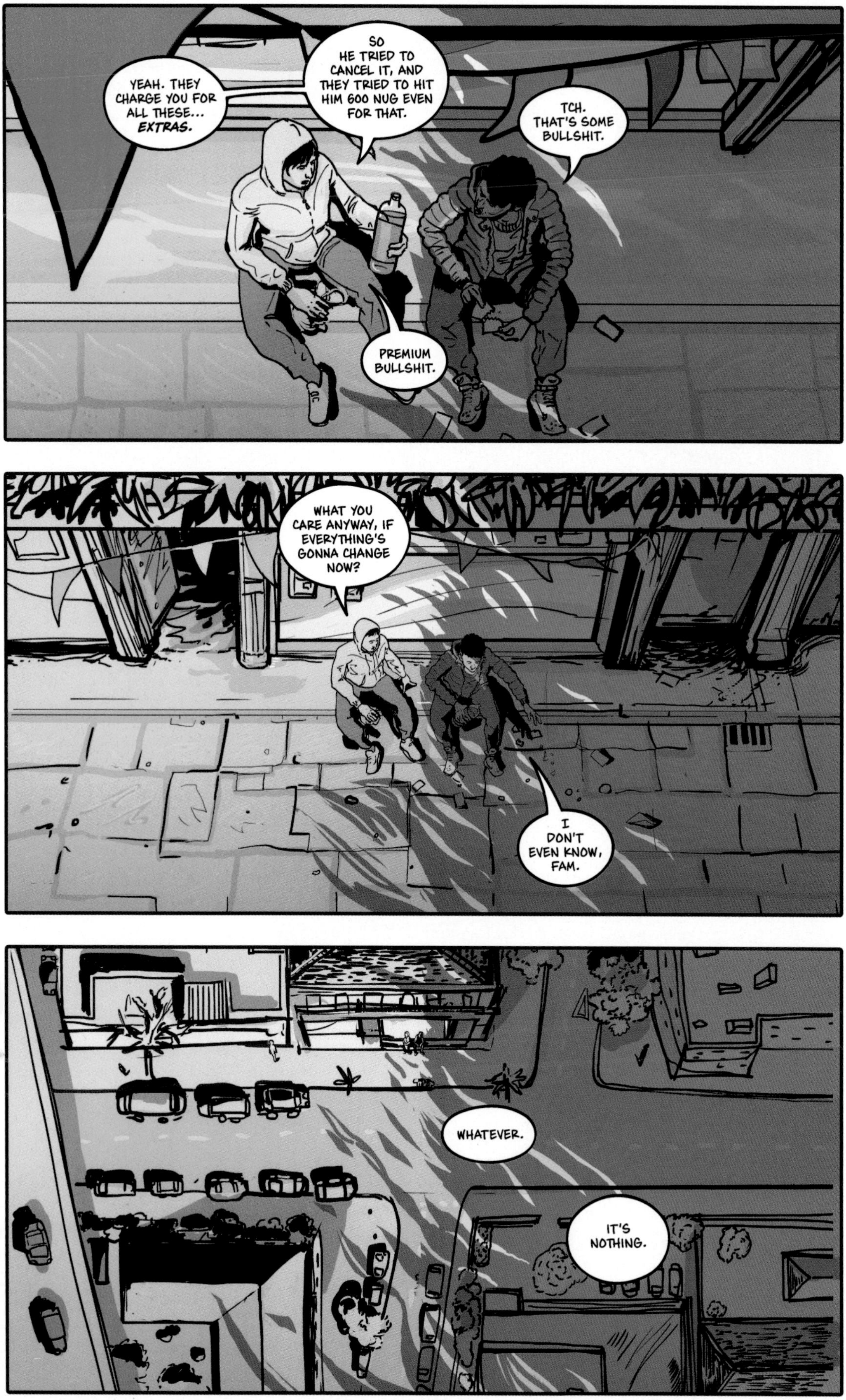

YEAH. THEY CHARGE YOU FOR ALL THESE... EXTRAS.
SO HE TRIED TO CANCEL IT, AND THEY TRIED TO HIT HIM 600 NUG EVEN FOR THAT.
TCH. THAT'S SOME BULLSHIT.
PREMIUM BULLSHIT.
WHAT YOU CARE ANYWAY, IF EVERYTHING'S GONNA CHANGE NOW?
I DON'T EVEN KNOW, FAM.
WHATEVER.
IT'S NOTHING.

GEN AINSLOW is a queer comics and prose writer from Albuquerque, New Mexico. This is Gen's first publication with Image.

LEIGH ALEXANDER is a writer of futurist fiction and interactive entertainment. She was recently narrative director on the acclaimed game *Reigns: Her Majesty,* and her digital culture writing has appeared in *The Guardian, The Columbia Journalism Review, Motherboard, the New Statesman* and more. She is the author of *Breathing Machine,* a memoir of early internet society, and her occasional ASMR video series "Lo-Fi Let's Play" explores ancient computer adventure games. More projects can be found at leighalexander.net

SEAN AZZOPARDI is a London-based cartoonist who has produced numerous mini comics and books for his Phatcomics imprint, including acclaimed titles such as *Ed, Twelve Hour Shift* and *Dark Matters.* Away from self-published titles he is working on Vol 3 of *Necessary Monsters* (First comics) phatcomics.co.uk ☻ @seanazz

DOUG BRAITHWAITE is an award-winning artist who has worked in the comic book industry for more than 25 years. He has drawn just about every major comic book character for Marvel and DC, working on such titles as: *Punisher, Superman, Batman, Green Arrow, Justice League, Thor* and *Wolverine.* He is currently exclusive to Valiant Comics.

LINKI BRAND is an illustrator working from Penicuik, Scotland – originally from South Africa. After obtaining a B.A. Graphic Design degree at North-West University (Potchefstroom) she worked at advertising agencies in Bloemfontein and Cape Town before moving to Scotland with her husband and two children. Since then her focus has shifted from graphic design to illustration. linkibrand.com

CHRISTOF BOGACS is a comics writer based out of Sydney, Australia. As well as self-publishing his own comics, his work has been featured in *PanelXPanel* and the upcoming *Corpus* anthology. He lives with his wife, several succulents and the lingering feeling that it could all go terribly wrong.

TREVOR BOYD is a comic book writer and filmmaker based out of Houston. He is currently completing a degree in Film at Sam Houston State University in Texas. "Fruit Punch" is Trevor's first published story, and he is grateful for the chance to help raise money for the survivors of the Grenfell fire and to be featured alongside such amazing creators.

ALEX DE CAMPI writes stories. The most recent ones have been *Bad Girls,* a late-50s Havana noir graphic novel out from Simon & Schuster; a story in *Ghost in the Shell: Global Neural Network* from Kodansha; and the trade of her critically acclaimed Image anthology series *Twisted Romance.* She also regularly contributes to *2000AD,* with Judge Dredd and Rogue Trooper stories. She lives in New York City with a daughter, a dog, and a cat, and may be found about the internets as @alexdecampi

PABLO CLARK is a Scottish-Spanish illustrator who likes drawing stories: comics, storyboards for feature films, TV shows and video games or just illustrations that try to conjure up another place. When not drawing he writes his own stories too. ☻ @inthedarkarcade

PAUL CORNELL is a writer of SFF in prose, TV and comics. He's written *Doctor Who* for every medium, *Elementary* for CBS, and everything from *Action Comics* to *Wolverine* for Marvel and DC. His creator-owned comics are *This Damned Band* and *Saucer State.* He's the creator of the *Lychford* series of rural fantasies. He's won an Eagle Award for his comics, a BSFA Award for his short fiction and shares in a Writer's Guild Award for his *Doctor Who.* Find him at paulcornell.com or on *Hammer House of Podcast.*

DEE CUNNIFFE is an award-winning Irish designer who worked for over a decade in publishing and advertising. He gave it all up to pursue his love of comics. He has colored *The Dregs* and *Eternal* at Black Mask, *The Paybacks* and *Interceptor* at Heavy Metal, *Her Infernal Descent* and *Lost City Explorers* at Aftershock, and *Redneck* at Skybound. ☻ @deezoid

LIAM DONNELLY is a Sad Gay Boy™/cartoonist based in Queens, New York. He likes roller derby, Lois Lane, and frequently changing his hair. His work has previously been published in *Lilies, Vagabond Comics,* and the queer magazine *DRØME*. You can follow his artistic exploits on Twitter and Instagram @baelliam

AL EWING is a writer of comics and prose based in Britain. He is best known for his work for 2000AD and Marvel, including *Judge Dredd, Mighty Avengers, Zaucer of Zilk, Loki: Agent of Asgard* and more. His novels include The *Fictional Man*, published by Solaris. He is presently writing *The Immortal Hulk* for Marvel. ⊙ @Al_Ewing

TRIONA TREE FARRELL is a Dublin-based colourist/illustrator with a Masters in Visual Critical Art. She has worked in many large companies in the comics industry, including Boom!, IDW, Vault, Darkhorse and Marvel as a professional colourist. In person she's a huge nerd and loves gaming and comics.

MIKE GARLEY is an EMMY-nominated writer who has written for *Adventure Time, Wallace and Gromit*, as well as creator-owned projects *The Kill Screen, Samurai Slasher*, and *Our Final Halloween*. Mikegarley.com patreon.com/mikegarley ⊙ @Mikegarley

MELINDA GEBBIE is an artist and writer based in Northampton.

KIERON GILLEN is a writer based in London. He is best known as co-creator of *The Wicked + the Divine, Phonogram* and *DIE,* all for Image comics. At Marvel, he has written for books including *Iron Man, Young Avengers, Uncanny X-men, Star Wars, Darth Vader* and many more.

SARAH GORDON is an artist, writer and animator working in London. Her work includes *Strip*, which was nominated for Best Comic in the British Comic Awards. ⊙ @notsarahgordon

ROBIN HOELZEMANN creates stories from a small town in the United Kingdom. She is best known for her creator-owned work on *Curia Regis*, an 18th century drama, and *The Witching Hour*, a gothic fable. She is currently working on a new graphic novel about a shop that sells wishes. When not illustrating a new comic or cover, she can be found playing D'n'D, baking, or exploring the outside world.

TOM HUMBERSTONE is an award-winning comic artist and illustrator. His work has appeared in *Phonogram* (Image) and the Eisner Award-nominated *Nelson* (Blank Slate Books). He also regularly contributes comics to *The Nib, New Statesman*, Vox, and Buzzfeed. His illustration clients include the BBC, *The Guardian, Vice*, and *Wired*.

ROB JONES is a British writer and letterer of comics, and part of Madius Comics. He has lettered for numerous small press comics and publishers. He co-writes *Griff Gristle, Tragic Tales of Horrere* and more with Mike Sambrook. ⊙ @RobJonesWrites and ⊕ facebook.com/RobJonesLetters

BEV JOHNSON is an LA-based illustrator and character designer who loves teaming up with people to tell stories.

ANTONY JOHNSTON is a *New York Times* bestselling author and screenwriter. His work includes graphic novel *The Coldest City*, which became the hit movie *Atomic Blonde* starring Charlize Theron; the epic series *Wasteland*, one of only a handful of such longform achievements in comics; and *Dead Space*, a videogame that redefined its genre. He lives and works in England. ⊙ @AntonyJohnston

REDA KAHLOULA is an Algerian cartoonist who spends his days drawing or complaining about not drawing enough. He got into comics by reading European BD before discovering the beautiful world of Shonen Manga, which he now thinks is the purest form of art. He was recently awarded the excellency prize for comics by the European Union.

For nearly 20 years SARA KENNEY has worked as a filmmaker on documentaries, drama and animation (BBC, Channel 4, Discovery). She recently wrote her first comic *Surgeon X* (Image) and is currently a Wellcome Trust Engagement Fellow exploring comics, health and the human condition.

GWEN KORTSEN AND ANGELA WRAIGHT have been making comics together for over ten years; they'd like to think they're starting to get good at it! If you like their story *A Logical Conclusion* you may want to check out their book *The Japanese Village* where the same two characters appear. They live in London now, but Gwen is from Norway and

Angela is from Portsmouth. Their website is suicidaltoys.com. Follow @AngelaWraight on Twitter for updates on their comics.

Lisa Wood, known by her pen name TULA LOTAY, is an English comic book artist. She is best known for illustrating *Supreme: Blue Rose*, written by Warren Ellis for Image Comics and *All Star Batman #7* with Scott Snyder. She was also an artist for Si Spencer's eight-part series *Bodies* for Vertigo. She illustrated issue #13 of *The Wicked + The Divine*, which was published in 2015 and nominated for a GLAAD Media Award for Outstanding Comic Book. She lives in Yorkshire with her husband and daughter.

LIZZ LUNNEY is an illustrator, comic artist and joke writer from the UK. She also works within the animation industry. See her full portfolio at lizzlunney.com ◎ @Lizzlizz

DILRAJ MANN is an artist and illustrator based in Lewes, UK. His art is largely inspired by the unexpected and often curious locals from the streets of London. He is the creator of the *Stroke* and *Queen* zines and his work has appeared in *Island and Kus!* among many others. dilrajmann.tumblr.com ◎ @dilraj_mann

RHONA MARTIN is co-editor of *24 Panels* and co-creator and co-producer of its sister publication *24 Stories*. Both "24" projects were motivated by her personal experience with PTSD; her wish to help create a wider understanding of PTSD and a desire for those who have experienced profound trauma to receive the help they need and ultimately regain inner unity and thrive.

PIPPA MATHER is a comic book colourist, currently working for 2000AD and Dynamite. She comes from the northwest of England, where she lives with her fiancé (letterer Simon Bowland) and cat (Jess). ◎ @colormepip

GAVIN MITCHELL is the artist for the Fighting Fantasy graphic novel *The Trolltooth Wars, Santa Claus vs The Nazi* and co-creator owned comedy detective *Spatchcock*. Gavin lives in south Wales with his wife, Emily and surrogate child, Boo the dog.

ALAN MOORE is a writer based in Northampton.

ALEX MOORE is an illustrator, storyboarder and comic book artist whose clients have included *Wired Magazine*, Ubisoft, the RAF Museum, *Toronto Comics Anthology* and more. She is also an Academic Assistant for Middlesex University's Illustration BA. cargocollective.com/alexmooreillustration ◎ @alexmooreillustration ◉ @notanotheralex

EMMET O'CUANA is a Dublin-born, Melbourne-based writer and critic. He is also an aspiring home cook. One day, he dreams of owning a miniature goat. emmetocuana.com

HASSAN OTSMANE-ELHAOU is the letterer behind *Shanghai Red, The Lone Ranger, Dream Daddy, Short Order Crooks* and more. He's also the editor of the Eisner-nominated *PanelxPanel*, and voice behind *Strip Panel Naked*.

LAURIE PENNY is a Brighton-based journalist, essayist, activist and author of *Unspeakable Things, Everything Belongs To The Future* and *Bitch Doctrine*. When she gets time, she also writes creepy political science fiction. laurie-penny.com ◎ @PennyRed

ERIKA PRICE is a comic artist based in the UK. Her current project is *Disorder*, a webcomic that uses horror as art therapy. When not making comics she can be found in bed, asleep, cuddling her cat. ◎ @erikapriceart

TOBEN RACICOT creates comics and is pursuing a PhD in Role-Play Game Studies at the University of Waterloo, Ontario. As a letterer, he collaborates on *Thorn Squadron, The Wild Cosmos*, and *Memoirs of a Starseed*. He's written *The Bad Guys: The Ballad of Greg and Chad* and *Crown & Anchor*.

CARDINAL RAE is a letterer whose work has been featured in books from DC, Image, and others.

JEFERSON SADZINSKI is a comic book artist from Curitiba in Brazil. His interest in sequential art first came from watching cartoons as a child. He still likes to imagine his own stories and draw them in his spare time. ◉ deviantart.com/jeffsadzinski/gallery ◎ @JefSadzinski

DANIEL SANTOS is a comic book writer from Perth, Western Australia, whose stories have appeared in several anthologies. His comics and occasional musings can be found at danesses.tumblr.com.

DÉBORA SANTOS is a comic artist and has been drawing since 2014. She is a part of a group of independent comic artists in Brazil called Netuno Press, having published five minicomics under this label. She also produces an event in her hometown dedicated to discussing comics production and illustration by women. She sometimes teaches drawing and is currently working for the university of her state, Ceará, making educational comics. ⊙ deborasantosart.tumblr.com ◎ @deborasantosart

RACHAEL SMITH is a comic artist and writer. She has created numerous critically acclaimed comic books including *House Party, Artificial Flowers, Wired Up Wrong,* and *The Rabbit* – nominated for Best Book in the 2015 British Comic Awards. She has worked on Titan's *Doctor Who Comic* series, and is a regular contributor to *Empathize This,* a website which gives a platform to marginalised voices through the medium of comics. She lives in Hebden Bridge in the UK with her cat Rufus.

JOANNE STARER has worked in publishing for nearly 20 years, beginning as an editorial assistant at Harris Comics before moving on to *Marvel Knights* and now, her current home, Paper Films. She lives in New York with a small but obnoxious cat.

RO STEIN AND TED BRANDT are an English comics art duo working together since 2014. They started out on Action Lab's *Raven: The Pirate Princess,* worked on titles such as *Champions, Mighty Captain Marvel* and *Steve Rogers: Captain America* for Marvel Comics, before their first creator-owned series, *Crowded,* launched this year from Image. They love making comics, but are mostly doing it for pizza money.

MIKE STOCK is a comic book letterer and graphic designer, he was also the digital editor for *Dead Roots* and *VS Comics.* A mainstay of the UK indy comic scene, Mike has had work published in the likes of Image and Markosia, as well as small-press titles like *The Kill Screen, The Pride,* and *Raygun Roads.* michaelstock.co.uk ⊙ @sheriffstocky

PAUL SWAIN, for some reason, seems more enigmatic than he really is. When he grows up, he'd like to be able to continue drawing pictures.

DESHAN TENNEKOON writes comics and children's books. He co-wrote a graphic novel called *Podi* (forthcoming, Oni Press) and writes storybooks for Think Equal, an NGO specialising in social and emotional learning. Occasionally he's asked to write things that aren't comics, like *Traditional Culture and Aesthetics of Sri Lanka* for the Encyclopedia of Asian Design (forthcoming, Bloomsbury Publishing).

STEVE THOMPSON is a filmmaker and writer as well as co-editor of *24 Panels* and co-producer of its sister publication *24 Stories.* He is the producer of New Wave music documentary, *Couldn't Miss This.* His first novel was *Street-Fighting Woman,* adapted to a graphic novel of the same name, as well as writing the comics *Animal Magic* and *3-Headed Narwhal* and his upcoming novel *Ill Vacation.*

RAM V is an award-winning author and creator of comics & graphic novels such as *Paradiso, Ruin Of Thieves* and *Grafity's Wall.* His short stories and comics have appeared in several anthologies and e-zines. Conspirator and trouble-maker at White Noise Studio. Ram currently lives in London– dog person, doodles, argumentative melancholic. ram-v.com ⊙ @therightram

DAN WATTERS is a writer based in Notting Hill, London. His comic work includes *Limbo* for Image, *The Shadow* for Dynamite, and *Deep Roots* for Vault Comics. He is currently writing *Lucifer* for Vertigo. danpjwatters.wordpress.com ⊙ @DanPGWatters

CASPAR WIJNGAARD is a comic artist based in England. Co-creator of acclaimed neon-noir series *Limbo* and the celebrated YA series *Angelic* both for Image. He has drawn for publishers such as Marvel, IDW and Dynamite. ⊙ @Casparnova ◎ @caspar_wijngaard

DREW WILLS is a queer comic book colorist and occasional illustrator from Albuquerque, New Mexico. While currently hard at work on many projects, this is his first published comics work. WillsandDrew.wixsite.com/portfolio ⊙ @WillsandDrew

Comic book artist and illustrator, LYNNE YOSHII, is an alumnus of the 2016 DC Comics Artist Development Workshop. She has done various work for DC, Boom! Studios and *Time for Kids* magazine.

24 PANELS WOULD LIKE EXTEND SPECIAL THANKS TO

Dee Cunniffe	Michael Perlman	Ross Wilkie
Tula Lotay	Susan Darker-Smith	Image Comics
Chrissy Williams	Sean Gardner	Gosh! Comics
11 O'Clock Comics Podcast	Hassan Otsmane-Elhaouto	

and to all the contributing writers, artists and letterers.